A
POCKET FULL
OF HOPE

Dedication
For my Family,
with much love.

A
POCKET FULL
OF HOPE

by

Lynne Whiteley

MENIN HOUSE

Menin House is an imprint of
Tommies Guides Military Book Specialists

Gemini House
136-140 Old Shoreham Road
Brighton
BN3 7BD

www.tommiesguides.co.uk

First published in Great Britain by
Menin House Publishers 2014

ISBN 978-1-908336-98-9

Cover design by Ryan Gearing

Typeset by Vivian Foster @ Bookscribe

Printed and bound in Great Britain

CONTENTS

ACKNOWLEDGEMENTS

To my good friends Pauline,
Sharon, Andrea, Maria, Margaret,
Karen and her Mom for the
encouragement to finish it
and to my beloved brother
for his perseverance in his research.
I thank you all.

1915

Beth

'This is for the little girl with no shoes on,' she called as she threw the chocolate over the balcony.

Beth looked up and saw the girl wave and point in her direction; there were no other little girls around. Beth waved back and ran over to where the chocolate had landed. The girl standing on the balcony was dressed in a pretty, white nightgown with lace around her pale neck; her long, black hair was tied back with a large, bright pink ribbon which accentuated her drawn, hollow, grey face and large, sad eyes. Beth might have envied her under different circumstances but, as young as she was, she understood this building was a place for the sick. So, picking up the chocolate, she smiled and held it preciously between her hands to try to give the other girl a feeling of pleasure for her kind thought. The girl stood alone on the balcony taking in the fresh air and quietly watching the children play their game around the bushes. Both girls became transfixed in a momentary stare; they smiled at each other again and waved. The pale girl defining Beth as the 'girl with no shoes' had not really hit home, for not wearing shoes was an everyday event.

Arnold, who was her older brother and who knew everything, had told her that this building was a home for grown-ups and children who were very sick and not expected to live. She had been playing hide and seek in the grounds of the Infirmary with him and his friends; the colourful gardens around the building were full of rhododendron bushes which gave them the cover to hide. Beth loved the vibrant colours of the flowers on the bushes and wished it could always be sunny and that they could play endlessly instead of having to return to the house where she lived with her mother, Arnold and baby Arthur. Their home was void of colour since the arrival of the new baby; his constant crying drained everyone.

She and Arnold had grown closer to each other since their father had volunteered to serve his country at the beginning of the Great War. He had responded to Kitchener's war cry and, like thousands of others, had been swept along with patriotic fervour, none of them realising that it would turn into a horrific nightmare that would last for four long gruelling years. Their father had gone proudly and told Arnold, 'Look after your mother and sister…you are now the man of the house.'

Although Beth had been told he was now a sailor and that his ship was sailing to a faraway country, she didn't really understand where or why he had gone. Arnold had gently tried to explain to her again after their mother had become angry because she was asking too many questions. He had taken her to see one of Kitchener's posters which hung on a railing at one of the nearby buildings, he told her it read: 'Your Country Needs You.' All she saw was an angry looking man in uniform pointing at her. Arnold tried to explain that was where their father had gone, but his explanation didn't help either. She just nodded and kept her misgivings to herself rather than disappoint him. She quietly hoped wherever their father was, there was colour; she missed him.

Arnold came running over to see what she had picked up. Showing him the chocolate, she ate half and gave him the remaining piece to him. They both giggled with delight at the sweetness of it.

'Come on now, we have to go home,' and taking her hand they both turned towards home. The little girl on the balcony watched them go wistfully through dark eyes. Beth waved to her before they turned the corner and out of sight, and she waved back to her and smiled.

Walking through the streets towards home Arnold decided to make a game of it for his troubled younger sister, so they marched home together like their father and the soldiers they had seen marching away to war. Everybody had cheered them and waved flags that day. Falling in line behind him she tried hard to match him step for step, heads high and in time they reached their street. Turning the corner they hesitated, they could hear not only baby Arthur crying but their mother wailing, an awful sound from her inner soul that stopped them in their tracks. All the neighbours were crowding around their door. They stood in silence and feared to go any closer both hoping the awful noise coming from their house would stop. A silent dread descended on them both. They had seen similar instances where a telegram boy on a bike delivered a piece of paper to a house which had turned the women on the street into a demented state. In the background baby Arthur continued to cry to screeching proportions.

They stayed at the corner transfixed until it was dusk, taking in the scene of various neighbours going in and out of their door in resigned silence. The lady who lived in the corner house came out onto the street. She approached quietly, her head down, lost in thought until she saw them sitting on the cobbles on the corner. Arnold had a protective arm around his sister hugging her close, his knowing eyes were wide with fear and Beth cowered silently into his body. The neighbour came quickly to their side enveloped them both in her arms for a moment, then said, 'Come with me.'

The lady took them inside her house momentarily away from the horror on the street; she was trying to delay the inevitable pain they would have to accept at such a young age like many others before them. For Beth the colours of the day had quickly faded, but she didn't understand why, the feeling frightened her. The neighbour gave them both a slice of bread and dripping to eat and after a long, uneasy silence where they feared to utter any words, she gently told them they would have to go home to help their mother.

Ellen, their mother, was now silently rocking to and fro in her chair. She didn't notice them come through the door into the dark room. Baby Arthur was being cared for by a neighbour, but they could still hear him. The kindly neighbour had brought them back home and gently told them to go to their mother's side. She turned to leave the house once more in silence, her shawl pulled over her head, weeping for yet another death and all the misery it brought.

Holding hands they approached their mother in silence and fear. She opened her arms to them and wailed so mournfully it was a sound that was forced deep into their psyche. Their father had been lost at sea, his ship had been torpedoed by a German U-boat off the Dardanelles.

A weeping Ellen cradled her children; her despair encompassed all three of them. Arnold held on to Beth's hand trying to give her some support, but the eyes that looked back at him were lost in a mist of confusion, sadness and fear. She didn't understand, but was aware something of tragic proportions had happened which made their game and the delight of the chocolate earlier in the day a distant memory. As the cold night closed in around them, baby Arthur still wailed like a banshee in the background next door.

The days following fell into a void and their mother became distant and morose. They nursed and fed Arthur as best they could on sugar and water and tried to compensate not really knowing what effect it would have on their mother if any at all. The neighbours fell away, not able to continue their initial support, their own problems once again coming to the fore. They were not easy times for anyone; their presence was replaced by sympathetic looks reflecting their thoughts of 'there but for the Grace of God go I.'

There was to be no funeral, the Government of the day had declared that the dead could not be brought home, so massive was the loss of life. Instead, there would be war monuments erected displaying the names of the fallen in all the cities, towns and villages where they had lived. Months later their mother received a black-edged letter to say, that as a mark of respect, there would be a special viewing of the photographs of the fallen at a local picture house and she was invited with the children to attend. Arthur, husband and father to her children, would appear for just a fleeting moment on the silver screen. Arnold and Beth sat in silence and watched the sea of faces appear before them; their father was just one of many and they were frightened of missing him. Suddenly his face filled the screen. He was wearing his naval uniform, his rank Able Seaman. Then the photograph quickly disappeared to be replaced by another dead soul; it was the last time they were to see their father's face.

They tried to fall into some sort of routine. Arnold went to school more as a means of escape. He tried his best to be the man of the house and support his mother and Beth, but Ellen descended into a haze of gin – it was the cheapest way of deadening the pain and the constant noise of Arthur's endless crying.

Seven months after losing their father, baby Arthur died and once again the house descended into mourning. Ellen's widow's pension was reduced as she now only had two surviving children. The baby was laid to rest in a pauper's grave in an untended part of the cemetery. A few days after his death Beth returned to the gardens of the Infirmary to try and recapture the memory of her last day of sunshine and fun. She stood under the balcony and waited in vain in the rain hoping for the little girl with the pink bow to appear, but she too had gone along with all the colour.

September came and with it a new school term for Arnold and what should have been Beth's first term, but she remained at home with her mother. Ellen could not summon any effort or interest to send her daughter to school and ignored any pleas that Arnold made on his sister's behalf. He had hoped after the months of despair that she would at last find the door to a new world opening before her and her imagination would fly. Instead, through no fault of her own, she was held back to exist in a house that was drowning in her mother's self-pity, a sea of misery and despair.

Eventually the letters started to arrive from the school authorities. At first they only advised that they were aware that Beth should have been in school and expected her to arrive at the appropriate times. Her mother ignored them all and threw them on the fire. Three months later, answering a loud knock at the door, a summons was placed in her hand and she was ordered to appear before the magistrates to answer the charges. Giving her daughter the summons and instructing her to ask a policeman if she saw one, Beth was duly dispatched with summons in hand and she walked to the courts in her bare feet. She knew where the Court House was, it was opposite the markets.

The policeman standing on the steps of the court building looked ten foot tall to her. She stopped and look up at him and held the paper out that Ellen had given to her. The policeman looked into the sad, tear-filled eyes staring up at him and his heart melted. He moved down the steps and gently picked her up off the cold stone. He took the summons out of her small hand and read it, then turned on his heel and carried her into the building. The magistrates were incensed; they ordered the little girl to be taken to the canteen and given food. A Black Maria* was despatched to pick up her mother without delay.

Arnold always returned straight home from school for his sister, he knew that she looked forward to him arriving back home as she had so little to lighten her day. Turning the corner he saw the Black Maria stop at their door and ran the rest of the way reaching the step at the same time as the bailiff who started to bang loudly on the door. Horrified he stood and watched as Ellen opened the door and was promptly placed in the back of the vehicle without any explanation.

'Stop!' he shouted. 'Who are you, what are you doing?'

'Who are you lad?' asked the bailiff.

'Where are you taking my mother... where is my sister?' he shouted in panic.

The bailiff told him to get into the back of the black van with his mother. The doors closed with a loud bang and the lock turned. The bailiff returned to the driving seat and the van started its journey back to the courthouse. His mother remained silent during the short journey and ignored all Arnold's questions. When they reached the court the policeman who Beth had approached saw them arrive and strode quickly towards the van. Beth had told him she had an older brother so he rightly assumed that the bare-footed boy was Arnold. Taking his hand he told him his sister was waiting for him and asked him to go with him. The bailiff, without comment, quickly ushered Ellen directly into the court room.

Beth sat at a large table and heard the policeman's footsteps approaching. The door opened and her eyes widened with delight when she saw her brother. She ran over to him and pulled him over to the table.

'Come and see, look Arnold... '

Another plate of food arrived and they both tucked into the first hot meal they had had in weeks with relish. Watching them eat, the kind policeman asked them gently what had happened at home recently and Arnold explained as best he could about his father and their baby brother. It was an all too familiar story. The policeman was getting used to children these days having such old heads on young shoulders, their childhoods taken away through no fault of their own. What chance did they have of a normal happy childhood, what was normal anymore?

Standing in front of the magistrates Ellen presented a small, sad figure. She kept her head bowed and eyes down. She was terrified of being committed to the workhouse, that dark Victorian place of horror which stood a short distance from where they lived. Its high black gates and reputation instilling fear into all the poorer classes if they fell on hard times; it was an ever present spectre.

'Please... not the workhouse. Please, please... I beg you... don't send us to the workhouse,' she whispered in panic.

The magistrate looked at her and heard her plea. He then listened to the clerk who quietly briefed him on the family's circumstances before asking for the children to be brought into the courtroom.

He was not a man without compassion. They arrived in the room hand in hand, frightened to the point that the tears were visible in their eyes, but clearly they dare not cry. Arnold noticeably gripped his sister's hand tighter and placed his arm around her small shoulder; the bench silently acknowledged their bond. Sympathy for them overruled any judgement or fine he had initially thought of imposing, and he smiled at them to try and ease their fear as best he could.

Ellen was severely told in no uncertain terms that Beth must attend school, that there was absolutely no excuse and if she ever came before him again then she would face dire consequences. He also told her that as she was a war widow the state would provide them with shoes and alms so her children should never go barefoot or hungry again.

With her eyes still cast downward, Ellen thanked him and they left the courtroom, the children still a little unsure of what was happening. The kind policeman read their faces and stopped them on the way out. He held both their hands, took them quietly to one side and explained that it was all going to be alright. He then gave them a penny each.

'Always remember I will be here. Here put this in your pocket... it is just a little thing to give you both hope instead of despair. You can come and find me if things don't change, either of you... do you promise?'

'Yes sir,' said Arnold. 'Thank you sir... we will.' His bravado finally left him and a tear trickled down his cheek. The policeman was touched. To try to change the sombre mood, he ruffled Arnold's hair and smiled at him.

'It will be alright lad. Don't worry now, just remember what I said... when you have hope you have everything.'

Beth looked at her brother concerned that he was upset, and then she took hold of the policeman's hand and smiled at him. A pair of warm brown eyes looked back at her and nodded, she silently wished it would be possible for him to become their new father. He had made sure that Ellen had heard his instruction to them to come back to him if things continued as they were. She turned and ushered them out of the courthouse and returned home without saying a word but calling to the alms house for shoes as instructed.

Beth finally went to school; she loved walking with Arnold and felt proud and grown up in the shoes they were wearing. She became fond of her teacher and it gave her a feeling of belonging and pride when she was praised. The high windows of the classroom let all the sunlight in, which reflected on to the pupils' paintings that bedecked the walls. The colours changed hues when it rained. She compared the rain drops that ran down the same windows to tears, and it always momentarily distracted her from her work.

When they were not in class Arnold, as always, kept her in his sights and during a break one day he took her into his classroom where there was a large map of the world on the wall. He showed her a pink coloured patch and a blue area and told her it was where their father had died. To Beth it was a strange looking picture that didn't really tell her anything, she had had similar thoughts to the one he had shown her before showing Kitchener's face. This one, however, was just a flat picture of odd shapes in different colours and lots of blue and black dots and writing. She took Arnold's pen from his desk and dipped it into the inkwell and put a small cross on the place he had indicated. From time to time when there was no one around she would creep back into the classroom to look at the mark she had made and convinced herself that her father would know she was there and that she was thinking about him. It was a nice feeling.

After her fright in court Ellen kept her word. Every morning Beth and Arnold left the house together for school with dry feet. Every time they outgrew their shoes she sent them alone back to the poor relief shop for a new pair. Her fear of the workhouse started to recede into a mist of gin and while the children were in school the men started arriving.

*Black Maria – Colloquial name for a Police Riot/Prisoner Van of the early 1900s.

Owen

His grandmother was ironing his shirt for school; he liked the warm area in front of the fire and watched her as she pressed it to perfection putting the iron onto the black leaded fireplace to renew the heat. His two aunts were also sat in the kitchen, repairing bed linen by gaslight and talking to each other in hushed tones. While his grandmother was there he knew there would be no criticisms, innuendos or sly slaps which, unbeknown to her, always happened when she was out.

Eleanor had brought him to her house just days after he was born. Six months earlier her eldest son Owen had drunkenly informed her that Theresa was pregnant with her first grandchild. They were living in what she deemed to be a slum with a dirt floor and no running water and the child would be born out of wedlock. The latter had rocked her Quaker roots to the core. A few days after the news had reached her that the child had been born, she left home to walk to their abode and sternly knocked on their door before entering. Theresa stood as she entered and smiled, her son sat at the table with a jug of beer, he looked at her with contempt; she returned his gaze solidly and kept her dignity.

She walked over and looked at the baby boy who was sleeping in a makeshift crib in an old drawer on the mud floor, smiled and quietly asked his name.

An embarrassed Theresa said quietly 'His name is Owen after his father... '

'Not my idea... ' slurred his father, who belched and picked up his glass of beer.

Eleanor looked at her son with disappointment and disgust then at Theresa with compassion, and held out her hand for Theresa to take hold.

'He is beautiful,' and after a pause, 'I am sorry, but I cannot let my first grandson live in this hovel and house of shame... I will take care of him don't worry... he will be loved and cherished... always.'

Shocked and hurt Theresa had cried out, 'No... please... no!'

Owen Snr ignored her protestations, turned away from them, picked the jug up and refilled his glass. 'Let her have him woman... enough.'

Realising it was futile to argue with him she had kissed her baby's tiny head, turned away from him and started to cry in despair.

Eleanor gently took hold of him, wrapped him inside her shawl and carried him home to nurture and bring him up as her own. That had been eight years ago and she had been true to her word.

His grandmother was his world; her Victorian and Quaker values ruled the house he now lived in. He was loved in return and she took great pride in his appearance and his development at school. His aunts were not so magnanimous and fell short of the Quaker way of life followed by their mother, taking any opportunity to keep reminding him of where he should be living and with whom. Not that he understood their vindictiveness.

He rewarded his grandmother by doing well at school and attending to the chores that he was expected to carry out at home without question. Every Friday after school he would walk the mile to the bakery where his aunts worked and would stand and wait across the road until the back door opened. One of his aunts would pass a large bag to him containing enough bread for the week before telling him sharply to go straight home and be quick about it.

His main chore was collecting the weekly bag of coal from another relative who worked at a city coal merchant. He would walk to the tram stop at the bottom of The Moor and ride a way into the city to the Cathedral before then walking to another tram terminus in Fitzalan Square. That would take him in the opposite direction out of town towards the coal merchant's yard in Attercliffe. He always enjoyed the journey to the yard and sat proudly on the top of the tram knowing that he would have to sit downstairs on the return trip. On arrival at the yard he would take receipt of the coal in a sack which differed in weight on a weekly basis. He would then drag the bag back to the tram stop and return by the same route back home. If he was in luck the friendly tram conductors would help him to board the trams, they got to know him after a while and all assumed his father was away at war.

The tram stop was a five minute walk from the house, but on average it took him twenty minutes to drag the heavy sack back home always fearing it would tear. He was now particularly careful and tried not to lose any of the contents as one of his aunts had followed him into the house one week holding a piece of coal and spitefully said that he had dropped it and just left it there in the middle of the road. His grandmother had quietly told him to be more careful in the future, so from then on he always made sure the sack was intact so that the same accusation could not be made against him again.

The tram conductors had assumed correctly that his father was away at war although this fact was still unknown to him, he had never questioned it. When he was four years old Owen Snr had joined the Guards like many others to do his patriotic duty again answering Kitchener's call to arms, at the same time loudly stating to all who would listen that nobody was going to give him the white feather.

During the time Owen had been at his grandmother's, Theresa his mother had again given birth to two girls and life was hard and worrying for her. Though painful to her she was grateful that her eldest son was cared for, she still thought about him every day and silently wondered how he was. Owen was oblivious to the fact that he had any sisters, all he knew was from the aunts who, given any opportunity, kept telling him that he didn't belong there and should go back to his own family. He didn't know who his 'own' family was so how could he go back? Their venom would rise whenever his grandmother was out of the house telling him if he said anything to her that he would be thrown out. He didn't understand why but he chose to say nothing to her.

Theresa appeared unannounced one cold night on Eleanor's doorstep. She was carrying her youngest child and Elizabeth her eldest daughter was holding her mother's hand. She was not sure what welcome they would receive but felt that Eleanor should know that she had received a telegram saying that her eldest son had been wounded in the Battle for Passchendaele. Eleanor looked at her and the children and listened to her news with horror. She acknowledged that her Quaker roots dictated that she must give them food and shelter. Owen stood in the kitchen and felt his grandmother's concern. He watched the girls hungrily eating hot food, not realising that this was the family that had been referred to by his aunts.

Theresa looked at him through a mother's eyes and saw what a good looking, proud, young boy he had become. He was clean, warm and nicely dressed, a son to be proud of. She cast her eyes down as he returned her stare from warm blue eyes; she was ashamed of their appearance and fearful of saying anything to him. His sisters looked at him with wary, curious eyes. Then the moment was broken by Elizabeth who smiled warmly over at her older brother and he smiled back.

His aunts were outraged that Theresa had been to their door, but Eleanor had overruled them and said it was their duty to support her son's family if the worst should happen. She then sat down with Owen and explained quietly who the visitors had been and that his father, who was now a soldier, had been wounded in one of the battles in France. He listened in silence and started to understand what his aunts had always taunted him with. His grandmother, in contradiction of Victorian values, told him she loved him and that while ever she was alive he would remain in her house and continue with his studies. He told her that he understood and went off to bed thinking about the woman who it appeared was his mother, and the young girls that were his sisters. As they had disappeared back into the cold night, Elizabeth had turned and waved goodbye to her elder brother and he had waved back; he also noticed they were not wearing shoes.

Later sitting alone and in silence after her charge had gone to bed, Eleanor prayed and wept without reserve for her son and grandson into the early hours.

Weeks passed and there was no further contact from Theresa until just before Christmas. She arrived at Eleanor's door with a postcard that had been sent from the hospital that Owen Snr had been evacuated to after being wounded. It was a bizarre picture of the inmates of the ward with her son to the fore, a canopy over his left leg indicating where the surgeons had amputated. The idea was to send a Christmas greeting to their relatives to show they were still alive although maimed, probably softening the blow a little before they were actually discharged and sent back home. Eleanor gave thankful, silent prayers that although her son had lost his leg he was still alive, there didn't seem to be any other injuries. In the photograph he was sitting up in bed staring fully into the camera. It had been widely reported that mustard gas had been used by the German forces at Ypres but it appeared that her son had not been affected in that respect. She thanked Theresa and before she left gave her a basket of bread and potatoes. She was grateful that she had come to give her the news and for coming during school hours knowing that Owen would not be there. She knew she had to tell him, but she would decide to do so on her own terms and when the time was right. Three months later his father was discharged from the military hospital and arrived back home.

Another three months passed Eleanor knew it was her duty to visit her son. After much thought she decided to take Owen with her so he could actually see where and how the family lived. She quietly acknowledged he must have unanswered concerns and questions and she hoped by reassuring him again that he would remain with her he was bright enough to see and understand her reasoning.

The visit was full of trepidation for both of them. Eleanor had once again packed a basket of provisions and given Owen two small bags of sweets for the girls. They set off for the house and walked in silence.

Theresa had told her husband that his mother was to visit them, he had not commented. Elizabeth was sitting outside on the step when she saw them coming down the lane, she ran inside shouting, 'They're here... they're coming... ' Her mother heard the shout, straightened her hair and apron and turned to look at Owen Snr. He returned her look with a glower and picked up his glass of beer as she went to the door to greet them. Eleanor acknowledged her with a nod.

As they entered the house Eleanor's gaze swept the room, she looked at the jug of beer on the table and at her son's glazed eyes and gripped her grandson's hand for mutual support.

Owen Snr turned, looked at his mother with a fixed glare then at his son. After a long pause he slurred, 'I am your father boy... you have come here to show some respect... yes?'

'Yes sir,' he replied quietly. His young son lowered his eyes, not able to hold the malevolent gaze aimed at him.

His father was sitting in a red velvet upholstered chair; it looked oddly out of place in the cold dark room they were in. There were half-burnt candles and an overriding smell of damp and the drains from outside. A pair of crutches was leaning against the wall next to a wooden leg fitted with leather straps. A grubby chaise longue sat adjacent to the wall.

The silence was broken by Theresa who gratefully took the basket from Eleanor and beckoned the girls to receive the sweets from Owen. Elizabeth approached her brother with a smile, she was pleased to see him again and in that moment he thought how pretty she was. He nodded and smiled back and gave them the small packages feeling relieved that he could lose his father's hostile stare. The three of them then moved to the side of the room without another word being spoken.

Eleanor had taken Theresa to one side and told her that if she ever needed food for the children she could come to see her, but as long as her son was spending his benefits in the alehouse she could not help by giving them money. Silently Theresa nodded her head, and with tears rolling down her cheeks thanked her, adding that she was with child again. Her honesty was met with stony silence.

They did not stay in the hovel long as Eleanor was not comfortable. She felt that she had done her mother's duty by visiting him and taking his son with her to enquire after his health; that being done they walked back home together in silence lost in their own thoughts. They did not discuss the visit although it weighed heavily on both their minds. Owen held her hand tightly all the way.

Beth

School was an escape and when Monday morning arrived she was always eager to leave the house as soon as she was ready. Some days, if Arnold wasn't ready, she left him to follow and walked alone. Other classmates always looked forward to the weekend and the two days off, but Beth's weekends were a mixture of her mother drinking and the appearance of men at the door who she didn't know but clearly her mother did. The pattern was always the same, a knock at the door then Ellen would tell them to go to the park or find someone to play with. She had on the rare occasion gone to look at the gardens in the infirmary, but it always reminded her of that awful day when her father had been lost at sea so she had decided never to go there again. She preferred to go and sit on the school wall where she felt comfortable even though she couldn't go into the school buildings. She knew as long as she stayed out of the house for a couple of hours when she returned the visitor would have gone.

There was no fear of the unknown during the school day, her teacher worked through the different subjects they were learning about and she thrived on the discipline. Now she was older she understood about the world map that Arnold had shown her when she first started, in fact her lessons were now held in that same classroom and the map was still on the wall. The cross she had made years earlier had faded but still visible to Beth because she knew where to look.

She knew there were lots of other children in school who had lost their fathers in the Great War; there were many homes without a man at the head of the family. Then there were fathers who had returned with such awful injuries, their wounds so horrific that it made you stare at them all the time, then if they saw you looking you would turn away feeling ashamed. In one way she was pleased that no one would stare at her father, he would never become a victim of morbid curiosity and there was some comfort in that. All the children in school seemed to accept these casualties of war in their stride, in one sense it put them on a level playing field as very few families were left unaffected in one way or another.

Ellen felt the need for male company more and more as the years started to pass. She still thought of herself as an attractive woman although she realised that because of the huge loss of young lives in the war years, the chance of finding a new man to take care of her and her children was realistically, non-existent. She chose to take brief liaisons to brighten her days, desperate for light conversation and the intense warmth of another body close to hers. It released her from her day to day existence and stopped her thinking of what might have been. She was very careful not to appear too demanding or needy for fear her admirers, as she viewed them, may stop coming.

As the years passed Arnold tried his best to earn a penny for Ellen as he hated it when the men arrived at the door; he would leave the house in resentful silence. As young as he was he felt he was the man of the house and tried his best to keep the promise he had made to his father, whether it be by collecting empty bottles to take back to the shop or just cleaning up tradesmen's yards in the area. He tried to keep alert for any opportunity and walking down the high street one day he passed the local newspaper office and noticed that there was rubbish piled up at the back entrance. He looked around and found the watchman and asked if the rubbish needed to be cleared away to the local tip. The man told him to wait where he was and he would ask the foreman. He stood mesmerised watching the papers running off the presses through the window and didn't realise that the foreman was standing behind him.

He smiled at the boy's obvious fascination at the production line in front of him.

'Now then lad...what can I help you with?'

Arnold turned and quickly took his cap off his head. 'Oh... I am sorry sir, I didn't see you... I was wondering if you needed all that rubbish moving from the yard?'

'Yes lad I do... but do you think you are up to the job, a young man like you? I have just dismissed the usual man for not turning in for three nights, he was unreliable... I like your initiative... if you can prove to me that you are reliable and come every night at this time then we will pay you two shillings a week. How's that? And you can use the newspaper's barrow to take the rubbish away.'

Arnold was thrilled. He thanked him and shook his hand then rolled his sleeves up and moved towards the barrow to start clearing the rubbish. When it was all cleared and the yard was tidy he said goodbye to the watchman then ran home to tell Ellen and Beth his good news. His announcement was greeted with delight by Beth who laughed and clapped her hands at her brother's good fortune. A distracted Ellen had just nodded in agreement as that day she had realised she was pregnant and a slight panic had set in.

She had decided not to tell them in the early days, her thought pattern being no point in upsetting anyone just yet, time enough. Unfortunately neighbours talk and neighbours' children in the same school tend to pass on any gossip they overhear from their parents. Arnold was the first to become aware of what was being said from one of the boys who lived on their street. He had staunchly denied it but it led to a fist fight in the school yard which resulted in him giving the boy who had made the accusation a bloody nose. The teacher caned them both in front of the class for fighting, but at least he had not asked what had caused the fight and for that Arnold was grateful. Beth had comforted her brother on their way home, she was oblivious to what the fight had been about.

For Ellen, as the months passed, inevitably her pregnancy became more obvious. To prevent her children from actually being told the truth maliciously, she sat them down one day to tell them that in the not too distant future there was to be addition to their family. Arnold looked at his mother horrified and with a stony glare ran out of the house. Beth initially thought how nice it would be to have a new baby in the house if it didn't cry all the time like baby Arthur had. She didn't really understand the implications or why her brother had reacted so out of character and run away.

The first indication that there was something wrong was when they were walking to school one morning and whispered comments were made regarding their mother from some of Arnold's friends. Beth had looked at them, then at Arnold enquiringly, but her brother had told her to keep on walking and take no notice of them. Then a girl in her class had told all the other girls that her mother was a disgrace as she was having a baby when she had no husband and the taunting had started. Arnold took the decision that he couldn't fight everyone in the school so he told Beth to ignore what they were saying and stay close to him; he explained that when the baby was born then the other children would have nothing to torment them with. Beth, trusting her brother implicitly, did what he asked and concentrated on her school lessons instead of reacting to the taunts. They now always walked to school then back home together with their heads held high and, because there was no reaction from either of them, their tormentors soon got bored and left them alone.

Ellen was becoming increasingly concerned about going into labour and being at home alone with just the children. She decided she would save a few pence out of the money that Arnold was making at the local paper and her weekly benefit to pay a local neighbour who acted as a midwife in the area. She paid her half in advance so that she was guaranteed to come when Arnold arrived on her doorstep to say it was time.

Ellen delivered a healthy baby girl then introduced her to her older children. Arnold just looked at her and nodded, he felt embarrassed and was not sure what sort of a reaction was expected. Beth, on the other hand, was delighted that she could tell everyone she had a baby sister not really understanding where it had come from but happy all the same. Ellen announced that her name was to be Evelyn and when she registered the birth, the space for the father's name on the certificate remained blank.

Arnold was now an old hand at the newspaper offices. He was popular, quick to laugh and always polite, the general feeling was that he was a good lad so when the opportunity presented itself he was given extra chores to do in addition to clearing out the rubbish. He hoped when he was fourteen in a few months' time and ready to leave school, that they would let him work there full time now that there was another mouth to feed at home.

The foreman who knew his history was pleased that he had proved his worth and one day just as he was leaving for home called him over and said, 'Arnold, we are pleased with how you have worked lad, and if you want it there will be a permanent position here for you when you finish school.'

He didn't have to answer, his face erupted into a huge smile, and doffing his cap, replied, 'Yes please sir... that would be great... thank you... thank you...'

'It's alright lad, you have earned it... your family should be very proud of you. Well done, well done... come here,' and, extending his hand, he took hold of Arnold's and shook it vigorously.

His high was short-lived because whilst walking away from the yard the memory of his father came into his thoughts, a fleeting moment taking him back to the last day he had seen him before he went off to war never to be seen again. The feeling overwhelmed him and he stood by the wall of the newspaper building for a moment and had to hold on to it for support. The years since the loss of his father had been full of despair at times and challenging at others. Arnold hoped that if his father had been alive he would have been proud of him, with the way he had coped and tried to do his best. If only he could have been there to congratulate him tonight, to shake his hand as any proud caring father would do, he would have given anything for that. Without warning the tears welled up and started to roll down his cheeks, and he sobbed uncontrollably in despair into the wall. After a while his tears suddenly abated as quickly as they had started and he took a moment to compose himself and wipe the wet streaks from his face on his sleeve. He then took a deep breath and continued home to tell Beth and his mother the good news.

Ellen knew that she was the main topic of conversation in the area but, like all gossip, she also knew it would only last until it was some other poor soul's turn to be in the spotlight. Evelyn was a demanding baby but not in the same way Arthur had been. Ellen and Beth both doted on her, the child's face lighting up every time Beth was around to entertain her. Arnold was pleased that his youngest sister had brought about a positive change at home, his mother had stopped her drinking and the men came no more. Now that he would be working and be a wage earner he could assume the role as head of the house and keep his promise to his father made long ago on the last day he was to see him alive. He continued walking home and for the first time in years felt at ease with himself.

Owen

Life continued much the same for Owen at his grandmother's house. He was older now so the aunts didn't have as much impact on his day to day life as he now knew about his parents and siblings so they no longer had a secret over him. He still worked hard at school, enjoyed his lessons and did his chores which is all his grandmother had asked of him. Eleanor felt tired, the pressure of bringing Owen up as her own had taken its toll over the years. She prayed to ease the pain and shame of her eldest son's way of life and his total disregard not only for his mother, but for the children from his union with his common law wife Theresa. If he was desperate for money then he would send Elizabeth to her door. Eleanor felt she could not deny the children but would only send food never the cash he asked for as she knew he would only spend it on drink. The rift grew wider between mother and son.

In the warm kitchen Owen ate his breakfast and then prepared himself for school. His grandmother was sitting in her usual chair but this particular morning as he was leaving she had called him back. She took hold of his hand, smiled at him, told him she loved him and that he must promise her he would always be true to himself. He thought she looked more tired than usual and was surprised when he saw there were tears in her eyes. He kissed her cheek and told her not to be upset, to rest and that he would see her later that day after school. He opened the kitchen door to leave then paused and turned to look at her once more before leaving. He smiled at her again, said goodbye, then closed the door behind him. Eleanor quietly and peacefully passed away in her chair the same morning, he never saw her again.

She had been on his mind all day and a premonition made him run home from school, when he arrived he found her chair empty and his aunts in a state of shock and despair. He was promptly sent to his room and told to keep out of the way. Bereft at losing his beloved grandmother he did as he was told and stayed alone in his room without comfort for nearly two days. Her daughters made the arrangements for the funeral, he was told when it would be and what was expected of him. If he felt hungry he fed himself and tried to be inconspicuous. Over the years he had become used to their spiteful ways but this was a new twist in the seat of power and he felt more than a little afraid of them.

When the day of the funeral arrived he was told to dress smartly and not to let his grandmother down by showing any grief; he was to walk behind the immediate family and to keep quiet. He did as he had been instructed, stood alone, and being the Quaker way, grieved in silence. Cold and solitary, his head bowed he watched in despair and disbelief as his grandmother lying alone in her coffin was lowered into a dark void in the cold ground. Desperate to control his sobs of grief he closed his eyes to shut out the nightmare and to stop himself from calling out to her, squeezing his nails into the palms of his hands. His beloved grandmother was now gone, she was to be left alone buried in the cold ground in the cemetery forever. He watched from a distance and in resigned silence as his aunts received all the condolences in turn from family and friends present. He wondered what the future held for him now that his beloved grandmother was no more.

His mother and father attended the funeral, he had watched as his father limped in to the place of worship with a resentful scowl, neither of them spoke or acknowledged him. Later his mother had quietly approached him and put a kindly arm around his shoulder and looked at him with loving, sympathetic eyes. It was a discreet touch designed not to draw any attention to either of them; she then turned away leaving him in his grief stricken silence once more.

Still standing apart from the adults and waiting for the instruction to return home after the internment, he noticed his aunts having an animated conversation with his father. Their voices were raised although he couldn't hear what they were saying. After some time the sisters indicated to him it was time to return home; on entering the house they told him to pack his possessions as he was moving back to his own family, from now on he was to view their home as his.

Night fell on a cold and miserable day. He walked slowly and in grief to his parents' house with his bundle and stood outside the hovel trying to steel his nerves before cautiously knocking on the door. His arrival was met with four sets of steady eyes from his three sisters and one brother, his father was sitting in the red velvet chair, his customary jug of beer to hand. The house had not changed, there was still the pervading smell of damp and open sewers, a far cry from the comfort and warmth of his grandmother's house that had been his home since he had been a baby. He stood in front of them all in this alien house, eyes downcast and looking at the floor. Once again he tried very hard not to cry.

His mother felt his despair and her heart went out to him. She took the bundle from him put her arm around his shoulder and whispered to her first born, 'It's alright Owen... it will be alright... please don't worry... please don't be frightened... I am here for you.'

'Quiet woman... ' shouted his father, 'and you... get out of my sight,' pointing a vindictive finger at him.

The other children crowded around their mother, all curious to see what the bundle held, they were all disappointed that there was no food inside. His aunts had checked that he was only taking his clothes before throwing him out of the house, but then relented and allowed him to include the books his grandmother had bought for him along with any of the items he used for school. Unbeknown to him and Theresa, and out of sight at the funeral, the aunts had given his father a few pounds and told him they were sending his son back as he was now his responsibility. This is what the disagreement had been about earlier, Owen Snr was to consider the money they had given him as his dues from his mother's estate and to never contact them again.

The heavy silence continued in the small room, the only sounds coming from his father lifting the jug of beer, belching and moving in his chair to make himself more comfortable. Theresa showed Owen the mattress on the damp floor where all the children slept fully clothed, and as they all crowded onto it Owen found himself on the edge. In silent despair, he tightly closed his eyes to try and once again shut out the nightmare, when suddenly Elizabeth's hand found his and held it tightly as if to comfort him. He responded to her touch and daring not to make a sound held on to it as silent tears rolled down his cheeks for his grandmother and himself.

He couldn't sleep in the alien surroundings and not certain of what he was expected to do the next morning, he quietly left for school without disturbing anyone. He went without breakfast and slowly walked the distance back to the familiarity and comfort of his school surroundings.

The headmaster, Mr Storer, saw him arrive. He was aware from Owen's aunts that his circumstances had changed. They had wasted no time in advising him that they had no further responsibility for his young pupil, that he was now in his father's care at a different address. He had not warmed to their demeanour. Approaching him, he sympathetically explained that as Owen had moved and no longer lived in the school's catchment area, he might have to attend another school elsewhere, he would check with the authorities and let him know. He listened and acknowledged what his headmaster had said and again despair consumed him. He walked as if in a dream into his classroom and started his lessons dreading the end of the school day when he would have to leave.

On rising Theresa noticed that her son had quietly left for school. She organised the other children and they all left for their school together. She liked to usher them out of the way before attending to her husband's needs. When he roused she always assisted him with the strapping on of his false leg so that he could get his mobility, it always took time depending on how much drink he had consumed the night before.

The previous night when his son had appeared at the door, he had looked at him and only saw a good looking, well proportioned young man. He decided that he had been in school long enough and that it was now time for him to go out and work for a living, earn his keep and support the family. This opinion had been formed through a drunken haze, what he didn't see was a vulnerable young boy with a broken heart who's world and security had just totally disintegrated. His life would never be the same again but there was to be no compassion.

Later that morning Owen Snr left the house on a mission and, with the help of one crutch, painfully limped his way towards the commercial area of the city determined to find his son a position of work. He had the money in his pocket from his sisters so he knew he could call for his drink en route. The wooden leg into which his knee fitted hurt when he walked any distance, so he drank to numb the pain. When out of his usual haunts he could always spin a tale and find someone to buy an old soldier down on his luck a drink or two.

His planned mission was not as easy as he thought it was going to be, he had enquired at a dozen companies and received the same reply – 'Too many people to choose from', 'Didn't need to take on a boy with no previous experience', times were tough for everyone. With each dismissal he became more belligerent which made his plea for work for his son totally unacceptable to any prospective employer. Eventually loudly cursing all the companies he had visited he turned back towards home and decided he would call in at all the hostelries to ease the pain in his leg.

The school bell rang signalling the end of the school day and his heart sank. Owen walked back slowly not wanting to return to the house he was now expected to call home. Having not eaten all day he alternated between hunger pangs and nausea brought on by fear. He stood outside the door and hesitated before he entered being unsure of who he would find there, the nausea was prominent. His mother turned and smiled at him as he opened the door after knocking first, the other children were all sitting on the mattress eating bread and jam. He was relieved to see the red chair was empty and his sad blue eyes reflected the look of relief to his mother.

Elizabeth was quick to read the bereft look and moved the little ones, indicating to her brother to sit next to her. Theresa gave him the same to eat and told him that when they had all finished they were all to go out and Elizabeth would show him where they all went to play. It was her way of trying to keep the peace in the house, her husband had been gone nearly all day and she assumed rightly that he would be the worse for drink when he returned. As always, one wrong look or word or if the children were noisy, it would give rise to an argument which could turn violent. She knew it would be best if they were out of the way especially Owen, who her husband irrationally held responsible for the family's problems.

Elizabeth felt proud having her brother at her side as they all walked down the lane together. The two of them had never had a proper conversation over the years, it had always been just looks of either curiosity or concern when they had seen each other at their grandmother's house. The younger ones had no qualms about asking him questions some of them enquiring, others just silly because of their ages. A couple of times he laughed at his younger brother Kenneth's questions. There was a nine-year age gap between them but the youngster liked to play the joker when out of the house. Usually they all took their lead from Elizabeth, especially at home, she only had to flash her eyes as a warning and they all adhered. She was now thirteen and very pretty. As they sat on the grass in the park Theresa and Sybil, the two younger sisters, asked him about his life at their grandmothers.

'Was she a nice lady... our grandmother?' asked Theresa. They all sat quietly to hear his reply.

'Yes she was... ' replied Owen sadly not looking at any of them. 'She was everything to me... '

'But you didn't know us then,' piped up Kenneth not understanding his older brother's sadness.

Owen smiled at him and said, 'No that's true I didn't... it is a pity none of you could have known her. Always remember your grandmother was a nice, kind lady... '

'I shall always remember her like that, because she was,' said Elizabeth quickly to the younger ones. 'Whenever we used to go to see her there was always cooking smells in a warm kitchen that made you hungry. Then she always gave us nice things to eat.' She then changed the subject and asked, 'Will you be coming to our school?'

He looked at her and answering truthfully said, 'I don't know, I hope not... it is the only link I have left of the days I lived with my grandmother. I would like to keep my promise to her... to try and do my best, but I don't know if I will be able to now because I have had to move.'

They all listened to his reply then Sybil broke the silence and said, 'Well I think it is going to be nice to have a big brother. Elizabeth can't boss us around anymore as she is not the eldest now.' Owen laughed again and so did Elizabeth, she looked at him and sincerely hoped that one day the sadness would leave his eyes.

Theresa heard her husband coming along the lane and opened the door quickly. She looked at him and from his demeanour detected that his quest had not been successful. Taking the initiative as he came through the door, she appeared very sympathetic and led him upstairs to unstrap his leg so that he could rest and sleep the drink off. Her strategy worked, he slept through the night and the next morning Owen and the other children had already left for school by the time he was ready to have his breakfast.

Owen walked on alone to the only school he had ever known and was careful this time not to catch the headmaster's eye in the hope that he might forget their earlier conversation regarding a transfer to another school.

Later in the morning Owen Snr left the house again, he had decided he would be more selective in the companies he would approach. He had decided he would look for companies with a work yard so that they might be able to start a youngster off just clearing rubbish out of the way and once in, he could progress from there. Being an industrial city there were many to choose from so walking in a different direction to the previous day off he went again. By late afternoon his result was the same as the previous day, so begrudgingly he decided once again to turn for home and enjoy some companionship in the public houses on the way back home to ease his pain and woes. Just before he reached the corner of the street he noticed a painting and decorating company with a large storage yard and decided to have one final attempt for that day.

Mr Appleyard was co-owner of the company Owen Snr approached. He was preparing to leave for the day when he overheard a conversation in the yard. He listened as a voice stated his business to the company foreman, emphasising his war record and how he could no longer care for his family as he had lost his leg at Passchandael. It was paramount he find a position of employment for his eldest son to secure his family's wellbeing. Mr Appleyard walked over to the gate to look at the man leaning on his crutch making the request to the foreman, he was a kindly man who liked to think that he did his Christian duty for the less fortunate. His immediate line of thought was that as the company's existing young labourer was about to enter his apprenticeship, this unfortunate man's son could be given a trial and, if he proved himself to be efficient and conscientious when he was fifteen, he too would be taken on as a paid apprentice to serve his time.

He approached the two men. The foreman acknowledged his employer and explained to Owen Snr who this gentleman was. After listening to the offer Owen Snr thanked Mr Appleyard and told him he was a gentleman. He doffed his cap and shaking his hand assured him that the boy would be there the next morning at seven o'clock prompt. He said he was not only sure his son would be fine but certain that he would see Mr Appleyard again on his fifteenth birthday; Mr Appleyard nodded his consent, turned and left. Highly delighted with his success Owen Snr placed his cap back on his head thanked the foreman and left the yard at all speed to celebrate, having no problem finding the usual faces to share in his good fortune especially as he was buying.

The classroom door opened and the headmaster appeared, the entire class stood automatically; he had come to find Owen. Mr Storer called him out of the classroom into the corridor and once again the fear in the pit of his stomach hit home before a word had been spoken. He told him that as he was a good pupil and taking into account his recent personal circumstances, he had appealed to the local education office and governors of the school for him to stay at Duchess Road School rather than have to move to another. He was pleased to tell him that they had agreed, so he would be able to remain there. Owen was thrilled, he thanked him and felt the relief flood back into his body.

Before he re-entered the classroom he took a moment to compose himself and wiped away the tears as his grandmother once again entered his thoughts. His euphoria soon evaporated as he cautiously approached the house after school; this hovel could never be classed as his home, there was always the fear of what awaited him hiding behind its door. He opened it cautiously and five pairs of eyes turned to meet his, he smiled, they all smiled back and moved over for him to sit down and join them for something to eat.

It was still early days, Theresa wanted Owen to feel that he was becoming part of the family. She had told the other children to wait for him so that they could all eat together and it pleased her that they had all taken to him. She knew he looked the odd one out as he was far better nourished and dressed than his siblings, but they didn't seem to mind. She tried to keep the fleas out of the clothes he had brought with him although she knew it was just a matter of time before they became as infested as everything else. That was the reason the children slept fully clothed on the flea-ridden mattress, there was no way of keeping them out, it just kept the bites down.

As they were all chattering the door banged open and in hobbled their father. He threw his crutch down and shouted at them all to get out apart from Owen. Theresa suddenly felt nervous and moved to help her husband into the red velvet chair. She hovered close, fussing over him, but he shoved her away with a rough push. Owen stood alone in front of his father and met his stare; his fear made the nausea rise and he clenched his fists tightly pressing his fingernails once again into the palm of his hands forcing himself not to cry.

His father's breath was sour with ale; he started to point his finger contemptuously at his son. He told him his school days were now finished, he had to earn his keep and provide for his family. He sneered that his grandmother had been too soft and to forget those days as first thing the next morning he was to go to Appleyard's and work there until his fifteenth birthday, at which time he would become a tied apprentice to their trade. He should consider himself lucky, do what he was told and not cause any trouble or he would have his father to answer to. When he had finished speaking Theresa indicated with her eyes to her eldest that he should now go out and join the other children, ushering him quickly to the door.

All the other children were sitting on a wall near the house waiting for him to join them. Elizabeth saw her brother leave the house but instead of turning towards them he started to run in the opposite direction. She called out to him but he ran on without acknowledging her and didn't stop until he reached the cemetery where his grandmother had been interned only a few days earlier. It felt like years since he had lost her. Finding her place of rest he threw himself on to the plot exhausted and wept yet again, he remained there sobbing alone until darkness fell.

Cold and desolate, but knowing that he had no option but to return to his father's house, he walked back and entered the hovel once again unable to speak for fear the tears would rise and never stop. His mother watched as he took his place in silence with the other children on the flea-infested mattress. Once again Elizabeth's hand found his to try and give any small comfort to him that she could.

The next morning Theresa rose early, she gave him some bread and dripping wrapped in paper and a bottle of water for his break. She watched in sadness as he walked slowly down the lane for the decorator's yard as instructed by his father. She knew they dare not defy him, and her heart ached for her son as he walked dejectedly round the corner and out of sight.

He found the company and was told by the gateman to sit and wait for the owner Mr Appleyard who would be arriving shortly; he felt numb. His employer duly arrived and saw the boy stand as he entered the gates, he walked towards him and smiled gently. Owen doffed his cap and cast his eyes down uncertain what other stance to take. Looking at the boy Mr Appleyard asked him his name and which school he had attended. He answered him dutifully with a 'Sir' after each question. Walking respectfully one pace behind his employer he followed him into the office for the paperwork to be completed. When Owen gave his address Mr Appleyard asked him why he had gone to Duchess Road School instead of one nearer to his home. He explained that he had always lived with his grandmother until her recent death and that was why he had so recently had to move. Mr Appleyard listened quietly and nodded, he then called for Georgie the other boy in the yard to come to the office and instructed him to show Owen around and explain what his duties would be. As he watched the two boys go he made a mental note to make enquiries about Owen when he saw the headmaster of Duchess Road School at his church the following Sunday morning.

Georgie was a little older and taller than Owen, he had been pleased not to have to go to school anymore and was grateful that Mr Appleyard had given him a chance to better himself and train as an apprentice. He was a streetwise boy and had come to the attention of the kindly gent outside the local public house returning bottles for the penny deposits. Mr Appleyard had thought it showed initiative. Georgie could see that Owen was better dressed than he was, but he appeared quiet and uncertain of what was expected of him and really quite sad and ill at ease. He was pleased to have another boy in the yard and hoped they would become apprentices together and told him so hoping that this might make him feel a little more relaxed.

At the end of the day Georgie was impressed that Owen was actually stronger than he looked, the years of dragging and lifting the sacks of coal for his grandmother had strengthened his muscles. His initial thought that he might have to carry this boy were dispelled when Owen matched him lift for lift. They clocked out together and headed for home, Georgie telling him that he would see him the next morning, that he was pleased that Owen had come to work there and that he had enjoyed their day together.

Owen nodded and said, 'Yes, so have I... thanks to you.' He smiled as he turned the corner thinking how nice it was to have a new friend. He continued walking but his good feeling was short lived when he sighted the house in the distance. Again the fear rose in his stomach when, on opening the door and walking in, he was met with the steely glare of his father.

'If I find out you have not done everything that has been asked of you today you will suffer the consequences.' Putting his beer down on the table he turned and picked up his crutch and held it menacingly, 'Do you understand what I am saying?'

'Yes,' replied his son.

'Yes... what?' The grip on the wooden crutch tightened and the eyes turned malicious.

'Yes... sir.'

His father looked at him with disgust, turned and threw the crutch down and picked up his beer once again. The other children sat in silence and watched in fear, they were used to his tirades and knew it was not an idle threat. Elizabeth shuffled over on the mattress and Theresa silently indicated for him to join them so that he would be out of his father's eye line. Owen followed the instruction and all of them remained quiet until their father had started to doze in his chair. They knew the format, once he had consumed enough beer then he would want to sleep and their mother would start the onerous job of getting him upstairs to his bed out of everybody's way.

The next day was Saturday so Owen and Georgie only worked half day, they finished at one o'clock. After they had clocked out Georgie suggested they go off to the park for the rest of the day and Owen readily agreed pleased that he didn't have to go back to the house.

Elizabeth, being off school, had missed him. She had waited for him thinking he would be back earlier. When he did arrive home he found her still sitting outside on the wall waiting for him, he smiled as he approached. She told him that she had been waiting an age for him to come home, that their father had gone out so it was alright and he need not worry. She wanted to hear all about his day so he sat down next her on the wall and told her all about Georgie and Mr Appleyard. She was pleased to hear that they were nice people and told him she hoped he would be happy there as she knew it had been another shock.

As they talked he told her he had decided to go to his grandmother's grave the next day to tidy the flowers away that had now died. He said he would pick some wild ones on the way to replace them. She asked if she could go with him and take the other children as Eleanor had been their grandmother too. Owen smiled again and nodded and said yes of course his grandmother would have liked that. The next morning they all set off together for the cemetery.

Theresa, standing at the door, watched her children, she knew where they were going and had packed some bread and water for them all so that they could make a day of it out of the domain of their father. Watching them go she afforded herself a rare smile before her husband finally roused himself from the previous night's drinking and banged loudly on the floor for assistance.

The same Sunday morning Mr Appleyard attended his church.

After the morning service it was considered etiquette on leaving the church that the parishioners thank the vicar for an uplifting sermon, and then the socialising could begin. The ladies would group together and discuss family matters relishing any gossip; the men used this time for promoting business if at all possible. Mr Appleyard turned from the vicar and acknowledged Mr Storer the headmaster of Duchess Road School. He told him that Owen had started work in his yard that week and hopefully he would go on to take up an apprenticeship. Mr Storer was visibly shocked to hear this news, he had thought Owen's absence for the rest of the week had been due to a delayed reaction to his grandmother's death. He explained to Appleyard that the boy had been brought up by her since birth, and how he had fought for him to remain in his school with the authorities after her unexpected death as he was an excellent pupil. He was now surprised and somewhat dismayed and disappointed to hear of this unfortunate development. Mr Appleyard apologised and told him that the boy's father had secured the position for him and the only reason he had mentioned it was that he was hoping the boy would not disappoint him. Mr Storer was quick to reassure him and re-iterated Owen's good character and commitment to his schoolwork. He sadly explained that the boy's circumstances had irrevocably changed for the worst and thought it most unfortunate for the boy. He was pleased that he was now under Mr Appleyard's sponsorship and hoped that he would succeed and for Mr Appleyard to extend his good wishes to the boy for his good fortune. Taking his leave Mr Appleyard thanked him for the encouraging report and stated that he would pass Mr Storer's good wishes on to the boy when appropriate.

Georgie Lee had started his apprenticeship three months before Owen, it was the day of his fifteenth birthday and his father a jovial man, had arrived proudly at the yard to sign his apprentice papers. With his cap in his hand he had graciously thanked Mr Appleyard for the opportunity he was extending to his son. A proud father, he had looked at Georgie dressed in his painter's white bib and brace and jacket, shook his hand and congratulated him. He worked in the steelworks and was delighted that his son did not need to follow in his footsteps into the dark, hot kingdom of the furnaces. After the signing everyone in the company lined up to shake the new apprentice's hand and to welcome him officially into the company, congratulations abounded. Georgie bursting with pride beamed at his friend Owen, knowing that he too would be following in his footsteps a few months later.

Their daily routine had fallen into a pattern and Georgie did his best to help his new friend along under the watchful eye of the older men in the yard. Mr Appleyard watched from a distance, they were a likeable pair and he felt sure that they would prove to be good apprentices as well as turning into good friends. Before the apprentice's papers were signed their wage was five shillings a week, Owen took this amount home and gave it straight to Theresa not realising that it was all handed over to his father but never in his view. Usually his father was out when he arrived home, apart from pay day, that was the only day he would be in the house waiting for his son's return. When he was fifteen and offered the apprenticeship his wage would increase to eleven shillings a week, of which five shillings would be deducted initially until his overalls were paid for. It was a strict company rule that no apprentice could appear on any site or be taken into a client's house if not wearing his full whites.

The day of Owen's fifteenth birthday arrived and he waited for his father to appear to sign the papers for his apprenticeship just as Georgie's father had. Mr Appleyard was already in the office and Owen had told him that his father would arrive for the appointment later in the morning due to his incapacity. Two hours later Owen Snr, limped through the yard and into the office ready to sign his son's indenture papers. Full of anticipation Owen stood with Georgie and waited to be called into the office, then to his horror his father reappeared a few minutes later and limped back out through the gates without any acknowledgement to his son whatsoever. He and Georgie looked at each other fearing the worst. Georgie felt for his friend and they both remained where they were looking towards the office in silence.

It had been a brief conversation. Owen Snr had been shown into Mr Appleyard's office by the company's head clerk Perkins who always witnessed any legal documents. He had prepared Owen's papers earlier and took his position behind his employer's chair papers in hand.

'Good morning Sir. Welcome on this auspicious day,' said Mr Appleyard smiling. 'This must be a proud morning for you.' He extended his hand but then paused as, reaching forward, he had become aware of the stale smell of beer.

A cold pair of eyes looked back at him, 'You can dispense with the pleasantries. Just show me where I sign,' came the curt reply.

The clerk moved forward, 'Well it is customary for the young apprentice to be present when his papers are signed and company policy for us to have a small celebration. It is after all the first step into manhood and his chosen career. It would be a pity if...'

'Pity? Don't talk to me about pity. Pity for who? He deserves no celebration, he is here to do a job and get paid for it and no more. Give me the papers. Where do I sign?'

The clerk looked at his employer and Mr Appleyard nodded in silence for him to place the papers on the desk and to give this man a pen.

'Right... now that is done he is all yours. Any problems from him let me know.'

Mr Appleyard held back his disgust and, keeping his tone of voice level, said, 'Owen has conducted himself extremely well in the short time he has been here with us, you should be proud. I am sure you have nothing to be concerned about.'

'What do you know?' he stood leaning heavily on his crutch. 'I am left like this fighting for people like you, you have no idea. I am unable to work due to fighting for this country's freedom, while you and your like are sat on your arses in fine offices. I have five mouths to feed and another on the way. If he is so good and you are so pleased with him, you will not object to giving me a five pound sub out of his forthcoming wages will you?'

The clerk was outraged that Mr Appleyard was being spoken to in this manner, 'I can assure you sir... '

'It's alright Perkins,' said Mr Appleyard staring at Owen Snr coldly, 'give this man what he asks for and let us be rid of him. After all we have work to do.' Sitting back down in his chair he said, 'You will have to excuse me I am rather busy, good morning to you.' He picked up his pen and Owen Snr was left in no doubt that he had been dismissed. With a feeling of disgust Appleyard watched him limp back out of the office with Perkins following to give him the five pounds he had asked for on account; he was left feeling perplexed and disappointed for his new apprentice. He stood, and with the papers in his hand, moved to the window to see Owen despondently watching his father leave. His friend Georgie was standing in his painter's whites next to his friend in readiness to support his celebration. It had proved to be an embarrassing gesture and they both looked bewildered and not certain what to do.

A few minutes later Mr Appleyard appeared in the yard, approached his new apprentice and shook Owen's hand vigorously. 'Welcome my boy to our company. We are very pleased to have you here. I am sure you will make a first class tradesman.' Mr Perkins and the rest of the workforce lined up and shook his hand as custom demanded. The new apprentice responded graciously thanking them all and tried to put his father out of his mind. Georgie, feeling his friend's despondency, stayed close to him for extra support placing a friendly arm round his shoulder.

Pay day arrived and they were both called to the wages office. Georgie being slightly senior was first and signed for a full pay packet of eleven shillings, now that the cost of his overalls had been repaid. Owen stood behind him in his whites and signed off the receipt of his pay-packet feeling elated until he realised that inside was just one shilling. He didn't understand until the wages clerk explained that his father had taken a sub against his wages of five pound which was to be repaid at five shillings a week, plus there was an additional reduction of five shillings per week for his whites. He and Georgie listened in silence, once more Georgie felt hurt and embarrassed for his friend, the only thing he could think to say to him was that things could only get better as Owen got older so for him not to worry.

Mr Appleyard had given much thought to the distasteful meeting with his father on Owen's apprentice day. He had taken the decision that rather than keep his apprentice off any of the sites where he would fall behind in experience they would deduct both amounts so that all that went home to his father was one shilling. Owen Snr had had his pound of flesh to drink his fill at his young son's expense, he would have to live with the consequences and his conscience, not that Mr Appleyard thought he could possibly possess one.

Beth

Life at home had become easier in some respects since the arrival of Evelyn, the old days of Ellen opening her door to strangers and being drunk on gin had ceased. Her youngest daughter was now four and the apple of her mother's eye. Ellen had lavished all the attention on her youngest that she had been incapable of giving to either Arnold her first born or Beth in equal measure. The older children had formed their own strong bond through their years of misery during the Great War, they were totally at ease with each other but now in their teens both were conscious they had no privacy. Arnold, now a young man had left school and was still working at the newspaper having been promoted to the production line. Beth had been doing the household chores since Evelyn had been born and Ellen had told her that she must look for a position in service now that she was old enough, but not for a live-in position as she still needed her at home. Her selfishness still remained as far as her older children were concerned, Evelyn was the centre of her universe to the exclusion of all others.

Word arrived via a third party that Ellen's mother had passed away. Both Beth and Arnold had never known their extended families so when Ellen told them, there was no emotional impact as they did not know the people she was referring to. Dutifully on the day of the funeral Ellen donned black and the party of four made their way to where the service was to be held. Although she was dressed in mourning, once again Ellen, being remiss with regard to anyone else's feelings, totally failed to appreciate why there would be a reaction to Beth wearing a bright red dress. They arrived to be met with outrage and jeers from her family who were still steeped in their Victorian values. Poor Beth could not understand their reaction or what she had done wrong. Arnold took his sister home away from their venom, these people meant nothing to either of them. They left Ellen holding Evelyn's hand to the wrath of her family. She was considered a pariah within both her and Arthur's family, not only for neglecting her children and consorting with men after her husband's death, but also the ultimate disgrace of having given birth to an illegitimate child.

Arnold concerned for his sister's welfare had asked his work colleagues to inform him if they ever became aware of any suitable positions for her, he didn't want her to go and skivvy in service. Arriving at the newspaper one morning his friend told him that there was a sign in one of the local shops advertising for a helper. Without delay he went to enquire exactly what the position was; it was at a family bakery just around the corner. His first impression was good, he was greeted by a homely silver-haired lady and she smiled as he introduced himself. He explained that he worked at the newspaper round the corner and that his younger sister was looking for a position and could he bring her along to see her. Mrs Richardson warmed to his manner and agreed saying she would remove the sign if Beth could come that day and if she liked what she saw she would hire her. Arnold ran back to the newspaper and asked his manager if it would be acceptable for him to have one hour off and make it up at the end of his shift, explaining the reason why. His manager readily agreed as his work record and discipline had always been good. He knew of his home environment and the promise he had made to his father and since the first day he had arrived at the newspaper he had not wavered.

Running all the way back home he quickly told Beth what had happened. She washed her hands and face, put on a clean smock, tied her hair back neatly and returned with him to the bread shop. They could smell the aroma as they turned the corner and she followed Arnold through the door. They both stood quietly to one side and waited until the existing customers had been served. Beth took the opportunity to look discreetly around the shop and at the lady she was hoping to impress.

Mrs Richardson smiled at the two young people in front of her. She thought her first impression of Arnold had been correct as he proudly introduced his sister, and Beth smiled at her in response. She asked to see Beth's hands and her boots and, satisfying herself that they were to her exact levels of cleanliness, said that she would give her a week's trial. She explained that as it was a bread shop she expected it to be spotless before opening so Beth would have to be there early. If the week's trial was a success then her hours would be extended to help her with chores in her house at the rear of the shop. She smiled to herself as she watched them walk down the street clearly thrilled with their good fortune. Arnold was delighted for his sister and walked back to the newspaper to begin his shift. He thanked his manager once again for letting him have the time off and telling him the good news.

Beth arrived prompt the next morning as instructed, hair tied back, clean smock, hands and boots extra clean. Mrs Richardson welcomed her and gave her instructions where to start; her wages were to be three shillings a week if she was taken on permanently. Arnold instructed her to tell Ellen a shilling less than she would be paid cash in hand, she was to give it to him and he would put in the same place where he saved his. She listened and understood what he was saying to her, as they were growing older into maturity they both recognised there was no way out from their predicament unless they made it for themselves. They owed their mother nothing.

She worked hard the first week and was delighted when she was told that she would be taken on permanently. Beth had taken a liking to Mrs Richardson, who had listened sympathetically when told of how young she and her brother had been when the news of her father had arrived so early in the conflict. Arnold accompanied her to the shop each morning and was there every night when she finished. Nearly always as she was ready to leave for home, Mrs Richardson would give her bread that had not been sold that day for the family. Ellen was happy to receive the provisions together with her children's wages each week and did not question that there may be a disparity. True to form she always expected Beth to continue her work when she arrived home much to Arnold's disquiet, he tried to help her whenever he could.

Some months later Arnold was waiting outside the shop for her as usual, he had some news that he couldn't wait to tell her. When she finally appeared he excitedly told her that he was going on a charabanc trip to Blackpool. This was the employees' annual outing provided by the newspaper, and this would be the first time he had been to the coast to see the ocean. Her delight for him was evident and she laughed and hugged him as they walked home, both imagining what the day would hold for him. She made him promise that he would remember everything so he could tell her when he returned. All the employees would receive five shillings to spend as a bonus for their good work and he promised he would bring her a souvenir of his day, perhaps a copy of a huge Tower that someone had told him that they had seen there.

From time to time the young boys at the city newspaper where he worked commented to him that his sister was pretty having seen her with him and at work in the bread shop just around the corner. He always responded with a smile and a good natured brotherly warning to keep away. He knew she was becoming attractive by the glances she would receive when he was escorting her to work; Beth was totally unaware.

He loved his sister and from time to time took her to the Palace picture house to see the silent films. Rudolph Valentino was her favourite and he knew she would watch enthralled, drawing audible breaths of wonder at her hero's on-screen adventures, becoming lost in the amazing world of moving pictures. She loved to see the glamorous actresses like Lillian Gish and Harlow in their beautiful gowns, and watched studiously how they danced. He knew once at home she would want to practice the dances she had seen and expect him to be a serious partner instead of becoming embarrassed and protesting loudly before finishing up in a fit of the giggles. Her love of dancing would never leave her.

As they were both now working Ellen condescended to give them money back to buy clothes and shoes, she knew they had to look respectable to keep their positions. She had now become used to the extra cash and had no wish to threaten that position. Growing older, Arnold acknowledged that they would in time go their separate ways, and hoped that the small amount of money they were saving would one day make that transition a little easier.

The day of the trip to Blackpool arrived, and Arnold dressed in his 'Sunday Best' together with boater set out for the newspaper office with Beth at his side. She was more excited than he was. It was only six o'clock on the Sunday morning but the day looked promising weather wise and she was determined to wave him off and join in the excitement of his first full day excursion. Dressed in her modest finery and a straw hat with yellow and white daisies on the side, they arrived at the newspaper offices and were amazed to see at least twenty charabancs for all the employees lined up on the High Street. They had all been allocated a number which was on the side of the transport so Arnold found the one he was to travel on. He made his presence known and collected his five shillings additional spending money for the trip. They had been told they would be leaving at seven o'clock prompt and the procession would not wait for latecomers. Before boarding he told Beth he wished she could come too, but she told him that this was his day, he had worked hard for the newspaper and he must enjoy all of it and as promised recount everything in full detail on his return. At ten minutes to seven o'clock everyone was instructed to board and promptly on the hour the procession started to leave. Holding on to her hat she waved and waved until he was out of sight then reluctantly turned for home still excited for him and making a silent wish for her brother to have the best of days. She was unable to imagine what sights he would see, or how vast the ocean was that had taken their beloved father away.

It was the early hours of Monday that Arnold arrived home, happily singing gently to himself. A little worse for wear he opened the door to find Beth still up and sleeping in the chair. She had made a decision to be there when he arrived back home and was anxious to hear all about his day. Unfortunately the early start had taken its toll and she had not been able to keep her eyes open and had succumbed to sleep. He took a little time and looked at her, the way her head gently rested on the wing of the chair, her hair tousled over her face. In that moment he thought what a lovely young girl she was turning into despite all the grief and hardships of their early lives together. In that quiet moment he felt they would achieve happiness in their own right one day and took her hand gently.

In that moment her eyes flashed open, her delight evident in her eyes when she saw him standing there. Leaping from the chair she demanded to know how his day had been. He told her it had been a wonderful day and because it was late he would tell her all about it in the morning as they were walking to work. Not wanting to disappoint her he gave her the small presents he had looked long and hard for, to try and give her some idea of what he had seen.

She looked at the postcard and back to Arnold in amazement. It said Blackpool Tower, a structure so magnificent she was pleased he had brought a picture as to try and describe it verbally would have been impossible. There at the back of the structure stretching to the horizon, a vast expanse of water, she looked at him and with a tremble in her voice asked if that was the sea, he nodded. It was then he gave her the large sea shell and said, 'Hold it to your ear and listen. It's the sea.' She held it gently and listened in silence.

Thinking of her father she closed her eyes and the tears started to roll down her cheeks, out of concern Arnold said, 'Hey don't be sad. I'm sorry I didn't intend for it to upset you.'

Wiping away the tears with the back of her hand she took hold of his and said, 'No don't worry I am alright. I like it… it sounds gentle.'

The next morning they set off for work as usual. Beth had placed her gifts in a safe place out of the reach and prying eyes of Evelyn. She knew Ellen wouldn't think about looking for anything. Arnold had brought his youngest sister a stick of rock with Blackpool written through the centre of it and for his mother a dish with the Tower painted on it. As usual they were still in bed when he and Beth left, so he left them on the table.

As they were walking to work through the city he told her about the trip in the charabanc and how many towns and villages they had gone through until they had reached the coast. What they had seen; villages in the green countryside with cottages and gardens as the route took them up to the Snake Pass to go over the Pennines.

'It's a different world Beth,' he had told her. He described the ladies walking along the promenade in Blackpool in their fine hats and dresses, the beach huts on the sand, people laughing while they bathed and played in the sea in colourful bathing suits and keeping the most exciting part of his day till last – Blackpool Tower. How high it was and how it dominated the landscape and finally his trip to the top to look out 'over the world.' She was enthralled, her eyes widening with each revelation and before she knew it they were outside the bakery and back to reality and looking disappointed. He promised he would tell her more after work and continued on towards the newspaper to re-live the day again with his friends and work colleagues.

Beth entered the shop and was concerned to find Mrs Richardson sitting behind the counter which at this time of the day was unusual. She was usually to be found in the bakery supervising the amount of loaves that had been ordered for the day and arranging the trays of bread and cakes for display in the shop. Beth looked at her and asked if everything was alright to be told she was not feeling well so could she quickly clean the shop and arrange the trays of bread for her. Happy to do so, she quickly cleaned the counter and glass pains in the door, swept the floor and arranged the loaves under instruction from Mrs Richardson and waited for the first customers to arrive making sure her hands were clean and that she looked presentable. She served the customers with a ready smile and conversation and felt pleased that Mrs Richardson had trusted her enough to serve on opening and to take the money. In turn Mrs Richardson acknowledged that Beth had coped under duress and decided it was time to change the staffing levels. She would look for a new cleaner and give Beth her position to greet and serve in the shop and keep the business thriving. So a few days later a new cleaner was appointed with the same exacting standards, Beth was promoted and to her delight gained extra responsibility and an increase in her weekly wage. Arnold told her to say nothing of her promotion or increase and saved the extra amount for her in the usual way.

The weeks continued with Beth enjoying her new status. She had grown close to Mrs Richardson in a way that she had not been able to do with her own mother, that position was reserved exclusively for Evelyn. Her half-sister lived in a totally different world compared to the environment that Beth and Arnold had been subjected to. She never went without shoes and had been taken to school by her mother with much excitement on her first day; there had been no sadness in Evelyn's young life. Her world was comfortable by comparison and full of attention from Ellen who only viewed her older children as their providers, she never thought to mention their father ever. Beth's nature would not let her feel any resentment towards her younger sister or mother for past sins, she and Arnold had started to make their own way in the world. They had their own memories of their father to keep them strong and together one day she knew they would find their way to future happiness on their own terms.

Mrs Richardson's health did not improve over the following months. Although the daily stress of the shop had been taken away and as she now knew that Beth could continue in her wake, she rapidly lost interest and became morose. Her husband was a master baker and after the many years of working together for other people they had finally established their own successful business, but it had all arrived too late. He watched his wife's health decline in despair. They were a loving couple, their biggest regret being that their union had not been blessed with children. Beth had acknowledged the love between them, they had all grown closer and they had started to view her as the daughter they never had. Although she realised that Mrs Richardson was not well, in her naivety she had no reason to suspect that the couple would not be part of her future.

They set off for work as usual that morning, it was a relaxed routine with the same route always being taken, daily pleasantries being passed in good humour with the usual faces en-route. Arnold and his smiling sister passing the time of day with everyone on their way to work, this was by now a daily occurrence and a source of delight in the locals' day. They arrived at the corner and both knew instinctively that this day was not to be as usual, the bakery was closed and the blinds still drawn over the windows. Emmy the new cleaner was standing outside the shop, she had been unable to gain early access to clean. Fearing the worst Arnold told Beth to wait with Emmy and went on to the newspaper office to explain why he would be late or even absent that day. The Richardsons' bakery was well known to all the management and employees being just around the corner, his concern was mirrored and he was told to let management know if there was a problem.

He returned to find Beth and Emmy still standing together becoming increasingly concerned. He banged on the door to the shop then went round to the living accommodation at the back. The response was the same, no sign of life, by this time both girls were tearful. The local constabulary was called and forcibly gained entry. Mrs Richardson had died during the night with her husband at her side, unable to contemplate continuing to live without her, he had made a noose and hanged himself in the bakery. Emmy left for home in shreds of tears and Arnold's manager gave him permission to look after Beth. He took her to the Infirmary gardens because he didn't know where else to take her, once again the rhododendrons were in bloom. They sat quietly together for hours, he held her tightly to try to ease her mind. Arriving home after dark a saddened Arnold explained to Ellen what had happened. She listened, then looked at a tear-stained Beth, the only words of compassion being, 'Well then... you had better look for another position.'

The police and coroner decided it was a straight forward case of Mrs Richardson's death by natural causes and Mr Richardson's by suicide due to him being depressed and unable to live without her. The local community turned out for their joint funeral in force. Arnold accompanied a distraught Beth suitably dressed this time in mourning black. Ellen had watched them go without a word, she was more concerned about the reduction in her monies.

Throughout the service Beth held onto Arnold silently weeping for this couple who she had loved and who had filled a void. She wept again for her father and wondered how many more times she would have to lose someone she loved.

Theresa's Children

Life at work had taken a distinct turn for the better for Owen as he had grown older under the auspices of Mr Appleyard. Georgie was still his work mate and best friend, they had come a long way together. He enjoyed his work and was comfortable in the fact that his employer was always there if he needed any advice. It had been clear to all and sundry when he had started his apprenticeship that his father was not and never could be a role model. Further conversations between Mr Appleyard and Owen's ex-headmaster convinced him that Eleanor had obviously been his guiding light from birth up to her death; the old adage 'see the boy see the man' would hold true. His principles had been set by his grandmother and would always be in total opposition to his father's point of view which was purely self-serving.

Life at home had continued to be one of caution where his father was concerned, there was always an unspoken tension between them.

Theresa tried her best to keep the peace between her husband and their son but she could deny her husband nothing. She could be seen regularly going to the corner shop to fill his jug with beer usually after a visit to the local pawn shop. If there was no money in the house she would visit the local pawnbroker and negotiate a few pence for her wedding ring, it was in his hands more than it was on her finger.

As their eldest son grew older and became a young man, Owen Snr would sit and stare at his son with simmering, dark eyes that were full of resentment. Theresa would look at this man and wonder why he harboured such hatred towards their eldest son. In a quiet moment her memories would take her back to an earlier time when life had been happy and her future awaited her without worry or fear; she would then remember the first time she had seen that look filled with hatred.

She had been an attractive girl in her youth, small and carefree with laughing, blue eyes and long, curly hair that shone in the sun. Their eyes had met through the crowd at an Easter Parade in carefree days before the war. She had been wearing a blue dress and bonnet. It had not taken long for her to become enamoured with him, and he knew all the right things to say to this impressionable, attractive young girl. She in turn felt proud amongst her peers being escorted by this tall, good looking young man on their weekly dates. It was not long, however, before she realised to her horror that she was pregnant to him. She chose to say nothing at first hoping to cement their relationship further. Her family were hardworking, honest and committed Christians and she was well aware how they would view their daughter becoming pregnant to a man they had never met or even knew existed.

Frances, her sister, had noticed the thickening of her trim waist and enlarged breasts and confronted her one morning. She thought she had concealed her sickness but Frances had become aware of her queasiness in the early mornings as they were leaving home for work. They worked in service together in the large house of their church minister. Hoping against hope that her younger sister would deny it, she broached the subject as they walked to The Manse one morning. Theresa broke down and admitted that she was with child, relieved that the burden was now being shared, but terrified of the consequences. Her sister was mortified; she could live with the hope that she might be mistaken but the confirmation of the fact terrified her for the impact it would have on her younger sibling and more to point on her unsuspecting parents. She had been with Theresa that day at the Easter parade and had noticed the eye contact between her sister and the good looking, tall stranger, but she had no idea that they had been conducting a relationship. She demanded to know when and where the liaisons had taken place and was terribly hurt when she realised Theresa had not confided in her.

They wept together and Theresa begged her older sister to keep her secret for the time being. She told her she would bring him to meet the family and everything would be fine. She loved her parents and she felt sure they would understand and support her. Their parents had brought them up by Victorian Christian values and the Ten Commandments, no doubt there would be horror and great distress that Theresa had become pregnant out of wedlock and to a man than they had never met. The liaison had been conducted in secret as if there was something to be ashamed of and therefore made it sordid.

Theresa sat on the park bench awaiting his arrival, she tried to relax but her nerves were evident in the way she fidgeted in turn with her hair, hat and her small pouch bag. She kept an anxious eye on the path that she knew he would take to meet her. He approached, walking in his usual confident manner and immediately noted that she looked dark around her eyes and on edge; it was hardly surprising given the week of stress she had endured. She broke down in tears as soon as he was at her side. Confirming his worst fears with frightened, blue eyes she begged him to return home with her to explain to her parents that they loved each other and would marry and make things right. He listened to her words spoken through tears in stony silence. His immediate feeling was one of being trapped so he told her to go home, prepare her parents and he would follow hoping this suggestion would give him time to think and steady his nerves. Arranging the time for three hours later Theresa composed herself to return home and showing him where to come said she would wait for him to arrive and would then formally introduce him to her parents. He said he would see her shortly and not to worry. He went directly to the local hostelry to contemplate his fate and their future.

She arrived home to be met by a concerned Frances, she explained to her sister that she had told Owen and he was to arrive a few hours later to be introduced to their parents. Together they would explain the situation and ask for her father's blessing. Frances, with heavy heart, took hold of her sister's hand and together they knelt and prayed that although it would be an awful shock their father would accept the situation and bless their union.

Theresa changed and announced to her parents that there was somebody she would like them to meet, that she had known him for some months and wished them to consider him as a suitor. Her parents expressed surprise and concern that she had been 'walking out' with someone without their knowledge, but they would meet with him, assess the situation and establish his intentions and prospects. After their discussion Theresa went to stand by the window to await Owen's arrival.

He arrived as they had arranged and rang the doorbell. She ran to the door to let him in while her parents walked down the hall behind her. On opening the door her smile soon diminished as she smelt the beer on his breath; he was leaning against the door, glazed, cold eyes staring straight at her parents.

Her father stepped forward and introduced himself, gently moving Theresa to one side. Her mother then moved to her side and put a protective arm around her, they thought they had both read the situation, but worse was to come. Her father invited him in and he clumsily fell through the door before righting himself in front of Theresa and her mother. Her father was of the opinion that his daughter would see this scoundrel for what he was and negate their relationship, until in the lounge Theresa looked at both her parents and bravely told them this was the man she was going to marry as she was with child. Her mother gasped with horror, Frances was soon at her side to lend support, her father was enraged. He looked at this drunken man then through hurt and bewildered eyes at his youngest daughter.

Throwing his hands up in despair he said, 'If you are serious about marrying this man who has brought shame to my house then you must leave and go where you will to continue your life.' There was an emotional catch in his voice, he fought to regain his composure. 'Go now and God be with you.'

She dropped her eyes in shame, she had seen the hurt in her father's eyes and knew he would not forgive her.

'Call yourself a man of God then do you… your piety disgusts me,' shouted Owen menacingly pointing his finger into her father's chest. 'You are no better than me.'

'Get out of my house,' her father replied quietly, turning his back on the both of them.

Owen stood outside while she quickly collected what clothes she could and left the house to the sound of her mother and sister weeping in despair. Her father kept his tears until he was alone.

They arrived at his mother's house with Theresa carrying her bundle. He had not spoken to her since they had left her parents, he had just weaved his way back home on unsteady legs. She had followed a few paces behind not knowing what to say to him. He had thought in his drunken state that this might happen but if so, being that her father was a religious man he would give them some money to ease his conscience, it had not happened; he had watched them go without a penny.

Arriving home, his mother Eleanor and his sisters looked at him then at the small fragile girl standing behind him with downcast eyes holding a bundle; she had clearly been crying. He slurred his words through an explanation and sat down on the chair in the warm kitchen and promptly fell asleep, leaving the women to discuss amongst themselves what was to be done. Eleanor looked at the girl standing quivering in front of her, she was saddened that her son had brought them all to this. She gently took hold of Theresa's hand and led her to another chair. She told her to make herself comfortable and to try to sleep, and that it would all be discussed in the morning when her son was sober. Eleanor went to her bed with a heavy heart but knew what she had to do to make her son finally take some responsibility for his actions.

That had been nearly twenty years ago and although Theresa loved her husband she acknowledged that Owen Snr was only concerned with his own wellbeing. She accepted that she and their children came second and her first born was and always would be held responsible by his father for everything that was wrong in their lives. She came out of her reverie to look at her eldest son and was grateful he had come back into their lives even though for him it had been traumatic. She hoped that one day he would again find the peace that he had known when his grandmother had been alive.

The years had rolled by since then and Owen was now a young man. He and Georgie were committed friends and held no secrets from each other. The day that his father had failed to support him on his Apprentice Day and taken a sub from his son's wages had become common knowledge within the company. Georgie and the whole workforce at Appleyards had felt compassion for him. Not until the following week during their break, when Georgie had asked about his family, did Owen tell him the full story regarding his early settled life with his beloved grandmother and the horrific change of circumstances upon her death a few days before he had arrived at Appleyards. Whilst telling his story his tears flowed once again, no matter that it was in front of his new friend, he wept without embarrassment. This one act forged their friendship for life.

Georgie, who had been moved by Owen's tears had also become distressed when regaling his friend's story to his parents together with the outcome of Owen's apprentice day. Georgie's father had told him to tell his friend that he was welcome at any time in their home and if he wished to leave what little money he could save after paying for his father's loan and for his painter's whites with them, then it would be in safe hands. Their conversation weighed heavily on his mind, after the pride he had felt for his own son on signing his apprentice papers he really could not comprehend how any man could be so callous to his own blood immaterial of their circumstances.

They had served their apprenticeships in safe hands through the Depression years and both assumed the ranks in a company with an excellent reputation. They had joined the older painters on the workforce according them respect in the time-honoured tradition, the old timers good humouredly teased the apprentices following in their footsteps.

As he grew older whatever items of clothing Owen bought for himself, they remained at Georgie's house so that he could change and have a night on the town looking smart and modern. He kept his trousers, shirts, jackets and shoes and money there, knowing full well that if his clothes had been left in the vicinity of Owen Snr they would be pawned and the money spent on drink, the years had not changed him. When necessary he only kept a work outfit at home that he knew wasn't worth pawning. If he didn't return to Georgie's after their night out and had to go home, then when he left for work the next morning his clothes would go with him then on to Georgie's house for safe keeping.

The older painters at Appleyards regularly went fishing and one weekend had invited the two younger ones along to compete in one of their friendly matches. It was to be their first experience of fishing, much merriment had followed when they had both turned up in their finery as if they were on a night out on the town. The older painters had laughed and told them to forget it and come the following week in something more appropriate. They had taken the criticism in good humour and knew that the older men would regularly bring it up in conversation when at work and all would have a good laugh at their expense without umbrage.

Owen's three older sisters were now in employment and also cautious of their father as the same principles existed for them, if it wasn't on their person it would be pawned. They felt for their mother and tried to make her life easier by giving her money from their wages, but he always managed to take the lion's share as she always gave in to him. The fact that they were all growing older he deemed to be a threat, so he constantly reminded them of his sacrifice made for the country during the Great War. How he had been tied to a gun carriage wheel as a punishment for insubordination and left in 'No Man's Land' for forty-eight hours and survived. That he was indestructible. They had listened to this time and time again and now knew how to respond to him, they would just nod and agree as any other reaction would provoke an argument which meant, when they left, their mother would take the brunt of his anger through a drunken tirade.

The family had had to move numerous occasions since being in the first house where Owen had come to live with them. The 'moonlight flits' had become a regular occurrence as the family had grown larger. They all became used to avoiding the rent collectors and bailiffs, their father still had a silver tongue when it came to needing a new abode to house his family. The unsuspecting landlords believed everything he told them until the rent became unpaid for weeks on end and another silent flight would ensue under darkness. He was always one step ahead of the game without any conscience. His family had grown older and these days one flea-ridden mattress wasn't enough especially when he expected them to hand over their wages to him for him to drink away, rather than pay any rent. It was a subject that was not up for discussion with any of them as far as he was concerned, they would do as he told them.

The three girls shared a double mattress on the floor sleeping top to toe, and Owen's younger brother Kenneth shared his. In the house there were seven adults, with two younger sisters of school age and a baby boy of eighteen months. In the ensuing years Theresa had lost two other children just after their birth and had been distraught; the toll of her lifestyle had not helped to sustain them during her pregnancies. They had both been born underweight and sickly, unable to produce the milk for them they had both died in infancy. Owen Snr took it all in his stride and had taken the baby corpses wrapped in newspaper to the local undertaker to be disposed of by the city council. He had shed no tears and had given over the baby bundles without remorse or conscience.

Owen's three older sisters accepted their home life as nothing unusual for the times they were living in, but all secretly hoped that whatever fate had in store for them it would be a better existence than their mother had always endured. Elizabeth and Theresa worked together at a local cutlery factory and Sybil had just started as cleaner round the corner from them in a bakery. All three of them usually walked to work together, always attracting the attention of the local unattached males with their confident air, laughing as they walked enjoying the attention and whistles.

The austerity from the war years had faded and it was now a time for the younger generation to enjoy their youth and set new standards whatever level of the community they were in. The Crash of 1929 had not really affected this generation's life style, they had always been poor so the general feeling was the only way was up. The strict Victorian values had gone and the frivolous 1920s had raised the bar, so in each city the dance halls became the place for socialising on a serious scale without old school formality. Popular music became accessible to all and in the cinemas now with sound, they sat enthralled, every girl dreaming of becoming a Jean Harlow or Greta Garbo; films, dancing and music became the centre of their lives.

Every Saturday, after being waved off by their mother, the girls would arrive at the local dance held in the training barracks dressed in their finery. Owen would be out with Georgie, and when their paths crossed they would take it upon themselves to become unofficial minders to the girls from across the dance floor. This invariably led to arguments with prospective dance partners that the two friends did not deem suitable especially if they had been for a drink before arriving at the barracks. The girls would express dismay at the time, but secretly be pleased that their brother and his good looking friend were there as a deterrent to anyone looking to take advantage. Elizabeth being the beauty of the family and feisty with it, would argue with Owen to leave them alone, she enjoyed the dances and being the centre of local attention. After her protestations she would turn and laugh at her brother, kiss him on the cheek and wink whilst still holding the hand of the young man that had caught her eye. Owen would always smile at her recognising she was happy and walk away but not before giving the suitor a steely look to let him know who he would be dealing with should there be any problems.

The girl's dance dresses were usually bought from a pawn shop on pay day before they went home and would be adapted to the fashion of the day by hand usually influenced by the outfits worn by the actresses in the movies. Elizabeth would endlessly trawl the fashion shop windows or the cinema promotion photographs to get her inspiration of how a plain dress could become stunning with a little ingenuity. She always passed her ideas on to her sisters much to their delight. On dance nights the other girls would be waiting to see what new creations the sisters were wearing, the men would be waiting to see them for entirely different reasons. They always made an entrance twenty minutes after the dance had started, always in time with a lull in the music for maximum impact, and all heads would turn. Elizabeth would lead the three of them through the door always with head held high and a radiant smile acknowledging the entire male contingent present, casting glances to them all with a teasing eye.

The dance music was supplied by amateur musicians copying the big bands of the day. The American numbers were big favourites and local singers earned a few shillings replicating their songs with the band to the delight of the youngsters. The guy with the soft voice covered the romantic Al Bowlly songs at the end of the evening. The last dance meant a chance meeting that could possibly convert to something more permanent. Elizabeth loved anything that came from America, the music, the fashion, the films and, because of her enthusiasm and style, she was invited to sing along with the vocalists from time to time. She loved it and felt she was becoming very sophisticated; her sisters were delighted that she had a presence and the confidence to sing in front of an audience and encouraged her with applause. Owen stood at the back and watched her with pride, she in turn, to lose her initial embarrassment would catch his eye and sing just to him. She would blow him a kiss at the end of the number much to the dismay of the local talent not realising that he was her brother and it was just an act.

Owen and Georgie also enjoyed these nights, they would eye over the other girls that were there all blatantly hoping to catch a suitor. He, in his brotherly way, thought the three best looking girls in the dancehall were his sisters and no one would have argued the fact. He and Georgie were popular with the ladies and both would give compliments out here and there as they trawled the hall. The ladies in turn, being well aware that Owen was the elder brother to the sisters, always took it as a huge compliment if he spent a little time with them passing pleasantries or asking them to dance. Both he and Georgie were considered a catch because of the ready smiles and their pleasant manner. The girls would respond to the compliments and readily agree to be escorted home. But neither Owen nor his friend, although they had started relationships, felt that they had met the one with whom they would like to be with for the rest of their lives. Life at that moment was good without complicating it.

That was until one Saturday night. They had arrived at the barracks as usual, dressed to impress, Owen having arrived at Georgie's house as normal to change and to compare apparel just as his sisters did. It was the usual routine, the atmosphere was always full of anticipation of what awaited whether it be fending off his sisters' admirers and risking a fight; enjoying a drink or two; or just enjoying the night successfully chatting up the girls in what they considered their domain.

His sisters were already there, creating the usual interest from the female contingency eager to see what they were wearing or how they had done their hair. The men always enjoyed their entrance, silently hoping that one of them would cast a favourable glance in their direction. Elizabeth would notice any promising new arrivals within minutes. She usually danced with a favoured few that she knew were not only good dancers but good looking as well. This not only gave her an audience it also gave her the opportunity to show what a good dancer she was, her poise and beauty being on view to full advantage. It was a well-run exercise and Owen knowing who the usual partners were would only become involved if an upstart insisted on a dancing with her and she objected. Theresa and Sybil, her younger sisters, also had their usual suitors but left Elizabeth to be the main attraction without rancour, always keeping an eye on her like Owen to see who she was with and if she looked happy.

The girls were all enjoying themselves, the music was good and all of them were swept along in the warm atmosphere of the evening. It was intermission time, they had gravitated back together as the lights came up around the dance floor and the musicians had left the stage to take a well-earned break. Owen and Georgie had just arrived and were standing next to each other chatting when Owen bent slightly to light his cigarette from Georgie's lighter. Lifting his head back up his eyes connected with a pair of sparkling, blue eyes staring directly at him from across the dance floor. He nodded acknowledgement but she dropped her eyes and turned to speak to her friend as if the moment had not happened. He looked at Georgie, smiled and winked.

Reading his friend's look Georgie asked, 'Have I missed something?'

'Well... we will have to wait and see won't we,' Owen replied drawing on his cigarette and looking round the dance floor as if nothing had happened.

BOOK TWO

Beth and Arnold

Beth had matured into beauty. She was modest in dress, had a ready smile and a kind word for everyone. Arnold was as proud of her in adulthood as he had been when they were children and felt just as protective. Life at home continued as before. There were two separate camps in the house, Beth and Arnold and their mother and half-sister, Ellen still put her own and Evelyn's needs first, nothing had changed. Although Evelyn had finished her schooling Ellen was loathe for her to start work; she felt her youngest daughter should be her companion and as both Arnold and Beth were working then there was no reason for that arrangement to end. The tragedy at the bakery changed all that.

It took some time for Beth to come to terms with the loss of Mr and Mrs Richardson. When their father had died she had not experienced a grieving process for him, at that age she had not really understood the implications of his death or growing up without him. Arnold had always been there for her as her protector so she had been shielded. When the Richardsons had died so suddenly and together she went into a state of shock not only grieving for them, it released all the latent despair for her father. When Arnold had brought her home from the funeral she could hardly stand she was so bereft, he had gently put her to bed and told her to rest. Returning downstairs Ellen coldly told him she could not understand what all the fuss was about or why Beth was so distraught and that she ought to pull herself together. Reacting angrily he told his mother and Evelyn to leave her alone in a tone of voice she knew not to answer him back. He told them vehemently that he would take care of her. The house descended into silence apart from the sound of Beth's sobs.

He rose early the next morning wanting to spend a little time with her before he left for work to see how she was. Sitting on the side of her bed he could see the despair etched into her pale, drawn face. She looked so different to his usual vibrant sister. He held her hand and gently whispered comforting words hoping she would hear him in her deep, melancholy sleep. Then he reluctantly left for work.

She was to remain in her bed for nearly three weeks. Each morning he would leave sustenance on her bedside table in the hope that if she roused she would be able to regain a little strength. It was to prove more of an emotional need, the loss of her father, the years of indifference from Ellen, the loss of the Richardsons who had returned her love; it was going to take time for her inner calm to return.

Ellen remained at a distance, the actual emotion of grieving a lost memory to her. Her life since the loss of Arthur had changed when Evelyn had been born and had led to the exclusion of her older children completely. In Ellen's mind they belonged to a different life altogether, in a weird way she acknowledged that they had become her benefactors, but it was as if they worked for her. To the outside world, anyone knowing Beth and Arnold thought that Evelyn was their younger sister, not half-sister, and that the three children had lost their father in the Great War. Ellen acknowledged that this was the perceived view of the family and did nothing to change the image of her being a tragic war widow left with three children.

At the end of each work day Arnold came home and, without acknowledging either Ellen or Evelyn, went straight upstairs to see how Beth was. If he could have taken her struggle on board to come to terms with her collective loss instead of it being her sole domain he would have done. He held her hand each morning and evening and whispered gently hoping to reassure her. He hoped and prayed that one morning she would wake and the despair would be gone and he would have his carefree, beautiful sister back again. He had placed fresh flowers in her room each day hoping that they would please her eye when she would at last emerge from her grief.

It happened on the twelfth day; he arrived home after work to find her awake and she smiled as he entered the bedroom. There was sad warmth in her eyes and she was still very pale but at least she had come back to him.

He came to her, held her hands and kissed her troubled brow affectionately with relief, her eyes closed and she returned her brother's love and the tears of relief flowed from both of them. She had fought her demons created from her recent and past loss of loved ones, she now looked at him with a renewed strength; together they would continue to support each other until they found independent love and security on their own terms.

It had taken a few more weeks for her to feel confident again and strong enough to look for another position. Arnold had silenced Ellen's protests by increasing his contribution to the family budget, but she still managed to make barbed comments always making sure they were out of his earshot but loud enough for Beth to hear.

She knew she had to emerge back into a daily routine instead of stifling in the house; the sunlight had to come back into her life once again. When Arnold was not at work over the weekend they went for long walks to get her back into the fresh air and slowly the colour came back into her cheeks, her eyes lifted back to their brightness, the laughter returned. Whilst walking home after their walk in Endcliffe park and passing the usual array of shops they were pleased to see the bakery shop extending into the next door empty premises; business was obviously good.

'Must be due to the local cutlery factories Beth,' said Arnold. 'Plenty of customers, perhaps we could call down tomorrow and enquire.' He didn't want to push her into it before she was ready.

'Yes, yes I will,' she said excitedly and he was pleased to see that she was looking through the window with her hands cupped around her eyes trying to see what the new layout in the shop was going to be. She had made a mental note of the owner's name over the shop entrance.

'It could be a new start,' he said smiling at her, 'and a much needed one.'

She left the house with him early the next morning keeping the same exacting standards as she had displayed for Mr Richardson and stepped out looking pristine. Her hair was neatly tied back, boots blacked and a freshly laundered smock ready for a new challenge. They detoured to the bakery and Arnold escorted her to the shop door hoping to find the owners inside. The bakery shop wasn't yet open at this early hour, the breads were still in the ovens. He stood at a discreet distance and watched as Beth knocked on the door and waited for someone to respond. A young boy appeared. She smiled at him, wished him good morning and asked to see Mr Newbould the owner. The young boy blushed slightly and asked her to wait a moment. He ran to find his employer and told him there was a nice young lady at the door who wished to speak with him.

Mr Newbould appeared brushing the flour off his large apron then off his hands and looked at the young lady in front of him. She smiled at him and dipped slightly and explained that they had noticed that he was enlarging his premises and that she wondered if he would be looking for new staff to serve in the shop. What he saw was a very presentable young lady with a confident pleasing manner.

'I am not sure yet my dear... I have to see how it goes before deciding whether or not to take extra staff on. Do you have any experience?'

'Yes sir, I used to work for Mr and Mrs Richardson,' her voice and lip suddenly started to tremble. 'I managed their shop... before...' Tears filled her eyes and she swayed on unsteady legs.

Mr Newbould was quick to respond to her distress and took a step forward and put a supportive hand out to assist her. 'It's alright my dear. Come and sit down for a moment.'

Arnold appeared at her side, explained who he was and took hold of her hand.

Mr Newbould also became visibly saddened at the mention of the Richardsons. He had known them both well from the Master Bakers Guild and had attended their funeral out of respect with many other bakers from the area, it had been a very sad time for everyone.

Beth tried to regain her composure and said, 'I am so very sorry. They were very dear to me,' and the silent tears streamed down her face again.

'Yes I can see that,' said Mr Newbould smiling gently. 'There is no need to apologise my dear they were good honest people.'

Beth wiped her tears away, 'I am so very sorry... I thought I was...'

'No apologies... please... none needed,' and he took hold of her hand. 'Now, the work on the new area should be finished in four to five days, so come and see me next Saturday and we will discuss your pay and hours. Your loyalty to the Richardsons is enough for me.'

'Thank you,' she replied. Arnold shook his hand and they walked away from the bakery leaving Mr Newbould in pensive thought as he watched the two of them go.

As they walked Arnold suggested she come to meet him after his shift, they could have something to eat at the local pie shop to celebrate her new position. She agreed and they parted company to walk their separate ways.

As she walked, she noticed all the surrounding streets were full of the workers arriving for their shifts at the numerous local cutlery factories and tool-making companies that Arnold had mentioned. Usually when she had been in this area the same premises were closed for the weekend and the streets empty, so the amount of people around really surprised her. There were men cycling or walking in the same direction discussing sport, and large groups of girls arm in arm, full of chatter about their weekend outings and dates making ribald comments to the men and laughing at their reaction.

These girls were the army of polishers required by the cutlers and were responsible for bringing the pieces of cutlery up to a shine from a matte state, they were known as Buffers. All of them wore brightly coloured headscarves wrapped around their heads and tied at the front to protect their hair. They had tape on their third fingers left hand to protect any wedding rings; it was a distinguishing image, a uniform of sorts. The polishing was a long and arduous process and at the end of the day they all had black faces from the residue of the buffing paste on the brushes. Within the industry, although the girls were deemed to be rough diamonds, they commanded an honest respect for their art. Any man wandering into their work area unannounced would be debagged to cackles of laughter, so the men on site gave them a wide berth. Beth smiled in reaction to the sound of their laughter and the sea of colour from their bright headscarves, it was good to be out amongst people again.

After a while she realised she was standing outside the Richardson's old shop, she had walked there automatically without a thought. The bakery and shop was obviously closed and in the window was the name and address of the solicitor handling the estate. 'All enquiries to... ' She stood for a moment and the tears flowed again, this time in silent homage. Sadly turning to leave she noticed the florist across the street, who had been quietly watching the vigil from her stall. The florist walked over, embraced her, then handed her four red roses. She looked into the sad blue eyes in front of her and said, 'We all miss you and the Richardsons, it was very sad what happened dear, but life must go on. You are very young and have everything to live for. You will always keep their memory alive when you think about them. Don't forget they had a good life together, be happy that you knew them, and when they come into your thoughts, however fleetingly, just smile. You must start to live your own life again and move on, they would want you to do that.'

Beth looked at the florist. She was a widow who had probably listened to and seen a lifetime of troubles through the war and since on her stall. Her lined face was sympathetic and her well-meaning eyes were warm. Beth took the red roses and thanked her silently, no more words were needed.

She turned back to the shop, kissed and placed two of the roses in the handle on the bakery door. Then closing her eyes she recalled the faces of Mr and Mrs Richardson. She sent them her love and knew they were together in death as they had been in life. Turning away from the door she acknowledged the florist with a smile and a nod of her head and walked on to the grounds of the Infirmary.

She felt relaxed just sitting alone in the garden. Mentally the rhododendrons brought back the memories of her father and the little girl who had stood on the balcony of the hospital so long ago. She glanced up at the balcony then moved to place one of the roses where she thought the chocolate the little girl had thrown had landed. The remaining rose was for her father. She found where she had been hiding in play on that fateful day and gently laid the rose on the well tendered grass. She remained there all day sitting quietly in the sunshine lost in her thoughts and laid her ghosts to rest.

Arnold sensed the change in her when he came out of work and saw her standing there, she looked like her old self and as she smiled and waved when he appeared through the exit of the newspaper. He didn't want to question her as to what had brought about the change, so just approached her as normal. They locked arms and went off to the pie shop for supper. Unbeknown to Beth, he had arranged with some of the staff from the newspaper who all knew her to be there for their supper at the same time. They all made a fuss and said everyone missed her smile and the bakery, at the same time being careful not to dwell on the fate of the Richardsons lest she should become upset. They proposed a toast for her new position, then the conversation switched to the announcement that had been made that day about the annual trip to Blackpool; they all cheered again and settled down to enjoy the rest of the evening.

Saturday morning arrived and she left once more with Arnold for the bakery, they had said nothing to Ellen about the possibility of a new position deciding to wait and see what her pay would be if she was successful.

She tapped on the bakery door. As it opened the aroma of the baking bread greeted her and she smiled at Mr Newbould as he appeared in the doorway. He was pleased to see she was looking much better than when they had parted company earlier in the week. He greeted her warmly and invited her to follow him into the new premises. Opening the door with a flourishing gesture he indicated for her to step in to see the finished renovation, he was clearly delighted with it. She stood in the threshold and just stared, instead of the basic shop unit with wooden shelves where the breads would be stacked, the shelves had been angled and a basket sat in its own section. The floor, instead of linoleum, was black and white chequered tiles which looked bright; the window had a wide display sill with cake stands and lace doylies. Next to the breads there was a display unit for jams and marmalades and a further section for puddings and pies. She turned and laughed at Mr Newbould.

'It's just wonderful!' she gasped.

If he had had any reservations about impulsively offering her a position earlier in the week they were quickly dispelled by her reaction. He indicated for her to enter and wide-eyed she took in all the minute details of what was to be her new work domain. The Richardson's shop had been very basic but with a warm atmosphere, she felt there was no reason why the same warmth could not exude from this shop too. It would be lively, she was certain, because of the girls she had seen working in the area, a different kind of clientele from what she had been used to but nothing to fear. Previously, being based in the centre of town near the newspaper, their customers were usually the men from the production line and the bread was baked to suit a man's taste. Here Mr Newbould told her, the female workforce bought bread to take home after their shifts and on pay days it included a variety of sweet items for the weekend. Stale bread not sold was saved and made into bread and butter puddings. The women would bring their dishes in and then pick them up duly filled after work with their bread orders. As the women worked in awful conditions this presentation, he thought, would appeal to them because if it returned them to a feminine environment just for a short time in their day, they would enjoy the experience and continue to buy there.

Beth ran to the door. 'Arnold come and look... come quickly,' he smiled and walked towards the shop pleased that she looked clearly delighted. 'Come and see... it's wonderful.'

Stepping through the door, he removed his cap, shook hands once more with Mr Newbould, and followed her around the shop smiling at her enthusiasm. He silently thought, 'Welcome back.'

The pay she was offered was more than she had been paid by the Richardsons because the hours she would work would be a little longer and turnover was obviously higher. He told her he would like her to serve as she had done previously and to take overall charge of the other girls. He also asked her to promote the jam and marmalade section which was a new line he was prepared to try. He told her if she had any other ideas to increase business then he would be willing to listen.

She was thrilled and walking home with Arnold she never stopped talking of the possibilities that could bring extra business into the shop. He told her to tell Ellen that she had been successful at securing another position and luckily it was at the same rate that she had been paid by the Richardsons; Ellen would be no wiser or even question it. She would be relieved that Beth was working again and that she and Evelyn could return to their existence of doing exactly as they wished again. In her mind this had temporarily ceased when the Richardsons had died and Beth had created a fuss, the fact that the status quo had not changed at all didn't occur to them.

All day Sunday her excitement continued and on their walk out she insisted on passing all the other bakeries and bread shops in the area to have a look at the competition. To her delight they were to find no other shop that came close in comparison. She felt that word would soon travel in the area of a new experience when shopping for bread provisions. People would come to have a look out of initial curiosity and hopefully buy, then keep returning to buy.

She arrived on the Monday morning earlier than the time arranged so that she could familiarise herself with all the different lines Mr Richardson baked and determine the prices. He was always on the premises from around three o'clock in the morning to fire the ovens and get the baking started for the early shifts coming in to the factories. He had greeted her warmly and told her he appreciated that she had arrived early of her own volition. There were two other girls working in the shop and when they arrived they both looked at Beth with a cautious eye. From her pristine appearance and general air she looked as if she was to be put in charge. They had worked for Mr Newbould for some months and were fine, he had no complaints about their work but comparing their appearance against Beth's he acknowledged that possibly they could begin to look a little more presentable and improve their image to match their new surroundings. Beth smiled at them both and said, 'Hello... I'm Beth. Could you both help me to familiarise myself with everything here? I know you must know everything, so I would find it very helpful if you could.'

Mr Newbould winked at her from behind the girls, smiled and said, 'I will see you shortly Beth to see how you are getting along.' He turned to go back into the bakery thinking that she had already got off to a good start.

The girls introduced themselves, 'I'm Annie and this is Sybil.' Both tidied their hair under their caps to try and look a little smarter. They were both wearing smocks as Beth had done at the Richardsons, both items clean but a little well worn. As she looked at them she determined that Annie was more or less her age, Sybil looked younger by a few years and her tasks were generally cleaning, but from time to time she was called on to serve if the shop became very busy.

'This is such a lovely shop,' said Beth. 'I am really looking forward to working here. I thought I would ask Mr Newbould to provide us with aprons and caps so we can all look the same, what do you think?'

Both girls looked a little incredulous at her. 'Well if you think he might say yes that would be good, so long as it is you that asks him,' said Annie, thinking, 'I she wants to go and get the sack on her first day then fine.'

'That's good,' said Beth. 'I will see what he says a little later. Now can you show me all the items we have for sale.'

There was the usual array of breads that were to be sorted into the baskets. The most popular were pound loaves. They were weighed on the scales on the counter to prove to the customer that they did indeed weigh one pound in weight in line with the ancient Corn Laws and were set at a fixed price. Should the loaf not weigh a pound, then the shop had to add another item to the purchase to make the weight up. Usually if children were sent to purchase bread they would always insist on it being weighed in the hopes that it was slightly under and a sweet item would be offered in lieu. The parkin and caraway seed cakes and puddings were usually timed to appear towards the weekend.

Annie explained that the bread that was a day old was sold off as slices with different toppings or scrapes as they were known, dripping, jam or honey, and the buffer girls and men from the tool works would either appear on their way into work or on their breaks and ask for a penny scrape. The stale bread also went into the bread and butter puddings and, finally, if there was anything left over on the Saturday there were arrangements in place with the local butcher and pig breeder. The local butcher turned the bread into breadcrumbs for his sausages and the farmer would collect all the other waste for his pigs. There was no waste.

She helped the girls to arrange the breads before opening. Their customers usually arrived in timed waves depending on which shift they were on, then there would be a lull until their lunch breaks. Noticing the shop was reopened quite a few of the girls couldn't resist a quick look in on their way into work and there were plenty of comments of, 'Ere…what a grand shop,' and 'We'll see you later.'

Mr Newbould re-appeared and called Beth over. Annie and Sybil had seen him come back into the shop and, fearing what his reaction might be if Beth was to ask him about the aprons and caps, carried on with their duties, cleaning and re-arranging the loaves.

'How are you getting on Beth?' he asked.

'I'm fine Mr Newbould thank you,' she replied.

'What I would like you to do is arrange the jams and marmalades on the display unit to see if we can create a little interest,' he said leading her to where the jars had been stored.

'Yes. I was thinking that we could always put a few jars in the window among the bread until the weekend items. I thought it may make the window look a bit more interesting.'

'Yes do that,' he replied nodding his head, 'It can't hurt.'

She continued, 'and I was also thinking that perhaps one day we three girls could all have the same smock, apron and cap. It would make us all look smart don't you think?'

Not committing himself he said, 'I will have a think about it and let you know.' He walked back towards the bakery door.

The other girls heard the conversation and nodded to each other. 'Well he didn't say no did he?' said Sybil.

'No he didn't,' Annie replied raising her eyebrows. 'We could look on it as a new outfit, at least nobody else would have worn it,' and she laughed.

The first wave of girls came in for their 'scrapes.' Monday was the only day it was fresh bread so there was no choice of a cheaper one and they were all three half pence. The word had gone round the buffing rooms about Mr Newbould's 'posh shop' so they all had come in for a good look. Beth had displayed all the jars on the unit and there was a designated counter for the orders for the bread and butter puddings next to the display unit. She smiled at them all as she served them, enjoying the general hustle and bustle and animated chatter.

It was a good first day and she felt elated. A they were all ready to leave Mr Newbould put his head around the door and said, 'Well done girls, and oh by the way Beth, I will get Mrs Newbould to order the aprons and caps for you all. I's a good idea. See you all in the morning.'

Annie and Sybil reacted with glee and locked arms with her as they all walked down the street away from the shop, Beth securely in the middle. Sybil was the first to leave them, not living too far from the bakery. Then Annie walked another twenty minutes with her before Beth turned away from her to continue to her house. She was pleased how the day had gone, both with the shop and with Annie and Sybil. Up until now Arnold had been the closest person to her and that would never change, but she felt excited about having girl friends for the first time and being in a predominantly female environment when taking the shops clientele into account.

She arrived home to the usual indifference from Ellen and Evelyn. They didn't ask her how her day had gone, she didn't expect them to. Arnold followed her in and without acknowledging his mother or sibling asked her quietly how everything was. He would have been genuinely surprised if she had said anything other than, 'It was good. I like the girls I am working with and Mr Newbould agreed to the aprons and caps I wanted to ask him about. Everything is going to be fine,' and she smiled.

It *was* fine. For the first time she could enjoy conversations with girls her own age; they all became friends which gave her the opportunity to go to the cinema with them. After each weekend Sybil always told them about the dances that she had been to with her older sisters and suggested that she and Annie start to go as well.

'But I don't have anything to wear for a dance,' she told them.

'Don't worry,' said Sybil, 'I only have one like everyone else, but my sister is good at making it look different every week. She adds bows or flowers and we dress our hair different every week as well… sometimes a comb or a snood… it's fun.'

'Well let me think about it and have a look at home to see what I could use or change,' said Beth.

Annie nodded, 'Yes and I will do the same. We can bring them to work first for you to have a look at and see what you think,' looking at Sybil.

'Course I will,' said Sybil laughing at their concern. 'There's all shapes and sizes go you know, you are not going to bump into anyone dressed like Mae West…so stop worrying about it.'

She told Arnold about their conversation and admitted to him that although she would like to go she didn't really have anything suitable to go in. She was afraid she would look out of place whatever she wore and feel silly.

'There is no need to worry or feel silly about anything, I am sure you can have a look around for a dress with the girls and buy it. Don't forget your savings that I have, you might as well have a bit of pleasure out of it... that's what it's there for.' He was pleased that she was starting to spread her wings a little and at last making friends of her own.

'Oh I hadn't thought of that. I forget I have some money saved. Well, I won't go silly. I will have a good look around first before I make my mind up. Sybil was giving us some good tips today.'

'Good that's sorted then,' said Arnold, 'and, oh, don't forget that next Sunday is the Blackpool trip again from work. I hope you are going to come and wave me off,' and laughed.

'Wouldn't miss it,' she answered back. 'Had better get my hat sorted out.'

So, as in the previous year, they both rose early and made their breakfast. Beth had made sandwiches for Arnold and whoever else was in the charabanc. She had brought fresh bread from the bakery on the Saturday for sandwiches so she knew there was enough for the journey there for all of them. She had told Mr Newbould of the trip so he had donated a slab of parkin as an advert for anyone living near his shop that might be in the charabanc with Arnold.

Beth always thought that sunrise was a quiet and beautiful time of the day and said as much to Arnold as they stepped through the door. The weather once again looked as if it was going to be kind to them. He was carrying the basket of food and drinks for the journey and was once again looking forward to the trip even more this year now he knew what to expect. The first time had been excited anticipation of what might await.

They arrived at the newspaper offices and once again all the vehicles were lined up with a number visible on the side of each of the panels. Arnold went and registered himself and came back to Beth with the number of the one he was to travel in and off they went to place the basket inside. They passed all his work colleagues on the way, all doffed their caps at Beth and she smiled, everyone was in good humour.

The whistle sounded at ten to seven, they all climbed aboard readying themselves for the seven o'clock departure, excitement as before was running high. Now that Beth knew quite a few of Arnold's work colleagues she walked on to the front of the queue and waved to them all as they passed in the different vehicles, calling them all by name and telling them to enjoy their day. Arnold's coach appeared and all the occupants waved and called back to her. She held onto her hat in the breeze and only stopped waving when they had all disappeared round the corner of the High Street to start their long journey. Once again she turned for home and silently wished them all another wonderful day.

Arnold and his pals sat back to enjoy the excursion and the driver good-heartedly called out the route they were to take and told them signs to look for. 'We will be going through Penistone then over the Woodhead this year and down into Manchester, through Preston and on to Blackpool.' They all cheered and told him to be quick. 'Just enjoy the trip... we will be there soon enough,' he called back.

As they passed through the villages en-route, the local inhabitants waved and the children ran alongside trying to beat the line of vehicles in a one-sided race. Up and over the Pennines and moors down to Manchester through the magnificent scenery the Peak District had to offer. Coming from a steel city they all agreed that this was the best part of the trip, and just enjoyed the views in quiet thought. It didn't seem long before the shout went up, 'Look, look... there's the Tower.' Everyone strained to see the magnificent structure far on the horizon, and cheered once again.

The charabancs all parked up for the day in a line. Arnold and his pals congregated to spend the day together. They had already discussed what their route was to be, so off they went to the promenade to see and be seen. The entire work force all dressed splendidly in their best clothes and hats all in the same frame of mind to spend time marvelling at the ever-moving ebb and flow of the sea, acknowledging and waving to each other as they passed along the prom.

Arnold and his friends had decided to walk the length of the promenade then take the sea front trams back to the amusement park before finally moving on to the Tower. Once there, they would take the ride to the top to survey all the surrounding countryside on one side and the vast sea on the other, then descend back down to ground level to wander around the arcades at will until it was time to start their return journey home.

As they walked they all kept their eyes open for the young ladies that were walking in the opposite direction towards them. They all hoped to catch an admiring glance or even a shy smile, they cajoled each other if a response was noted before the lady averted her eyes while walking past. They would then wait to see if the same lady turned for a second glance and gave a smile away. There was great delight if she did and always a chance of connecting with the same pair of eyes later on in the day as everyone appeared to take the same route, promenade, amusement park, the Tower.

Arnold was no different to his friends it was all part of the day and he thoroughly enjoyed watching the fairer sex parade in their finery, equally hoping to catch admiring glances from a possible suitor. Then he saw her walking towards them dressed in a rose pink dress with a matching rose on her straw hat, laughing across the line of her friends to something that had been said. As she turned her head back her hazel eyes locked on to Arnold's and she laughed again. He lifted his hat and nodded slightly, she held his gaze. The two lines walked past each other and two heads turned for a second look and a further exchanged smile.

'Let's turn round and go back,' he said to his friends. 'Did you see her? Let's go back.'

'No, this is the direction we have all agreed on, we can't change it just for one. We would be all over the place and not see anything if we all turned round every time we saw a pretty face. Come on Arnold there is every chance you will see her later.'

Feeling disappointed, he turned once more to look and so did she. She smiled and waved, then continued walking with her friends.

'Right,' said Arnold, 'if anyone sees that hat again I want to know. The day is far from over, I must find her again.'

'Don't worry when we are on the tram coming back, you will have another chance to see which direction she is heading,' said Tom, 'and if you go on the top you can wave again when we pass them.'

Arnold nodded, 'Good idea, let's hurry up.'

Tom's eye's rolled upwards, he knew that this was going to take over their day if they didn't find her again.

Throughout his life Arnold's priority had always been to safeguard Beth and although as he had grown older he had come to admire the turn of an ankle and a pretty face, he knew that his goal was to find someone similar to his sister not necessarily in appearance but more importantly with the same caring temperament. They had both grown up grounded individuals which, considering their early childhood without any parental support, was a great achievement. Admittedly Beth had succumbed in the wake of the deaths of the Richardsons but had emerged out of her nightmare a stronger person, her heart ruling her head, always wishing the best for people. She would never change he knew that, she had set the bar.

They climbed aboard the tram and started the journey back to the amusement park area, Arnold scanning both sides of the promenade for any glimpse of the girl dressed in rose pink. Every time one of them spotted any shade of pink they would shout 'over here Arnold, is this her?' and so it went the full length of the trip back to the end of the promenade from where they had started walking. There was no sign of her.

'She has got to be somewhere,' said Arnold becoming exasperated. 'You are not looking properly,' and much to his dismay they all laughed.

Tom steadied himself and said, 'C'mon don't worry... she is here somewhere, we'll find her.'

Keeping to their original plan they continued towards the amusement park, they had been told that new rides awaited but Arnold only had one thing on his mind. They passed the entertainment booths with the barkers all competing for their attention and money, extolling the virtues of the Bearded Lady, The Strongest Man in the World or The Man from Borneo 'Never to be seen again.' The man in the ringmaster's outfit would shout, 'Come in and see with your very own eyes', but no amount of persuasion was going to deter Arnold, he would find her again.

Adelaide was sitting in the sun with her three friends sipping sarsaparilla after their long walk up the promenade. As she looked around Sarah said, 'I can't remember what he looked like. What he was wearing?'

'I couldn't exactly tell you,' replied Adelaide. 'It was his blue eyes I noticed and his smile, he looked nice.'

'Well it will be like trying to find a needle in a haystack with all these people here, nice or no,' Sarah replied emptying her glass. 'I enjoyed that.'

The four girls lived and worked in Burnley in Lancashire. Adelaide's parents ran a haberdashery shop over which they lived. Sarah worked for them and she and Adelaide had become firm friends. With them on their excursion were

Sarah's sister and her friend who both worked in the mills. The four girls liked to come to Blackpool for the day at least twice a year, getting away from the dark mill town, saving a little for their trips every week.

'Well where are we going now?' asked Sarah.

'Ferris Wheel I think. I do like to see everything from the top, so fasten your hats securely,' said her sister standing up. 'Let the sarsaparilla settle first, don't want to be sick.' They all laughed and agreed. She took the glasses back into the sarsaparilla bar and they set off in the direction of the Wheel.

Arnold felt as if the fun had gone out of the day. She had made such an impact on him he felt he could no longer enjoy himself until he found her again. He fervently hoped he had not read the connection wrong, but where was she, in the midst of all these people would he find her again or would he be forced to leave Blackpool without seeing her ever again?

'C'mon let's go on the Ghost Train,' said Thomas to one of the other men. 'I am ready for a good fright.'

'You are supposed to take a lady on the Ghost Train and protect her. I don't want you screaming with fright like a girl, if you go on it you will go on your own.' He turned to the others, 'Who's for the Zipper Dipper? Now that's a man's ride!'

They all nodded in agreement and Arnold had no alternative but to follow the flow, so towards the Big Dipper they headed.

The girls all waited patiently in the queue for the Ferris Wheel. When each car ground to a halt the new customers would climb aboard into the chair that had just been vacated. Moving down the queue Sarah's sister and her friend climbed into the first one available, Adelaide and Sarah taking the next one. Gradually as it emptied and filled up one by one they moved up the arc of the wheel to start the ride proper, Adelaide's eye sweeping the ground hopefully for a glimpse of a face seen earlier.

Approaching the Dipper they could hear the screams from inside the cars hurtling down the steep track and back up again at speed. 'Now that's a man's ride alright.' said Archie. 'Don't want to hear any screaming from you lot, don't want you showing me up in front of the ladies.' They all laughed and decided to make a wager. 'The first one who screams buys the first glasses of beer in the Tower.'

They all joined the queue after buying their tickets and stood and watched the drained faces of the emptying cars, young men and women swaying from side to side on wobbly legs after the gravity-defying speed ride.

They climbed aboard and sat and waited for the car to start moving forwards. It slowly began to climb the steep incline in front of them, all showing bravado bearing in mind the wager that had been made. Making himself comfortable, Arnold steeled himself for a bumpy, fast ride round the track. The car continued slowly up the first high ramp giving them a view over the whole park, he glanced to his right and saw the hat gliding down on the Ferris Wheel and shouted, 'She's there…look,' pointing at the wheel. 'Everyone shout for me.' They all turned and looked over to the Wheel then started calling out 'Ferris Wheel… over here... Ferris Wheel,' waving as they shouted.

The wheel continued its descent then started to climb again just before the dipper car reached the summit of the first steep incline, over it went at speed, the shouts being lost in the sound of the car rattling on the track. Arnold shouted in frustration and wished the ride to be over; round the circuit it rumbled before returning to the beginning and starting its second lap. He knew it would slow again for the second big climb and hoped that she would still be on the Ferris Wheel where they could attempt to shout again. It would take time for her to alight the ride and, bearing that in mind, he hoped that they would have vacated the Dipper before her ride ended.

The climb started again and they all turned towards the Wheel to start calling and waving again. Sarah's sister heard the commotion and turned to look where it was coming from and shouted to Beth in the car behind them. 'Isn't that your friend over there waving from the Big Dipper?' just as the car Arnold was in disappeared once more over the summit of the track.

Arnold was a little more relaxed on the second circuit, even if they had left the Wheel before he arrived there at least he knew that she was in the amusement park somewhere so hopefully their paths should cross again. He whooped with laughter very careful not to let it sound like a scream.

Adelaide had looked towards the Dipper just in time to see the last car disappearing over the summit and heard the sounds of screams rising over the music being played in the park below. She smiled and felt a little excited but then reserve set in, there was still a protocol to follow so that a young lady did not appear to be too forward. What she didn't want, was him to be waiting when they got off the Ferris Wheel and expect her to approach him, that couldn't possibly happen. The girls rallied around her sensing her dilemma. Sarah then suggested that they join the ice cream queue for a cone, knowing that the stall would still be in the view of anyone leaving the Dipper.

The Dipper finally ground to a halt and Arnold was the first from the car and headed to the exit gate. The others laughed at him but all were genuinely pleased that he had spotted her again. He approached the Ferris Wheel and to his dismay realised it was full of new customers and moving the full circle again. He sighed and looked from side to side to see if he could spot the vision in rose pink. His friend Thomas appeared at his side and said, 'It's alright I have spotted where they are. Just appear calm and no rushing in like a bull in a china shop or you will lose her. A lady likes to be courted properly.' Thomas had been walking out with his girlfriend now for nearly a year, so felt he could advise him how not to react when he came in her vicinity again.

The girls were all waiting in line to be served their ice cream, and were aware of the party of friends approaching them although to the eye all the girls appeared to be in deep conversation. Thomas being the one who was deemed by the others as 'nearly engaged', approached them with confidence and lifted his hat.

'Excuse me ladies, good afternoon to you all. My name is Thomas Sinclair, I am here with my friends today and they would very much like to buy you all an ice cream if that would be possible. I can vouch personally for their respectability, my betrothed and I have known them all for some time.'

In that one sentence he had explained his marital status and initiated a possible formal introduction between the two parties. The girls all looked at each other for a consensus of opinion before Sarah said, 'Thank you Mr Sinclair that would be very nice,' and smiling back at him, 'I think we would all like that very much.'

The girls moved over to sit on benches nearby and Arnold and the others joined Thomas to assist in purchasing the ice creams.

Arnold approached Adelaide and held out her ice cream. 'Hello…good afternoon…my name is Arnold Johnson and I am very pleased to meet you.'

A pair of hazel eyes looked into his and replied, 'Thank you Mr Johnson. My name is Adelaide Gibson and I am very pleased to meet you too. Thank you kindly for my ice cream,' and moved her hand to take the cone out of his. He sat down next to her on the bench careful not to sit too close. All the others introduced themselves and happily chatted about Blackpool and their trip.

Within a few minutes it was evident that both of them had relaxed following the initial introductions. There appeared to be a mutual attraction. He explained where he lived and worked, that he and his friends were on a works day out, that he lived at home with his sisters and mother and laughing told her that he liked her hat very much. She liked the way his eyes crinkled when he laughed and felt at ease before going on to tell him that she lived with her parents in Burnley and that she and her friends were in Blackpool just for the day too. They all remained in the amusement park for some time after the ice creams were finished. The rest of the group then headed to the other rides secretly hoping to take one of the three girls on to the ghost train at least. Adelaide was obviously taken with Arnold and Thomas had already told them he was betrothed so there was no competition there.

The pair of them were quite happy to watch their collective friends have fun on the other rides, they were quite content just to sit in the sunshine or wander at ease and get to know each other. 'Tell me about your family?' she asked.

'I have a sister Beth, we are very close especially since our father's death.' She noted the sadness in his voice. 'I would do anything for her and love her dearly, I am sure you will like her,' hesitating slightly and hoping that she wouldn't think he was being too forward. He quickly backtracked and said, '...would like her if you ever met her that is, she works in a bakery.' After another pause he said, 'We live with our mother and other sister.' He stopped there and Adelaide sensed he didn't wish to discuss it further.

'I have a sister too,' she said trying to keep the conversation light. 'She is older than me and married with two children. I live with my parents over the shop, and yes I am sure I would like your sister... if I ever meet her. What do you do at the newspaper?'

'I work on the production line of the paper. It's interesting work. I have been there since I was fourteen.'

'Yes, I would imagine it is,' she replied.

Their friends returned and said it was time to go on to the Tower or they were not going to get everything done that they had planned. As the two groups had the same agenda there was no problem so they all set off together back down the promenade towards the Tower. Adelaide and Arnold bringing up the rear quite happy just to be in each other's company and both very conscious that when their day together ended they would be leaving in totally different directions to go home.

Whilst walking he had told her that he had to find something special for Beth to take home.

'Tell me about her, what sort of things does she like?'

'Oh that's easy, the talkies and especially the musicals, she makes me practice the dances with her when we come out.' They both laughed. 'She has just decided to start going to dances with her friends.'

'Well there is the ballroom in the Tower, I am sure they will have things to buy, something that she will like,' said Adelaide.

'That's a great idea, I wouldn't have thought of that. She has been worrying about what to wear, thank you,' he replied and smiled looking directly into her eyes.

They followed the rest of the group inside and Arnold told them he was going to look around to get something for Beth and he would see them later. If they wanted to go on somewhere that was fine he would see them back here at seven o'clock as they had to be back on the park where the charabanc was parked for eight o'clock. They all agreed and Sarah looked at her friend and nodded. The trip had turned into a fun day for them since they had all met up and she sensed that for Adelaide, Arnold could turn out to be someone special.

Leaving the group they turned to start the search for something special for his sister. 'Last year I took her a picture of the Tower and a sea shell. She has never been to the coast you see so I wanted her to have an idea of what it was like here. The sea shell was so that she could hold it to her ear and hear the sea, our father was lost at sea during the War.'

'That is one of the loveliest things I have ever heard. Did she like them?'

'Yes, I knew she would. Although when she heard the sea in the shell she cried for a moment... for our father. She wasn't sad about it, it was more of a comfort I think. She said the sound was gentle. She has treasured it since and now listens without tears.'

'You love her very much I can see,' said Adelaide and touched his hand to show him she understood.

'Yes I do. We have been very close since the death of our father. It has not been easy.'

She noted he didn't mention his mother or other sister, and decided not to ask him. 'Come on let's go and see what we can find for her this year that will be as special.'

They looked in all the souvenir shops as they passed but Adelaide had put the thought into his head regarding dancing and the ballroom. He was interested to see what might be in the ballroom shop first rather than deciding on something from the souvenir vendors.

Being the weekend the ballroom was open for a tea dance so they looked through the door. Adelaide wanted him to see it so that he could describe it to Beth; she had been touched by his obvious concern for his sister. Pointing over to the stage she told him that was where Reginald Dixon appears to play the organ for the dancers, and the same stage where Gracie Fields appeared regularly to sing, he was thrilled.

'Beth will love hearing all that,' he said.

'Over here Arnold, here is the shop,' she said pointing in the direction.

Inside the Ballroom Emporium was an array of shoes, dresses, clips for hair, bracelets and stockings. There was an expensive section but the management recognised that in the main their clientele would be the hard working population having a day trip out at the expense of their employers, as indeed Arnold was. So, with this in mind they had kept the prices for the full range within the visitors reach. The Tower Ballroom was becoming synonymous with dancing and glamour for the working classes.

'You will have to guide me through this lot,' said Arnold.

'Don't worry I will, now what size is she?'

'She is probably a little taller...but I would say much about the same size as you.'

'What colour eyes does she have?'

'Does that matter?' asked Arnold.

'Of course it does, it gives me some idea.'

'They are blue.'

'Then we will find something to match her eyes. I don't think you can go wrong with that.'

'Whatever you say, so long as it is not too showy, she wouldn't like that.'

Walking towards the line of dresses Adelaide picked out a couple of dresses, just to see what he thought. One was forget-me-not blue, the other a little darker. They were a similar design neither was showy, just a nice cut with the back of the skirt being a little longer than the front, mid-calf and a waist line that could be dressed with a belt or left plain. One had long sleeves with a long cuff with pearl buttons, the other a short puff sleeve.

'What do you think of these?' she asked holding one in front of herself then the other.

'I think you would look very nice in either one of them,' he said smiling.

'Not me silly. Do you think she would like the styles?'

'Well yes, I suppose she would,' said Arnold a little unsure.

'Well which one do you prefer,' she persisted, 'or shall I look for another one?'

'Oh no...that will only make it a more difficult choice.' Then, after a moment's pause, 'I think she would like the darker one with the long sleeves.'

'It is a nice dress, understated elegance,' said Adelaide holding it up and looking at it again. 'She will look lovely in it and if you buy two combs with pearls on even better,' she enthused and laughed.

'That's it then. I would never have thought about buying anything like that for her. She will be thrilled, she has had a difficult time of it this last couple of months and has been quite ill. She is alright now thank goodness and I think this will just give her that extra lift.' He looked at the dress again and smiled, 'Thank you for helping me Adelaide. I am very grateful and also very pleased we have met,' he said looking into her eyes.

'So am I,' she returned his gaze and touched the back of his hand again, it felt the natural thing to do.

He let her choose the combs to match the dress and paid the cashier. When both items were wrapped and placed in a gift box they turned to leave the shop and Arnold looked at her and said, 'I think I owe you a high tea.'

'That would be lovely,' said Adelaide, so off they headed to the tea shop situated on the roof garden.

The hours past with the two of them lost in easy conversation. They were both dismayed to realise that the time was fast approaching for them to join the others so Arnold could start his journey home.

They arrived to find their friends all waiting and there was lots of friendly banter when they appeared with Arnold carrying his parcel for Beth; the box showed it was from the Ballroom Emporium. Adelaide was carrying a small bunch of flowers that he had bought her, on the premise of helping him but really it was something he wanted to do anyway and he hoped she knew that.

'Buying flowers and dresses for women now are we?' they all laughed.

He took it all in good humour, smiled, and told Adelaide, 'Take no notice, they are only jealous that you are with me.'

She looked back at him, 'Don't worry I won't.' Then, looking at Sarah, asked her, 'Have you all had a good time?'

'Yes great... looks as if you have,' she replied.

Looking happy and at Arnold she answered, 'Yes, the best.'

They all walked back to where the vehicles were waiting to take them home. The girls went with them to wave them off, their trip home only a short train ride by comparison. They had all enjoyed their day together so before the whistle went to climb back on board, the rest of the boys gave Adelaide's three friends platonic kisses on the cheek and diplomatically left Arnold to say a fond farewell to his lady. Her friends also moved away to give the pair a little privacy.

'Adelaide, please can I see you again? Can I come and visit you if you don't think that would be too forward? It would have to be on a Sunday I am afraid... please say yes,' he said looking at her with hope in his eyes.

'Yes, yes of course you can. I would really like that. Sunday would be fine, the shop is closed on Sundays. But how will you get to Burnley from Sheffield?'

'I will get there don't worry. Give me your address then I can write and tell you when.'

Quickly she wrote down her address and told him not to lose it.

'Don't worry there is no chance of that, and I will write I promise. Thank you for a wonderful day.'

The whistle sounded, they locked hands and he kissed her very gently then turned to climb aboard the charabanc for his journey home.

Just as Beth had waved when he had started out on his journey earlier that day, Adelaide walked at the side of the vehicle until it picked up speed. She then stood holding the flowers tightly in front of her with one hand and waving goodbye with the other until he was out of sight. He sat back in his seat smiled and felt as if his chest was going to explode with emotion.

As before, Beth was sitting in the chair dozing when he arrived home. She heard the key in the door and rushed to open it for him. As soon as she saw him she knew something was different, he looked elated and as he came through the door lifted her off her feet and turned her round the kitchen.

'Beth I have had the most wonderful day and have met a wonderful girl,' he said when he put her down.

'That wonderful?' she laughed at him. 'Tell me who she is... is she pretty?'

'The prettiest girl in Blackpool today and in the whole of Burnley – that is where she lives. She is called Adelaide, but first I have something for you.' He re-opened the kitchen door to retrieve the parcel for her, he thought she might be sitting up waiting for him so he wanted to surprise her after quickly telling her his news.

'No tell me... quickly... it's more important than me opening a box, that can wait a moment I am sure.' She took the box and sat back down again, 'Come, tell me all about your day and your wonderful lady, then I will open my gift.'

'Alright...we met in the amusement park. We had seen each other whilst walking down the promenade. She was with her friend Sarah, her sister and friend but they were going in the opposite direction. I thought I wouldn't see her again but then spotted her hat when she was on the Ferris Wheel and we were on the Big Dipper, it had a pink rose on it,' Beth laughed at the detail.

'So when our ride finished we all went over to the Wheel and there she was. Thomas spoke to them first, him being nearly engaged and all that, so then we all introduced ourselves, had ice creams, and Adelaide and I spent the rest of the day together. I have her address and I have told her I will write and go over on Sundays.' He stopped for breath and Beth waited for the next instalment.

'We went in the Tower, had high tea and she told me about her family and I told her all about you. She helped me choose your present,' quickly adding, '...well I chose it really, she just gave me some good ideas. I hope you like it, I think it's special, not just because Adelaide helped me... you will love her.' He lifted the gift box again for her to open, eager to see her reaction but also a little bit nervous about her not liking it. 'Please open it now, you have heard my news and this is important to me.'

She took the box again and lifted the lid gently, she removed the tissue paper and gasped. She looked at him and tears filled her eyes, 'Arnold... it looks wonderful. Is this really for me?' The tears starting to stream down her cheeks.

'Don't be sad... please don't be sad,' said Arnold horrified at her tears.

'No I am not sad, it is the most beautiful thing I have ever seen. Look at the colour and buttons, and the combs… I have never seen anything so beautiful. This was your day and you bring me this?' she took his hand and held it against her wet cheek. 'How can I thank you?'

'Beth, I don't need or want your thanks, I just need to know you are going to be alright. I may be getting in front of myself but I think I might have found the girl I want to be with and that will mean leaving you which will break my heart. But it is something that was going to happen one day; that is what we have been saving for, our futures with someone we want to be with.' He took her hand and kissed it. 'Try the dress on for me and let us be happy for each other. You can now go to your dances dressed like a movie star and I can go and see the girl that has captured my heart.'

'Are you sure you want me to try this on now? It's late,' said Beth.

'Late doesn't matter, I just need to know you like it and it fits so that I can write straight away and tell Adelaide,' he smiled. 'Go on, let me see it… I am too excited to sleep.'

She emerged in the dress and he immediately knew that they had made the right choice.

'How clever of Adelaide,' she said, 'it fits perfectly. I love it.'

'You look wonderful,' he said. 'A real life Ginger Rogers,' he laughed.

She smiled and kissed his cheeks, 'Thank you, and thank you Adelaide. I will write too and give her my thanks. What a nice person she must be to have chosen this for me.' Packing it carefully back in the box she held it close and bade him goodnight.

'See you in the morning. What a wonderful day,' he said sighing and kissing the top of her head. 'By the way don't say anything about the dress, what they don't know doesn't hurt them.' Placing one stick of rock and a packet of humbugs on the table he turned the light out and went to bed.

They left as normal for work the next morning, the small items he had brought for Ellen and Evelyn still there on the table, neither of them aware or even interested in the fact that he had arrived back home safely from his trip.

Leaving him en-route to the bakery Beth couldn't wait to get there to tell Annie and Sybil about the beautiful dress. Then she had second thoughts that it might appear to be boasting and might even dissuade Annie from going to the dance. She decided just say that over the weekend she had managed to find a dress that would do and explain later that it was a present from Arnold.

The girls arrived for work and they all took time to discuss what the weekend had held for them. Beth enthused about Arnold's trip to Blackpool without mentioning her dress. Sybil as usual re-iterated the night out with her sisters; both Annie and Beth always enjoyed hearing about her weekend and what the girls had been wearing for the dance. Elizabeth always came up with great ideas for them and Annie, hanging on to every word, hoped that the same ingenuity could be applied to her plain dress that she had brought into the bakery.

'I have brought my dress in for you to have a look. I hope you can give me some ideas on how to make it a bit special,' she said to Sybil. Then, turning to Beth, 'I really want to go to the dance next Saturday with you.'

'Don't worry,' said Beth, 'I am sure Sybil and her sisters can work their magic. I can't go without you can I?'

Annie smiled, thankful for the support and said, 'I can hardly wait.'

'That goes for all of us, it will be nice to have you both there as well as my sisters. Now, show me your dress,' said Sybil.

Beth looked at her friend, 'I can't wait to see your dress and see what can be done with it but… tell you what, leave it until we have opened up and the first wave of customers have been in. Remember we are here to work, don't want Mr Newbould to think we are wasting time do we?'

Annie nodded, 'Yes you are right, and you never know, if I show it to Mr Newbould he might have some ideas.' She laughed at the silliness of the idea.

Sybil's sisters arrived before their shift and ordered the usual scrape on bread, 'And don't scrimp it,' said Elizabeth laughing to Sybil.

'And don't you go getting me into trouble,' replied Sybil introducing her family. 'Take no notice you two, these are my sisters Elizabeth and Theresa,' she said to Beth and Annie. They all acknowledged each other with a nod and a smile. Beth noticed that even dressed for work with her headscarf tied round her head covering all her hair, Elizabeth somehow still managed to look stylish and outshine her other sisters.

'Heard a lot about you,' said Annie to Elizabeth looking excited.

'Hope it's all good… it better be,' she replied. 'So what's our Sybil been telling you then?' looking at her younger sister with a glint in her eye.

'Oh… nothing bad,' said Annie backtracking. 'She just said that you were good at updating dresses for the dance and we are coming on Saturday so I hoped you would look at mine and give me some ideas... please?' she sounded a little nervous.

'Course I will, we'll be back at dinnertime break so I will have a look at it then...what colour is it?'

'Red,' said Annie.

'That's OK, lots you can do with a plain red dress, see you at dinner time,' said Elizabeth and off she went with Theresa for their shift. 'Bye.'

Annie was thrilled. 'Isn't she lovely?' she said to Sybil who just raised her eyebrows and nodded.

'Yes she is,' replied Beth watching them walking together down the road towards the cutlery factory. 'What do they do Sybil?' she turned and asked.

'Oh they're not buffers,' said Sybil turning her attention to the bread. 'They are packers, they put the cutlery in their boxes and canteens, mind... the way she dresses for work you would think they were buffers... says she doesn't want any of the dust on her hair or anything, it's awful stuff.'

'Well I think she's lovely even in her work clothes, and Elizabeth is such a lovely name,' said Annie. 'Is she the one that gets up and sings sometimes?'

'Yes,' said Sybil beginning to tire of all this praise of her elder sister. 'That's our Betty, she's the one.'

'Betty,' said Annie, 'who's Betty?'

'Our Elizabeth, that's what she is known as at home,' said Sybil with a wry smile and walked out into the yard bringing the conversation to an end.

After meeting the sisters Annie felt a little apprehensive that she might become the centre of attention in front of all of them when Elizabeth came back. She didn't want to be in trouble with Mr Newbould, so she decided just to show Beth and Sybil for a first reaction when the shop became quiet. Her dress was cherry red and in panels that moulded to her body, it had a V-neck and the sleeves were slightly puffed on the shoulder and finished at the elbow, it was calf length and slightly flared at the hemline.

'That's nice,' said Beth, 'the colour suits you.' Annie beamed.

'Yes, I was lucky I got it from the pop shop for my sister's wedding.'

'Annie that's fine,' Sybil joined in. 'We have a lot of black bits in our box at home so I am sure it can be trimmed in some way, round the neck or sleeves, or a bow. Better than white with your hair being dark, and what about a red snood?' she asked. 'Leave it with me and I will get some black sorted tonight when we're at home, we can use white another time.'

Annie was becoming more excited by the minute. 'I can't wait to see it,' she said putting it back in the bag just as the sisters arrived back in the shop on their lunchtime break.

'I've had a look Betts, it will be fine. Plain red so it can be trimmed with black,' said Sybil to her sister. Elizabeth nodded.

'I'm sure it will be lovely, whatever you decide to do with it,' said a grateful Annie. 'I can't wait for Saturday,' looking at Beth and beaming.

The dress came back on the Thursday. Sybil took it out of the bag and Annie gasped. It was now adorned with a black frilled collar which fell into a large soft bow at the front. The sleeves had a subtle trimming of black just on the edge. Eager to see how it would look she held it up in front of her and asked for Beth's opinion.

'That is really chic, Annie, you will look lovely,' said Beth honestly. The wide collar and the way it fell into the bow accentuated Annie's waist, the black trimming on the sleeve just finished it off. 'What about pinning your hair up for a change?'

'Yes I could do,' said a thrilled Annie carefully putting the dress back into the bag. 'You haven't told me what colour you will be wearing on Saturday.'

'Mine is blue, so don't worry we won't clash.'

Saturday finally arrived and the shop was filled with much excitement. Annie was hardly able to contain herself. They closed at lunchtime and arrangements had been made to meet later. Sybil would be coming with her sisters as usual, Beth and Annie had agreed to meet outside the barracks.

Walking home Beth felt a nervous excitement for what the evening might hold. She knew she would enjoy watching the dancing and listening to the music. Would it be like the talking pictures, would anyone ask her to dance? Worse still what would she do if nobody asked her to dance? Still lost in her thoughts she heard a familiar voice call her name and knew Arnold was following her, she turned to wait for him.

'I have decided to take you to the pictures tonight, so no arguing,' he said and laughed.

'Not tonight thank you sir I have other plans, but I tell you what you can do and that is help me practise my steps before I go out,' she giggled.

'No mercy please… not again. You don't need any more practise, you will be fighting them off for a dance. I will take you and pick you up when it's over, I don't want you walking home alone, is that alright?'

'You know it is,' she replied and linked his arm for the rest of the walk to their door. 'More importantly, have you written to Adelaide yet?'

'Yes I have told her you love the dress and have said that I would like to visit in two weeks if her parents approve. She has plenty of time to reply then.'

'That's wonderful I am sure they will. Did you tell her I am going dancing tonight?' she enthused.

'What do you think?' came the reply, 'and by the way say nothing when we leave tonight, I doubt if they will ask where we are going anyway but just in case let's just leave as normal.'

They arrived at the door and two pairs of eyes looked up as they came through the door. There were no greetings, both were used to Beth bringing bread and sometimes bread and butter pudding home on Saturdays so they were always sat waiting in anticipation. Ellen looked up to see if Beth was carrying anything. She placed the bag on the table and went to remove her coat. It happened every Saturday they sat and waited for her to come home, then pounced to see what the offerings were in the bags and took their pick. She and Arnold were always left with what they didn't want, not that it worried them Beth always had an extra bag just for her and Arnold under her coat; they had learned to play the game to their advantage.

She took her time getting ready. She knew Evelyn would not think to come to see what she was doing, they really never had any contact or proper discussion. Her mother and sister's world was their own, any outsider would not have known that they were part of the same family. As far as Arnold and Beth were concerned there was no more to be said, Beth had a brother, Arnold had a sister and that was that.

Ready to go, she glanced in the mirror and stood transfixed for a moment. This was the first dress she had ever had that was new, one that had been bought just for her. As long as she could remember they had always had clothes from the alms houses after they had lost their father, and since she started work like everyone else she went to the pawn shops. There were always bargains to be had at some poor soul's expense, pawnbrokers everywhere thrived in difficult times. Everyone used the 'pop shops' without any embarrassment, it was a normal way of life if they couldn't afford to redeem their goods then they lost them.

Arnold tapped on the bedroom door and called her. Hearing no reply he gently opened the door and called her again. He found her still staring into the mirror. 'Beth... is everything alright?'

'Oh yes, I'm sorry,' she turned and looked at him.

He looked at his younger sister and his eyes misted. He took her gently in his arms and held her quietly for a while, both of them sensed that their paths would probably now start to move in different directions.

'Is this really my sister? You look lovely.'

'Yes its just little old me,' she laughed.

'Not so little anymore. I am very proud of you Beth, don't ever change... promise me.'

'Of course I won't silly, and I am just as proud of you and think Adelaide is a very lucky lady.'

'C'mon, let's go, the young men at the dance don't know what awaits them, you will be danced off your feet.'

They left the house without fuss as normal and set off in the direction of the barracks. Saturday was always a busy night with everyone dressed for the weekend after toiling at work all week; a few hours of enjoyment whether it was in the picture houses, alehouses or the local dance hall was all everyone wanted.

Annie was waiting for her. She had pinned her dark locks up and found a red lipstick to match her dress and looked very different to the Annie that worked in the bakery shop. She looked confident and very attractive and had already attracted admiring glances from the crowd waiting to go in.

'My word,' said Arnold. 'Annie you look lovely, the two of you are really going to set the cat amongst the pigeons tonight.' He hoped a couple of compliments would settle their nerves, not that they need have any.

'Thank you kind sir,' said Annie blushing slightly.

'Off you go, I will see you at eleven thirty. Annie we will take the long walk home with you as well if you want. It will probably take that long for you both to tell me all about it anyway,' he said laughing. 'I am off to meet Thomas and the crowd, have a good night.'

'He's a real gent that brother of yours, Beth,' said Annie putting her arm through her friend's.

'Yes he is. Come on let's go and see what this dancing is all about... ready?'

They left their coats in the cloakroom and both admired each other's dresses. Annie looked striking in the black and red and Beth graceful in blue. She had rolled her hair under and clipped the sides back with the combs which highlighted her eyes.

They followed the other girls into the dance hall and took a little time to become comfortable with their surroundings. They could see the other girls taking side glances, obviously recognising they were new to the arena and without doubt competition.

'Come on Annie hold your head high, we are being vetted,' said Beth confidently. 'Let's go and find some seats and see what happens.'

The musicians had already set their instruments up and just after eight o'clock the first chords were heard. The dancing started and it wasn't long before Beth and Annie were asked for a dance. A little bit tentative, Beth nodded her consent and once on the dance floor lifted her arms to her partner to start the waltz. Annie, behind her, followed suit holding her breath and praying that she wasn't going to make a mess of it. For the rest of the evening after one dance finished, there was another suitor to request the next and their confidence on the dance floor was growing.

After about twenty minutes, carefully choreographed to be timed between dances, the doors opened and Elizabeth, Theresa and Sybil made their entrance. There was an audible groan from the rest of the girls present, this weekly ritual being viewed as nothing more than a floor show by the girls but the boys loved it, and there were always whistles of approval to be heard on their arrival.

Annie spotted them first. 'Look Beth, here is Sybil and her sisters. Oh, gosh don't they look sophisticated. Who would have thought they could look like that after seeing them in their work clothes.'

'Annie, did you take a look in the mirror before you came out. You look just as lovely. I am surprised you recognised yourself,' said an amused Beth, laughing to put Annie at her ease again.

'Hah you're right. Actually I didn't!' she replied returning the laugh and turned her attention back in the direction of Sybil and waved. She was disappointed when the wave wasn't returned.

'Don't worry,' said Beth, 'we will see them, it's early yet.'

Sybil didn't see the wave as she was caught up in conversation with Theresa, whilst Elizabeth was taking stock of who was there and in particular any new talent. The usual crowd of admirers were there to hand now that their entrance had been made.

The music started again and the dancing partners came thick and fast for all the girls apart from Elizabeth. She knew exactly who she would partner during the evening, that is if there was no other new talent to choose from. As always, as she danced she always kept an eye to the other dresses that were being worn around the room and it wasn't long before she spotted the blue creation that Beth was wearing. She didn't realise it was Beth as with all the girls their transformation from working clothes into evening wear for a dance was amazing. She did note how the dress moulded the figure, the stylish sleeves with the pearl buttons, how it moved when the wearer danced, the matching hair combs, understated elegance not usually seen in their dance hall on a Saturday night. Beth danced oblivious to the fact that she was being scrutinised.

It didn't take long for Annie to connect with Sybil on the dance floor. They greeted each other whilst dancing and said they would chat when the dance had finished. Annie thanked her partner at the end of the dance and went to find Beth so they could meet up with the other girls. Sybil was standing with Theresa when Annie and Beth approached, they all greeted each other and admired each other's dresses.

'I think you have both made quite an impact tonight in those dresses,' Theresa told them. 'Annie the black against the red is great on you and Beth you just look lovely, really elegant. Have you any more at home like that?'

'No,' she answered. 'I wish I had. My brother bought it for me as a present.'

'Some present,' said Theresa turning to Sybil. 'We will have to have a word with Owen... or better still the old bastard,' and they both laughed.

Elizabeth joined the group. She had noticed them talking across the dance floor and as the said blue dress was in the group came out of curiosity to see who the wearer was. She obviously recognised the updated dress that Annie was wearing so there was no problem joining them.

'Hello, Annie, the dress looks lovely on you,' and turning, 'and who is this vision?' before she realised that it was Beth from the bakery shop. Slightly taken aback she said, 'Oh hello, what a beautiful dress. You look lovely, I didn't recognise you Beth.'

'Thank you, that's very kind of you.'

'Well I wouldn't have recognised you,' said Annie. 'What a transformation Elizabeth,' she smiled and nodded her head in acknowledgement then turned to her entourage for one lucky soul to light her cigarette.

'Are you enjoying it Annie?' asked Sybil.

'Oh yes, now that we have been asked to dance, we'll not be nervous anymore will we Beth.'

'No I think we will all be fine,' she replied with a smile, looking over to Elizabeth holding court and thinking how nice after toiling at work all week in a cutlery factory Elizabeth could become a different person, just like story line out of the movies.

They continued to accept the offers to dance and with each dance they became more confident; the interval approached for the musicians to take a break. The gathered crowd applauded as they left the stage for the intermission and the lights came up around the hall.

Beth and Annie resumed their seats and chatted in general about the partners they had danced with, laughed about some and praised others then retired to the cloakroom for Annie to refresh her lipstick. They returned to their seats to wait for the musicians to reappear, having collected a drink from the refreshment bar on their way. Quietly sitting at the table Beth glanced over to where Sybil was standing with Theresa, and noticed the two men who had joined them. Elizabeth was standing next to Sybil to one side in conversation with one of her dancing partners, as always her eyes alert and totally aware of what was happening around the dance hall.

Beth watched him lower his head to light his cigarette from the lighter his friend was holding and kept her sights on him until, to her horror, he lifted his gaze and they locked eyes. He acknowledged the connection inclined his head to her and smiled. She averted her eyes and turned to Annie and said, 'Talk to me quickly,' sounding a little flustered.

'Why what's wrong?' said Annie.

'Nothing really,' replied Beth, 'just say something.'

'I don't know what to say,' said Annie.

'That will do... don't worry that's enough,' said Beth regaining her composure again and glancing back round the hall.

Elizabeth had caught the glance between the two them. 'Well, well, well,' she thought, and turning to her brother she asked, 'How are you this evening Owen?'

'I am just fine thank you Betts,' he answered staring at the girl in the blue dress.

The intermission over, the musicians appeared back on stage with the usual singing duo; the music continued and the dancers returned to the floor. Beth and Annie were then surprised and delighted when Elizabeth appeared on stage and joined the other two girls to perform a number by the Boswell Sisters. This was Elizabeth's high point of the evening and she performed like a professional.

Beth watching her performance soon became aware that Elizabeth's gaze was transfixed, whereas the other two girls were singing to the audience in front of them. She followed her gaze from the stage to see that the person she was singing to belonged to the same person she had locked eyes with a little earlier. He was smiling as she sang to him. Feeling embarrassed and a little disappointed she quickly looked away from him and returned her gaze to the stage.

'Wasn't Elizabeth good,' said Annie clapping furiously at the end of the song.

'Yes,' said Beth quietly, 'very good.'

The rest of their evening passed quickly and before they knew it Arnold appeared just as the band had played the last number.

'Well, what a shame, and there I was just about to ask you both to dance,' he laughed. Seeing a look of disappointment on Annie's face, added, 'Not really Annie I am only joking. Beth will tell you I have two left feet. You would probably never dance again,' and he laughed. 'How has your evening gone?'

'It's been wonderful,' said Annie, 'I have really enjoyed it.'

'Yes and so have I,' said Beth.

'Right are we ready then?' he asked. 'Ladies,' extending his arm in the direction of the door.

Arnold placed a protective arm around Beth as they waited to leave the hall and said, 'I am so pleased you have enjoyed it, gives me something to tell Adelaide.' He opened the doors for them and they left the dance hall.

Owen watched the doors close and cursed himself for not speaking to the girl dressed in blue. She had obviously found someone else to escort her home much to his annoyance. They were obviously familiar with each other as she had been laughing with him, her relaxed manner made her even more attractive to him.

He checked to see if the girls were all together and said abruptly, 'Come on Georgie, I have had enough, let's go,' and headed for the exit without waiting for an answer.

It was Monday morning again and all the girls arrived at the bakery within minutes of each other. Annie was full of chatter about the night out at the barracks and how much she had enjoyed it, humming to herself some of the songs that had been played.

'I hope we are going again Beth, and you too Sybil, obviously,' she said while going about her duties.

'Oh we are there every week, the entire family practically. It's the big night out for all of us,' Sybil replied.

'Did Elizabeth enjoy it? She was very good on stage, she ought to start singing herself,' Annie continued stacking the loaves at the same time. 'Wished I looked like that and was brave enough to get up and sing.'

'Our Betty has enough confidence for all of us don't you worry,' Sybil replied. 'She knows where she wants to be and it's not going to be the Drill Hall every Saturday night for the rest of her life. Might be good enough for us lot but not my eldest sister.'

'Does she have a boyfriend?' said Beth joining in the conversation casually.

'She has one or two, they like to think they are special but she has other ideas. There's nobody in particular,' replied Sybil cleaning the counter.

'Hmm... must be nice just to have a choice. Then again she is very attractive,' said Annie leaving them and going into the bakery.

As if by clockwork all the buffer girls started to appear on the cobbled streets, passing the shop on their way to their shift, some calling in to pick something up for their break some just calling 'Mornin' through the door. Elizabeth and Theresa appeared and ordered their usual. Annie, now back in the shop and still showing her excitement from the weekend, looked at Elizabeth and gushed, 'Oh I thought you were wonderful on Saturday night. I have never known a singer before,' and grinned from ear to ear.

'Thanks,' was the reply. 'Did you both enjoy it?' she said looking at Beth.

'Yes, thank you, we both had a good time.'

'See anybody you fancied?' Elizabeth asked with a smile.

'Oh... I saw lots,' said Annie and laughed.

'What about you Beth?' Elizabeth continued, and raised a well manicured eyebrow.

'Yes there were some good looking guys there but I think we were both concentrating on our dancing, were we not Annie?' she smiled then turned towards the next customers who had just come in.

Elizabeth turned, 'Well, there's plenty of time.' They picked up their purchases and told their sister 'see you later', left the shop and continued on their way to work.

'I hope you are going to calm down about seeing our Betty join in on one song,' Sybil said to Annie. 'There'll be no living with her if you carry on. '

'Well I just think she's lovely, that's all,' said Annie defending herself.

'Yes, and don't we all know it,' retorted Sybil heading towards Beth to help her carry in another basket of bread.

In another part of the city Owen and Georgie were heading into work. As they walked Georgie turned to Owen and said, 'You ended up in a funny mood on Saturday night what was the problem. Is your father having a go again?'

'No,' replied Owen not breaking his step.

'Well, are you alright? You know you can tell me.'

'I'm fine,' he said this time looking at Georgie. 'Really... I 'm fine.'

'No, you're not, I can tell. Are you going to tell me?' he asked again.

'No,' said Owen and carried on walking.

Georgie stopped and laughed out loud, 'Must be a woman in there somewhere then, there's got to be,' he replied. He followed his friend into work and didn't raise the issue again.

It was only Monday but Annie was already wishing the week away. 'I think I will have a look round for a red snood for my hair this week instead of having it up. I think red would look better than black. What do you think Beth?'

'Yes it would, black would look nice as well but I think the red would stand out more.'

'That's what I thought. What are you thinking of?' Annie continued.

'Well it's only Monday Annie, long way to go yet. We'll see, I will have a think about it. Can't change the dress.'

'No you can't, it's new and it's lovely... matches your eyes,' Annie drifted off again into her own world and Beth smiled at her. Their conversation did prompt her to think what she was going to change. The snood idea was a good one but she didn't want to wear one if that was Annie's choice, it would wait for another week. It could either be white to match the pearl buttons with pearl earrings or a blue one to match the colour of her dress. Then her thoughts drifted to, 'I wonder if he will be there?' Then... 'Stop being silly Beth,' promptly coming out of her reverie she decided she would style her hair up this week and use the pearl combs again. The pearl earrings would nicely finish off the overall look, satisfied with her choice she relaxed.

As always the week did pass and finally it was Saturday morning and their half day. Annie had told Mr Newbould all about their previous Saturday night every day and how much she was looking forward to the following Saturday. He had listened in good humour and was relieved when their half day arrived so he wouldn't have to listen to the same report for another whole day. At least on the Saturday it had changed from what their evening the week before had been to one of anticipation for that night. He didn't mind his staff of three and their chatter, they were all happy working together and carried out their duties well. The female clientele were happy to chat with them and spend their hard earned cash, so no reason to complain, his profits were good.

The girls all left together. As Mr Newbould locked the doors he called, 'Have a good evening all of you, especially you Annie. No doubt I will hear all about it on Monday morning,' and laughed. Then he added in jest, 'You can take me one week, I'll show you how it's done!' They all giggled at the thought of it, waved back at him and carried on down the street towards home.

Half day in Appleyards was also full of anticipation for the younger members of staff, the current apprentices had forged their bonds as Owen and Georgie had done. These two were held in esteem by the younger ones. They always enquired on a Monday morning what they had been up to over the weekend and intimated that if they had been wherever Owen and Georgie were, they would have given them a run for their money with the ladies. All was taken in good humour by both parties, the older ones laughing at the challenge from the young pretenders.

'So what are we doing tonight then?' said Georgie.

'The usual,' replied Owen, 'Only I thought we would go a bit earlier.'

'Any particular reason?' enquired Georgie trying to sound nonchalant.

'Should there be. Just thought it would make a change,' answered Owen.

'So do you want to arrive with the girls and make an entrance?' he laughed.

'No, we'll have a few drinks then get there before they arrive.'

'Any particular reason?' said Georgie again looking straight at him this time.

'No,' said Owen. 'Cut it out.'

'OK then. All will become clear no doubt,' was the sardonic reply. 'See you at mine.'

Arnold came home from work elated, he had received a letter from Adelaide. She had confirmed that her parents had no objection to him calling and being introduced. He had the letter delivered to the newspaper office as he didn't want to chance Ellen or Evelyn picking it up and opening it out of curiosity or spite. So, to be certain he had told Adelaide to reply to the works address after checking that it would be alright for him to receive mail there. He told Beth that he would be travelling to Burnley the following Sunday week by train, and needed her to check before he left that he looked more than presentable. He then had to decide what to take as a gift.

Beth had laughed at his nervousness and said, 'Not like you to be nervous Arnold, I am sure there will be no problem. Why don't you take some flowers for her mother and some chocolates for Adelaide… or some toilet water for her mother and flowers for Adelaide?'

'Not sure about the second one, don't you think the toilet water may be a little bit forward for her mother? Think I like the flower idea best,' he said looking at her.

'That's fine, you will be able to buy flowers in Burnley off the train I would have thought, instead of buying them here.'

'She was very pleased to hear that you liked the dress and enjoyed the dance. You will like her Beth I know you will, and she will like you,' he said smiling at her.

'I am sure we will become good friends from what you have said. I think I will write her a short note for you to take, thanking her for suggesting and helping you choose my dress in Blackpool and how much I like it,' she answered returning his smile.

'She'll like that I reckon,' he said nodding to her. 'Hope her parents are alright and not too strict,' a look of concern coming over his face.

'Stop worrying, write back and tell her what time you will be arriving. Are you meeting her at the station and then going to be *introduced?*' stressing the last word and laughing at him.

'Yes, I think that will be best rather than me trying to find the address. At least I won't be as nervous if she is with me,' he said turning serious again.

'Don't be nervous they don't sound like our family. If you can call ours a family,' she said quickly trying to ease his concerns. 'That would be like walking into a lion's den. I hope you are not thinking of her coming here?' she sounded concerned.

'No chance, the only person she has to meet is you, nobody else,' then added, 'and you can either come with me to Burnley one Sunday or better still we could meet her in Blackpool. How would that suit you?' he waited for her reaction.

'Oh... that would be marvellous, are you sure?' she said laughing and hugging him.

'Don't be silly... I did promise you after all,' he replied. 'I will arrange it all next week when I see her again so don't worry. The more I think about it, it would be nice for us to all meet up there so you can see it for yourself.' Then, adding cautiously, 'That's if it all goes alright that is and she wants to see me again and her parents agree,' a note of worry coming back into his tone.

'I am sure it will be fine. I won't get excited just yet but I am sure you have nothing to worry about. She is a lucky girl,' she added touching his arm.

'No it's me that's the lucky one, wait till you meet her. I will write the letter back now and post it when I have taken you to the barracks.'

'No, for heaven's sake. You don't have to walk me there Arnold, I will be fine.'

'Yes I do. I might not get too many more chances to be seen out walking with the best looking girl in the area,' he laughed. 'Especially when she is all dressed up to go dancing.'

He called up the stairs to see if she was ready and watched her walk down towards him. The blue dress really was an eye catcher and she had taken time and pinned her hair up, the two pearl combs holding it in place and the pearl earrings matched them beautifully. Quiet elegance, she had come a long way since those early days without shoes he thought; he was very proud of her.

'Look at you... all grown up and ready to go and make someone very happy... when he meets you.'

She appeared through the door to hostile glances from both her mother and Evelyn. They were tucking into the bread and butter pudding she had brought home at lunchtime, timing it for when Arnold or Beth were not in the room. Their selfishness still knew no bounds but the sight of Beth in her blue dress stopped them in their tracks, their peevish eyes missed nothing.

'Didn't know you had that, where's it from?' said Ellen churlishly. 'Where have you got the money from?'

'I didn't get one, it's not fair,' said Evelyn echoing her mother's nastiness. 'Why didn't I get one?' she said turning to Ellen.

Arnold turned on them both, 'Don't start all that, either of you,' he hissed. 'She is the only one that works round here, or have I missed something all these years. Anything more you want to say about it you will say it to me... is that understood?' his tone left them in no doubt, 'Well is there?'

Silence fell round the table, they both turned away, ignored his question, and carried on eating.

As they left the house Arnold realised that leaving Beth in the house with them would not be an easy thing to do when that day eventually arrived, she read his thoughts and sensed his concern.

'Arnold, I am a child no longer you must not concern yourself with my welfare, when the time comes for you to go and live your own life. We always knew that one day we would go our separate ways. You have always been there for me. I could ask for no better brother,' she said gently holding his arm.

'Yes, I know,' he said, 'and it is early days with Adelaide, but I always thought I would remain here close by to keep a brotherly eye on you.'

'You are only going for the day next weekend, stop worrying, and who is to say if things work out Adelaide wouldn't be happy to come and live here?'

'Suppose... getting in front of myself here again aren't I?' and he laughed nervously.

'Let's wait and see. I am sure it will all be fine, don't worry, but don't make me your priority...do you hear?'

'Right, enough said... let me drop you off... then I will go and post my letter then meet the others to have a pint or two.'

Annie was waiting for them and Arnold paid her the same compliment as he had the week before, once again making her blush and look a little embarrassed.

'Now don't go all coy on me, I mean it, you look very nice,' he added.

'Are you coming in tonight Arnold?' Annie asked him hoping he was going to say yes.

'No, sorry I have plans to meet friends, but I will be back to walk you both home again. You never know Annie this time I might get back before the last dance,' he laughed, 'but don't bank on it, your feet would regret it. See you both later. Go and have a good time the pair of you,' and giving Beth a quick peck on the cheek, off he went.

'I do like your brother Beth. Does he have a girlfriend?' she asked.

'Yes, but she lives in Burnley so he doesn't get to see her every weekend,' she wanted to keep the explanation simple.

'What a shame,' said Annie, 'Never mind, plenty more fish and all that... come on let's go.'

Familiar now with the routine, they checked their jackets into the cloakroom then on to the powder room to see that all was well with their appearance, they chatted confidently.

'What do you think to the snood Beth?' asked Annie tucking stray hairs back into the thick hair net.

'Looks really nice, the red against the black collar and your hair,' Beth replied honestly. 'Did you buy a black one too?'

'No, couldn't afford two this week, but I do know they have them in black.'

'Well, I was thinking could you get a white one for me?'

'Course I will... you ready?'

They came out of the powder room and headed down the corridor towards the dance hall.

Owen and Georgie had just arrived and were approaching the double doors into the dance hall when Owen caught a flash of blue out of the corner of his eye. He turned and their eyes connected. Once more Beth returned his gaze and this time did not avert her eyes.

'Come on Georgie... be a gentleman and open the door for these ladies,' he said loud enough for them to hear. He took one door and Georgie followed suit with the other, both doors opened with a flourish and the girls made their entrance.

'Thank you,' Beth laughed at him.

'You are more than welcome,' said Owen smiling back at her as they walked through the door. He then turned and winked, 'Nice timing Georgie boy...

nice timing.'

'Oh, now I see... that's answered my question I reckon,' he replied. 'Knew there was a female in there somewhere despite your denials. Do we have a plan?'

'Well, we will have to wait and see what happens won't we?' Owen laughed watching where they went to sit and taking time to see if anyone was waiting for them. 'What do you think of her friend?' he asked.

'She looks nice. Think they'll dance with us?'

'Well, I don't think I will have any problem,' said Owen with a grin, 'not so sure about you. Let's wait and see. You can ask for nothing... tell her you are really Rudolph Valentino or Fred Astaire in disguise,' and laughed again.

'Oh, yes, and why won't you have any problem then?' asked a scorned Georgie.

'It's all mapped out I reckon and I'm feeling lucky tonight,' he replied crossing his fingers just for an extra bit of good luck. 'So don't worry Georgie boy... we come as a pair,' and punched him lightly on his arm.

Beth and Annie found a table and sat down, Owen watched and relaxed seeing that there was no one waiting for them.

'Where did they come from?' said Annie. 'Everybody was looking when the doors opened like that,' she giggled.

'Not sure,' said Beth feeling a little flushed and thinking, 'well he was with his friend and Elizabeth is nowhere to be seen, let's see what happens when she arrives.'

The hall filled and the band started their repertoire, as usual fifteen minutes into the programme between dances the main doors to the hall opened and the sisters swept in.

'Here come the girls,' said Georgie, 'bang on time and looking great.'

Owen acknowledged his sisters with a smile, they certainly made an impact. As usual Elizabeth was leading the pack and being gracious to the male contingent lining up for recognition. Sybil and Theresa followed in her wake, happy to play supporting roles to their elder sister. It was a well rehearsed routine and a far cry from their mundane daily routines at work.

'Look,' said Annie. 'Here they are playing to the gallery,' and she stood and waved over in Sybil's direction. Sybil didn't see the wave so there was no response returned; Annie sat down again a little disappointed.

'Let them settle down Annie… you know it's a floor show first, we can chat with her later,' said Beth more intent on watching the smile across the dance floor being aimed in the sisters' direction.

The music started again and Beth and Annie accepted offers to dance. Owen watched Beth's progression around the dance floor, such was her concentration that she failed to notice him watching her every move. When the dance ended she thanked her partner and returned to Annie who was already back at the table.

'Well he had two left feet,' said Annie, 'shan't dance with him again.'

'Poor you… thank your lucky stars it wasn't Arnold,' said Beth laughing at her friend. 'The night's young yet Annie, it can only get better you'll see… oh here we go again… fingers crossed,' as they were invited on to the floor again.

Owen had a look round to see if whoever it was that had escorted her home the week before was in the hall; he didn't think he was but it was early yet so there was still time for him to arrive. In the meantime he watched who she danced with until he was distracted by Georgie.

'Well… are we going to make a move then?' he asked looking at Owen's serious face. 'Don't worry it might never happen… whatever it is… oh look… we're being honoured.' He turned, 'Good evening ladies, all looking lovely as usual may I say.'

'Thank you kind sir… of course you may,' said Theresa with a smile.

'You are not looking too bad yourself Georgie,' she said turning to her brother her demeanour immediately changing. 'You were in here early tonight Owen.'

'Yes,' said Sybil agreeing with her sister. 'Any particular reason?' a sharp tone had crept into her question.

'Is there a problem here?' came the reply. Noting the tension he turned to face them, 'Why the questions girls?'

'Come on, everything is fine. It's Saturday night,' intervened Georgie trying to lighten the conversation. He took his lighter out to light his cigarette and Elizabeth moved forwards into the fray for him to light hers.

'Thank you Georgie… always the gentleman,' she purred into his eyes. 'So how are things?'

'Fine Elizabeth… just fine thank you,' replied Georgie now a little cautious. She held his gaze, 'Owen still leaving all his worldly possessions at your house is he?'

Owen heard the question and spun round, 'So who wants to know? Do we have a problem here Betts? Girls?'

She took a long draw on her cigarette and sighed, 'He's been at it again... we could have done with you there tonight. It turned really nasty when we wouldn't give him any more money. She finished up in the hearth then shoved us all out of the door when I picked the poker up. But you wouldn't know all that would you... you had already left!'

'Stop it there right now. You know there is nothing I can do, he is not having anything else of mine to pawn. He's had enough out of me already and I am not going to do time for him,' he replied coldly.

'Well, we all had to gang up on him and it's not fair. We have hidden what we can at Francis' but the old bastard won't give up you know that. He'll probably send her round to beg, she'll be black and blue in the morning,' Elizabeth continued drawing intensely on her cigarette.

Losing his temper, Owen snapped back, 'That's the problem, until she stops begging and borrowing to get him his booze he is not going to change is he. He coaxed a couple of pounds out of me again last week, for the kid's food he said, "give it you back tomorrow my pension day" he said. I should know better, I won't see that again. I have told them... no more... I have fallen for it too many times, and the kids still go hungry,' he paused. 'He's a lying, evil old bastard you know that and he will never change.' He turned away from her with one final remark, 'Damn it! I am not having this tonight Betty, it's Saturday, leave it out!'

'Let's go for a pint I need some air Georgie,' and his friend followed him through the doors in silence.

Beth couldn't help but watch the obvious disagreement between them and once again felt disappointed as he left with his friend. There was obviously a connection with Elizabeth so it was better left alone with Sybil working in the bakery.

'You've gone quiet all of a sudden,' said Annie. 'Oh look there's Sybil, shall we go over?'

'You go over, I am just going to the ladies. I'll join you in a few minutes,' replied Beth and headed for the doors. Looking through the windows on the corridor leading to the ladies she could see the pair of them walking away from the barracks. She stood and watched them disappear round the corner and once again felt disappointed.

Annie walked across the dance floor. 'Hello Sybil,' she said beaming. 'I waved at you earlier when you arrived, but there was a lot going on as usual. You alright. Hello Theresa, hello Elizabeth,' she said excitedly.

Elizabeth cast a scornful glance in her direction then moved away, Annie looked a little crestfallen.

'Take no notice Annie, she's in a bit of a mood tonight,' said Sybil.

'Family matters,' added Theresa, hoping to stop any further conversation there.

'Oh that's alright,' said Annie quickly. 'Families huh? Well you know what they say... ' and giggled self-consciously.

'Yes we do,' said Theresa quickly cutting her off and following her sister. Sybil felt a little embarrassed for her workmate and for her sisters' rudeness.

The uncomfortable moment was broken when Annie saw Beth walking towards them, she turned back to Sybil and said, 'Oh... here's Beth... we'll see you later.'

Beth read her face, 'What's wrong Annie?' she asked. 'You look upset.'

'Oh they all seem to be in a bit of a mood tonight so I have said we will see Sybil later,' Annie replied. 'Made me feel really stupid.'

'That's alright Annie, don't be upset and you are certainly not stupid. Come on let's go back to the table and see if we can get you a dance without your feet being trampled on,' said Beth trying to lighten the mood a little. 'We'll put a sign up saying keep away if you have two left feet,' and Annie laughed.

They were soon back dancing and Annie recovered from the earlier upset and was determined that it would not spoil her evening. She couldn't understand what the problem had been, she had only said hello. Beth smiled as she watched her friend start dancing again, pleased that she had the ability to put any unpleasantness aside. Dear Annie, she thought, wouldn't hurt anyone, so she was not quite sure why someone would want to be nasty to her without any reason. She turned to see where the sisters were, they were standing to one side of the dance floor immersed in a deep conversation. Beth thought that Elizabeth didn't appear to be her usual confident self for a Saturday night, although still in conversation her eyes were continually being drawn to the entrance doors, as were Beth's.

In the public house Owen downed his pint. 'Will it ever end Georgie? He is such a bastard to us all... not just to me, to all of them and I am made to feel I am responsible for all of it. If I am ever lucky enough to have my own family, my God I will never treat them as he treats us.' He placed his glass on the bar, 'I suppose I should thank God for my days with my grandmother. Then fate dictated that it could not continue for whatever reason. I had to return to my maker and live a life in hell. He looks at me with such hate and venom, and my mother is so weak she accedes to him in everything. It is not her fault, it's his poison, it's in all of us I suppose... has to be,' he shrugged his shoulders and looked away.

'Owen, it's not in you. You have always spoken of your grandmother with love. Your father or your aunts never possessed the love your grandmother was capable of, for whatever reason, it is not of your doing.' He paused to take a drink of his beer, 'Let him destroy everything within his reach apart from you – you have the strength. You have your grandmother's love inside you but your sisters don't understand that... how could they? It is not their fault this hate exists in him but neither is it yours.' He looked at his friend with concern, 'I have known you for many years now, don't you think I would recognise if this so-called poison existed in you. I have also seen your father at his worst, you are not and never will be him. Do you understand what I am saying?'

'God forbid, I have no wish to be anything like him... ever,' said Owen in a plea of desperation.

'Trust me dear friend, you are not. You would be no friend of mine if you were. Do not let him invade your very being, you are your own man and a good one at that.' Georgie looked at his friend and could see his pain and wished he could ease the threat of Owen Snr. 'Now... let's go back to the dance and try and enjoy our weekend,' he said draining his glass. 'When we get back you will ask your lady to dance... yes? That is what we came here tonight for if I am not mistaken. Now drink up and let's go... come on.'

'Don't know if I am in the mood any longer Georgie,' said Owen sadly looking into his beer glass. 'He has the capacity to ruin anything that is good. Whatever it is he cannot bear to see anyone happy or trying to better themselves, he is so full of scorn and malice even to the younger ones and he will never change. I fear for them, they know very little happiness.'

'Any right minded person would do,' Georgie said quickly, 'but you cannot carry the guilt for everyone when you have nothing to be guilty about.'

Owen continued, 'If only my grandmother had not died, but then I am being selfish. You know I still have nightmares about the night I was sent back to live with them, vile flea-ridden pit that it was. Mind it's not much better now; no right minded man would want his family to have to live in those conditions.' He covered his eyes with his hands, 'then again he is not in his right mind is he?'

'No he's not but on the other hand, had your grandmother not died we probably would never have met,' Georgie responded trying to help his friend become a bit more positive. 'And I don't really want to think about that... not having you as my best mate.'

'What you have never had Georgie, you never miss.'

'Trust me I would have... now, let's try and make the best of it tonight or he will have won another one over you. Not going to let that happen are you? Come on, I will dance her friend off her feet if it helps, I promise,' he added laughing.

'She is probably dancing with someone else by now,' said Owen already resigned.

'Well, if she is we'll come straight back in here and get drunk as skunks then. I promise, I can't be fairer than that. And I will buy... what are mates for?' Georgie said standing to leave the table. 'Come on now, enough of long faces, we're the boys. Let's go and show them all, including your sisters.'

Owen drained his glass and looked at his friend, 'Thanks Georgie. You are a mate... that's a fair deal,' and smiled ruefully.

Elizabeth felt remorse that the argument had happened over their father. She knew Owen was right that he had the capacity to play one off against the other and once again he had succeeded. She knew that she had wrongly taken her anger out on her brother. She knew that their father would always load the gun, he was malicious and manipulative.

Their mother, to her cost, was terrified of his reactions when he was drunk. He would demand she fetch more beer when there was no money left to buy it and would turn on her and the younger ones if she didn't find it from somewhere. He always spent all his pension on drink, it was his right to do so he said, and their mother was left to feed the family and pay the rent due out of the money she was given by her four eldest children. As he always bullied her into submission he always took the lion's share of that as well, there was never enough. She had run out of things to pawn including her wedding ring, there was nothing left. That is why they all took their valuables, such as they had, out of the house away from his thieving fingers.

Earlier in the evening when the sisters had appeared downstairs ready to go to their weekly dance he had reared up and demanded they give him some money, if they had money to go out then they must have too much. Elizabeth, being the strong willed one, had said they had all paid over their board for the week and he was getting nothing more and they turned to leave.

He moved towards the door and blocked their way with his crutch. 'Look at the three of you,' he shouted, 'you all look like whores. No daughters of mine are going out looking like that.'

'Who are you calling whores you malicious old bastard,' retorted Elizabeth shouting with anger. 'Drunk again father are we... just for a change? If we are old enough to work to keep this house and you in drink, we are old enough to go out without your permission and dress as we like.'

He came back at her, 'What you don't know is that your brother tells me how much you are all earning. He says you should be giving your mother more money and not going out tarted up looking like you are all on the game. You bring shame on this family... all of you!' The crutch was still raised.

Her mother tried to position herself between the two parties ready for what was going to follow. The younger ones were cowering in the corner watching with eyes not only full of hunger but now with fear. They were all well used to his drunken tirades from an early age but it didn't stop it being a frightening experience each time he erupted.

Her mother spoke, 'Owen, leave the girls alone... don't hurt them... they deserve a night out. I will go and ask for some more credit... I will get it somehow... let them go.'

'Deserve... they deserve what? Get out of my way woman... they deserve nothing apart from what they are going to get. Get out of my way!' he ranted and thrust their mother aside with such force that she stumbled and fell into the hearth; the younger children cried out in panic.

He wavered on his false leg and turned his crutch but Elizabeth noticed that he was now holding it by the wrong end, not to use as a support but to use it as a weapon in his rage. Sybil and Theresa moved to help their mother to her feet and Elizabeth stepped back out of his reach and seized the poker from the side of the fire.

'Come on then old man... let's see who gets in first then. You on one leg and drunk ... or me... this is not the first time we have been here over the years. I doubt if it will be the last... so come on... if you are brave enough... but I don't think you are. As usual, a big man when it's women. Well let's see shall we?' She held the poker menacingly, her arm raised to strike him, steely eyes waiting for him to move.

Her outburst stopped him again momentarily as it had over the years, and after a moment he slowly turned the crutch around to its correct position. He looked into his eldest daughter's eyes, and even through his drunken haze he could again see her rage and determination. He paused, then moved to one side, dropped the crutch and sat down again in his chair and shouted at them, 'Get out of my house and don't come back or you will be sorry... all of you... whores the lot of you, a disgrace.'

Their mother ushered them to the door and told them, 'Go out now... out... take no notice of him. You know he doesn't mean it. I'll get him some more somehow then he will sleep.' Her daughters looked at her in disbelief.

'Mother, you should hear yourself. You know exactly what he is. Why do you say he doesn't mean it? Why do you kid yourself after all these years? He's never going to change, he is an evil, selfish old bastard,' shouted Elizabeth back at her. 'He's never been any different and he never will be.' She was furious.

'No, no... he doesn't mean it, he says it's his leg. If he was better he wouldn't be like this. It will be alright now, you go... go and enjoy yourselves... I'll get his jug and go down to the beer off... they will give me some for him I am sure,' she said rubbing the arm she had fallen on.

The three girls looked at their mother with a mixture of frustration and anger and Sybil shook her head. 'Here, get him some with this,' and she thrust a few pence into her mother's hand. They left her in the lane and walked on to the barracks subdued and sickened by yet another confrontation.

'I hate him,' said Sybil.

'Me too,' added Theresa, 'but what can we do, he's never going to change?'

'The only thing we can do is stand up to him. Never a man around when you want one is there?' said Elizabeth still fuming over what had happened.

'One day I will do for him... the old bastard!'

'He's not worth it Betts,' said Theresa, 'we all know that.'

'Come on,' said Sybil, 'let's try and calm down and have a good night in the real world where people are hopefully normal.'

'Hmm... is there such a thing as normal?' asked Theresa. 'Not around these parts.'

'There had better be... somewhere,' said Elizabeth still seething. They had continued on their way in silence towards the barracks, all of them disheartened.

Elizabeth was still thinking about the earlier incident with their father, it had set the tone for the evening and looked as if it was going to spoil the whole night for everyone. She was brought out of her black mood when she saw Owen and Georgie arrive back in the dance hall and she lifted her head to acknowledge him again.

Owen lit a cigarette and glanced around the dance hall and a pair of steely eyes connected with his sister's for just a second before moving his glance on quickly to look for the girl in blue. Elizabeth read his look and immediately felt guilty that instead of causing a confrontation she had not explained to him quietly what had happened earlier. Their father was master in his skills, the more pain he could inflict on his family the better for whatever reason. No one was better than him at creating hurt and humiliation, he had done it for years; a natural born liar and they all knew he would never ever change. Although his older children were now adults he would never accept that they could have a life or opinion of their own, they owed him everything as far as he was concerned and no one would ever tell him any different.

Georgie stood by his friend's side in silence, he could feel his tension. He accepted that there was going to be an atmosphere between Owen and his sisters after what had transpired earlier. Quietly looking around the hall he was surprised to see Beth standing with her friend, both of them talking to Sybil

Trying to be diplomatic and upbeat he said, 'Hey now that's a result. Owen look who she's talking to.'

'Who?' asked Owen sounding totally disinterested.

'You know who... over there... keep up,' nodding his head in the girls' direction. 'If that's not an 'in' I don't know what is... come on.'

'I don't think I am in the mood,' came the response.

'Well I am... suit yourself,' he replied moving away from Owen. 'You coming or what?'

He hesitated, then caught the determined look in his friend's eyes so nodded in resignation. They moved across the floor and he briefly acknowledged Sybil without saying a word.

'Hello again Sybs,' said Georgie, desperately trying to break the ice. 'You going to introduce us to your two friends then?'

Sybil looked at Owen with caution. He nodded, feeling a little relieved she said, 'Oh... yes of course. This is Annie and this is Beth, we all work together. Girls I would like you to meet my brother Owen and his friend Georgie.'

Beth looked surprised said, 'This is your brother Sybil?' very quickly working out that he was Elizabeth's brother too. So no conflict of interest there after all.

'Yes, hello. At last, a proper introduction, thank you Sybil,' said Owen. She acknowledged his thanks, returned his smile and walked away back to her sisters.

'Hello Sybil's brother,' said Beth and laughed. 'Fancy that... me working with your sister all this time.'

Owen looked into the blue eyes and instantly felt relaxed again. 'Yes. amazing. Would you like to dance?' asked Owen.

'Very much,' she replied.

Georgie looked at Annie and said, 'Well, would you like to dance as well?'

'Not if you are going to trample on my feet,' she replied looking straight back at him and wondering why her invitation to dance hadn't been as romantic as Beths.

'I'll try not to, but I can't promise,' said Georgie laughing. 'Come on girl let's give it a try.'

Elizabeth watched the introduction across the floor and smiled. She had acknowledged the connection between the two of them the week earlier and was pleased it had all finally come together for them. She watched Beth lift her hands and they started to dance. Her brother was staring at the girl he was dancing with, oblivious to everyone else. She felt a pang of jealousy as she watched their closeness, then guilt again when she thought of their fall out earlier in the evening. She knew he was right about their father, if anyone had the right to hate him it was Owen over and above anyone else. She decided she would apologise to him before the night was over and try to put things right between them.

They danced with ease and when the music ended he turned and said, 'That was over far too quickly another... please?'

Beth nodded, 'Yes I would like that.' Just at that moment she saw Arnold standing on the side of the dance floor watching her, she waved and he acknowledged her contact.

Owen followed the wave and recognised him as the escort from the previous week, feeling disappointed he turned to her and asked, 'Oh... I'm sorry would you rather dance with him?'

'Good heavens no. Why do you ask?' looking at him surprised.

'Oh... I thought he escorted you home last week,' he replied a little too quickly.

Beth looked over at her brother again and he indicated that there was no rush to leave, for her to take her time. He sat down at a table, watched the dancers and patiently waited for the evening to end.

'Yes, you are right he did and now it is my turn,' she replied looking back at Owen and laughing. 'He's my brother, so that evens it out.'

'Oh, I'm sorry,' he said smiling and sounding relieved. 'I didn't want to tread on anyone's toes. Now I have seen off the imagined opposition I would like to carry on dancing with you for the rest of the night, if that is alright?' looking back into the blue eyes.

'I would love that... it's fine,' came the reply, her eyes twinkling in the lights.

Arnold watched his sister's body language while she was dancing, she looked relaxed and happy, and kept looking into the eyes of her dancing partner; it came to his mind that they made a nice looking couple. A flood of emotion welled up as he realised that the time was probably not too far off that they would indeed go their separate ways. He had been her protector for years and to be fair to Beth, one day he would have to let her go with his blessing. She was a lovely young woman, he loved her dearly but she deserved every happiness out of her adult life with someone that would love and cherish her.

To their mutual disappointment the last dance was announced by the band leader. 'We hope you have all enjoyed it tonight. Moonlight & Roses is your music for the final dance this evening. We look forward to seeing you all next week,' he turned to the other musicians and the first chords blended together. They started to dance once more.

'Can I see you next week Beth... please?' said Owen whispering into her ear.

'Yes, would like that,' she replied feeling a slight thrill in the pit of her stomach.

Not wanting the music to end they danced oblivious to everyone else. Finally as the music stopped he took hold of her hand and kissed the back of it. 'That was wonderful. Now, can I be introduced to this brother of yours, just so that he knows I can be trusted with you?'

'That would be nice. I really think he would appreciate that,' and they walked to side of the dance floor to where Arnold was seated. He saw them approaching and stood to be introduced to Beth's partner.

'Hello Beth, have you had a good evening?' he asked out of courtesy giving her a kiss on the side of her cheek.

'Wonderful evening thank you,' she said. 'Arnold, I would like you to meet Owen. I shall probably be seeing him again next Saturday.'

She turned, 'Owen, can I introduce my brother Arnold.'

The two men took measure of each other's eyes and shook hands. 'I am very pleased to meet you Owen.'

'Likewise Arnold,' replied Owen. 'I hope you don't mind if I arrange to see your sister here again next week?' he asked.

Arnold laughed, 'I know better than to incur her wrath. Of course not, if she is happy to see you,' he looked at his sister and she nodded. 'That's sorted then,' and smiled at them both.

At the same time Annie returned to the table with Georgie, they too had spent the rest of the evening dancing together. Georgie had kept an eye on Owen at the end of each number to see if he and Beth stopped dancing and parted but it hadn't happened. He quite liked Annie and she was obviously happy to remain at his side.

'Hello Arnold,' Annie introduced them. 'Georgie, this is Beth's brother Arnold. He usually takes us home after the dance,' she explained. The two of them also shook hands warmly.

'Hello Arnold, pleased to meet you,' said Georgie. 'That's a bit of a handful I would have thought. Escorting these two home,' and started to laugh.

'Yes,' said Arnold responding, 'but I can't complain it looks good on my score sheet if people don't know I am Beth's brother. Two good looking girls on my arm... just how lucky can you be?'

Just then Elizabeth walked across the dance floor and joined the group. She had been watching the introductions and felt this was the opportunity to join Owen's group to try and make amends. She knew there were a couple of apologies to be made.

Smiling warmly, cigarette in hand, she approached the party. 'Good evening all... again,' her gaze sweeping round all of them. 'I don't believe I know this gentleman?' turning to Arnold. 'I am Owen's sister, Elizabeth,' and held her hand out to him, looking at her brother with one pencilled eyebrow raised in expectation.

'This is Arnold... Beth's brother,' Owen replied, returning her gaze solidly and still sounding decidedly cool.

The moment was broken by Arnold, 'Well hello there. I am very pleased to meet you,' he said shaking her hand.

After the introduction she turned to Annie, 'Annie dear... darling I am so sorry if I sounded a little short this evening. I am afraid I have had a terrible headache. I have not been able to sing for it, do forgive me.' Owen and Georgie glanced at each other then back to his sister to see how long this act was going to continue.

'Oh that's alright Elizabeth... no harm done,' replied Annie relieved that they were now back on speaking terms. 'I do hope it has gone now?'

'Yes dear, thank goodness,' Elizabeth nodded to her then turned her attention to Beth. 'Hello Beth. You are looking lovely as usual. No doubt you now know Owen and I are related? Such a small world isn't it? You both danced so beautifully together tonight... natural partners I thought.' Owen caught her eye and she noted that there was still a hint of warning in them.

'Thank you,' Beth smiled back at her. 'Yes strange, I agree it is a small world.' She had registered the tension. 'Annie are you ready?'

'Yes,' said Annie, 'I'm ready,' not really aware of the innuendos around her.

Beth turned to Owen, 'Thank you for a lovely evening.' Leaning in a little closer to him she said quietly, 'I will see you next week. I am looking forward to it already.' She smiled and then turned, 'Goodnight everyone.' Owen winked and smiled back at her and, taking Arnold's arm, she let him escort her out of the dance hall with Annie in close attendance.

He watched them go then turned back to his sister and, without any emotion, said, 'Alright Bets... now what was all that about?' at the same time lighting his cigarette.

'You know what it was about. I just wanted to say I was sorry to Annie before she left, but mainly to say sorry to you. I was out of order Owen, it wasn't your fault and I didn't intend to spoil your evening. Seriously, you know what he's like, he winds everybody up. It became really nasty and mother was hurt.'

'You didn't spoil my night, it couldn't have turned out better actually,' he replied, 'and you are not going to spoil it now, so apology accepted... end of... I don't want to talk about that old bastard any more. He is only good at threatening women and the kids, that's the top and bottom of it. I have finished with it, don't talk to me about him again... you hear?'

'Yes... I hear,' she replied, smiling and planted a kiss on his cheek. 'You know I don't mean it, I love you to bits.'

'Hmm,' he responded fixing his gaze on her. 'I said I don't want to discuss it again. Come on Georgie we're off.' They turned away from her and headed to the door.

Elizabeth smoked her cigarette slowly and watched her brother and his friend leave the dance hall. Again she felt saddened about how the evening had started, her brother hadn't deserved her anger. However, she was also pleased for him as he was obviously interested in Beth. She knew Beth had a nice nature and that she would be good for him. She was being honest when she had said they had made an attractive couple, she could recognise these things.

Walking down the road away from the barracks Georgie asked, 'So... after a very rocky start I reckon that finished up a pretty good night... yes?' with a wry smile.

'Yes the best I have to say. Strange how things turn out. And how did you get along?' said Owen turning to him, 'as if I don't already know.'

'She's great, good looking, sense of humour, what more could I ask for?' he replied.

'Good night all round then,' and they continued their way home.

Annie happily chatted all the way home mainly to Arnold as for half of the time Beth was lost in her own thoughts. What a lovely evening it had been. How nice he was and the flutter of a ripple ran through her again. It was a nice feeling which happened each time she thought about him.

They soon reached Annie's house. 'Can't wait for next weekend. See you Monday Beth, goodnight Arnold, thank you,' and into the house she disappeared waving to both of them before closing the door.

As they walked on, Arnold asked her, 'Do you like him?'

'Yes, I think so, he seems very nice and he can dance,' she laughed. 'So that lets you off the hook. Isn't that amazing that he is Sybil's brother,' she explained. 'There are three sisters... Theresa works with Elizabeth, they both come in the shop every day.'

'Well, if you see his sisters every day I am sure they will put you right. She's an attractive lady, that Elizabeth,' said Arnold. 'Don't see many like her around here.'

'No,' said Beth. 'She is. Whenever you see her whether it is in work clothes or at the dance hall she stands out. Sybil and Theresa are attractive too, but she seems to have something extra. She gets up and sings with the band sometimes,'

'Quite the star then?' said Arnold.

'Yes. Why are you interested?' said a bemused Beth.

'No, no, not me. Goodness gracious, too stylish for me, looks expensive. Out of my league totally,' he laughed with an air of panic. 'I know my level Beth. Adelaide will do nicely thank you and she reminds me of you,' he explained.

'Well thank you. I don't know whether to take that as a compliment or an insult,' she protested.

'Now then, you know what I mean. Lovely to look at, modest with a nice nature, that's more my style and I would say that description fits you pretty well.'

'Well alright, if you say so,' said Beth. 'Will let you off then.'

'I do,' said Arnold quickly in reply. 'End of conversation.' They turned the corner into the street they lived on. 'Well here we are, back to harsh reality. Don't get excited, we'll probably not get a welcoming committee and I bet all the bread and butter pudding you brought home has gone, so no supper either.'

Owen was also lost in his own thoughts as he and Georgie walked towards home. Georgie could sense his friend was now relaxed. He was pleased that after the disastrous start to the evening it had turned out so well. Strange how things happen, he thought, after a while he broke the silence, 'Owen why don't you stop at mine tonight instead of going back there? You don't know what sort of mood he will be in,' he said out of concern.

'No thanks mate. I have to go back to face him off. He knows what will have happened with the girls and if I stay out of the way he will think it's a victory. Don't worry nothing will happen now, he did the damage earlier. He will probably be sleeping it off at this time of night anyway, she will have made sure of that, so that the girls can get back in without any further trouble.'

'OK, if you are sure. If there is any bother you come back, just throw a couple of stones at my window that'll be enough and I will come and let you in. Good night,' he said before leaving Owen at the end of the street.

'You're a good mate Georgie, thank you... night to you too,' Owen called out.

'No problem, that's what mates are for isn't it? I'll see you tomorrow,' he replied without turning.

Owen continued on his way, rather than his thoughts being occupied with what might be waiting at the house, they were filled with Beth. Those blue eyes, that great smile, the way it felt right when they danced together. Roll on next Saturday, he thought, and continued his journey home with a spring in his step.

He opened the door to the sound of his father snoring loudly. He was sleeping downstairs on the battered chaise longue in the corner. When he had had too much ale and couldn't negotiate the stairs with Theresa's assistance, she would take off his false leg and pull a night shirt on him and leave him to sleep it off as usual on the same flea-ridden couch that they had been given when he had returned from hospital during the Great War.

Owen looked at his father without any emotion, he had no feelings for the man who had sired him apart from a cold loathing. He sat for some time just looking at him snore and dribble his way through his night's sleep, and Owen's memories took him back to his childhood. How could this man be the product of his beloved grandmother? Where had her mother's love gone so wrong to produce such a vile individual who was so hateful to his own family?

The love his grandmother had shown him, her first grandchild, had been beyond reproach; so where, a generation earlier had it all gone wrong as far as her own children were concerned? The family was Quaker in origin, so empathy was a pivotal discipline in their religion. Owen Snr had empathy for nothing or nobody. In his world he ruled, whatever the cost to his wife, children and anyone else with whom he became connected; they were all beneath him, their wellbeing immaterial.

Even Owen Snr's sisters, his aunts, were of a similar disposition, they too had also been spiteful by nature. He thought briefly of the times their spite had been taken out on him when a young boy, and again wondered why. He had not seen them since the day of his grandmother's funeral when he had stood alone, cold and in despair. Then on the same day they had forced him to leave the only home he had ever known like a common criminal and sent him to live in a slum without any compassion whatsoever. He had had no option but to try and survive with people he had never known even though they were his immediate family.

Owen was lost in these thoughts whilst staring into the face of the man who was his father, when suddenly Owen Snr's eyes flew open. He gasped, horrified when he saw the fixed stare of loathing from his eldest son and tried to get up and take control of the situation.

Owen bent forward slowly and pushed him back, 'Yes old man be afraid. I could have got rid of you in an instant by putting the pillow over your face. You would have had no idea, no chance of survival and, even better, nobody would have known or cared for that matter.'

He sneered back, 'Get away from me. I have seen off worse than you. Don't you ever think you can get one over on me... you never will.'

'One day old man, when you are not expecting it, you'll see. So you had better get ready to meet your maker.'

Theresa awoke and ran down the stairs when she heard the commotion. Her son seemed calm but Owen Snr was struggling to get off the chaise longue as Owen was standing over him. As always, trying to be the mediator, she got between father and son just as the girls walked in from their Saturday night out.

'My God is he still at it?' said Elizabeth. 'Don't you ever get tired of being a bastard?' she shouted at him.

'Don't you dare call me a bastard. It's him... he threatened me,' he shouted back and pointed at Owen.

'When?' she asked. 'When did he threaten you. He has not been here all night, you're delusional or still drunk, probably both. Had a nasty dream have we?' she laughed.

'Don't you laugh at me you bitch. It was just before you came in,' he snarled.'
I tell you both now, it's the last time either of you two will ever threaten me.
You can get out of this house... now!'

'Threats what threats. Anybody else hear these threats?' she asked without
anger looking at her sisters and mother.

'No,' said Sybil and Theresa in unison. Their mother dropped her eyes and
remained silent.

'You bitch, I'll show you both. Don't you try and get the better of me. Get
me my leg woman... now!' he shouted at his wife, still struggling to get off
the chaise longue.

Elizabeth walked over and picked up the false leg. 'This? You want this?'
waving it in the air. 'Then come and get it yourself old man, we are sick of
you and your demands,' she said walking up the stairs to bed carrying his
leg. 'Night all... night Owen.' Her sisters quickly followed her and closed the
stairs door.

'Go back to bed mother... go on it will be alright,' said Owen keeping his
eyes fixed on his father, his voice still low and even.

'No you don't. You will stay here,' he spat at his wife. 'She will stay here...
help me woman... go and get me my leg... now!' he shouted at her. Owen
detected a note of desperation in his tone.

'She'll do no such thing. Go to bed mother, don't worry I won't hurt him...
not tonight... sweet dreams you drivelling old drunk. Go back to your slovenly
drunken slumber. Just remember, you have ruined my life for years and this
is the day it ends.'

'Not while I have a breath left in my body,' he raged. 'You are the cause of
all of this. You... coming here thinking you are better than everyone else. You
will pay your dues to me and show respect.'

Owen turned away then looked back at his father, 'Respect? What do you
know about respect? You have to give it to receive it?' Then he whispered, 'Oh
and don't forget what I have said... one day... and you won't see it coming!'
He turned and accompanied his mother up the stairs. He noticed she looked
tired and not surprisingly was on edge. 'Stop worrying,' he said to her as they
climbed the stairs.

She nodded back to him quietly, 'It's his leg, he wouldn't drink like this if... '

'Mother... enough...I have heard it all before. Now go and sleep, are you in pain?' he asked gently.

'Not much... I will be alright,' she replied and he noticed a slight tremble on her lips.

'Don't worry Bets and I aren't going anywhere just yet, so you don't have to worry about the youngsters. Now, leave him to his own devices. Go and try to sleep.' For the first time he held his mother in his arms just for a brief moment to try and give her a little comfort. She nodded, sighed, and went into her bedroom and closed the door quietly so as not to disturb the younger ones.

As he settled to sleep he made a pledge that no family of his would ever look upon him as a tyrant, one in the family was enough. He turned over, closed his eyes and pictured Beth's face and silently thanked her for being there tonight and wished her a silent good night.

On waking the following morning he could hear his mother again trying to placate his father from the previous night's ructions. He had obviously had a bad night and was probably dwelling on his older children getting beyond his control and finding the strength to threaten him. That and coping with his usual hangover. As always their mother took the brunt of it. Steeling himself he came down from the attic he shared with the younger boys and found Elizabeth sitting on the stairs waiting for him.

'Here we go again,' she said to him nodding downstairs. 'I want to speak to you. Let's go straight out for some breakfast at least it might give the others some peace if we are out of the way... otherwise he'll start again.'

'Fine with me. I was going to Georgie's anyway.' He had his previous night's clothes in a bag to take with him. 'Come on let's get it over with... don't be drawn... just ignore him,' and took her arm as she stood and they descended the rest of the stairs, Owen first.

He opened the door into the main room in the house where they all lived. It housed the black cooking range and small sink in the corner with one tap. They were both met with a black stare of hatred. He was now sitting in his chair; he had already strapped his leg on as he had sent their mother to retrieve it before the older girls were awake. His crutch was propped at the side of his chair to hand if needed. Their mother looked her usual tense self. She was standing at the sink and turned as the stair door opened. She only briefly ever relaxed when he was sleeping the ale off in their bedroom well away from the rest of the family.

'It's alright mother... don't worry... we're not staying,' said Elizabeth. 'Give our breakfast to the kids,' and out they went completely ignoring their father and closing the door.

As they walked together Owen asked what she wanted to talk about.

'Nothing serious,' she answered. 'I just wanted to apologise again for last night and put it right between us.'

'There is no need to apologise again, you did that last night, so don't worry we're fine. We both know where the problems lies. I just didn't appreciate it kicking off like it did in the dancehall that's all as if I was to blame. You could have explained what had gone off.'

'I know you are right, it was me shooting my big mouth off. I was totally out of order Owen and I know it,' she said sounding contrite. 'I am pleased it didn't spoil your evening entirely. From what I know of Beth she's a nice lady, Owen, you could do worse and you look right together.' Feeling comfortable that any tension between them had now gone she slipped her arm in his as they continued walking.

'What do you mean?' he asked.

'It's just something that happens sometimes, you look at people and get a feeling that they look just right together. It's being easy in each other's company and that's how you two looked last night even when you danced together. Are you seeing her again?'

'Yes, next Saturday, hopefully,' and he smiled.

'From what I saw I think it is a given. That's great,' said Elizabeth. 'Now let's go and eat I'm starving. Nothing like a couple of good arguments to get your appetite going,' and she laughed again.

They had breakfast and both felt pleased that the argument between them from the previous night had been laid to rest. When they parted company Owen was to go on to Georgie's house and Elizabeth had decided to trawl the shop windows on the High Street to look at any new fashions on display.

'See you later,' she said to Owen.

'Yes,' he answered. 'No doubt we will be walking back into a lion's den.'

'Don't worry about that,' she said. 'As long as we all stick together he's no chance. Don't worry about it.'

'I won't... and Bets... thanks.'

'What for?' she asked.

'For being there. Like you have been since that first night I came into that hell hole. I still owe you.' He brought her hand up and kissed the back of it.

'You owe me nothing,' she replied squeezing his hand in return before turning away from him, 'I'll see you later.'

Beth woke, stretched and smiled to herself every time she thought of the dance the night before. Every time she thought of Owen the ripple appeared in her stomach again and again. Fancy him being Sybil's brother. She heard Arnold come down from the attic and climbed out of bed to get dressed to go downstairs.

He had lit the fire and put the kettle on to boil when she appeared. As usual they were left to their own devices first thing in the morning, Ellen and Evelyn kept out of the way.

'I have been thinking, just as a precaution Beth, give me your dress to keep with my things. It's just a thought, but after last night it might mysteriously get a mark on it or a tear in it if it is left in your room. They wouldn't dare go through my things in the attic.'

'Do you think... surely not,' she replied.

'Just let's start as we mean to go on. If I am going to be away at weekends in Burnley, it's just a precaution that's all. You know what they are capable of and if you are on your own.'

'Well, I am going to have to stand on my own two feet then aren't I. It's been a long time coming Arnold, you can't be there fighting my battles forever,' she said taking the kettle off the boil.

'No I know that. Much as it grieves me, just don't give them any opportunity that's all.'

'I won't. Let's have breakfast then I will put it on the attic stairs for you,' she conceded.

'No, go and do it now while we are thinking about it, it's sorted then,' he persisted.

'Alright, you make the tea,' she turned and went back up the stairs.

She returned to the kitchen to find her tea waiting. 'You enjoyed it last night I reckon... yes?' he smiled at her.

'Yes... did it show?' she laughed.

'Just a bit,' he smiled. 'That's how I feel about Adelaide.'

'Well a little different. You and Adelaide nearly spent the whole day together

,we only had a few dances,' she said as she made their breakfast.

'Yes, but I can tell it made you happy. You had danced with one or two others as well in the night but he was different... or am I wrong?' he asked.

'No you're not wrong,' she smiled, 'and I think he is very nice and I am pleased that I will be seeing him this Saturday.' She turned and put the toast on the table. 'Don't think you have to accompany me to and from the barracks, you don't. You have an early start on Sunday morning for the train, it's important you look your best,' she said.

'Well, I might walk you there and make sure that he will escort you home,' he said biting into his sandwich.

'No, Arnold. You can walk me there if you must. I will decide if he will escort me home during the night. You can't assume that, he might not want to. You have just said we have to start as we mean to go on, so there you are. I have just made a decision,' she said looking back at him.

'Oh, well his problem if he doesn't. Look at what he will be missing, but then I suppose I'm biased,' and he laughed at her. 'Come on let's finish and go out for our walk. I have a feeling there are not going to be too many more times to enjoy each other's company on a Sunday as we usually do,' he added sounding a little sad.

'Don't be sad, it will be on to bigger and better things hopefully. Anyway you are not going anywhere yet, her parents might not like you,' she laughed at him. 'I am only kidding,' she added quickly when she saw the disappointment on his face. 'Let me clear these things away then we're off.'

'Right, just time for me to go and put your dress in a safe place,' and he disappeared back up the stairs.

They took their usual route past the church then up to the entrance of the park. Beth liked to walk around the lake then sit for some time just watching the world go by. Every Sunday found couples walking, children feeding the ducks and playing, there was always lots of laughter around, families enjoying their free time spending it together. They usually sat in the same area near the rhododendron bushes.

After sitting quietly for some time Beth turned to her brother, 'Do you think our childhood would have been different if the Great War hadn't happened? Would our father have brought us here?'

Arnold smiled, 'I am certain he would have from what I can remember. I always like to think of him laughing, that is how I see him in my mind's eye. Sadly I don't remember what he looked like, it's just a mental image of somebody laughing,' he paused, 'but it's a nice image. Does that sound strange?'

'No,' said Beth. 'I like to hear your memories of him. I can vaguely remember somebody being there, but like you not what he looked like.'

'No you wouldn't, you were too young to remember. But you were the apple of his eye and you know, I can never remember him shouting at us,' he said wistfully.

'I don't think I will ever forget that horrible day Arnold, as young as I was. My memory of when he died is of an awful dark day filled with sadness and poor Arthur continually crying. Then it just all descended into a black void and silence. I look at these children and wonder if we were ever like them. They are all so happy, not a care in the world, and that is how it should be in childhood.'

'Yes it is, and we were like them before he died Beth, it was a short-lived happiness but it was there, that you can be assured of. He was a good father, he loved us I am sure,' said Arnold taking hold of her hand. 'We're getting very serious all of a sudden…what's wrong?'

'Nothing really… I just feel the need to talk about it and you are the only one I can do that with. I think about baby Arthur sometimes and wonder if father had been there would he have died?' she continued.

'I can't really answer that one. One thing for sure Evelyn wouldn't have been here and a certain other somebody would have had to make more effort I reckon. I don't think he would have put up with her selfishness and we would have had a proper childhood.' He looked at her and continued, 'I like to think he would be very proud of us for what we have achieved against all the odds. The workhouse only loomed once and I think we averted that, not her in court that day…do you remember that?' he asked. 'We were both young and very frightened.'

'Yes, I remember it and the nice policeman, he gave us a penny didn't he?' she smiled wistfully. 'I remember him being very tall.'

'Yes, and he gave us hope,' Arnold agreed, 'and he told us to come and find him again if things didn't get better. He was shrewd enough to tell us in a loud enough voice so that she could hear.'

'Yes… and we got shoes for the first time.'

'Yes, we did, but we had to go and get our own, she didn't take us,' he answered crossly.

'Arnold... if it hadn't been for you, what would have happened to us?'

'Don't go there... it didn't happen did it... and it was a long time ago.'

'No, I know it didn't, but I think we came very close when you think about it now,' she said.

'Yes, there but for the grace of God and all that. We did escape the workhouse but only because she was hauled up in front of the magistrates, if that hadn't happened then we may have become inmates,' he added seriously.

They both sat quietly for a moment thinking about what might have been. Then Arnold said, 'Enough, that is all in the past. It's gone and those days will never return again. I think we are both ready to move on with our lives now. We both have a little money put by, we don't owe anybody anything, we make our own decisions,not such a bad position to be in... is it?'

'No it's not,' she replied responding to his lighter mood. 'And I don't think we will have to speak of it again either after this conversation. It's like putting it all to rest so that we can and will move on.'

'Good,' he replied. 'I think that deserves a cup of tea and a cake to celebrate. Whatever our futures hold Beth, whoever it is with, it cannot ever be as bad as those early days so don't dwell on them... they have gone...forever.' Standing he said, 'just think this time next week I shall be on my way to Burnley and you will be recovering from being danced off your feet.' He extended his arm for her to stand and kissed her gently on her forehead. 'Come on, let's go.'

Georgie's face was one of relief when Owen appeared. 'What's wrong?' said Owen.

'Nothing, I am just glad to see you that's all. How was it when you got back?'

'Oh, the usual tirade, that I am to blame for all of it. To cut a long story short the girls arrived just after me so he had a two pronged attack, one from me and one from Bets. She took off to bed with his leg so that caused another ruction. He will live to fight another day no doubt... don't want to talk about him, let's change the subject.'

'Alright, I reckon we are on for next Saturday night what about you?' said Georgie changing the subject and laughing.

'Well I know I am,' said Owen smiling.

'Well if you are, so am I... I think.'

'That's alright then, because I know I definitely have a date,' confirmed Owen.

'Great,' said Georgie, 'what do you want to do today?'

'Nothing much. Just want to stay out of the way and hopefully he might be sleeping it off when I get back later tonight. I don't think we will have a repeat of last night for a while, something to look forward to I suppose,' he said ruefully.

'That's fine, my mother says you can stay for your Sunday dinner. I told them about the upset last night,' said Georgie, 'hope you don't mind.'

'Not if it keeps me in your mother's good books and fed. You can tell them the second instalment later about Bet disappearing with his leg,' he laughed. 'Let's go for a quiet drink and bring her a stout back. I know the way to a woman's heart,' he said slapping Georgie on his back. 'Watch and learn Georgie boy, watch and learn.'

Monday morning arrived and Beth and Arnold set off for work together as usual. It was if there were two separate factions in their house who had no family connection whatsoever. Whenever they left the house in the morning their mother and step sister were never in evidence, when they returned in the evening they were barely acknowledged. The only interest shown was if Beth came back with something from the bakery, such was their greed they would not ask, they would just take whatever was in the bag. Beth had learnt to keep any special items for Arnold and herself in a separate parcel, what they didn't know they couldn't gripe about.

Monday mornings at Owen's house fell into three shifts and Theresa always tried to make sure Owen Snr was still in bed upstairs as each wave left the house. Always the first to leave was Owen, followed by the girls then the older children left for school. That just left the youngest ones for breakfast after they had all departed; they too were all resigned to eating whatever was available, if anything, in silence. The first sign of their father being awake would be when they heard the bang on the bedroom floor to summon his wife to help him. They would take their lead from their mother when he appeared and remain quiet and cautious, their wide eyes never leaving her.

Beth laughed when she saw Annie approaching the shop, she could see by her demeanour that she was happy chatting to the factory girls she was walking with, telling them about her weekend. She had warned Mr Newbould that he should expect to have all the events of her Saturday evening explained in great detail, he had rolled his eyes and replied, 'Yes alright, but I am going to tell her that I will listen to it just once this week, not every day,' and laughed. 'Or am I being an optimist?'

Beth just smiled back at him as Annie arrived at the door. 'Hello Beth, good morning Mr Newbould. Oh, did we have a lovely time on Saturday night?' taking off her coat and not breaking her step.

'Yes, yes, so I understand Annie, I am very pleased to hear it. You can tell me later when I have time to listen. We all have things to do at the moment as it's the first day of the week,' he answered her, not unkindly. He winked at Beth and walked towards the bakery door.

'I have not stopped thinking about Saturday night,' she said helping Beth prepare for the customers. 'I hope Georgie will be there again I do like him, and he can dance... he never stepped on my feet once.'

'He'll be there Annie, don't you worry,' replied Beth. 'I am pleased to hear you like him.'

Just then Sybil arrived with her sisters. Elizabeth saw Beth, smiled and waved. 'Good morning both of you. Owen has told me to tell you he is looking forward to seeing you next Saturday Beth. See you both later.'

'Thanks,' called Beth. 'There you are Annie, I told you he would be there so you don't have to worry. Now let's get on.'

Georgie was waiting for Owen to walk the rest of the way to the yard together. 'Morning,' he said as Owen approached. 'Monday again, not be long before the weekend's here. At least we have something special to look forward to,' and laughed.

'You can say that again,' he replied.

'Morning. Monday again, not be long,' to which he received a friendly cuff round the ear and laughed even louder.

'You're in a good mood,' smiled Owen.

'Nothing wrong with that, makes a change,' said Georgie. 'Nothing better than a good weekend, even though it did have a rocky start,' and continued walking.

Arnold was also in good humour and deep in thought as he walked on to the newspaper. Uppermost on his mind was that it was only six more days and then he would see her again. Her letters had been friendly and she had written of how much she was looking forward to seeing him and she would be waiting at the station to meet him. He just had to remind Beth to write her short note of thanks regarding her help with the dress, and over the next couple of days he would look for a small gift. He had decided he would buy the flowers for her mother when he arrived in Burnley, then wondered should he take something for her father then decided against it, he didn't want to appear to be too forward. The flowers for her mother would be enough, probably when he became acquainted with her father he could possibly take him for a drink that was if he liked a pint... he might not.

Thomas saw him approaching deep in thought and called to him, 'Come on Arnold, might never happen whatever it is.'

He looked up, 'Sorry Tom I was miles away.'

'Yes, I could see... somewhere around Burnley I reckon... right?' and laughed.

'Could say that and it will be a prettier face than yours that I will be looking at when I get there, thank goodness,' he replied laughing back at his friend. 'Let's get to it,' and into the newspaper office they went.

Saturday lunchtime finally arrived and they all left their respective places of work full of anticipation and hoping for a good weekend.

Annie full of excitement had waved goodbye to Mr Newbould, he had watched them all walk down the street with an air of confidence. They were a good set of girls, they worked hard and he wished them all the best from life. He smiled to himself as he thought about the varied conversations that had taken place during the week regarding hairstyles and dresses just for this night. Whatever decision had to be made, Annie always asked him for his opinion much to his and his wife's amusement. She had brought Beth the white snood she had asked her to get, and announced that she had decided to wear her hair down for a change. Mr Newbould had told them whatever they wore and however they styled their hair they would be the best looking girls there, and he wished he could come too, but Mrs Newbould wouldn't let him. The girls had taken this in good humour and told him with mock sympathy that they were sorry to hear that and they would miss him before all descending into shrieks of laughter.

As Owen and Georgie left Appleyard's yard Georgie had asked, 'What time tonight then do you reckon?'

'Early... I want to be waiting outside when they arrive. There is no mistaking who they are with then, if that's alright with you?'

'That's fine with me. Do you want to go for a drink beforehand?'

'No let's go for a couple now instead. Don't want to be waiting for them smelling of beer, it would remind me too much of you know who... first impressions and all that.'

'This all sounds as if it could get serious. Never known you to plan ahead,' Georgie said a note of caution in his tone.

'You never know your luck Georgie boy, then again they could blow us out after the first dance.'

'Well, if that happens it will be a short night. I will take you to the pub and let you cry on my shoulder,' he replied laughing.

Arnold had changed his mind quite a few times during the week about what he wanted to buy for Adelaide as a keepsake. Each time he had seen something he thought would be appropriate he had asked Beth for her opinion until they finally agreed on the chocolates and a presentation box of cotton handkerchiefs that were hand embroidered with forget-me-nots. Beth had written her note of thanks, and Arnold knew that Adelaide would enjoy the contact from his sister. He picked up the handkerchiefs from the haberdashery shop and headed for home. When he arrived Beth was already there, she had brought fresh bread for them and left the day old items for Ellen and Evelyn.

'Make the sandwiches and let's go out for an hour, it's a nice day,' said Arnold. 'I feel this weekend could see the beginning of a change in our lives so we might as well make the most of it.' She nodded and wrapped the sandwiches in muslin and out they went leaving their mother and sibling to rifle through the paper bags that remained.

They walked to the park, using their usual route. Beth's arm linked through her brother's, bidding good day as they walked to all the people they were used to seeing. Without any words being spoken, Beth understood that her older brother was on the threshold of making a decision for the first time in their lifetime where her wellbeing was not uppermost in his mind.

'You remember our conversation about the friendly policeman that gave us the pennies and told us not to lose hope?'

'Yes.'

She looked at her brother as they walked and her eyes misted over just as he turned to return her gaze.

'What's wrong... Beth what is it... tell me?'

'Oh, I am just being silly, take no notice. If all our wishes come to fruition this will be the beginning of our lives that will lead to us being apart... but for the best of reasons,' she explained quickly. 'What will I do without you?'

'Don't you worry. I will not be going anywhere until I am assured you are to be well cared for, how could I?'

'That is hardly fair on either you or Adelaide, you have always been there for me. I could never repay the debt I owe to you Arnold. What would have happened to me without you being here?'

'Beth, we have already discussed all this and I say to you again there are no debts to be repaid... you are my sister... I will love you always and will be there for you always no matter what happens in my life or yours, so take comfort in that. I will escort you and Annie to the dance tonight as arranged, then I will go and meet Thomas for a quick drink and you will enjoy yourself. I have no doubt of that. You will not think of me once and that is how it should be,' he said reassuringly.

'Yes, I'm sorry. I am being very selfish and silly,' she replied wiping her eyes.

'No you are not, you do not have a selfish bone in your body. No more nonsense. I shall just make sure you will be alright this evening before I leave you, that is all.'

'Alright thank you. Can I come to the station with you tomorrow morning just to wish you luck?' she blew her nose and looked up at him.

He took hold of her hands and kissed them, 'Yes of course you can, but only if tonight goes well for you. Now let's eat.'

Beth dressed for the dance, the blue dress had re-emerged from Arnold's room intact and she was pleased with the overall look when she put her hair in the white snood; the understated pearl earrings once again completed the look perfectly. Arnold tapped on her door to see if she was ready and once again paid her the first compliment of the evening when she appeared.

'Beth, you look even lovelier tonight for some reason, if that is possible,' he said smiling at her. 'I wonder why that is?'

She smiled at him, 'Well thank you but I know you're biased. If I look as happy as you do, that will be fine. Does it seem a long time since you saw

Adelaide?'

'Yes it does. I know it is only a couple of weeks but it seems an age. Never mind tomorrow is nearly here, I hope she recognises me,' he added in mock panic.

'I am sure she will... how could she not?' laughed Beth as they reached the bottom of the stairs.

Ellen and Evelyn sat in surly silence and vetted what Beth was wearing again this time without comment. They did not want to provoke another outburst from Arnold like the week before, they knew nothing of his plans for the following day and he had no intention of telling them anything with regard to Adelaide until he felt it was absolutely necessary.

They walked towards Annie's house so that he could escort them both again. Annie made sure she was ready before they were due to arrive. As she stepped through the door Arnold gave a wolf whistle which made her laugh in embarrassment and she blushed again. She had got used to his compliments and he didn't let her down.

'Annie I would not have recognised you... you are looking very glamorous with your hair down. My goodness, what am I doing escorting you two to a dance then leaving you to dance with someone else?' he asked looking at her in mock bewilderment.

'Arnold, you say the loveliest things. I wish everyone was like you,' she said looking a little star struck. 'Thank you, kind sir,' and did a slight curtsey in return.

'Hey steady on here Annie, I am supposed to be complimenting you not the other way round. Come on now, let's get you to your dates,' and he offered his arm for her to link as Beth's did.

As they turned the corner towards the barracks they were both delighted to see Owen and Georgie waiting for them outside so that they would be escorted in. Excitedly they commented to each other.

'Now girls, stay cool,' said Arnold. 'Can't have them thinking you are both easily smitten just yet. Think what Bette Davis would do.'

Listening to his prompts without comment they both smiled and confidently approached their dates.

'Lovely ladies, welcome,' said Owen looking at Beth tenderly. At the same time Annie beamed at Georgie. Then extending his hand, 'Arnold, it is good to see you again,' he said warmly and they shook hands.

'Likewise,' he replied. 'Well here you are gentleman, the two best looking ladies in town, but then I am biased,' and they all laughed. 'I will leave them safely in your charge now. Have a good evening all of you.'

'I will see you in the morning to go to the station. Don't leave without me,' Beth said to him sounding a little concerned.

'Of course I won't don't worry,' and he kissed Beth gently on her cheek. 'Now go and enjoy your evening,' he whispered.

As they walked towards the entrance Owen looked back for a second to see Arnold still watching them. 'Look after her,' he mouthed to him. Owen nodded back to him and escorted her through the door. Arnold walked on to meet his friends feeling slightly forlorn but at the same time pleased for his sister. He felt his instinct where Owen was concerned was correct and that he could now relax.

The night was everything Beth could have wished for; they danced and danced to the exclusion of everyone else.

'Have I told you how lovely you look tonight?' said Owen

'Yes,' said Beth smiling, 'just a few times. Thank you.'

'Well it has taken a few weeks to get here but I am glad we finally made it. Just to make my night can I take you home?' he asked. 'I don't think Arnold would think very much of me if I didn't. Can't have you walking home alone.'

'Yes, if we don't fall out between now and then. It's early yet,' she laughed.

'No chance,' he whispered into her ear and kissing it gently said, 'You are stuck with me.' Beth felt the ripple in her stomach once more.

The music ended and they went to join Annie and Georgie who had just sat down at their table. There was a sense of contentment in the air between the four of them.

'Did you see the girls arrive?' said Annie.

'No,' said Beth, 'I didn't.'

'Neither did I,' said Owen pulling out a chair for her to sit down.

Georgie swapped glances with his friend and smiled. 'Missed their entrance huh, you'll be in bother,' he laughed.

'Much more important things to take care of at the moment,' said Owen smiling at Beth and taking hold of her hand. He then turned round to see where his sisters were holding court.

Elizabeth was looking in their direction, saw him turn and waved. He nodded back and indicated to Beth where they were standing, she and Annie waved over to the girls on the dance floor.

'Oh doesn't she look glamorous,' said Annie in awe.

'Yes... they all look lovely as usual,' answered Beth without rancour.

'Not as good as you Annie,' said Georgie. 'I think you look smashing with your hair down.'

Annie smiled, blushed slightly and said quietly, 'Thank you for saying that to me Georgie, it was a nice thing to say.'

'Well it's true. Come on the music has started again let's dance and oh... just one more thing... I don't want you getting up on the stage to sing because you might go off with another admirer.' They both laughed and took to the floor and started to dance.

A little later in the evening Elizabeth joined the singers on the stage for a Boswell Sisters number and Beth was touched to see that for the first time she didn't sing exclusively to Owen. She widened her gaze to the admiring male contingent smiling widely as she sang. She really is an attractive lady thought Beth, and she obviously thinks as much about her brother as I do mine for which I can't fault her. I hope we can become good friends.

She came to find them all after the song had finished. Sybil and Theresa had already wandered over for a chat.

'That was great as usual Elizabeth,' said Annie her usual giddy self.

'Thank you Annie. I like the hair tonight... suits you,' she replied much to Annie's delight. 'Hello Georgie... you behaving yourself?' He laughed out loud.

'Hello you two, are you two alright?' she asked turning to Beth and Owen with her cigarette ready for lighting. Her brother obliged and they exchanged a warm glance.

'Everything is just fine thank you Elizabeth. I enjoyed the song, we all did, well done,' said Beth smiling at her.

'Thank you. Like to please darling. You are positively glowing tonight Beth... do you know that?'

'It has got to be because of the company she is in,' said Owen with a smile in Beth's direction and pulling her close.

'I'm sure,' replied Elizabeth. 'See you all later, come on girls let's go and see what's happening around here,' and turning on her heel she glided her way through an admiring audience with Sybil and Theresa in her wake.

'That sister of yours is something else,' said Georgie laughing.

'Yes... she has her moments,' said Owen with a wry smile. 'But I reckon her heart's in the right place.'

The evening came to end when the band leader announced the last dance. 'Ladies and Gentlemen we hope you have enjoyed your evening. The last dance tonight is a slow foxtrot. We have a special request for Moonlight and Roses... a very goodnight to all of you... we hope to see you again next week.'

Beth and Owen took to the floor, she raised her hands to his and once again their eyes connected as the music and lyrics started... *Moonlight and Roses, bring wonderful memories of you. My heart reposes in beautiful thoughts of you.*

'This is my request for you,' said Owen. 'We danced to it last week when we met and I feel it is our song. Is that alright?'

'It's more than alright... it's wonderful,' said Beth. 'Thank you,' and he kissed her gently on her cheek.

They danced as if in solitude and when the music stopped Owen whispered, 'Please don't let go of my hand. I don't want this to end.' He gently pulled her closer to him placed his hand on the back of her head and kissed her hair, the ripple appeared again.

'Don't worry I won't,' said Beth closing her eyes and enjoying the sensations. They stood in each other's arms for a moment longer before walking back to the table closely together hand in hand.

When Beth and Annie went to retrieve their coats from the cloakroom Georgie looked at Owen and smiling at him said, 'Well... you look as if you have enjoyed your evening.'

'Oh... and are you going to tell me you haven't then?' said Owen in response sounding a little surprised.

'No... it has been a great night. I really like her. I was just checking that we were both in the same frame of mind that's all. Are you taking her home?'

'What do you think. So you can't let Annie walk home alone can you?' Owen looked at him raising his eyebrows.

'Now would I?' said Georgie sounding outraged. 'A gentleman like me?' and laughed again.

The girls returned from the cloakroom and Georgie turned and said, 'Right ladies... let us get you both home before I turn into a pumpkin.' Beth put her arm through Owen's and turned to leave the dancehall. Annie took the cue from her friend and did the same with Georgie.

As usual Annie was full of chatter so as they left the barracks none of them noticed the figure standing in the shadows on the corner of the next street. Arnold had been waiting just to check that the girls were being escorted home. Satisfied, he smiled to himself and turned on his heel for a brisk walk home. Beth or Owen did not need to know that he had been there, it was for his own peace of mind rather than anyone else's. He would be back in the house before Beth so everything would be fine. As he walked he thought how happy his sister had looked as she had come out of the barracks arm in arm with Owen. He crossed his fingers that his trip tomorrow would produce the same result, he couldn't wait to see Adelaide again and hoped that she was feeling the same.

Beth and Owen parted from their friends at the end of Annie's street and continued their way towards Beth's house.

'Tell me, is there just you and Arnold at home?' he asked as they slowly walked along.

'No... we have a half-sister,' replied Beth, 'but if I am honest we don't have anything in common with either her or our mother. It was not a particularly happy childhood for either of us as our father died at sea in the Great War. Arnold has always been my protector since then, we might as well have been orphans for all the help our mother was,' she said sadly. 'So now you will probably understand why I am so close with my brother. I would hate you to think he is over-protective or interfering.'

'Of course not, good heavens I totally understand. I happen to think all the children from our generation had a really rough time of it through no fault of their own. Arnold has done a wonderful job... credit due to him, it can't have been easy.'

'No it wasn't... far from it,' Beth said quietly. Then after a moment, 'Sybil has said that there are quite a few of you at home.'

'Hmm... yes,' said Owen, 'there are,' sounding a little cynical. 'I am the oldest... the youngest is eighteen months old, seven of us. They lost two others.'

'Good heavens, it must be nice to have a large family,' said Beth. 'Are you close?'

'No,' he replied. 'I am probably closest to Elizabeth. I didn't live with them until I was fourteen so they never knew me. It's a long story and it will keep for another day, I promise.' He smiled and squeezed her hand. 'Let's change the subject.'

Beth sensed that whatever the story was there was sadness somewhere in him similar to the one she carried for her father. 'Of course... don't worry I am sorry for prying,' she said quickly.

'No you are not prying. I started it asking about home, it's not your fault don't worry.'

'You seem to be close with Georgie,' she said. 'He does make me laugh. He and Annie make a good couple. So long as he doesn't tread on her feet when they are dancing he will be in the good books,' she said laughing.

'Yes, Georgie is my best mate. Don't know what I would have done without him and his parents. I have a lot to thank them for. They are genuinely nice people and nice people do exist in this world, which is nice to know. There I go again getting serious, I'm sorry.' Then, changing the subject again, 'What does Arnold do for a living?'

'He works at the newspaper on the High Street. He has done really well he started there before he left school. He used to go and clear the rubbish away then they decided to take him on and he has been there ever since. He is off to Burnley tomorrow morning... I am very excited for him,' she said showing her delight and continuing. 'He met a young lady on the works trip to Blackpool, she lives in Burnley and he is going to see her again tomorrow. He is going on the train in the morning, it leaves at a quarter to nine. I have told him I shall go and wave him off and wish him luck.'

'That's a nice thing to do,' said Owen.

'It's become a habit. I usually wave him off on the works trips. He has been to Blackpool twice now and has promised he will take me to meet Adelaide there. That is the lady he has met.'

'Lucky Arnold, Blackpool twice. Well, I hope he has as great a time as we have had tonight.'

'I am sure he will. He is going to meet her parents as well,' said Beth laughing. 'He is a bit worried about that part of it.'

'Oh dear, yes well, it has to be done I suppose,' Owen replied. 'I shall be in no rush to introduce you to mine so don't worry on that score.'

Beth laughed, 'Well that makes two of us. Arnold is the only family I have really and you have already met him.'

'That's alright then, I am relieved. You already know my sisters so let's make a decision, one day we will tell each other our family histories, but not just yet I don't want you getting the wrong impression.'

'Sorry, first impressions and all that... already formed, not a lot you can do about it now,' she replied and smiled wryly.

They continued walking in silence, just pleased to be together, with Beth's arm linked through his. Sounding disappointed she suddenly said, 'Well this is my house. It's been a lovely evening and thank you for walking me home Owen.'

'Hey my pleasure. I hope we can do it all again next Saturday... can we?' he asked looking into the blue eyes and holding both of her hands together.

'Yes, please,' said Beth returning his gaze.

He took her into his arms and lowering his head gently kissed her slowly. She responded and once again felt the thrill of the ripple in the pit of her stomach.

'Goodnight,' she said, 'I will see you soon.'

'You bet,' he replied and holding her face in his hands kissed her on the end of her nose. 'Night... sweet dreams.' She stood in the doorway and watched him walk back down the street and waved as he was about to turn the corner. She then closed the door and stood leaning against it for some time not wanting to lose the moment.

Arnold heard the door close, relaxed and promptly fell asleep thinking about Adelaide and what tomorrow would bring.

He was up bright and early as usual. Then Beth appeared to make some breakfast and a sandwich to take. 'Are you nervous?' she asked him.

He sat cleaning his shoes. 'Yes,' he replied not looking at her.

'Don't be,' she said walking over to him and resting her hand on his shoulder. 'Everything will be fine you'll see... stop worrying.'

'What if she has changed her mind and sends her friend to tell me it was all a mistake. She might not really like me after all,' he said putting the shoe down.

'Don't be silly and stop being negative. I don't think she would have written to you to ask you to come all that way if that had been the case. She sounds too nice a lady to do anything like that. Come on, finish cleaning your shoes and we will walk to the station.'

'Are you sure you want to come to the station?' he asked putting his shoes on.

'Yes,' she replied. 'If I don't, you might talk yourself out of it,' and laughed. 'Let's go and don't forget your presents.'

As they were walking down the street Arnold turned to her and said, 'Beth, I am so sorry I didn't ask if you enjoyed yourself last night. I am so wrapped up in my own thoughts this morning. Very selfish of me. Was everything as you wished it would be?'

'Yes, I had a wonderful time. I was that good I expect to be doing the same all over again next Saturday,' she answered, smiling at him and tightening her grip on his arm as they walked on.

'Did he bring you home?' he asked not looking at her.

'Yes he did,' she replied.

'Good, I have nothing to worry about there then?'

'No you can strike me off your list of worries,' she said laughing again. 'That just leaves Adelaide... and her parents.'

Watching the concerned look come back on his face she quickly added, 'For heaven's sake Arnold, I am only joking. If you were not my brother I would be proud to walk out with you. Apart from that I think from what you have said Adelaide sounds the sort of lady that knows what she is looking for. So let us have no more of this doubt... enjoy your day... all of it even the train ride,' she chided.

He smiled and said, 'Alright, there you go, all doubts dispelled. Yes, I will, I promise.'

He had bought his rail ticket earlier in the week so when they arrived at the station he said, 'Let's go and have a cup of tea, we have enough time before the train arrives.'

They sat in the tea room and waited for their tea to arrive.

'Here you are ready to go on a train... all that way... how exciting,' said Beth looking pleased. 'You must tell me all about the journey on the train when you get back, as well as Adelaide and her family of course... everything.'

'I will don't worry. What are you going to do today?' he asked.

'Oh, I think I shall just have a long walk to all the usual places. It's a lovely day again, it would be a shame to waste it. I am in no rush to go back to the house.'

'That sounds good, you will enjoy that, but don't get too lost in your thoughts and become upset. I know what you are like when you start thinking about things,' he said holding her hand.

'Don't worry, I won't, I am still enjoying thinking about last night too much to become upset,' and the ripple tickled her stomach again and she smiled at him.

They walked to the platform where the train would arrive and sat on a bench for the remaining ten minutes. Beth was quite content to sit and watch all the departures and arrivals of other passengers, Sheffield Midland Station was busy. Arnold was lost in his own thoughts too, thinking about Adelaide.

'What a mixture of emotions railway stations are Arnold,' she said looking around. 'People laughing and crying when they arrive and others crying when they are leaving. I could just sit here all day and watch all the comings and goings.

'Well, it would probably save your legs, but you would be in tears every five minutes sympathising with them knowing you,' he replied laughing.

'Yes, but there are tears of happiness as well, that is very different,' she said looking across the platform and smiling at a little boy's joy when his father alighted his train, quite obviously returning home. Once again her father came into her mind fleetingly.

'Yes it is, and let's hope that from now on we only have tears of happiness. I think we have had enough of the other kind to last a lifetime, don't you?' he asked picking up her hand.

'Yes, you are right, no more unhappy thoughts or tears... I promise,' she replied looking at him. 'Oh, this is your train,' and she stood and pulled him up from the bench. 'Now... no tears mind,' and laughed.

They walked to an open door. Arnold then turned round and kissed her gently on the cheek and said, 'Thank you for coming with me. I will just find a seat then we can chat until it is time to leave.'

He found an empty compartment and put his parcels and raincoat on the seat then came back to the door to talk to Beth through the open top window. In no time at all it was eight forty-five and the guard's whistle blew. He waved his flag and the train started to move away from the platform. As she did with the charabancs she walked along the platform until the train's speed picked up enough and started to pull away from her and leave the station.

'Bye bye Arnold,' she called as she was waving. 'Have a lovely day. Give Adelaide all my love.' He waved back until her could see her no longer, turned with a smile, and returned to find his seat.

She stood for a moment and watched the train disappear then turned from the platform and walked back towards the main entrance of the station. She smiled as she handed her platform ticket to the ticket collector and as she stepped through the gate a voice said, 'Good morning... lady wanting escort home?' she turned and there was Owen.

'Hello, what a nice surprise. What are you doing here?'

'I just thought I would come and escort you back home. Don't want you wandering the streets by yourself,' he said holding his arm out for her to take. 'If that is alright and you have nothing else better to do.'

'Of course it is. I am very flattered. I was going to head to the park,' putting her arm through his and smiling.

'Your wish is my command, park it is madam,' and they turned in unison away from the station once again comfortable in each other's company.

Adelaide had butterflies in her stomach; she woke early and started to think again of what she should wear to meet him. She had previously decided on the same outfit she had worn to Blackpool. This had been decided in a moment of panic, she thought it would serve as a reminder to him in case he had forgotten what she looked like. Then thinking about it again, she thought she would change the dress but keep the hat with the rose on, the hat she knew he would definitely remember.

She looked at the clock it was eight-thirty, the train was due to arrive in Burnley at ten thirty-five so time to make a move. Her mother was downstairs making breakfast when she entered the kitchen.

'What time are you leaving to go and meet your young man?' she asked.

'Mother, he is not my young man yet. He is coming to get your's and father's permission to see me first.'

'Well Adelaide I don't think he would be coming all this way if he wasn't serious would he, and neither would you let him. I am sure that after today we will be referring to him as your young man,' she said arching her eyebrow and smiling. 'Now, what would you like for breakfast?'

'Just something light please,' smiling back at her mother. 'I shall be leaving at a quarter to ten.'

She caught the bus to the railway station and, after checking the arrivals board, stepped on to the platform ten minutes before his train was due. The butterflies were still there.

Arnold felt nervous and kept checking his watch to determine how long it would be until he arrived in Burnley. He went to the toilet facility and checked his appearance for a final time combing his hair and washing his hands and straightening his tie.

The train came to a halt on the platform. Adelaide had decided to stand near the wall of the waiting room rather than right at the edge of the platform. She thought it would give her the best vantage point and hoped the train wouldn't be too full.

He opened the train door and stepped on to the platform, as he alighted she had turned to look towards the front of the train where she could see the doors opening. She lifted herself on to her toes to try and see over the mingling crowd but could not see him. He looked down the platform but it was busy with people alighting and others waiting to board the train. He couldn't see her either and a slight panic set in until he noticed in the corner of his eye a flash of pink to his left against the stone wall. He turned and there she was, but she still hadn't seen him. He decided to stand still until the rest of the passengers had moved away and took the time to look across at her, he was pleased that she looked exactly as he remembered. She was still scanning the crowd and beginning to feel a little concerned until she glanced back towards the rear of the train and there he was right in front of her.

'Hello you, I seem to recognise that hat,' he said, all his nerves disappearing.

Smiling at him and holding her hands out her said, 'I am very pleased you do. It's lovely to see you again Arnold, I am so glad you came.'

He took hold of her hands and kissed her very gently on the lips. 'I have been waiting to do that for weeks. You look lovely, how are you?'

'I am fine now that you are here. I was beginning to panic there for a moment,' she laughed. 'I had a horrible thought that you might not come after all.'

'Now would I leave the loveliest lady in Lancashire waiting all alone on a lonely railway station?' he laughed back. 'I don't think so.'

She giggled. 'Let's go and have a cup of tea and a chat first before I take you home.'

'I would like that, before I have to meet the locals. Are they friendly?'

'Of course they are and looking forward to meeting you.'

They found a tea room and ordered a pot of tea. 'I need to buy some flowers for your mother Adelaide,' he said. 'Don't let me forget.'

'That's a nice thought, she will like that.'

He gave her the gifts he had brought. 'I also thought you may like these... and there is a note from Beth.'

'That is so lovely of you, thank you,' she looked at him. 'I shall look forward to reading what Beth has to say. You said in your letter that she loved the dress and combs. Did the colour suit her?'

'She looked stunning. You were absolutely right about the colour matching her eyes. She has met someone too. I have only met him a couple of times but he seems very nice and he has made her very happy.'

'That is good news, I am pleased for her.' She opened her gifts and gave him a kiss on the cheek, 'Thank you so much, these are just lovely.'

'You are welcome,' and he looked at her and took her hand. 'Adelaide, I have not been able to stop thinking about you these last weeks so let's dispel any fears. I am hoping you could feel the same way about me.'

'I think I already do,' she replied looking at him and smiling. 'Now, let's go and meet the family. Please don't worry they don't bite. My sister is calling in later and she is looking forward to meeting you.'

They left the tea room and walked arm in arm to the bus stop calling for the flowers on their way. Arriving outside where she lived, Arnold straightened his tie again and nodded to Adelaide that he was ready. 'Stop worrying,' she said, 'it will be fine, I know it.'

'Hello mother, father, we're here,' she called and took off her hat. 'Where are you...come and meet Arnold?'

Her mother and father appeared in the doorway. 'I am very pleased to meet you sir,' said Arnold extending his hand to her father. 'Hello Mrs Gibson... very pleased to meet you. I thought you might like these.'

Her mother looked at the flowers then at the young man in front of her, 'Hello Arnold, we are very pleased to make your acquaintance too. What a very nice thought, thank you. I will put them in water straight away.' Adelaide smiled at her mother as she left the room with the flowers.

'Come and sit down lad,' said Mr Gibson. 'I think you have made a hit there with the flowers. Come and have a chat. Would you like a glass of beer seeing that it is Sunday?' he asked. 'I like a glass of beer on a Sunday... don't bother in the week usually.'

'I would yes, thank you sir,' Arnold replied becoming more comfortable by the minute.

'That's good. I will just get them, then you can tell me all about yourself and you don't need to call me sir.'

Adelaide nodded to him and added quietly, 'I will just go and help mother. I think you are a hit,' and smiled as her father came back into the room carrying two glasses of beer.

Mr Gibson gave Arnold his beer, 'There you go lad... cheers.'

'Cheers,' said Arnold, 'good health.'

'Good health. Now, tell me all about yourself Arnold,' he said settling into his chair and lighting his pipe then damping it down.

Arnold sat with him for a good hour and explained about his father and Beth and briefly touched on his mother and Evelyn but did not go in to full detail. He explained what he did at work, what his prospects were and asked for Mr Gibson's permission to carry on seeing Adelaide as his intentions were serious and true.

At the end of the conversation Adelaide's father had given his blessing for Arnold to walk out with his daughter albeit from a distance. He also commiserated with him with regard to his father and commended him on his commitment to his family. He felt from what he had told him that his future prospects were good. He then called his wife and his daughter into the front room to give them his decision and suggested a toast to the young couple despatching Mrs Gibson for the sherry. The rest of the day went extremely well. Adelaide's sister and family arrived after lunch for an informal introduction, by this time he felt very relaxed in this family's presence.

His train back was due to leave at seven forty-five, so around five o'clock Adelaide announced that they would go for a walk before going on to the station for Arnold's return trip home. Her family bade him a fond farewell and told him to come again soon. They wished him a safe journey and the two of them left the house to spend the last of the day together.

Walking away from the house Adelaide said, 'What did I tell you. I knew there would be nothing to worry about they all loved you.'

'Thank you for having such a nice family, Adelaide. You don't know how lucky you are. I only have Beth really, we are not close to our mother or younger sister, in fact it is the opposite. We are not a proper family like yours so I am so very sorry to say that I can't return the compliment,' he replied all of a sudden sounding serious and looking concerned.

'Don't worry. I am really looking forward to meeting Beth. You have spoken so highly of her, I am sure we will get along,' she said holding his hand to allay his concerns. 'If she is your only family then that is good enough for me, nobody else matters.'

'Thank you for understanding. I have suggested that we all meet up in Blackpool one weekend so she can meet you. She has never been on a train or to the coast and I know she is anxious to see the sea one day because of how our father was lost.'

'That is a lovely idea Arnold I would like that too. I am sure we can arrange it for one Sunday.'

They walked arm in arm in silence both contemplating his leaving. 'It seems to have passed so quickly,' said Adelaide. 'I don't want you to go.'

He stopped walking and turned her to him. 'Don't worry, this is only the beginning. Perhaps next time I can come for the weekend not just the day, then we have to arrange a meeting in Blackpool. I am sure with letters during the week and going to work the time will pass quickly. I have never felt like this about anyone Adelaide, you are very special to me... very special.' He bent his head slightly lifted her chin and kissed her very gently then held her for what felt an eternity.

'I have become very fond of you too. I think of you all the time and was frightened that perhaps I had made too much of our brief meeting in Blackpool,' she replied tears starting to well in her eyes.

'No you didn't... and neither did I... our feelings will grow from here so don't become upset. Let me reassure you, it is not going to end even though we are apart. It is going to grow. I will come to you every weekend if I have to, if you need convincing.'

'I would love you to come every weekend. I can ask my mother if you can come and sleep overnight on the couch, I am sure she will say yes. I will ask as soon as I get back home and write to you tonight and post it tomorrow.'

'I don't want to appear presumptuous Adelaide. If I have to come only on a Sunday that will be enough, they have been very kind today I have no wish to take their hospitality for granted.'

'No I don't think they will see it like that so long as I am happy. Apart from that, mother was thrilled with the flowers, you are definitely in the good books.'

'Well, let us see what they say when you get home. I don't want to assume anything where you or your family are concerned, you are too important to me.'

They stood on the platform waiting for his train to arrive, hardly daring to speak to each other. When the train arrived, he opened the carriage door then turned and held her very close to him. Keeping an eye out for the guard he said, 'I will see you again very, very soon, don't worry.' He kissed her just as the guard blew his whistle and climbed on board as the flag for departure was being waved.

She held his hand through the window and walked with the train as Beth had done until speed became the victor. They waved to each other until he was out of sight. Arnold went to find a seat and sat down to contemplate his day, he felt wonderful.

Adelaide wiped a tear away, then caught her bus for the return journey and sat thinking about him all the way home with a smile.

Beth had also had a wonderful day, more so because it had been so unexpected. She and Owen had spent the whole day together after he had found her at the station. They had walked from the station to the park and spent a relaxed time talking and laughing over lunch in the tea rooms there. Later they walked back towards town for high tea before Owen suggested they finish the day with a trip to the cinema to see the film of the moment 39 Steps. That was fine until they realised that Fred Astaire and Ginger Roger's new film Top Hat was also showing at an alternative cinema so there was only one decision he could make, Beth was delighted.

When finally they arrived back at the end of her street she said, 'I will leave you here. I would rather you didn't take me to the door for obvious reasons. I am sorry I cannot invite you in,' she said her eyes downcast.

'We agreed not to talk about families did we not? Don't let's spoil a great day and don't get upset about it if they are not worth it. I understand totally. I would much rather have introduced you to you my grandmother than any of my so-called family and that includes my sisters, she would have loved you,' he said lifting her chin so that she had to look at him. He kissed her and said, 'Just tell me that we have a date for next Saturday still?'

It lightened her mood, she smiled and said, 'Of course we do. Today was just a super surprise. Thank you for coming to find me and thank you for coming into my life.'

'My pleasure,' said Owen kissing her quickly again. 'Now let me watch you walk down the street, then I know you are back safely. Give my regards to Arnold. Tell him I hope he has enjoyed his day as much as I have.'

'I will, you can be sure. Goodnight Owen,' said Beth looking into his eyes.

He watched her walk down the street and before she disappeared down the alley between the houses she waved and blew a kiss. As she opened the door into the house she came face to face with Ellen and Evelyn who were sitting in their usual chairs, both scowled as she came into their view.

'Must be nice when you can go out all day on a Sunday,' said Evelyn looking at her mother.

'It is, be assured,' said Beth smiling at them both. 'You want to try it sometime... there is a whole world out there believe it or not.' Turning away from them she went straight up the stairs to bed determined they were not going to spoil her day.

She roused from sleep when she heard the front door closing indicating that Arnold was home Her first instinct was to rush downstairs and ask him how his day had gone, then she decided not to. If his day had been successful his news would wait until the morning. As he had not returned early she decided she would leave him to his thoughts for the rest of the night and hoped they would be pleasant ones and he would sleep easy.

She was dressed and downstairs before he roused for work on the Monday morning. He opened the stairs door and entered the kitchen, she looked over to him and with a smile asked, 'Well how was it?'

'Wonderful... she is wonderful... her family is wonderful... we had such a good time Beth. I didn't want to leave,' he said and a looked a little sad.

Beth walked over to him and took hold of him in her arms, 'Arnold, I am so pleased. Tell me have you made any more plans?'

'Yes, she is to ask her parents if I can travel on Saturday afternoon instead, stay overnight, and sleep on the couch and return on the Sunday. It would give us a proper weekend then. If not then I shall just go on Sundays,' he added sounding resigned. 'Beth... they are really nice people... a real family, not like us here.' He lifted the cup of tea she had made for him, 'That reminds me were you alright on your own yesterday?'

'Hmm... ' she laughed, 'yesterday was wonderful for me too. Owen was waiting for me when I came out of the station after waving you off. We spent the day together and went to the cinema last night to see *Top Hat*,' she giggled. 'I didn't know he was going to be there. I had told him that you were going to Burnley on Saturday night at the dance so he thought he would surprise me and be there when I came out of the station. Wasn't that nice... and the movie... well that was just wonderful.'

'Sounds as if you had as good a day as me. I am so pleased Beth, he clearly likes you as much as you like him.'

'He must do... he passed on *39 Steps* so that I could see the new Fred Astaire dance film. Must be smitten... that Bette Davis routine must have worked,' she looked at him and laughed.

'That's a wise man... must ask him for lessons,' he said laughing back at her. 'Come on... work beckons.' He opened the door and they started to walk down the street arm in arm. 'Roll on next weekend, for both of us,' he said.

'Yes please, you sound just like Annie!'

'I should get a letter from Adelaide this week, letting me know whether I can go on Saturday and stay over,' he added as they walked on, 'and by the way she said thank you for your note. I have also mentioned meeting in Blackpool and you coming too, she was thrilled at the thought.'

'That would be lovely. I shall really look forward to that,' said a delighted Beth. 'I think we both have lots to look forward to Arnold and it's a nice feeling.'

'Yes it is, and doesn't it make a nice change,' he said squeezing her hand.

'Yes, it does.'

It was the usual Monday morning at the bread shop. Mr Newbould greeted the girls and was now resigned to the fact that he would have to bite the bullet and enquire how their weekend had gone.

Annie as always was excited and brought Georgie into the conversation at every opportunity, telling him that she would be seeing him again the next Saturday and how she couldn't wait. Beth just laughed at him when he glanced over to her and rolled his eyes before escaping back into the bakery. Sybil arrived with Elizabeth and Theresa in tow. They entered the shop with her for their usual order before going on to their work place.

'Hi Beth... well sweets... Owen seems to have had a good weekend,' said Elizabeth. 'I am pleased you two have finally got together. I think you will be good for him. I meant what I said on Saturday night you two look right together.'

'Thank you Elizabeth, that is very kind of you.'

'No worries, I just hope I am as lucky one day,' she said smiling. 'Come on Theresa let's go, another day another dollar and all that. See you all later.'

Georgie was sitting on a bench in the yard when Owen arrived. 'What a good weekend then Georgie boy,' said Owen tapping him from behind gently on the top of his head. 'Enjoy it?'

'Course I did. Thought I might have seen you yesterday with your clothes.'

'No I have brought them this morning, needed them yesterday. I spent the day with Beth,' winking at his friend.

'Well, next time tell me then I can arrange something with Annie,' he responded sounding a little hurt.

'Sorry mate, it was a spur of the moment thing and it turned out better than I could have hoped. She had gone to the station with Arnold so I just wandered down to see if I could walk her back, but she wasn't doing anything so we just spend the day together and finished up at the cinema last night.'

'Well nice for some.'

'It was the best I have to say,' said Owen. 'Sorry old mate if you were expecting me... will make it up to you don't worry... You seeing Annie again then?'

'You bet, she's great.'

'Marvellous,' said Owen. 'Pleased for you.'

At the newspaper Thomas was waiting for Arnold and saw him approaching and assumed by his gait that his weekend had gone well. He had a bounce in his step and was whistling loudly as he walked along. 'Morning,' said Thomas. 'Somebody looks in a good mood this morning. All went well did it? Her father didn't run you out of town then?' and laughed at his friend.

'Yes I think you could say it was a success,' replied Arnold, 'without me sounding smug.'

'So when are you off again?'

'This weekend hopefully... should know by Wednesday,' said Arnold sounding confident.

'That's good,' Thomas responded. 'Can you hear that noise?'

'What noise?'

'Not sure, but it sounds like the wedding march to me,' he answered running into the newspaper laughing before Arnold could cuff him.

He didn't have to wait long for his letter, it was waiting for him when he arrived at work on the Wednesday morning. Adelaide had written that all the family had thoroughly enjoyed his company at the weekend and his parents had no objection to him staying overnight on future visits if he didn't mind sleeping on the couch in the front parlour. He was thrilled. His initial thought was to write straight back and say he would see her the next Saturday but then after much thought decided he would travel the weekend following instead. As much as he wished to see her again he didn't want to alienate her parents by taking advantage of their good nature every week. So, he decided he would walk to the station during his lunch break to determine his options. He could then write to Adelaide when his shift had finished giving all the timings, then mail it back to her on his way home.

He finished his shift and sat down to write his reply. He knew she may well be disappointed that he would not be travelling again that week but he gave his reasons why and assured her that she had his heart. He had also decided that the week following his long weekend he would suggest that they meet in Blackpool and he would bring Beth along so that they could be introduced and get to know each other. He had also enquired about the Blackpool train times and was pleased that there was an early one that arrived there mid-morning. He then finished by saying he would await her reply before surprising Beth and sent all his love and best regards to her parents.

Adelaide received his response on the Saturday morning. Initially she was disappointed that she would have to wait another week before she saw him again, but then on re-reading it could understand his reasoning. Posting her reply straight back she told him that to have him there for nearly a whole weekend would be wonderful and hoped that the week would pass quickly and sent her love. She was delighted she would be meeting Beth in Blackpool and hoped they would become great friends. Her parents returned their best wishes and said they were looking forward to seeing him again the following weekend.

He had decided he would meet up with Thomas and their work friends on the Saturday night after he had escorted Beth and Annie to the barracks. He felt that probably he would not be socialising with them for much longer at the weekend so they could have a good night and one last Saturday night escorting the girls to the dance would not go amiss.

She thought he was unusually quiet the next Saturday night, then before they turned the corner to Annie's house he stopped and said, 'Next weekend I shall be going to Burnley on Saturday straight from work and not coming back until late Sunday night. Is that alright Beth?'

She stopped walking, 'Arnold, what on earth are you asking me for? Don't be silly, of course it's alright.' She took hold of his hand, 'What is it... what is worrying you?'

He looked at his sister, 'I know we have had this conversation before but it doesn't stop me feeling guilty about leaving you.'

She looked at her brother's troubled face and said, 'I have a feeling that Adelaide is a very special lady. It makes me happy that you now have some happiness in your life and if anyone deserves it Arnold, you do. My welfare has been your priority for far too long now. Don't you think that makes me feel guilty?'

'That's different, now you are being silly.'

'It is no different at all,' she sounded defensive. 'That makes two of us then... yes?'

'I suppose so, I'm sorry. But you are one special sister,' he said holding her close.

'Yes, but that is only because I have one special brother. Now... enough said,' and once again starting walking towards Annie's house. 'I am delighted to hear you are going for the weekend. It makes sense instead of going all that way for a few hours. You must have made a good impression on her parents, I am delighted for you.'

'Yes, it must have been the flowers,' he laughed as Beth knocked on the door and Annie appeared.

Quickly composing himself, 'Hello Annie,' he said. 'Looking lovely as usual, that Georgie is one lucky man.' He winked at her and offered his arm in anticipation.

Annie beamed and blushed, 'Well thank you as usual kind sir,' and linked her arm through his and away they went.

Owen and Georgie were once again waiting outside the barracks and saw them approaching. Not wanting to encroach on their time together Arnold, after the usual pleasantries, bade them all a nice evening, smiled and kissed Beth on her cheek. Taking Owen to one side said quietly, 'I am relying on you to look after her for me, to treat her right.'

Owen looked back at him straight in the eye, 'Don't worry, Arnold, you know I will... that is a promise and it won't be broken,' he replied and they shook hands.

Owen then took Beth's hand in his and they watched her brother walk away. Before turning the corner he looked back, stood for just a moment then waved. Then he was gone.

'Is everything alright?' Owen asked noticing the tear falling down her cheek.

'Yes don't worry, it will be from now on. I will explain inside,' she answered regaining her composure.

Beth & Owen, Adelaide & Arnold: Part 2

Arnold packed his overnight things and took them to work on the Saturday morning, only Beth knew where he was going and when he would return. Ellen and Evelyn may comment to each other about his absence to her but nothing would be said generally, it never was.

Once again for his next trip Beth had written a short note to Adelaide, in it she had mentioned their planned meeting. He had told her that he and Adelaide had already discussed the two of them meeting up in Blackpool one Sunday and asked if she would like to go, Beth had been thrilled. He had bought a silver pin brooch for Adelaide, and Beth had convinced him to take her mother flowers again as thanks for her parents' hospitality.

They left the house as usual and walked part way together before going in different directions to their workplaces.

Turning to him before parting she said 'Have a lovely time Arnold... please give Adelaide my love.' she said kissing his cheek and giving him a hug. 'I will be thinking about you both.'

'I will... and the same to you... you and Owen enjoy your evening.'

'Don't worry, it's all in hand... I have told Owen that you will be away for the weekend so you never know I might be seeing him tomorrow... failing that I could be seeing Annie... we'll see... don't you go worrying about me... I will be fine... now off you go... ' she squeezed his hand and was determined not to cry.

He nodded his head in agreement and kissed her back. He walked on, turning as always to acknowledge and wave to her before he disappeared round the corner and out of sight.

Owen had told Georgie that he would probably be seeing Beth on the Sunday again as Arnold was away for the weekend and suggested if he and Annie wanted to meet up with them at some point then that would be fine. Georgie was in agreement and added that he was sure Annie would be as well.

Beth left the house in silence and walked to Annie's house. They all met up as usual outside the barracks and decided instead of going straight in they would go for a drink first.

Owen and Georgie went to the bar. 'Are you up for it tomorrow then?' asked Owen.

'Yes if Annie is... I am sure she will be... it will make a change from only seeing you or nobody on a Sunday,' Georgie replied laconically.

'Yeah right... I actually only come to see you on a Sunday so that your mother can spoil me with one of her dinners... ' he turned to go back to the girls with a laugh.

He turned to Beth, 'Did Arnold get away alright?' he asked quietly.

'Yes I think so... he didn't come back so I think he must have done,' she smiled.

'Any problems at home?' he asked after a pause.

'No... we don't speak anyway, so even if they wanted to ask they wouldn't... they probably think he is working an extra shift.'

'What about tomorrow then... can we go out for the day again? I have mentioned it to Georgie if that is alright, to see if they wanted to meet up a little later... that way we get to spend time on our own first,' he said taking hold of her hand and kissing it.

'That would be lovely... you are really spoiling me... I did enjoy it last Sunday,' she said looking at him and smiling.

'Yes so did I... ' kissing her hand again. 'I will arrange it with him later.'

They arrived in the dance hall. Owen's sisters had already arrived and were holding their weekly court. He smiled and waved over to them all and they responded, Elizabeth turned and smiled widely to all of them.

'I do have to admire Elizabeth's flair for fashion... she really is wasted in the factory,' said Beth. 'She looks very glamorous again Owen.'

'Don't ask me where she gets it from,' he replied, 'it is definitely not from the old man or my mother... she has always been good at make believe... she used to tell the young ones stories that she had made up at night to settle them and get them all to sleep... she has a good imagination... which is not a bad thing... it took them all out of their squalid existence for a while I suppose.' He looked over at his sister again with warmth. 'I hope one day she finds what she is looking for, but I don't reckon it's around here with the likes of us.'

'No I think you may be right, Sybil said the same thing a few weeks ago,' agreed Beth.

'Come on, enough about my family, let's dance,' he said pulling her close to him. 'I have found what I am looking for so let's not worry about anyone else,' and he led her on to the dance floor.

Elizabeth held her cigarette and watched them dance round the floor lost in each other's gaze. 'One day,' she thought, 'one day that will be me looking happy and in love,' and she turned back to her line of admirers silently feeling pleased for her brother.

Adelaide was waiting for him in the same place when his train arrived. He walked quickly towards her, they embraced and looked at each other. 'It is so good to see you... I have missed you,' said Arnold holding her close and kissing her on the cheek.

'Same here,' she replied smiling at him. 'Do you want to go home or shall we go for a walk first?'

He took hold of her hand. 'I don't want to share you with anyone at the moment, so I think we should walk then sit somewhere on a bench and talk. I would just like to be together on our own... sorry no disrespect to your family.'

She laughed, 'None taken and don't worry I would like that too. It might be a bit difficult to fix it for all the time you are here though, but I will see what I can arrange.'

'Oh, Adelaide I apologise that came out wrong. I thought your family were really nice, it is just that I want to be with you on our own as much as we can without appearing rude.'

'No I know. it has been a long two weeks and I have missed you too. I am so pleased you are here,' she said pulling him close.

'Well... in that case we are not going to lose any more time. Miss Gibson, your arm please.'

They took their time and had a relaxing afternoon in each other's company and arrived at Adelaide's house in good time for tea. Arnold had purchased flowers again on the way.

'Hello, Mrs Gibson it's lovely to see you again,' he said smiling at her. 'These are for you and can I just say I am very grateful to you and Mr Gibson for letting me stay the night.'

'Hello again Arnold. You are very welcome... we are delighted to have you here again and thank you so much for my flowers. You really are spoiling me,' returning his smile with genuine warmth.

'It is just a small way of showing my appreciation.'

As he presented them to her it occurred to him in that moment that he had never bought his own mother flowers ever. He had never had the inclination and probably never would. He felt no guilt at the realisation of this fact and smiled gently at Adelaide's mother as she fussed over the blooms.

Mr Gibson appeared in the doorway and said, 'Nice to see you again lad... welcome. Come and have a sit down and a chat. It's nice to have a man in the house, it makes a change from a house full of women.'

Arnold laughed and glanced at Adelaide's mother who looked at her husband and said, 'Tea will be ready in thirty minutes Stanley. Just remember who he has come here to see and it's not you, so don't bore him silly or he might not come again.' She winked at Arnold and disappeared into the kitchen.

Looking at his wife he said, 'Well I reckon that's told me then Arnold lad.'

'Yes, I reckon it has,' said Arnold smiling ruefully and trying to sound sympathetic.

Adelaide had suggested earlier when they were walking that they could go to the music hall in the evening, he had readily agreed and said, 'Adelaide... I would be quite happy to sit and look at a brick wall so long as you were there with me. I usually get dragged off to the Fred Astaire and Ginger Rogers movies with Beth, so the music hall would be great for a change. Is there anywhere we can go for supper afterwards to finish the evening off?'

'Yes of course we can,' but then added, 'but thinking about it, I am not sure that the best of Burnley can compete with Fred and Ginger on the entertainment scale. I'm sorry.'

'Oh don't worry about that,' he answered. 'I only go for Beth... I can't dance!'

They left her parent's house and set off to enjoy their evening. Arm in arm they walked towards the bus stop. She was wearing the pin brooch he had bought her.

'They make a nice looking couple Stanley,' said Adelaide's mother to her husband as she watched them walking down the street together through the window.

'Yes... he's a nice lad. He's not had it easy with losing his father so young and with a younger sister to care for. She could do a lot worse.'

'So long as he is caring that's enough for me, and if he has more or less cared for his sister for all that time he can't be that bad... it shows he has a good heart. Adelaide told me that he is taking his sister to Blackpool to meet her next week. He wants her to see the sea with their father being lost on his ship as she has no idea what it looks like... a caring thought that.'

'Yes, he's a good lad alright, I don't think we have anything to worry about there. He hasn't mentioned his mother or other sister again though has he?'

'No he hasn't but that is up to him. We take him as we find him Stanley. He is alright so far and if he makes Addie happy there is nothing more to be said.'

Mr Gibson nodded in silence and moved to light his pipe; his wife walked back into the kitchen feeling happy for her daughter.

The music hall was full and the atmosphere was good. Everyone sang along with the popular songs being performed, laughed and heckled the comedians and generally enjoyed their evening. Arnold looked at his lady a few times in the dimmed lights and thought to himself how lovely she was. She laughed openly and honestly and in that respect reminded him of Beth, she possessed the same loveliness but in a different way.

Adelaide caught him looking at her a couple of times and smiled back and squeezed his hand, 'I am so glad you are here Arnold. Is everything alright?'

He whispered, 'Everything is just perfect, I could stay here like this forever. Now that I have found you I am not going to let you go Adelaide, you know that don't you... please say you feel the same way.'

'Yes I do.' She kissed him gently, 'I think that should say it all,' holding his hand tightly.

'Yes it does,' he whispered back to her, 'it says everything I was hoping to hear.'

Leaving the music hall they called in for supper at a local pie shop. 'What a grand evening Adelaide and we still have all day tomorrow. It is very good of your parents to let me stay.' He paused, 'It would be no good you coming to visit me, there is no way I would want you to stay even if we had the room I am sorry to say.'

'Arnold please don't worry. I am looking forward to meeting Beth next week and, as you say, she is basically your only family and that is enough for me.'

'Yes, realistically she is my only family. At some point I will tell you the full story, shocking that it is, but please not just yet. I would hate for your parents to judge me on the past deeds of my mother. I would hate it to spoil everything,' he looked at her with concern.

She took his hand, 'I think they have already formed their opinion of you

Arnold and I can assure you if they had not warmed to you, you would not be here now, so stop worrying. What is in the past is of no consequence to me. I hope you are my present and my future and that is the only thing I am concerned with. At some point you can tell me if you must but I will not press you to do so.' She took hold of his hands tenderly, 'And I am sure my parents won't either.'

'Thank you... you don't know just how good it feels to walk into a family home where you all support each other as families should. I suppose we were unlucky being born just before the war, it took a dreadful toll. It wasn't easy for Beth and I as children.' He looked at her and for a moment his eyes filled with tears, 'I am so sorry Adelaide, I am spoiling our evening, forgive me.'

'No you are not, you need to tell me these things as they are a part of what you are and what you will continue to be. Just remember that it is your past... I am your future. I think we have much to look forward to you and I,' and she leaned forward and kissed him, 'wouldn't you agree?'

'Yes I would and it feels wonderful to actually say so, thank you,' and he kissed her back.

Owen escorted Beth home after the dance, they had fallen into an easy routine when walking home. Her arm was through his, they were relaxed and totally comfortable with each other.

'I have arranged for us to meet up with Georgie and Annie at one o'clock tomorrow so what would you like to do in the morning?'

'I really don't mind, just being with you is enough, ' she smiled and hugged his arm a little closer. 'The surroundings are immaterial. One thing is certain I don't want to be housebound.'

'So no competition there then for your affection?' he said in response.

'No competition anywhere as far as I am concerned.'

He stopped for a moment, turned and held her in silence, and after a moment said, 'Beth... I cannot imagine you not being in my life... does that sound silly after only a few weeks?'

'No I feel the same. You are in my thoughts all the time. I have tried not thinking about you but it doesn't work.' As she lifted her head they kissed with a passion that would remain with them always.

They took a little longer than usual to say goodnight, neither wanting to be the one to finally say goodnight. 'I shall be here at nine o'clock in the morning for you.'

'You don't have to... '

'Yes I do. I might even come and knock on the door and ask for you personally,' he said looking at her.

'And I might just let you do that. It would be an interesting exercise either way. I wouldn't make it before lunchtime if I were you, you could be standing there all day if I go out,' she replied laughing at him.

They parted reluctantly not wanting to let go of each other. Beth turned towards her door, 'I shall see you in the morning then... sweet dreams, sleep tight... mind the bed bugs don't bite and all that... ' and blew him a kiss as she opened the door.

He walked home feeling exhilarated until he turned the corner on to the lane where they lived, whenever he approached the door it was always with caution. Would his father be waiting for him, he would soon know when he opened the door. He was in luck, his mother had obviously got him upstairs before he had become too drunk. Owen heaved a sigh of relief that his good humour was not going to be spoilt by yet another vile argument.

Rising early the next morning, he left the house and walked towards Beth's arriving just before nine o'clock. He found her waiting at the corner for him. 'Hello and good morning... I didn't want you to knock on the wrong door,' she smiled.

'Well good morning to you fair maid. Would you like to go for some breakfast with an admirer?' kissing her on the cheek and holding his arm out for her to take.

She smiled, 'Oh... Yes please,' putting her arm through his and pulling him close.

They took their time walking to the tea rooms and chose a corner table next to the window. The waitress appeared and took their order. 'I wish we could do this every morning,' he said taking her hand and sighing.

'You know what they say... you should always be careful what you wish for,' she said looking back at him and sounding a little cautious.

'Not this time Beth... I know exactly what I am wishing for,' he said lifting her hand to his lips and kissing it gently. Changing the subject he asked, 'What time does Arnold get back?'

'Not until later tonight. He plans to catch the last train. I do hope he has had a lovely time, he has arranged for me to meet Adelaide in Blackpool next Sunday. I am quite excited about it,' she said looking at him and leaving her hand in his.

'Yes you said. I have been thinking about that... do you think he... they... would mind if I asked to come along too? I would love us to spend the day there together, if it wouldn't be an intrusion.'

There was a slight pause and she looked at little pensive before she answered, 'Well... I suppose that would be better than me playing gooseberry,' she said, then... laughing at him, 'I was beginning to think you would never ask. I would love you to come. I can't think of anything I would like more and no it definitely would not be an intrusion, trust me,' squeezing his hand again and looking excited and happy.

He looked at the smiling blue eyes staring at him, and took both her hands in his across the table, 'Beth... do you have any idea how I feel about you? If I am speaking out of turn please tell me but I have to say this. You are in my thoughts first thing in the morning and last thing at night. If you don't feel the same please tell me now then no-one will get hurt... well my pride might be a bit bruised, but no more serious than that. I suppose I would get over it given time... Georgie might be able to help me if I was to get suicidal.' He looked at her with pleading eyes and tightened his grip on her hands.

The moment was broken by the waitress bringing the tea tray to the table. Owen let go of her hands and they both sat in silence until the tea paraphernalia had been set out on the table. The waitress took her leave.

Taking his hands in hers again Beth looked at him and said quietly, 'You could not have expressed how I feel about you any better than that... apart from Annie being in support for me instead of Georgie.' She smiled, 'You have turned my world upside down. I cannot wait to see you again when we are apart. Arnold has always been there for me as a brother and I love him dearly, and without him I really do not know how I would have coped. My feelings for you are totally different, but just as intense if not more.' After a moment she said, 'I hope that gives you your answer.'

He looked at her and he could see the tears in her eyes. He stood and lifting her hands so that she stood away from the table, he took her in his arms and kissed her softly. Lifting her face he said, 'You are my world too... I want to be with you all the time. I think we are saying the same thing here... yes?'

'Oh yes,' she replied quietly. 'I do believe we are and I could not be happier. Thank you... now... are we going to have some tea to celebrate today before it goes cold and then we can celebrate next weekend in Blackpool proper... yes?' laughing and hugging him tightly.

Picking her up and holding her tight he said, 'Yes, yes, yes, pour the tea, this will be our first celebration but a very special one. Just you and I ... next week we will share it with the people you love. I know that is important to you and I can't think of a better celebration for us all.'

They met up with Georgie and Annie at the arranged time and continued to enjoy what had turned into a very special day. Both their friends sensed their closeness and Annie had become very excited when Beth had told her that Owen was to travel to Blackpool with her and Arnold the following Sunday when she was to meet Adelaide.

Owen saw a faint look of disappointment on Georgie's face and he quietly indicated for him to walk to one side with him and have a cigarette. The girls were still lost in their excitement about Beth's impending trip to notice they had moved away.

They lit their cigarettes in silence and Owen looked at his old friend, 'Something tells me you are disappointed with Beth's news.'

'No... it's not that... I am pleased for her. It just occurred to me that it would have been nice for the four of us to go, all of us being close and all that,' Georgie replied looking a little sheepish.

'I hear what you are saying but this is not going to be the same sort of trip that we four will have, that will wait for the next one and we will all look forward to it... trust me. This trip is primarily for Beth to meet Arnold's lady but also it will be the first time she will have seen the sea. I know none of us have seen it yet, but she has unresolved issues from when she was a young child when her father was lost at sea. I think it will be a very emotive trip for them both. Something that is just between the two of them finally paying their respects together and being able to move on with their lives. It is my way of giving her support when I think she is going to need it. I am in love with her Georgie... this is serious, this is the one... but it does not affect our close friendship and it never will.'

'Oh Christ forgive me Owen. I am just being daft and not thinking. I suppose I am very lucky to have had a good home life and my parents there all the time. The war didn't really affect us that much with Dad working at the steelworks, he didn't have to go. After listening to your upbringing and from what Annie has told me Beth doesn't have much of a home life either, it makes me look a bit selfish. Sorry mate, take no notice.' He looked at his friend and nodded, 'you take her and let her put it to rest... but remember to enjoy the day as well. There will be a lot happening no doubt what with meeting Arnold's lady. When you get back there is enough time to plan when we can all go together.' He then patted Owen on his shoulder, smiled and tutted, 'So old friend... it's serious is it? Well it had to happen one day I suppose. Our luck had to run out, some lucky girls had to get us,' and he grinned over to Annie and winked. 'That's my girl,' Annie responded with a giggle.

Their day continued in good humour, four good friends enjoying each other's company; afternoon soon became early evening and a discussion started about what they should do for the evening. A few pints and a pie being Owen and Georgie's first choice or the picture house, then the debate moved to the choice of film 'Bride of Frankenstein' with Boris Karloff which again was their choice or Errol Flynn and Olivia de Havilland in 'Captain Blood' which the girls said they would prefer. So a compromise was reached and it was agreed one pint and a pie and 'Captain Blood'. All parties felt happy with the decision and an enjoyable evening ensued.

On leaving the cinema Owen asked Beth, 'What time does Arnold arrive back?'

'I'm not sure I think his train arrives back around eleven thirty?' she answered. 'Why?'

'Well... would you like to go and meet your brother at the station, just to finish a perfect day off for you both. I was just thinking about your conversation with him about emotions at railway stations that you told me about. I just thought you might like to go and meet him off the train, to round his and our weekend off so to speak. He is probably feeling a little down after a good weekend and having to leave the lady that holds his affections.'

'What a lovely idea. I would love that. Are you sure you don't mind after I have monopolised your day?' she said not able to conceal her delight.

'Would I suggest it if I minded... of course not,' he smiled. 'I think it has been an important weekend for us all and it keeps me with you for a bit longer.'

They said their warm goodnights to Georgie and Annie and set off for the station.

The station was relatively empty compared to the last time Beth had been on the platform seeing Arnold off. It was late evening and trains were arriving on schedule. Passengers were alighting and busily continuing their way home not expecting anyone to be there to welcome them with it being such a late hour.

They sat in silence waiting for his train to arrive on the empty platform. Beth felt totally relaxed sitting next to the man who had become her life, comfortable just sitting there with Owen's arm around her making her feel safe, warm and loved. She waited for the brother who had been the closest person to her since childhood with an inner feeling of peace and contentment.

The announcement broke the silence: 'The train arriving at Platform three is the eleven-thirty arriving from Burnley via Manchester continuing on to Derby via Chesterfield.'

Beth stood and Owen let her move alone to the edge of the platform not wanting to encroach into their space. The train came to a halt and the doors started to open and its passengers alighted. Arnold opened the door and stepped down from the train wrapped in his own thoughts. Owen smiled as he watched it unfold from the seat she had just vacated next to him. She saw her brother, waved and ran towards him; it took a moment before he realised it was Beth running down the platform towards him, he opened his arms and spun her round.

'Oh... what are you doing here?' he asked her looking delighted.

'It was Owen's idea,' she said laughing. 'How has your weekend gone?'

'It has been wonderful... and yours?'

'Oh... I think it would be safe to say it's been wonderful too.'

They walked back to Owen and Arnold shook his hand, 'Thank you Owen... thank you.'

'What for... escorting my favourite lady to meet her favourite brother. No thanks needed' Owen laughed and shook his hand warmly. 'How was your weekend?'

'It was excellent... and yours?'

Owen just smiled and looked at Beth, 'I think we have all reached a new place in our lives Arnold ... and for the better... yes?'

'Yes... I think we have and I have to say if you are where I am it is a wonderful feeling. My sister looks very happy and that is what I am thanking you for.'

'She is wonderful Arnold and she has captured my heart. She deserves to be happy... I think we all do.'

They all turned to leave the empty platform and Beth, walking in the middle, linked her arms with the two most important men in her life and hugged them both close.

Owen walked part of the way with them until they reached the place where he would continue his way home alone. Arnold stood away from them until they had said goodnight. 'Once again thank you, you always seem to be thinking about what I need, what I would like, how I feel... I love that,' said Beth kissing him gently.

Looking into her blues eyes, 'No more thanks Beth from either you or Arnold, it is not a chore, because I love you. There I have said it,' he sighed and nuzzled her ear. 'Beth I cannot imagine my world without you. I don't even want to think about it.'

'No and neither do I. I think I am in with love you too. I say think because I have never been in love before, but if this is what it feels like then I must be.' The ripple in her stomach appeared once more and she gasped at the sensation and said, 'and it's a wonderful feeling.'

They kissed again and reluctantly said goodnight; Beth then turned to Arnold to continue their way home both waving to Owen before they turned the corner out of sight.

Walking slowly so as to take their time back to the house Beth pulled Arnold close to her and said, 'So... you now know about my wonderful weekend... tell me all about yours? How is Adelaide and her family?'

'She is just perfect. I have a note for you from her and her family are very, very nice, they too send their good wishes by the way. We went to the Music Hall on Saturday evening then for supper. Yesterday we walked to the main recreational park, listened to the band, then her sister and family came to the house for tea. It is so good Beth to feel part of a family, something we have only ever dared to imagine... but it does exist.'

'Is that how you feel, part of their family?' she asked.

'I know that may sound very odd, and in no way does it affect you and I,' he said quickly. 'It is more of how they make you feel... welcoming and interested in you as a person. I suppose they see how happy Adelaide is and only want the best for her... and... I make her happy,' he laughed, 'she says so. In fact it is a little more than that Beth... like you and Owen... I think... in fact I would say I have met my lady.'

She squeezed his arm. 'Arnold that is wonderful, just what I wanted to hear. I am so looking forward to meeting her next week. I shall write to her tomorrow and tell her so.'

'Yes... and she is looking forward to meeting you too,' he answered.

'Now, I hope you don't mind,' she said sounding a little hesitant, 'it won't just be me meeting her. Owen will be there with me as well, will that be alright?'

He stopped walking and looked at her, 'Beth, it is your choice, if you would like Owen to come along then that is absolutely fine. I am delighted he is coming with you he seems to be a good, caring man.' He kissed her on the forehead and said, 'It will be a wonderful day for us to share together... a special day for all of us.'

They walked on, then after a moment he said, 'Tell you what...why don't you buy a new dress and hat? You have the money you know that. It will make the day that extra bit special.'

'Oh yes, I could, that would be lovely. I think I might have a look for one... Annie would help me choose... if you don't think it would appear extravagant.'

'Beth... whenever have we had the chance to be extravagant. We have never known the meaning of the word.' Arnold chastised her gently, 'You have worked for it, it is your money, now you have a good reason to go and enjoy buying yourself something new for a very special day in more ways than one.'

She looked at him, 'As usual, the voice of reason my brother, you are right. It is a nice feeling to think that I have some money of my own to be able to spend, so, yes, I will have a look around and if I find something I like I can tell you how much I will need.'

'That's good, I am glad you agree. We have waited so long Beth to emerge out of those long, dark days and put it all behind us mentally. I think we are now both ready to move on as individuals with people we love. We both have a small amount saved which will let us do that so really at the moment things couldn't be better.'

'Hmm... have you told Adelaide anything about our home life?' Beth asked, the conversation turning serious again.

'No apart from father being lost at sea… I haven't gone into detail yet about what happened afterwards. I have mentioned that we have a half-sister and that we live with them, but have not expanded on it further,' he sighed. 'Adelaide is shrewd enough to pick up that there is something amiss somewhere and has said when I want to tell her all of it she will understand, that is why it has been so nice being part of their family. Even though it has only happened a couple of times I can see how family life should be. Have you said anything to Owen?'

'Briefly… I have told him that we are very close and the reasons why… that we have nothing in common with the other two at home, but like you not all the grisly details. I think he also has issues family wise. He did say he would tell me one day, like you with Adelaide I suppose. There is an underlying sadness within him no doubt.'

'Well it will probably bring you closer if there are issues on both sides and no doubt they will all be worked through in time, together, which is how it should be. I tried to explain to Adelaide that I didn't want her family to form their opinion of me based on our mother's actions or her non actions as the case may be.'

'From what you have told me about her Arnold she sounds a very sympathetic lady… look at her helping you to choose something for me in Blackpool, she didn't have to but did it willingly from her heart. I am so looking forward to meeting her next weekend.'

'Yes and she you. Oh well here we are again… the warm welcome of home… I would like to have been a fly on the wall this weekend with me not being here and you out on both days. I bet the curiosity is killing them.'

Beth laughed, 'Yes probably… not that they will ask. I wouldn't tell them anyway… our lives have nothing to do with them… so better they don't know anything.'

'It is more likely to drive them mad. She will be worried about her money, especially with me being away. Who cares… Beth we have paid our way for years so I don't care one jot. Come on let's go in and have a cup of tea before bedtime. I doubt if they will be up fretting about us.'

They entered the silent house. Beth made the tea and they ended their weekend quietly together discussing the highlights of their weekend, happy for each other and looking forward to the next one.

They left for work the next morning as usual and closed the door of the quiet house. As they walked, the conversation turned to their Blackpool trip the following Sunday. 'I shall go and organise the train tickets at some point this week. Shall I get Owen's ticket as well at the same time?' he asked.

'You might as well... what time will we be going?'

'The first train is around seven thirty. Adelaide's train arrives ten minutes after ours and she will leave fifteen minutes before our last train back which I am pleased about as I can see her safely on the train then she won't be hanging around on the station on her own.'

'Good timing then,' replied Beth nodding to him. Changing the subject she said, 'I have decided I will ask Annie to come with me to look for a new dress this week, I think she would be disappointed if I didn't.'

'Yes I think you are right she would be. By the time Saturday arrives she will be very excited for you, it is a good friend that can be genuinely happy for you.'

'Yes she is a good friend... and a kind one. I can't imagine she would think ill of anyone.'

Leaving Beth at the usual place Arnold continued his way to the newspaper, Adelaide occupied his thoughts as he walked. The weekend had been just what he had hoped for and his spirits were high when he saw Thomas approaching their mutual workplace from the other direction.

'Good morning Arnold, you are looking in the pink again... good weekend I assume?'

'The best... ' Arnold answered his friend. 'Just the best... come on let's get to it and clock in... I'll tell you all about it later.'

Annie was thrilled when Beth asked if she would help her find a new dress and hat for the coming weekend. 'Ooooh I would love to... it will be fun having a good look around in proper shops instead of the pop shop,' she laughed. 'Did you hear that Mr Newbould, we're going shopping for a new dress for Beth, seeing that it is going to be a special weekend.'

As usual their good humoured employer joined in the repartee, 'Well if that is the case I must be paying you too much. New dresses hey... what next... I don't know.'

Beth smiled at him recognising that he was joking. Annie wasn't too sure at first but then relaxed when she noticed that they were both laughing in her direction.

'Right, Annie, bread is ready for display,' said Beth bringing the laughter to an end.

Sybil appeared at the door with Elizabeth and Theresa. 'Morning all,' called the sisters, 'see you later,' and continued on to their workplace. Sybil took her coat off to make ready for the day's work to start.

For Beth the days passed quickly; she and Annie had spent time together out of their working hours during the week and she had succeeded in her quest to find a new dress. It was pale primrose yellow with a white belt that accentuated her waist and being cut on the bias gave out to a full hem line finishing mid-calf. Her new hat was just a shade darker with the brim edged in white in the new style designed to be wore at a jaunty angle. It looked fresh and stylish, the colour complimented her, it was ideal for a trip to the coast without being over fussy.

Annie was thrilled for her. 'Beth it looks lovely, so stylish and elegant... ' and as they left the shop she added, 'Thank you for letting me come with you to choose it. I can imagine you there now with Owen and meeting Arnold's lady. I shall be thinking about you all day'

As they walked Beth smiled at her friend and gave her a hug, 'And thank you Annie for coming with me. What would I do without you as my friend. Are you and Georgie going out on Saturday night?'

'Yes we just thought we would go to the pictures with you and Owen not going to the dance this weekend. It will be nice just to be on our own and enjoy being together... not that we don't enjoy being with you and Owen, ' she added quickly.

'No I didn't think that. It will be nice for the pair of you just to do exactly what you want to do without having to please anyone else. We all enjoy being together but it is important to have some time on your own as well. I am sure you will both have a lovely weekend.'

'Tell me all the arrangements for your trip,' said Annie excitedly.

'Well... Arnold and I are meeting Owen on Saturday afternoon after work and for Owen to pay Arnold for the train ticket. We shall no doubt go for a drink first then for something to eat. Arnold's idea really. He has only met Owen briefly when he has taken us to the dance so he thought it would be a good time to spend a few hours together before we all go to Blackpool. I am pleased that they will have some time chatting and getting to know each other.'

'Must be nice to have an older brother that is always thinking about you,' said Annie wistfully. 'When do you meet his lady?'

'Sunday morning... her train arrives just after ours, he wanted to be there when she arrives.'

'Are you nervous about meeting her?'

'No... knowing my brother as I do Annie I think, in fact I would say I know, she will be very nice. He deserves to be happy, he has taken care of me for as long as I can remember. It is about time he started just thinking about himself, leading his own life and finding happiness. From what he has told me about her I think he might have just done that.'

'Like you and Owen then?'

Beth laughed, 'Yes... hopefully... like you and Georgie. It's a good place we are all in at the moment, Annie... let's hope it lasts with no worries,' she said looking at her friend, pulling her closer to her as they walked back to the bakery.

'Did you say you were leaving your dress and hat at work,' asked Annie.

'I am... if I walk into the house with these you can bet that inquisitive eyes will not let it rest until they know what is in the bag, best they go home with me after work Saturday lunchtime.'

'Must be weird to live in a house with people who are your family but aren't really because you don't have anything to do with them. Don't you ever talk to them?' asked Annie.

'No... there is nothing to say to them. We have nothing in common and as far as being family, she is a mother in name only. Arnold and I are the only family we two have. It has been that way since we were young children... you have no idea'

'Do they know about Owen or Arnold's lady and your trip?'

'No... Annie they don't. It is not worth the hassle. They only care about themselves; as long as we put our wages on the table every week they are not interested in anything else. '

Annie sighed, 'Beth I'm sorry... here I am babbling on like a fool and asking all these question... it must be very painful.'

'No it's not actually, not now, we did have some very dark times when we were younger but that is all in the past now. We are stronger for it and I now have you and Owen in my life and I love you both dearly. I don't need them they are two very selfish individuals... let's change the subject.'

'Yes... well then... are you going to show Mr Newbould your new dress? If you're not can I?' her usual excitement brimming over.

Beth laughed, 'Now Annie, I don't really think he would be interested do you?'

'Well I am going to ask him if he wants to see it anyway. You know he likes to know what we are doing and what we are wearing.'

'No Annie... you think he does, ' and she laughed louder. 'He is such a nice man he certainly wouldn't disappoint you by appearing disinterested.'

'Well I am going to show him anyway, ' she replied refusing to be dispirited as they approached the bakery.

Saturday arrived, Owen had arranged to meet Beth after her shift, they would then meet up with Arnold for the rest of the day.

Sybil was already there when Beth arrived and Elizabeth was standing outside smoking her cigarette waiting for her. 'Good morning Beth... just thought I would wait for you to say I hope you all have a lovely day tomorrow.'

'Well that is very nice of you thank you. Heavens don't be late for work because of me,' said Beth sounding concerned.

'Goodness... don't worry about a little thing like that. Theresa is clocking me in so no problem,' she replied with a throaty chuckle. 'Owen told me it will be a special day for you, in fact both of you... so enjoy it all... the train ride, the ballroom everything. I will be thinking about you... wish I was going.' She laughed as she took Beth's hand and said, 'Enjoy... I am very pleased for you both.'

Smiling back at her and feeling touched she said, 'Thank you Elizabeth... we will.' She watched Owen's sister walk away from the bakery towards her workplace as usual looking totally out of place in the stark factory surroundings.

Owen arrived at the shop just before closing time. Mr Newbould appeared just before the girls left, 'Hello Owen... nice to see you. Now you make sure you look after this young lady tomorrow.'

'You can be sure of that sir... you ladies all ready?'

Beth smiled and gave him the bags to carry holding her new dress and hat together with an extra one holding fresh bread for sandwiches for their journey. She took his arm and turned, 'Bye Mr Newbould see you on Monday.'

'Bye girls... have a good weekend all of you,' and they left him to lock up the shop.

They all walked together until it was time for Sybil to turn for home, then Annie. She hugged Beth and told her to have a lovely time. Beth and Owen responded by telling her to have a good weekend with Georgie 'and don't stand for any nonsense from him,' said Owen laughing before she left them.

They walked at ease through the main shopping area to where they were to meet Arnold. He laughed when he saw them approaching, kissed Beth and told Owen, 'Well... carrying all the bags already are we Owen... looks like you are a man spoken for.'

'No problem Arnold... and from what I hear you are going in the same direction mate so don't speak too soon.' They shook hands heartily and laughed at each other.

Once again Beth linked arms with both of them and said, 'So... where are we going?'

'Let's go for some lunch first then we can decide later,' said Arnold. 'I need to buy a small present for Adelaide which I thought you could help me with because I am running out of ideas.'

Beth smiled. 'Of course I will, let me think awhile. Let's go then... lunch it is.'

They all chatted easily over lunch about their respective week at work and how they were all looking forward to their trip the following morning. Arnold took the opportunity to have a serious word with Owen when Beth was away from the table.

'While Beth is away from the table and without speaking out of turn Owen, I hope you don't think I am overly-protective of my sister?'

'Not at all Arnold, all I see is a caring brother, and there is nothing wrong with that at all.'

'No there isn't, but basically all I need to know is that you are true in your intentions and I have no need to be concerned for her. If that was the case believe me I would put my life on hold.'

Looking straight back at him Owen replied, 'Arnold, I respect your concern and what I would say to you in truth is that your sister has become my life. You have no need for concern, you have my word. I understand that tomorrow is important to you both, it is the first time she will have seen the sea, which she associates with losing your father. I also understand that she will be meeting the lady that you hope will become your soul mate for the first time, which possibly could take you away from here and her. It is an important day for her in more ways than one and I would like to be there to support her... for both of you actually if you don't think that my presence will be intrusive.'

'Thank you Owen and no I don't think that at all. I have seen a distinct change in my sister for the good. I am not a dictating father substitute; we have come a long way together Beth and I and I am sure she will tell you the full story one day. I am hoping you and I will become good friends, after all we have a common bond.'

'You have no need for worry Arnold. I give you my word,' he said looking him straight in the eye and extending his hand.

Shaking his hand in gratitude Arnold replied, 'Thank you... we will speak no more of it.' They both stood as Beth returned to the table unaware that the conversation had taken place.

'Arnold,' she said as she returned to the table, 'I have been thinking of what you might like to take for Adelaide. I think a nice photograph frame may be appropriate and then you can have a photograph taken together tomorrow and she can place it in the frame as a keepsake.'

'That is a nice thought, yes, we can have a look when we leave here to see if there is anything that catches our or rather your eye.'

'And I thought I would take her some rosewater or lavender soaps, we can have a look for them at the same time.'

I am sure she would appreciate that Beth. It strikes me you are both very similar in nature, which is good with regards to buying gifts for each other,' he smiled. 'Let's me off the hook.'

The shopping trip followed lunch. In good humour they trawled the shops until the gifts for Adelaide were identified and, with Beth's approval, purchased.

The three of them enjoyed their day together and as it was to be an early start in the morning they decided to go for a drink then on for supper. Beth had watched with pleasure as her brother and Owen chatted comfortably with each other. This was the first time they had actually had the opportunity to talk at length, it boded well for their trip the next day.

They parted company and Owen arranged to meet them at the station the following morning. As he walked home he was determined that if his father was still up, in his chair and in one of his belligerent moods he would not be drawn into the usual argument, he would ignore him. He knew the girls would be at the dance and silently hoped that they had been able to leave the house without the usual ranting. He acknowledged it all depended on how much drink the old man had consumed.

Arriving home he found his mother sitting alone, his father was already in his bed. His mother turned as he opened the door, looked at him and smiled 'It's alright son, he is sleeping it off as usual. Don't worry there will be no fighting tonight. Bets told me that you have a special day planned for tomorrow with your lady, so rather than run the risk of the usual fight I thought I would get him out of the way so you can relax. Not fair that he should spoil it for you.'

Owen heard the loud snoring emanating from upstairs and smiled back at his mother. 'Thank you for that... I had taken a deep breath before opening the door... difficult not to react to him when he is off on one.'

'You don't mind Bets telling me do you?' she asked. 'I am very pleased to hear that she is a nice young lady, Sybs says so as well.'

'Of course not, and thank you for being pleased for me. You have very little to be pleased about... every day seems an endless struggle.'

'Yes it is and I don't think it will change in the short term but don't you worry about that. I love all my children Owen, you might not believe it but you being my first born you are very special to me. We have never really had the opportunity to talk about what happened all those years ago, but I am very glad you came back into our lives so that you could get to know your brothers and sisters.'

'Mother... it was at the expense of losing the woman I knew as my mother. I am sorry if that hurts you but none of us can turn the clock back. She was everything to me. I try not to think about the day she died or the day I had to return to you, I had no option. If I had known what a bastard he was I could have ran away I suppose... but where would I have gone? I suppose coming back to you was the lesser of two evils.'

'Yes, I do understand and I truly regret and feel ashamed that it happened the way it did. If it is any consolation I lost my family when I became involved with your father, so I can relate to how you feel in respect of your grandmother.

She was a good woman with a good heart. I chose my path to stay with him and I cannot waste time on regrets. The dye was cast years ago for better or worse Owen; losing my family was upsetting but losing you…well… I hope I will never feel such pain again.' She looked away from him.

'But you choose to defend and make excuses for him mother, does that make you feel better about it?'

'No, I am in the same situation as you my son. Where would I go? I have to stay for my children and as you say the better of two evils. I have my conscience to haunt me for the rest of my life. My children, hopefully, will be my salvation. Don't judge me too harshly Owen, I wouldn't have and didn't plan it to be this way... he wasn't like this when I first met him. I too had my dreams, believe me,' and the tears welled up in her eyes.

'Come here,' he said opening his arms and she moved across the small room to him and into his arms. 'I know you wouldn't have planned it to be this way... nobody would... he blames me not you. I am sorry you all have to live and suffer this way because of me, at least I have the option of getting out one day and hopefully this is the start of a new beginning for me where I can make my own decisions instead of them being made for me.'

'And I wish that for you too my son... for you to find your own happiness after what has happened. It was not your fault any of it. Make your life with the lady of your choice. It pleases me and I understand from your sisters that she is very nice and I hope one day to meet her. I accept that you would not want to bring her here. Tell me what time you are leaving in the morning I know it is important to you and I would like to see you off with my blessing?'

'No... I shall be leaving early around six thirty in the morning. I would hate for him to be disturbed at that time and take it out on you and the younger ones for the rest of the day.'

'Don't worry he will not know. I am glad we have had this chat Owen I feel responsible... I... '

He held his hand up and said, 'Stop now... no more guilt. You have more of your sentence to serve looking after the smaller ones, they need you. At least I can move on and it is enough to know that I have your blessing,' and he kissed her gently on her forehead.

True to her word she was up and had the fire lit before he came downstairs, she smiled at him as he opened the door and picked up a cup for him. 'Don't say a word…I did say I wanted to see you off.' Just as she turned to fill his cup with tea the stair door opened again and Elizabeth appeared.

'What is this?' he asked bemused.

'Just want to make sure that you go and that you don't stand the poor girl up... as if you would,' said Elizabeth laughing. 'We just thought it would be nice to see you off that's all, have you got a problem with it? If so I shall go back to bed.' She looked at him with a raised eyebrow, sat down and lit a cigarette. Their mother placed two cups of tea on the table and watched as her eldest son took his place next to his sister.

'Well that is very nice of you both, thank you,' he smiled.

'Now don't go getting all emotional on me. It is what close families do... allegedly,' she replied taking a sip of tea and sounding a little ironic. 'What time are you leaving?'

'Why is there a brass band waiting around the corner?' he looked at her questioningly.

'Christ no... please... ' she said looking up. 'We don't want the old man waking up just yet... God forbid. Just a couple of waves from your mother and favourite sister that's all so don't go getting all excited,' she answered drawing on her cigarette again and looking at him again.

Sipping his tea and eating the slice of toast his mother had placed in front of him he said, 'Alright Bets... hear what you are saying... not excited... just touched that's all. I didn't know you had it in you,' and a pair of smiling eyes looked back in her direction. 'How was last night did you enjoy it?'

'The usual... nothing to get excited about,' she replied inhaling her cigarette again.

'One day don't worry... it will happen, just be patient... and when it does it will hit you like a ton of bricks, trust me.' He took hold of her hand, 'You are one special lady... sister or not... trust me.'

She looked straight at him, 'I hope so, I can't think about being left here on my own when you have gone. One day I suppose, but on to a more serious matter, she is a lovely lady Owen. I wish you all the best together, you and Beth,' she said squeezing his hand back.

'I know you do and for that I thank you... and for always being there. You are important to me you know that. I know we have had our disagreements but I couldn't wish for a better sister, not bad considering that I didn't know I had one or two or three at one time,' he said laughing and catching hold of his mother's hand at the same time. 'I do think Beth is my future I have to say. Thank you for your good wishes and don't get despondent Bets it will happen,' he said looking at his watch. 'It is time for me to go.'

They watched him walk down the lane and both waved and before he turned the corner Theresa turned to her eldest daughter, 'I feel as if I have lost him again.'

'Yes,' said Elizabeth, 'but for the best of reasons this time. Don't worry you haven't lost him again totally, it is his time to find happiness on his own terms and I reckon he might have just done that... be happy for him.'

Owen arrived at the station a few minutes before Beth and Arnold approached from the opposite direction. He looked and saw her on Arnold's arm waving and smiling at him and so he waved back.

'You look just lovely,' he said to her as they joined him and as Arnold gave her arm over to him he said, 'Good morning Arnold... your sister looks sensational this morning I have to say.' He turned and looked into her eyes and kissing her cheek said, 'Hello you.'

'Hello you... thank you for your compliment kind sir,' she replied smiling.

'The first of many...I am sure,' as he drew her into his arms.

'Well I hope so.'

'You can be sure of it,' he said looking into her eyes then remembering they had an audience. 'Oh...sorry Arnold.'

'No... for heaven's sake don't mind me,' he said. 'I am just hoping there will be a repeat performance at the other end... pray for me.'

They both looked at him and just to reassure him Beth replied, 'Arnold I am sure Adelaide thinks the world of you. If she is not there then we will let you play gooseberry without any recourse. Don't worry I will hold your hand to make up for it... but I am sure there will be no need.'

Once the journey began Beth was riveted to the window pointing each time something caught her eye that delighted her. Owen sat at her side equally as enthralled, especially when the train ran into the long tunnel that took them out of the Yorkshire hills and into Lancashire. The Pennine villages nestling in the countryside being a far cry from the industrial city the three travellers inhabited. The only green areas they were used to were the municipal parks they frequented at weekends.

'I had no idea that people lived in such beautiful countryside,' said Beth sounding wistful. 'I know we are used to the large houses with their big gardens at home but these villages are just so lovely... how nice to be able to look out of the window and all you see is countryside... it looks so peaceful.'

'How the other half live eh Beth?' said Arnold. 'It's a different world alright,' and all three sat looking out of the window lost in their own thoughts as the countryside flashed past.

Arnold kept an eye out for when the Tower would appear on the horizon, its size reduced by the distance, so Beth and Owen could not at this stage appreciate its size.

'Look... there it is,' he said pointing out of the window, 'The Tower... I know it only looks small from here but trust me it is a huge height.'

They watched in silence as the Tower grew larger before the train finally pulled into the station and came to halt. They took the lead from Arnold as he rose. approached the door and opened it. The train had arrived on time so on alighting he went to check the schedules to see if Adelaide's train was on time and the platform number; he wanted to be waiting as her train arrived.

Beth and Owen stood back and waited for him to satisfy himself that everything was as planned. As he returned to them Beth asked, 'Is everything alright Arnold... is her train on time?'

'Yes, she will be with us in fourteen minutes according to the station master... so... I shall just wander over to the other platform to wait, then come back and meet you in the tea room.'

'That will be lovely... go and meet your lady. Join us when you are ready, there is no rush,' she replied and kissed him gently on his cheek. Owen smiled at him and nodded.

He turned and walked away from them towards the bridge that would take him over to the platform where the train from Burnley would arrive.

As they walked towards the tea room Beth not being able to contain herself said, 'I am so excited for him Owen. She sounds a lovely lady; I am excited about meeting her too, I hope she won't be disappointed.'

'Why on earth should she be disappointed... don't be silly... ' he looked at her questioningly. 'You are just as lovely so stop worrying. Knowing Arnold she is bound to be special... just like you'

'Yes, but you are biased,' she said squeezing his arm and laughing.

'Nothing of the sort, you are just paranoid. Come on let's order some tea and wait a while for them to appear.'

The announcement sounded out: 'The next train to arrive at platform six is the ten thirty-one from Bolton calling at Burnley and Lancaster.'

She stepped down from the train and within seconds he was at her side and whisked her off her feet with such force that she had to hold on to her hat. She laughed and he kissed her and she kissed him back with the same enthusiasm.

'I have missed you again,' said Arnold. 'Just let me hold you and look at you for a moment.'

'Yes, I have missed you too. It has been a long week.' She looked round when he finally he released his grip, 'Is Beth here?'

'Of course she is, they are waiting for us in the tea room. she is with Owen... come on they can't wait to meet you,' taking her hand he turned towards the bridge.

They both stood away from the table as the door opened and Arnold led his lady into the tea rooms towards them holding her hand. Beth smiled and walked towards her, opened her arms and greeted her with a kiss on her cheek, Adelaide responded in the same way.

'Finally... it is so lovely to meet you Adelaide. Arnold has told me such a lot about you... all good I would hasten to add.'

'Yes, likewise,' replied Adelaide turning and smiling back at Arnold. 'I have a feeling we will become good friends.'

'I think we will too. I feel as if I already know you. Now, can I introduce you to Owen,' said Beth holding her hand out to include him in the greeting.

'Hello Adelaide... my pleasure,' he kissed her hand gently. 'I am delighted to meet you.'

'Shall we join you for tea and plan our day? said Arnold satisfied that all the introductions had gone off very well. 'Where do you reckon first Owen?'

'Fine on the tea front,' said Owen sounding bemused. 'But you tell us as to the rest of it, this is our first trip. We are in your hands are we not Beth?'

Arnold looked at Beth and read a look of concern in her eyes, 'Of course,' he said. 'I think the promenade first then don't you, to take a long awaited look at the sea.'

She nodded, 'Yes please. There is something we need to do first, then we can go and enjoy ourselves,' she looked at her brother and he nodded.

'Yes and we can buy some flowers on the way don't worry.'

Owen squeezed her hand to give her support and she smiled back at him. 'We are all here to support you don't worry,' he told her.

They left the station after a further pot of tea and general chit chat which enabled Adelaide to find her feet and become comfortable. Walking towards the promenade Beth became quiet. She was holding onto Owen's arm and her grip tightened, 'Are you feeling alright?' he asked.

'Yes... don't worry I am fine. Or rather I will be after what I feel I have to do,' then changing the subject, 'I need to find a florist first.'

'Look... there is a stall over there,' said Owen pointing over to their right. 'Hopefully they should have what you need. You are not to worry if they haven't, we will look elsewhere.'

They walked over to the stall and Beth chose the flowers that pleased her eye. 'I will get these for you,' said Owen taking his wallet out of his inside pocket.

Squeezing his arm Beth said, 'No... please... I have to buy them myself. As much as I appreciate your gesture I need to do this with my own money. He was my father... this is something I have to do to show my respect to him. I will be able to feel that I can move on then after all these years. Don't think I am shutting you out Owen, it is important to me and I need to feel that we do this right... on our terms.'

'Don't worry I understand. All I can say is that I will be here to support you, whatever you need me to do, just ask.' He put his arms around her and cuddled her to him.

'I will don't worry,' she replied looking into his eyes.

She chose her flowers with care... lots of colours and what she hoped her father would like. 'I think that will do,' she finally said to the florist passing the flowers over to her. 'Could you put a red bow around them and make sure... if you can... that they will float in the sea?'

'I most certainly can,' said the florist. 'They are obviously very special... don't worry dear leave it to me.' She turned to the back of the stall and started to arrange each of the blooms that Beth had chosen. When she had finished the arrangement she passed it back to Beth. 'I have placed some forget-me-nots in there as well... just as an extra lovey... I hope that is alright. And don't you worry it will stay afloat for a long, long time.' She took hold of Beth's hand and gave it a squeeze.

Beth took the display, the tears hovered as she thanked her. 'Oh yes, of course it is alright... that is just so lovely. Thank you so much.' She turned to Arnold, 'Look... are these not the loveliest flowers you have ever seen?' He took her arm and agreed that the arranged flowers were something very special.

'Let us go now... it is time after all these years Beth. With Owen's permission... give me your arm.' Arnold looked at Owen, he nodded in reply and he held his arm out for Beth to take as she had done many times over the years.

'Of course,' said Owen, 'and I will escort Adelaide if that is alright Arnold?' Arnold smiled at Adelaide, she acquiesced and they all made their way quietly towards the sea front.

It appeared before Beth realised, a vast expanse of water so great she could never have imagined it. The largest she had ever seen to date was the boating lake within the park back home. For a moment she stopped walking, she was mesmerised and stood in silence not knowing what to say, Arnold felt her freeze.

'Beth... it is alright... don't worry I am here... and so is Owen for you. Let us go on to the pier, we can then throw the flowers into the sea. The tide is going out so it will gently take the flowers and your loving thoughts with it... he will know and feel it.'

She looked at him and smiled. 'Do you think so Arnold, after all this time... how will he know?' She stopped and looked at him with pleading eyes brimming with tears once again.

Quietly he held her close and replied, 'I do and he will. He knows he has always been in our hearts and he will know we are here... come.' Not wishing to make her more upset he turned her and together they walked towards the pier. Adelaide and Owen followed them in silence not wishing to intrude on their personal grief.

Walking down the pier Beth could see the end of it approaching, the wide expanse of blue water surrounding them with the reflection of the sun dancing on it, it looked so beautiful. She sobbed quietly with emotion as they walked on to the end of the wooden pier clutching the flowers as if her life depended on it. Arnold held her hand tightly in support and felt his emotions rise too.

They both knew it was more than a personal need to give and show respect to their father, it was an ache within them that had to be finally laid to rest. It had been a long, long time since he had been part of their lives and their feeling was one of deep sadness that it had taken so long but it had been out of their hands. Beth could hold it no longer and broke down in tears and sobbed uncontrollably and held onto her brother for support.

Adelaide and Owen stopped walking and stood some way back in silence to give them the privacy the occasion merited. As they stood witness, Adelaide felt the tears rise, stinging her eyes and starting to fall down her cheeks in support of the man she loved. Arnold and his sister were both totally overwhelmed by their grief. Owen sensed Adelaide's distress and for a brief moment loving thoughts of his beloved grandmother came to mind as he remembered the day of her funeral and his heart went out to Beth. Blinking back his tears, instinctively he placed a supportive arm around the lady at his side just to give her some comfort in her solitude. Together they too mourned a precious life lost, of a man that although they had never known him, had been instrumental in their future happiness.

As if frozen in time, brother and sister quietly held on to the flowers for a short time, then in unison threw them into the sea and watched the tide gently accept them and slowly start to move them away. Arnold held her close and they whispered the Lord's Prayer together in silence as they watched the flowers continue on their way. After a few minutes he turned and beckoned Owen to join them, Adelaide remained where she was as Owen moved towards them. As Arnold let go of his sister he symbolically gave her keep over to Owen, it was done with such feeling between them that Beth hardly realised what was happening. When she did take her eyes from the slowly disappearing flowers and turned it was Owen's eyes that her sad blue eyes locked with instead of her brothers.

Owen held her gently and kissed her, 'I'm here don't worry... that was beautiful in its simplicity Beth and I am sure your father knows and approves. Are you feeling alright now?' following the trace of her tears down her cheeks with his thumb.

'Yes I am,' she replied looking back at the distant flowers sitting in the water continuing their journey. 'I wonder how far they will travel?' she mused for a moment longer. Owen let her stand lost in her own thoughts and watched them float into the distance and just held her close. Neither spoke until she turned after a while and said, 'I will be fine now... it needed to be done and now I finally feel he will be at rest after such a long time. Thank you so much for being here with me,' she smiled and moved closer to him. She turned to see Arnold embracing his chosen lady; she realised they could now both move on with their lives and have the strength to face whatever the future held for the four of them.

Adelaide and Arnold joined them again and together the four watched as the floral tribute faded into the far distance, not until they had entirely disappeared from view did Beth move.

'It's time to go now I think... time to move on... don't you?' she said to Arnold at the same time holding on to Owen's hand.

'If you do,' replied her brother with Adelaide standing close to his side.

'Yes I do,' Beth said and kissed him gently on his cheek, 'I will always love you.'

'And I you... ' his eyes smiled at her and he kissed her hand.

She smiled back at him. 'Thank you for today... and Adelaide and Owen... thank you too, it has been very special having you both here.' She turned for one last look in the direction of the floating flowers and said, 'Rest in Peace father. I now think it is time to leave here and go and enjoy the rest of our day.' They turned and headed back towards the promenade all happy in the knowledge that she had finally laid all her ghosts to rest.

Taking their time, both couples walked arm in arm together along the sea front to the far tram terminus then took the ride back on the open-top bus towards the Tower. Beth and Adelaide chatted comfortably in each other's company. They decided they would have a leisurely lunch in one of the tea rooms in the Tower, then take a look at the ballroom that Beth had heard so much about before taking the lift to the viewing balcony at the top to look out over the sea, town and countryside laid out before them.

Arnold and Owen had had a brief chat, unbeknown to Beth and Adelaide about what they would like to do; Arnold had said he would like to spend some private time with his lady and he hoped that they wouldn't be offended. Owen had smiled and said, 'Hey that's fine I was thinking of taking Beth for a couple of dances at the tea dance that starts at five o'clock if that is alright with you? And take her for a look at the dress shop there where you bought her the blue dress.'

'Perfect,' said Arnold. 'I just thought it would be nice to take a browse around Stanley Park together, then we could all meet up for a drink later before Adelaide's train leaves.'

Owen nodded in agreement. 'That will be great... everybody is pleased then. Thank you for letting me come with you today Arnold, I feel very privileged, it has been a very special day.'

`Yes it has and it is not finished yet.' They turned back to their ladies who were merrily chatting together discussing all manner of things like old friends.

They walked past the sideshows resisting temptation to enter no matter how the barkers cajoled them with amazing facts regarding the freaks inside, real or imaginary. They laughed at the people screaming on the rides in the pleasure beach choosing the leisurely rides rather than the fast ones, visited the ice cream parlour where Adelaide and Arnold had first met and generally enjoyed the atmosphere which Blackpool always promised its visitors.

They had browsed the gift and souvenir shops along the promenade and Arnold had discreetly purchased for Adelaide a bracelet made up of semi-precious gems that he intended to surprise her with when they were alone in Stanley Park. Walking back towards the Tower he told her that they were parting company with Beth and Owen for a couple of hours and that they would meet up with them again later. She smiled, 'Thank you for that,' and squeezed his hand.

They left each other at the Tower and Beth was surprised and delighted when Owen told her they were going to the tea-dance in the ballroom.

'That's wonderful... I can't believe it... thank you.'

'Well I think you deserve it... you only had a quick look. I just thought it would be nice to have a dance as well, but before we do there is somewhere else I want us to go first.'

He took her hand and approached the shop where Arnold had purchased her blue dress. The shop was a dancing emporium with everything from shoes to accessories that matched the wonderful array of dresses, every colour and style imaginable on display.

Beth was speechless and moved among the racks looking in wonder at the choice displayed around her. 'Now... would you like the lady to help you choose one or... as I suspect... would you like to choose your own?'

'No I can't... Owen I don't need another dress for dancing. This is a new one that I bought for today... I can use,' but he stopped her short.

'Beth, this is a very special day and I would like to make it a little more special by taking you dancing in a new dress. I insist... my gift for my lady,' he stopped her protestations with a kiss. 'Now... do I call the sales lady or are we going to do this together?'

She laughed, 'Together... if you insist.'

'I do... come on... '

They worked their way through the racks and chose three for Beth to try on to see which they preferred. When she emerged from the changing room to show him, he had just smiled each time she appeared and said that he would comment only when he had seen all three.

'It has got to be the blue one again Beth,' he finally said when she had tried them all on.

'But my other is blue,' she protested.

'Yes, but a totally different shade and style. Blue suits you... it is definitely your colour... my lady in blue,' he said quietly. 'Looks stunning,' and he nodded to the sales lady.

Beth returned to the changing room and was quickly followed by the sales lady carrying a pair of dancing shoes the same colour. 'Your gentleman has asked if you can leave the dress you were wearing here so that you can go to the tea dance in your new one,' and she smiled widely, 'and here are the shoes that match. I have guessed your size if they are not right do tell me.'

'Thank you... that is very kind of you.'

Emerging from the changing room again wearing the matching outfit she took Owen's arm, 'What can I say?'

'Not a word... let us go... no time to waste,' and as they left the shop Owen turned back to the sales assistant, 'Thank you again for all your help. We will see you later,' she nodded and watched them leave with a smile.

'Yes... go and enjoy the dance... ' and to Beth 'you look lovely.'

They entered the ballroom to the strains of a waltz and she laughed as Owen quickened his pace towards the dance floor, 'Come on... not a moment to lose.'

'You don't think this outfit is too much do you, people are staring,' she said a little cautious as they waltzed, aware of the glances coming their way.

'Not one bit. Look at the surroundings Beth... they are magnificent... you fit in perfectly. If anything the stares are because they can't believe anyone could look so lovely.'

They danced through the programme with elegant timing, lost in their own world, few words being spoken; they had no need for conversation.

Owen reluctantly kept his eye on the time, conscious that they had to meet up with Arnold again and that Beth had to return to the shop to change.

Time for Beth stood still, lost in a world of music, dancing and glamour. 'I don't want today to end,' she whispered into his ear as the music ceased.

'No my love... and neither do I, but we have to meet Arnold in around thirty minutes so unfortunately I am sorry to say, I think the next dance will have to be our last one,' and he nuzzled her ear back.

'Oh dear is it that time already... Owen... this has just been heaven, the ballroom, my dress, the shoes... everything. I love it... all of it... it has been wonderful. How can I ever thank you for coming with me today?'

He took her face in his hands, 'There is one way... by becoming my wife... will you marry me Beth... please say you will?'

The music started again, she looked at him, 'Yes... I will.' He spun her round and they danced around the floor oblivious to the other dancers locked in each other's arms.

Elizabeth

She stood leaning against the door next to her mother and drew on her cigarette as they both watched Owen walk down the lane on his way to meet his lady at the railway station for their day trip to Blackpool. Watching him she thought to herself, if he hadn't been her elder brother she would have been attracted to him, the thought brought a wry smile to her lips.

Her mother brought her back to earth. 'From what you have said Bets she is a nice lady, ' her mother said wistfully as she watched him walk away from them.

'Yes... she is... I reckon they will be fine. She loves him... you can see that, and he will treat her right. He won't be an old chip off the block like that old bastard upstairs.'

Before he turned the corner he waved back to them. Elizabeth blew him a kiss and ground the spent cigarette into the pavement and turned back into the house. 'I hope he has a great time.'

'Fancy... Blackpool of all places... how nice. Not that I would know but I would imagine if that is where they are going it will be nice,' said her mother closing the door behind them. 'Bets... do you think he will introduce me to her one day?' she asked with a note of trepidation in her voice.

'Probably... he has got to come clean about his family one day I suppose. Beth knows me, Theresa and Sybs and is relaxed, so there would be no problem with anyone else apart from... ' and her eyes moved upwards. 'I can't imagine him being in a rush to introduce her to the old man if at all... can you? Anyway enough of him, I am off back to bed while it's quiet and he is still out of the way,' yawning she opened the stair door and disappeared. Her mother nodded and sat back down with a cup of tea. The house was quiet as they were all still asleep 'the calm before the usual storm' was the thought that went through her mind.

She smiled to herself as Owen, her first born came into her thoughts. She readily acknowledged he had not had the happiest of times since his grandmother had died and he had had to return to them. He had overcome the bullying and constant harassment by his father, he had managed to fight his way back and remain his own man, a good man. If Owen could do it the rest of her children could too, and now he had met a nice lady who he could make a good life with. Theresa nodded to herself and smiled at the possibility.

Her thoughts then drifted to Elizabeth, the beauty of the family without doubt. She had enough drive and determination for all of them, she definitely wouldn't settle for a lifestyle that mirrored her mother's and hopefully the other girls would follow suit. Her confidence shone through in everything she did, the way she presented and held herself and her capacity to climb onto a stage and sing at the dances; although her mother had never seen her she knew from her other daughters that she had a talent. She could be fiery, but that probably made her more attractive and a challenge to any man. She wouldn't be downtrodden like her mother, the way she argued back with her father proved that, she would be nobody's fool she had been that way since being a child.

Theresa had fallen pregnant quickly again with Elizabeth after Owen had been taken, she chose to keep it to herself and said nothing. She had secured a position in service and kept some of the pittance she received to one side as she knew how Owen Snr would react to a second child. Losing their first born to his mother had had no impact on him at all, it was a problem solved as far as he was concerned; he had told her the child was not to be mentioned again. She was quite a few months into her pregnancy before it had become obvious. Owen Snr had accused her of carrying another man's child one night in a drunken rage. Despite her protestations he persisted, which resulted in Theresa picking up the poker to defend herself and protect her unborn child, she faced him down for the first time since they had met.

'I will have this baby and no-one will take it from me this time so you had better get used to the idea.' She had spat at him; he had noticed the resolve in her eyes and turned towards the door to go back to the alehouse. She had placed protective hands over her stomach until he had left, then turned to the sink and retched out of fear until hot tears streamed down her face and she had fallen on to her knees still with her arms wrapped round herself.

When Elizabeth had been born she was alone apart from her neighbour who acted as midwife in the vicinity. She had agreed to help her during the confinement when the time came. She gave birth to her first daughter and cried as she placed the new born baby to her breast to comfort her. Owen Snr had arrived home after the birth, looked at the child sleeping in a drawer that had been made into a makeshift crib, and said 'Keep it away from me... whatever it is,' and gone back out to his usual haunt. Theresa watched him go without answering, silent tears once again running down her face.

Elizabeth was a good baby and beautiful, she laughed and chuckled at her mother but if her father entered the house she would become quiet and watchful even at this young age. It was as if she had taken on the warning from within the womb with regard to her father; he gave her no credence whatsoever, her mother never let her out of her sight.

The following months after the birth of her daughter Theresa tried to keep her husband at arm's length fearing yet another pregnancy. She would make sure his beer was to hand if he requested more in the house, always taking her daughter with her to fetch him his jug. Her thought pattern being that the more he had to drink the quicker he would have to sleep it off; and in the main it was a strategy that worked until he would fight her to have his own way. When Elizabeth was nine months old she realised she was pregnant again and wept in despair. They were still not married, not that that would have given her any warmth or any security, her fate she felt had been sealed years ago.

The drums of war had sounded in 1914 and the country had been dragged into conflict with Germany when Archduke Ferdinand had been assassinated in Austria. Immobilisation had started with a vengeance and Kitchener's war cry to arms had reverberated around the land with volunteers rushing to enlist without a second thought, such was the fervour.

Owen Snr in this instance did the same as his fellow countryman and had volunteered. He was despatched to the Guards and wore his uniform with pride until the reality kicked in and he realised it was a life of strict discipline, orders and hardship especially when he was posted abroad and found himself involved in the first battle for Ypres in the early days of the war.

The months rolled by and as before, with her previous pregnancy with Elizabeth, she said nothing until it became evident. The same neighbour came to assist when she went into labour and once again she gave birth to another baby girl she named Theresa. Elizabeth was present in the room when she gave birth, her father was still away fighting for his country.

Their life had fallen into a quiet routine at home now that Owen Snr was away at war. She could claim her benefit and use it to pay their rent; that at least gave her security regarding the roof over their heads. Although she worried about him when she read the headlines on the newspaper placards she had peace of mind that there was no conflict within the house. That feeling evaporated one dark day some months later when the telegram boy knocked on her door just as dusk was falling.

She had nervously taken the telegram from him and her hands had shaken with fear as she opened it. It read that he had been wounded and transferred to a military hospital but gave no further details regarding his injuries. She had sat for some time re-reading the telegram before she decided what she should do. Elizabeth felt her mother's anguish and had stood at her side in silence until her mother told her, 'Come Elizabeth we must go.'

Holding her mother's hand they had walked some way before arriving at a house that was unknown to her. She sensed her mother's hesitation before she had knocked on the door. It was opened by a lady who had asked what they wanted, the question had not been asked kindly. Elizabeth kept hold of her mother's hand and looked forward into the house; an older lady had appeared, looked at Theresa, and instructed the other lady to let them in.

Theresa ushered Elizabeth through the door and as they entered she immediately sensed the warmth of the place. It was a pleasant feeling far removed from their house where she lived with her mother and younger sister. Her eyes were all encompassing as they passed through the hallway into a warm kitchen. There was a boy sitting by the fire looking at a book, he stood as they came through the door and looked at the older lady enquiringly.

The older lady had given them warm food while she and their mother had talked quietly; the boy had watched them eat but had said nothing. Elizabeth finished her food, reassured her younger sister that everything was alright then smiled across at the boy and he had smiled back.

Their mother finished speaking with the older lady then told them it was now time to go home; she had been given a basket full of bread and potatoes. The girls, not wanting to leave the warmth of the kitchen, reluctantly turned to their mother and walked back towards the hall.

The older lady and the boy came to the door with them and as they approached the road Elizabeth turned and waved and the boy smiled again and waved back. The door was then closed and they were enveloped by the cold, dark night once more.

They walked in silence until it was broken by Elizabeth. 'That was a nice house... and a nice lady... and who is that boy?' she asked her mother as they walked.

Her mother sighed heavily and blinking back the tears answered, 'Who are they? The nice lady is your grandmother and the lovely boy... he is your brother.' Elizabeth caught the emotion in her mother's voice and instinct told her not to question it; they continued home without any further conversation.

They went once more to the house a few weeks later, Owen had not been there and Elizabeth had been disappointed. When they left she had said, 'Thank you,' to the lady and smiled. The lady had patted her head and smiled back at her, Elizabeth thought how kind she looked.

She had quietly hoped that the visits would become a regular thing but they did not go again. Instead, one day there was a flurry of activity, furniture was delivered to the house and their mother appeared to be on edge; she was constantly looking through the window and straightening the house until one afternoon there was a loud knock at the door. Elizabeth watched her mother take a deep breath, straighten her hair and hesitantly opened the door.

She saw the man at the door. He looked coldly at her mother then barked an instruction to the man behind him to help him through the door. As he banged the door open out of her mother's hand with his crutch and entered the house, instinct made her catch hold of her younger sister's hand. Both girls looked at the man in silence, he ignored them; her younger sister looked at her with a flash of fear in her eyes. 'It's alright... don't say anything... let's go over here,' and she led her over to the corner of the room which was out of his eye line. They sat quietly together and watched.

Her mother had fussed as the orderly had attempted to help him onto the chaise longue that had been delivered for him. 'Leave me be woman... go and fetch me my jug... now!'

Their mother looked flustered. She had turned and beckoned the girls to come with her and they had all walked down to the local alehouse. 'Who is that man?' asked young Theresa.

'Your father... ' her mother had replied. 'When we go back just sit quietly the pair of you or... go out to play out of the way.'

As they returned to the house Elizabeth had suggested to her sister that they stay outside to play; their mother re-entered the house alone.

'I don't like that man... Lizbet,' Theresa said.

'Just stay close to me and you will be alright... don't say anything to him.'

'No, I won't,' came the reply.

They saw their mother appear once more with the empty jug in her hand and go back down the lane in the direction of the alehouse again. When she came back she called them over and said, 'Just stay out here and I will come and fetch you when it is time to come in.'

'I'm hungry,' said her youngest daughter.

'I will pass you something out to eat don't worry. It shouldn't be long before you can come back in... just stand by the door.'

'He won't come out will he?' asked Elizabeth cautiously.

'No, don't worry he won't,' replied her mother. 'He will be asleep soon,' and looking resigned she had gone back into the house. True to her word the door opened again and she passed out bread and jam to her daughters to stave off their hunger, and forcing a smile had said, 'Don't be frightened... it's going to be alright.' She prayed she was right.

She had closed the door again and turned to look at him. A feeling of resentment swept through her; from arriving at the door he had not said a civil word to her or the children. He was filling his glass again and muttering to himself, lost in his own thoughts. Rather than force an argument she chose to say nothing. She hoped that he would sate his appetite for ale and soon fall asleep on the chaise longue so that in the short term she and her daughters could regain the peace they had become used to.

As the weeks passed a new routine fell into place. Theresa became subservient to him to keep the peace; her daughters understood and practically became mute when they were in the same room as him. When he was sleeping his ale off they all huddled together and spoke quietly, Theresa constantly trying to keep her daughters at ease. At the same time she would keep her eye on the sleeping form fearing he would wake and start yet another argument.

Elizabeth was now at school, initially she had been concerned at leaving her younger sister when their father had returned home, but their mother had told her that it would not be long before Theresa would be going with her and just to be patient. During school hours she kept her eye on the clock knowing what time she would be able to go home and lost herself in her lessons to make the time pass more quickly. When the school bell rang and she returned home she would always find young Theresa sitting on the step waiting for her.

Their mother had received word from Eleanor that she and young Owen would visit and pay their respects to her son: the day before their arrival she told both Owen Snr. and her daughters the news. Owen Snr had listened to her without comment, his dark eyes brooding as usual. Elizabeth had smiled and when they were out of earshot of their father had said excitedly, 'Isn't that nice... they are coming here to see us... tomorrow will be a good day, it is something to look forward to.'

'I hope so,' replied her younger sister.

She had sat on the step waiting for their arrival and inwardly was excited about seeing her brother again. She saw them turn the corner and ran in and shouted to her mother, 'They are here... they are coming,' then went to stand with her sister to wait in silence.

The visitors were greeted by their mother, the sisters watched quietly as their paternal grandmother came through the door into the squalid house. Elizabeth thought she looked like a proper lady, their brother was standing by her side looking nervous, he quickly glanced at Elizabeth but did not smile. The silence had been abruptly broken by their father, 'I am your father boy... you have come here to show some respect... yes?'

She had stood with bated breath as her brother had replied ,'Yes sir.' His face was taught with fear as he looked into a pair of dark, sullen eyes; his grandmother had hold of his hand for support, a tense silence fell. Theresa felt the fear in her son and broke the moment by moving forward to accept the basket that Eleanor was holding. As she placed herself between father and son she turned and indicated to the girls to accept the gifts from their brother. They quickly moved towards him and with a look of relief he handed over the packets of sweets at the same time smiling at his sisters.

'Thank you,' said Elizabeth looking at him and beaming.

'Thank you,' said Theresa following her older sister's lead.

The only sound from their father was a belch as he drained yet another glass of beer.

Elizabeth could see her grandmother was uncomfortable in the house and wasn't surprised to hear her say, 'Come along Owen... it is now time to go,' and they both turned towards the door. Theresa turned with them and Elizabeth and her sister followed them out into the lane. The siblings stood together as their mother and grandmother spoke in hushed tones to one side of them for a few minutes. Young Theresa searched for her older sister's hand again as they all became aware that their mother was crying. Owen stayed with them not knowing quite what to do.

Eleanor turned away from their mother, her face filled with pity. 'Owen... come,' she said quietly as she set off back down the lane. Before he turned to follow her he quickly glanced at the girls, then back at his mother for just a moment, then turned and followed his grandmother away from the house.

Elizabeth followed them to the corner and watched them walk out of view. She gripped on to the packet of sweets and felt a pang of disappointment that neither of them had turned round before they had disappeared.

Their mother composed herself before she went back into the house with her youngest daughter. When Elizabeth returned, she took hold of her sister's hand again and moved away from their father, back into the corner. He was asleep in his red chair oblivious to anyone else, dribbling down his jacket in his drunken stupor. The children sat quietly and watched their mother empty the basket that had been brought earlier.

'We will eat tonight Theresa,' she said whispering into her sister's ear, 'so save your sweets for another time.'

The girls continued to sleep with their mother upstairs, their father remained downstairs and alternated between the chaise longue that he used at night to sleep and the grubby, large, red velvet chair. Their mother would take them upstairs out of the way to sleep and remain with them until they would wake to the sound of him banging his crutch on the table. That was her signal that he wanted her and without delay she would descend the stairs to take care of his needs. There had been occasions when Elizabeth had called down the stairs to her mother after muffled shouts of protest could be heard and the sounds of what sounded like a scuffle. Her mother would call back to her to stay where she was and she would be back with them shortly. Elizabeth did as she was told and did not question further when her mother would reappear back in the bedroom her clothes and hair dishevelled and her face tear stained.

Both girls were at school now. Elizabeth had taken her sister on the first day of term and made sure she was settled in her class before she went on to her own. She was relieved that her younger sister was away from the house with her during school hours, they never knew what the atmosphere would be like until they arrived back. Their mother had told Elizabeth if the door was ever locked when they returned not to worry, just remain close outside and she would open the door when it was alright for them to come back in. Once again Elizabeth just nodded and did not question the instruction.

One day when they returned, their mother was waiting for them, their father was out. They presumed he would be in the alehouse now that his mobility had returned albeit with his false leg and crutch, there would be nowhere else he would be.

'Come... I have something to tell you both,' and she placed the slices of bread and a piece of cheese out for them to eat.

The girls looked at her, 'Are we going to our grandmothers again?' asked Elizabeth chewing on her bread and looking excited.

Their mother hesitated, 'No,' she replied averting her eyes from them, 'Another baby is coming... so you will have another sister or brother soon.' She regained her composure and smiled at them, both girls received the news without any emotion whatsoever.

'Let's go out to play Theresa,' said Elizabeth taking her bread and cheese with her; her sister followed. Their mother watched them go and sat and wept yet again. The subject wasn't discussed again until the new baby decided to arrive before daylight one morning and Elizabeth was woken by her mother and told to go and fetch the neighbour that she had used before to help her. 'Quickly... she is expecting you, get dressed and take Theresa with you. When you come back don't make any noise just sit on the stairs out of the way. Get a piece of bread... when it is time go to school leave as normal... but you must be quiet.'

She watched the girls holding hands and move quietly down the stairs so as not to wake him. Elizabeth looked through the stair door, he was laid on his side facing the wall. She decided to get the bread first as it was quiet to make sure they ate, then gently opened the door to get out of the house. Once outside she quietly closed the door again and they both ran down the lane to get help for their mother.

They returned with the neighbour and went straight upstairs to their mother, their father had not moved. Theresa had organised the bedroom as much as she could, the leather strap to grip onto was strapped to the brass bedhead and she had placed the thick rag to bite into within hand's reach; the drawer was ready again for the new arrival. The girls stayed with their mother until she felt things were moving on too quickly, she kissed both of them and said, 'Go now, it is time for you to walk to school, when you come home the new baby will be here. Try not to make a noise when you leave.'

The neighbour watched them go and looked at Theresa. 'Is he being difficult again? I noticed him dead to the world when we came in... it must be nice.'

'Difficult,' Theresa laughed, 'is that the word for it these days?'

'I was trying to be kind,' she laughed back. 'Anyway let's have a look how we are doing. You have two good girls there Theresa, are we trying for another... what's he want?'

'What's he want? Nothing to do with him love... any of it,' she said moving to get a little more comfortable. 'I make them on my own you know,' letting a little sarcasm creep into her tone.

'Like we all do, ' replied the midwife laughing. 'Well, looking at you girl... I don't think you are going to be too long.'

'I hope not I would like it to be all over before the girls get back from school. He'll not be happy me being up here.'

'Well, he will just have to fend for himself then won't he, it won't not kill him.'

'He'll not see it like that,' Theresa replied wincing at one of the contractions.

'I have seen them all Theresa love, the ones that run out, the ones that faint, don't worry, I'll sort him,' she replied giving a wry laugh. 'You just attend to what is important... there is a new life beginning here, poor little sod.'

The contractions were coming every few minutes and Theresa was biting down on the rag for relief so as not to make a noise, when all of a sudden the familiar banging of the crutch started.

'There, there lovey, come on you are doing alright... what's that noise?'

She removed the rag, 'It's him... I have to go down and sort his needs,' she replied.

'Not this morning you don't. I'll sort him,' she turned away and went down the stairs.

She opened the stair door into the room he looked up and glowered, 'What are you doing here?'

'Well, it usually has to do with a new baby arriving,' she retorted.

'Get out woman, you'll get no money from me... it's not mine... none of them are,' he shouted. 'Tell her to come down here and help me.'

'She is not in any fit state, so for once you will have to do it yourself this morning. We have more important things to do,' and coming closer to him she stared him in the eyes and said, 'Oh... and I understand it's another virgin birth... congratulations.' She passed him his leg, looked nonplussed, then turned on her heel and disappeared back up the stairs.

Theresa laid back on the bed with sweat pouring down her face. She wasn't sure whether it was the pain from her labour or fear from just hearing him shouting. She instinctively touched her swollen stomach, 'Come on baby... come on... ' When the midwife came back into the bedroom she said, 'I heard him shouting at you... are you alright?'

'Oh don't you worry about me. I have told you I have dealt with them all... bastards the majority... it is never anything to do with them. Anyway, I have told him he will have to sort himself out this morning, we have more important matters to attend to... so relax and stop worrying. You will stress the baby and we don't want any complications... we have enough on without him downstairs showing off.' She smiled at her patient and took hold of her hand gently. Not too long afterwards they had heard the downstairs outside door bang loudly.

'Well that's one problem sorted girl... just the three of us now. Come on, you are doing nicely,' and she wiped her patient's brow.

The birth went well, another little girl was delivered and entered the world with a hearty cry. 'There you are lovey... ten fingers... ten toes... all there like they should be... she's lovely.' She cut the cord and wrapped the child in the pieces of torn sheets that had been placed in the drawer ready. She handed the baby back to Theresa, who placed the newborn to her breast.

'Another little girl,' said Theresa a little tearful, 'another one to carry the burden of childbirth through her life.'

'Well... you never know things might be better for our kids. We can always live in hope. At least your girls were out of the way... no point seeing their mother in pain... the memory stays with them.' Then, changing the subject, 'I will call back later don't worry, you have time to have a nap before the girls come back and baby should be sleep. Is there anything for them to eat downstairs?' she asked.

'The usual... pieces of bread... Elizabeth knows what to do. When they come in from school I will keep them up here with me out of the way. No way of knowing how bad he is going to be when he gets back.'

'I will see you later. Just to make sure everything is as it should be,' said the neighbour and she picked up her shilling, the fee for the delivery, that was waiting on the chest of drawers.

The girls came in from school cautiously, saw he wasn't in his chair and ran up the stairs to their mother. She had been listening for them and as they came into the bedroom she indicated to them to look in the drawer on the floor next to her, 'Look... you have a sister.'

Elizabeth just looked at the baby but said nothing, her sister Theresa took hold of the tiny hand and asked, 'What will we call her?'

'I think we will call her Sybil,' said her mother.

'That's a nice name,' her youngest daughter replied.

'Why has she come here?' asked Elizabeth looking directly at her mother, 'there is nothing for her to eat.'

Her mother looked back at Elizabeth and thought for moment, holding her gaze she replied, 'Well... I think she was looking for some sisters and decided she would like to come here and live with you. She won't be eating much for a long time yet... now do you both want to go out to play or stay up here with me and Sybil?'

'I want to stay with Sybil,' piped up Theresa. 'Isn't she tiny... look at her little hands?'

'Yes she is,' replied her mother. 'Elizabeth would you fetch the bread from downstairs and we can all eat together up here? she asked cautiously.

Returning to the stairs Elizabeth quietly went back down, she relaxed as her father hadn't returned and found the bread and dripping. She brought it back to Theresa as she had been asked to do.

'Will Sybil have some?' asked the young Theresa enamoured with the baby.

'No silly,' said Elizabeth, 'she can't eat thank goodness... she has no teeth. I don't want any babies when I grow up,' she said looking at her mother. 'I will tell them they can't come to live at my house.'

Her mother tried to make light of it. 'Well... you might change your mind when you grow up to be a lady Elizabeth.'

'No I won't ever,' came the reply.

As dusk fell the neighbour who had acted as midwife returned as she promised. 'Just checking to see if everything is alright Theresa. Let me have look at you.' The girls sat in the corner while she examined their mother, the new baby had been on the breast and was sleeping soundly.

They heard him coming back up the lane and the girls instinctively moved towards their mother their eyes wide. The neighbour read their reaction, stood up, straightened the bed, looked at Theresa and said, 'Don't you worry now... I will be back in a moment,' and disappeared again down the stairs.

She reached the bottom of the stairs as he opened the door. 'What are you still doing here? I told you to get out of my house. Where is she, idling upstairs? Get out of my way and tell her to get down here.'

'You will leave her be until tomorrow. For your information you have a new daughter and they are not to be disturbed so leave them alone.'

'You stop interfering, her place is down here,' and raising his voice he shouted, 'Get down here woman now...or I shall come up there and pull you down.'

She shouted up the stairs to give Theresa some comfort. 'Stay where you are Theresa he is not coming anywhere. I will be back soon and will bring some more water up for you and the girls to bathe.' Turning quickly back to him she pulled herself up to her full height, looked at him with determined eyes and warned him, 'and if I hear any more threats from you I shall go and fetch the constable. He probably knows you anyway. You will leave her alone and let her rest do you understand me... do you?' Her voice was steady and determined.

He scowled at her and she stood her ground until he moved away towards his chair. 'I am sure you can fend for yourself, after all you are a grown man, an ex-army man to boot are you not? You cannot surely expect a woman who has just given birth and two young girls to wait hand and foot on you. I will be back later rest assured,' and out she went. Muttering under his breath it wasn't long before he was snoring in his chair, the sound drifted upstairs to their relief.

True to her word the neighbour came back with a large enamel jug full of hot water, took one look at him, tutted to herself and opened the stair door. The girls heard the door open and went to see who it was. They told their mother she was back. She had brought them both a small candy treat each, something they had only ever seen in the bakery windows, eyes and smiles brightened with delight.

'Your baby sister asked me to get these for you... a sort of hello.' She ruffled their hair as they looked for approval to their mother.

'That is very kind of you... thank you,' said Theresa, 'they don't get much.'

'It is only a small thing, not much really in the realm of things. If it makes them think this is a day for happiness all to the good with the new baby and all.'

'Let's hope so, they have very little else I'm afraid. It's his leg you see,' said Theresa a little defensively.

'Yes... I am sure it is,' cutting her short. 'Now girls come along let's get you washed then you will be fine in the morning for school.'

Before she finally left told she Theresa quietly, 'Any problems you send the girls for me... and I mean any problem... do you understand?'

'Yes,' said Theresa, 'thank you. I think I will be alright to see them off to school in the morning.'

'That is fine so long as that is all you do. No lifting... especially dead weights, do you understand what I am saying, we don't want a prolapse do we? You alone have three children to mind and I don't have to explain what would happen if...' she looked at Theresa without finishing the sentence. 'Do I?' Theresa nodded. 'Elizabeth come and fetch me if you think your mother is not well or upset.'

'I will.' she answered.

The girls fell asleep soon after the neighbour had left and Theresa picked up her new daughter to feed her. She looked into the little one's face, 'What sort of a life have I brought you into?' she thought as the baby suckled from her breast. Feeling comfort from her child she looked at her other two daughters and thought how lovely they both were. Thoughts of her own family came into her mind and the post natal tears then started to fall and she wept for all of them; her lost family, her plight and for Elizabeth her eldest daughter, a child that was growing old and cynical before her time.

The baby woke again during the early hours of the morning for her feed. Theresa fed and changed her and settled her once more into the makeshift crib without waking the girls. She rose before daybreak just to get the feeling back in her legs after being confined to the bed and crept down the stairs. He had moved on to the chaise longue during the night and was sprawled face downward towards the wall fast asleep. She thanked the Lord under her breath and moved to the corner of the kitchen where she tried to keep the foodstuffs out of the way of the cockroaches. The dry stale bread and a small hard piece of cheese was still there that she had secreted away before her confinement. She returned upstairs and fed her baby once more before the girls roused. They ate their meagre breakfast in silence.

They came down the stairs together, Theresa in front of the girls, and she looked towards the chaise longue once more. There had been no sound of the crutch being banged against the chair leg so they assumed he would still be sleeping. As she opened the door Theresa paused and the girls waited behind her, he was still laid on the chaise longue but on his back.

'I'm thirsty,' whispered Elizabeth.

'Me too,' said her sister quietly.

Their mother nodded. 'Just stand here... I will get you some water,' and she walked towards the old cracked pot sink which housed a single cold water tap.

As she passed him his dark eyes flashed open and he grabbed her leg.

Theresa cried out in shock as she felt his grip on her leg.

'Defy me woman would you. Letting that old hag in here to speak to me like that, without respect, in my own house.' He reached out for the crutch.

The girls screamed and young Theresa ran to aid her mother to try and pull her away from his grip. 'Get off her... get off.'

Her father reacted quickly and knocked the little one off her feet with his free hand. 'You'll be next missy... just wait till I get up.' Her mother was struggling to release his grip from her leg when Elizabeth ran over to the fireplace and picked up the poker, she turned and jabbed it as hard as she could into the stump of his leg. Standing perfectly still, her steady eyes never left his face as he looked at her with incredulity and winced in pain.

'Leave my mother alone... or I will fetch that lady back and she will bring the constable... she's promised me.' Her father released his grip.

Theresa composed herself and picked her youngest daughter up off the floor then gently turned Elizabeth, still with the poker in her hand, away from her father. She ushered them towards the door. 'Give me that Elizabeth please... out now... go to school the pair of you... I will be alright don't worry.'

Elizabeth looked at her mother then back at her father and gently said, 'Let's go Theresa... don't cry... I'm here,' and the young sisters walked out of the house into the lane.

Theresa closed the door quietly and turned to face her husband who was still rubbing his disfigured leg where his young daughter had hit him. With resignation in her voice she said, 'I'll get you something to eat... ' as if nothing had happened.

The girls came out of school and made their way home: unusually they found their mother waiting for them on the corner of the lane. She had baby Sybil cradled in her arm and the young Theresa fussed over her. Elizabeth looked directly at her mother, 'Is he in?'

'No... are you frightened,' said her mother holding her gaze.

'No,' replied her eldest daughter quickly with no emotion in her voice and she carried on walking towards their house.

The years passed and the feeling of animosity between Elizabeth and her father did not diminish. Even at her young age she felt she could not be subservient to him, and as each baby was born she became the appointed protector of the children. She watched her mother through her painful years of childbirth and the misery of two babies born dead. She could not understand why her mother needed more babies and why they kept coming when she knew it antagonised their father.

She came home from school one day with her sisters and younger brother behind her, she shepherded them into the house as usual. One look at her mother told her she had been crying; not wanting to alert the younger ones to her mother's plight she did not broach the subject until they were all out of earshot.

'Your grandmother has died, God rest her soul... although you only met her a few times she was a good woman... you need to know that.'

'Yes I know... I could tell when we went to visit. Then she came here with our brother, I liked her, the house was warm... not like here... it was a nice place.'

'Yes, I know,' replied Theresa quietly holding her daughter's hand. 'Just remember her... she would like that.'

One week later her older brother walked unannounced through their door. As he entered their domain, she stood with the rest of his siblings in silence and stared at him, he looked distraught and isolated. Their mother made a move to put him at ease which antagonised their father, he had dropped the bundle he was carrying and they all crowded round to see what it contained.

He stood silent, eyes downcast. Brushing them to one side Theresa indicated for them to get onto the mattress and for him to join them. Elizabeth had moved over on the mattress to make room for him to sleep on the edge, she saw the look of utter despair in his eyes and smiled at him but he did not respond. Feeling concerned at his plight, when he lay down on the mattress fully clothed she stretched her arm out and took hold of his hand. There were no words spoken, he just held it tightly in return and his body shook with silent involuntary sobs.

Elizabeth tried her best to make him feel comfortable in his new surroundings but she appreciated how he must feel at having to come and live in the hovel they had to call home. His home had been a warm, clean house with carpets with a smell of polished furniture; the kitchen had been welcoming with a warm fire and cooking aromas, it had been a good place for someone to live. Then there was their father, 'Who would want to come and live with someone like him?' she thought to herself after living with such a nice grandmother in a lovely warm house.

The next morning he had already left when they had aroused from sleep and she had felt concerned and disappointed. He had returned from school later and entered the house still very cautious and had looked relieved to see that their father was not in the house. After they had all eaten together their mother had sent them out; Elizabeth had started the conversation and they all joined in. His sisters and younger brother Kenneth were curious to know where he had been and about their grandmother; Owen had answered their questions and had even laughed a little. Elizabeth was pleased that he still felt he could after all his sadness.

The next morning they all left together. 'We will see you later Owen,' said Elizabeth to him. 'Wish you were coming to our school,' she was trying to lighten his mood as he still looked lost. He had just smiled at her ruefully then turned away from them and had set off alone in the opposite direction.

Later when he had arrived home they were all waiting for him so that they could all eat together. Elizabeth moved over at the table so he could sit next to her, she thought he looked at little happier. As they were eating the door suddenly banged open and their father entered, they all fell silent. She noticed he didn't look drunk, just menacing, they all became tense. 'Out... all of you... go,' he shouted. 'Apart from you,' and he had looked directly at Owen.

She quickly took the younger ones out of the way. 'Let's all sit here and wait for him.' So they all sat and finished eating on a wall further up the lane. A few minutes later she saw him come out of the house and run down the lane clearly in a state of distress.

'Owen... we're here... where are you going?' she shouted.

'Where's he going Elizabeth?' asked Kenneth.

'I don't know... ' she replied as they all watched him disappear round the corner.

They sat and waited as dusk approached. It was now turning cold so reluctantly their sister told them, 'Come on... we must go in now.'

'But where is he... will he be coming back?' asked Sybil shivering. 'It's getting dark and it's cold.'

'I don't know... ' said Elizabeth, and after thinking about it for a moment thought to herself, but then where else can he go? 'Come on... and nobody make a noise when we get in.'

She had taken them home and once inside she had moved them over to the mattress where they huddled together for warmth in silence. Their mother had nodded to her eldest daughter that she had done the right thing, but Elizabeth noticed the look of concern on her face.

Finally the door opened and in he came, a look of resignation on a pale tear-stained face. Without looking at any of them or saying a word he came over to the mattress; she made room for him and he laid down. Elizabeth once more sought out a cold hand and again held it tightly, he held on to it as if his life depended on it.

The next morning he had left again before she woke. She asked her mother, 'Has he gone to school already?'

'No,' replied Theresa, 'he now has a job... he is working.' The banging started on the floor; her mother looked at the ceiling then back at her daughter.

'Work... why has he had to go to work? He liked school and promised his grandmother that... ' said Elizabeth.

Her mother cut her off, 'Yes well... these things happen,' casting her eyes downwards. 'I have to go... he's banging... off you go to school... get the others,' and she walked towards the stairs door in quiet resignation.

Elizabeth walked to school in silence, the younger ones were full of questions as usual but she was in no mood to talk to them, her thoughts were with her brother and remained there all day. After school she sat with the others on the mattress and waited for him to come home. She had warned the other children not to mention him when they got back into the house if there father was there, they had taken her lead once more and again sat quietly and waited.

The door opened, Owen entered slowly and Elizabeth watched as he again locked eyes with his father. She and the younger children had held their breath as their father had picked up one of his crutches and aimed it at her brother. He had questioned him about his first day at work and left him in no doubt that if there was any complaints from his employer there would a greater problem for him to face at home. After his tirade he had placed the crutch down and picked up his beer.

Owen had stood there until he had caught his mother's eye. Elizabeth picked up on Theresa's silent instruction to him to move over to the mattress and moved over to accommodate him. He came over quietly to join her and when seated her hand crept over and again held his hand out of sight from their father. Together they watched as he consumed his beer and not until he had fallen asleep did they relax.

The next morning he left early again and Elizabeth was disappointed that she had slept through. He had told her he would only have to work half day with it being Saturday so she sat and waited and every time the younger ones came over to ask what she was doing, 'I am waiting for Owen... he shouldn't be long now,' she told them. From time to time she would wander down to the corner and stand there instead; it gave her a wider view whichever way he approached. The hours crept by and her mood changed between frustration, annoyance and concern until he finally appeared.

She ran to meet him. 'Where have you been?' she asked, a slight tone creeping into her voice. 'I have been here for hours.'

'Oh... I'm sorry if you have been waiting for me,' said Owen. 'I have been with Georgie who I work with... he suggested we go to the park,' he looked at her a little embarrassed.

It was Elizabeth's turn to look a bit embarrassed realising that her tone had sounded a little sharp. 'Take no notice of me... I just thought with you finishing early you would be home early that's all. Then again why would you be in a hurry to come back here? My fault... I'm sorry... did you have a good time?'

'Yes... we will all have to go there one Saturday. There is a boating lake, it's nice,' he smiled. After a while he told her, 'I have decided to go to my grandmother's grave tomorrow it gets me out of the way,' and he glanced at the door.

Elizabeth looked at him, 'Don't worry we are alright at the moment he's gone out.' After a pause she added, 'You know tomorrow, would you mind if we went there with you? Just to take some flowers... I know we didn't really know her... but... '

'She would like that I think Elizabeth, yes why not. We will make a day of it and they went in the house safe in the knowledge that their father wasn't there.

Elizabeth organised the younger ones the next morning and they all had their usual meagre breakfast chatting and asking questions about where they were going.

'Wait and see,' answered Elizabeth to their questions.

Theresa had kept some bread back for them to take; she hoped as it was an adventure for them their hunger pangs would take second place in their thoughts. She waved them off and closed the door on a quiet house and reflected for a moment her eyes taking in the poverty of their surroundings. She smiled to herself as she thought of her eldest son and his kindness and was pleased that at least they could have one day out and away from the squalor.

They all walked together; they headed out of the slums towards the rural part of the city where the cemetery was situated on a hillside. Owen had obviously been this way before and pointed out things that he thought might please them. He knew that when they were surrounded by the fields and trees that bordered the cemetery where the horses grazed they would become excited.

Elizabeth was as thrilled as the others to see the horses at leisure in the fields. 'Just look how free and beautiful they are... they look so different to the ones that pull the carts up the lane.'

They took their time through the fields and picked the flowers that they needed for their grandmother's grave. Elizabeth let the younger ones pick whatever pleased their eye. It didn't seem to matter if there were colourful weeds included, it was their personal tribute to an unknown grandmother; they all wished they had known her based on what their elder brother and sister had told them about her.

They all crowded around the grave. Elizabeth lost in her thoughts for a moment traced her grandmother's name with her finger in silence and told the younger ones to be careful where they were treading. When finally they had cleared the dead flowers away and all laid their tiny tributes near the headstone they turned away to find a place to eat on a raised bank beyond the gravestones makingsure they could still see the one that signified where their grandmother lay at rest. After they had eaten the younger ones went off to play.

'I like it here... it's quiet... do you think she knows we are here?' asked Elizabeth quietly as they ate.

'Yes, I would like to think so,' he replied sounding sad and looking over to her grave. 'I miss her... it seems an age ago since I lost her and life changed.'

'I'm sorry... I know what it feels like. Mine and Theresa's life changed when he came back from the war, at least when we were on our own we had food to eat... he changed it all.'

'Yes... ' he paused, 'but it won't always be like this Elizabeth as we get older. I know it might seem a long way off but it will happen.' Then gathering his thoughts, 'Come on, we have done what we came to do let's find the others, go back through the fields and let them carry on playing.'

They returned back into the city at leisure, nobody wanting to rush back to the damp, dark place they had to call home. Elizabeth opened the door quietly and looked to see if he was there, the chair was empty.

'Come on... he's not here,' she called back to the others watching her and they all followed her in. The younger ones walked towards the waiting flea-ridden mattress ready to sleep after their day out in the fresh air. Their mother wiped their hands and faces and settled them down and turned to her older children, 'Well... it looks as if you have all had a good day.'

'Yes,' they all said in unison.

'Let's get you sorted.'

'How long has he been gone?' asked Elizabeth.

'A few hours,' came the reply. 'Don't be difficult if he comes back soon, I would like the younger ones to get to sleep first.'

She shot a look back at her mother, 'I wasn't thinking about being difficult... I was just wondering if he had left anything for us to eat that's all.'

'Bread and broth,' said her mother not responding to her daughter's tone.

Her mother tried her best to eke out the meagre money he gave her. The food she bought for them she tried to keep hidden from him. Usually, after coming back from the alehouse, he would demand she go out with the jug for refills, she felt she had no option. It was a decision she made daily, did she spend nearly all the money she had on his beer, which when he had had his fill he would sleep and leave them all alone or on food for her children and subject them to a life of hell? Their basic food was dry bread with a scraping of dripping or jam or a weak broth made out of the vegetables that the greengrocer had put on one side to give to the pig farmers but would sell off cheaply if pressed. She would cut the rotten bits out of the carrots, turnips and potatoes and cabbage and leave the pot on the fire adding further pieces or meat bones as she came across them during the week. Try as she might there was never enough for them to have full stomachs after their father had taken the lion's share. He would take his fill without conscience.

'One day... when we are older we won't have this problem... will we Owen?' Elizabeth said casting a look at her brother.

Her brother returned her look but it was their mother that answered, 'Let's hope not Elizabeth.'

'No hope about it mother, believe me it won't happen,' and she turned to the cooking pot to see how much he had left.

She enjoyed school, at times it gave her the luxury of being able to become lost in her own thoughts, she was literate and knew her maths. Out of school, her time was not her own as she was either keeping an eye on her younger siblings for her mother, or taking the lead and reassuring them when their father was in their midst. She was a steady pupil and was encouraged by Owen to learn as much as she could, he had told her he missed school and if she tried hard in her lessons it could possibly help her climb out of the poverty they were both in. Prior to Owen arriving she had not really had anyone to confide in, she enjoyed their chats when they were together without the younger ones, which wasn't very often.

Now in her teenage years when walking to school she had become aware that the older boys would smile and try and catch her eye or nudge each other when she was passing by. She laughed if they whistled or would turn and smile at them, it became a game and it didn't take long before she realised that she enjoyed the attention.

Her two younger sisters, Theresa and Sybil, were now old enough to care for the younger ones so Saturdays became her own. She would leave the house and walk into the city to spend time looking in the shop windows at the fashions displays. She passed various cinema houses on the way into town and enjoyed looking at the photographs outside of the stars appearing in the movies. She became lost for a short time in a world of leading ladies, handsome men, how the actresses styled their hair, the design of their dresses and shoes, and every Saturday the same thought would run through her mind... one day.

She watched how the shop window displays reflected the seasons, and how the colours and styles changed to accommodate the colder weather. She would sit on a bench outside the Cathedral opposite Cole Brothers and watch the ladies enter the large, enticing store through the revolving door only to depart some time later with their purchases. She thought how wonderful it must be to be able to afford brand new clothes every few weeks, clothes that no-one else had worn before, new shoes on their feet. These self-assured ladies carrying their latest purchases home looked happy, their stylish clothes and fur coats made them look like film stars and she realised that a fashionable world actually existed right here in her city not only in the movies.

She would sit on the same bench and as the months rolled by she came to recognise some of the ladies coming out of the stores with their parcels as being regular customers. As with the film stars she decided on her favourite looking ladies and marvelled at their easy capacity to look elegant, always feeling excited when she saw them; the ladies themselves were totally unaware of the smiling young girl who sat opposite watching them.

Sometimes she would walk to meet Owen and Georgie at lunchtime after their work finished, and regale them with tales of who she had seen and what they had been wearing; they both knew she enjoyed her forays into town so would listen good heartedly and try and appear as impressed as she was.

Georgie made her laugh, she felt comfortable in his company and was pleased that her brother had his own close friend; it gave him an escape from the darkness of home. They in turn told her about the big houses they had been working in during the week, describing the colours, furniture and how many rooms the rich people lived in, and she would listen avidly. She had often looked over walls and seen the big houses, but it was a bonus to know what the inside looked like and how they lived. The nicest house she had ever been in was that of her grandmother's years ago. She could still remember the feeling as the door had opened and she had stepped from the cold ground outside into a warm world of comfort; a house with more than one room to live in downstairs, the memory had been etched in her mind.

During one of their conversations Georgie had asked how long she had before she left school and what did she think she would do when she left.

'Well... I would love to work in one of the stores that I see the ladies going in... but I can't see much chance of that can you. Look at me, I can do my maths but you have to look the part as well?' she said sounding a little despondent.

'You are too pretty to work serving somebody. Don't worry... one day...I am sure they will be serving you,' and he smiled at her hoping to lift her spirits.

'Well I shall need my own money before that can happen,' she replied a little pensive. Then she looked at him, 'But do you know what I think you might be right ... yes...one day they will,' and her laughter made him laugh too.

The opportunity to start work came from her school as the headmaster had been approached for school leavers to work in the cutlery industry at a nearby company. The cutlery industry ran hand-in-hand with the steelmaking in the city. During the Great War armaments had been produced in great number, which had resulted in German zeppelins bombing the city as a reprisal. Out of the devastation, new housing for the population had been built in the suburbs and buildings erected for factories in the bombed areas in the city. Although this planning had taken some years to come to fruition it coincided with Elizabeth leaving school. The factory owners had approached the local school for trainees, the girls to become buffers and the boys as apprentice cutlers to boost the local economy.

She arrived home from school on the day the factory people had been to the school and announced that she would be starting work the following week.

'About time,' growled her father. 'It's about time you went into service... learn to know your place with your peers.'

She looked at him, 'I'm not going into service... going into a proper job to earn myself some money... and get myself out of here one day.'

'You will give over what you earn,' he shouted back.

The steely blue eyes looked at him with determination, but she held her tongue out of consideration for her mother and siblings and turned her back on him. Her mother stepped in the breach between them to offset any further argument, her husband growled and picked up his jug.

She reported to the time office of the cutlery factory the following Monday morning and waited with the other girls from school who were also to work there. Owen had wished her luck and her mother had seen her off and given her pack up; she knew her daughter would have a long, hard day in front of her. True to form and unbeknown to Elizabeth, her father had followed her to the time office an hour later, explained his daughter had just started work that morning and demanded they give him a sub against his daughter's future wages just as he had done with Owen. He was told in no uncertain terms that it was piecework his daughter would be employed to do, so there was no guarantee on what her earnings would be until she proved herself. He was also told it was against company policy, so without further ado the time keeper had closed the window on him. He had banged on the shutter with his crutch and shouted that he was an old soldier and should be shown some respect. The time keeper had taken no notice and shouted back, 'It's history now... go tell it to someone who will listen... you will get no money from here.'

He had limped back home and demanded that Theresa fetch him his beer. He threw down his crutch and shouted at her, 'I blame you for having made that girl too headstrong... not going into service... she has ideas above her station that one.'

'She only wants to better herself,' Theresa said fighting back, picking up the jug and walking towards the door. 'You cannot blame her after the life she has had... ' and banged the door defiantly as she went out. He sat in his chair and was still glowering when she returned; she placed the jug on the table and avoided his stare. As she turned towards the pile of grubby washing that was on the floor next to the sink she felt the force of his crutch across the back of her legs and fell forward. 'Don't you talk to me like that again woman... it's no wonder they don't show their father any respect.'

Struggling back to her feet she held on to the sink to steady herself before turning. 'It's still respect we want is it... well probably had you ever done anything for your children, then they might show some respect. But until that happens I don't reckon they ever will and whose fault is that then heh? Go on pick the crutch up again, that is just about your limit, hitting your wife and children... and you talk about respect... get the beer down your throat and give us some peace,' and she kicked the crutch out of his reach.

He poured the beer out spilling some on the table in his anger. She turned, picked her youngest child up off the mattress and moved away from him going outside so that she could calm her nerves and sit for a while in the cool air until her legs stopped stinging. She was grateful that the other children were all out of the house at school and not subjected to yet another violent argument. He had started early so with any luck he would be sleeping it off when they all came home. She didn't want him brooding over the situation with Elizabeth all day and for him still to be sitting in his chair when she came home, better that she keep a steady stream of beer supplied then get him up the stairs and out of the way.

Elizabeth watched the girl intently as she demonstrated how the black cutlery pieces were buffed to a shine by the brushes whirring round on the machine. At the side of her seat was a large basket of black cutlery pieces waiting to be picked up and finished off by an expert hand. The girl was wearing a brightly coloured headscarf to protect her hair from the fine shower of dust emanating from the brushes as they spun round at a great speed. Her fingers and face were black and so was the long brown paper apron she wore over more brown paper that was wrapped round her legs and tied with string. The paper was used to protect her legs from the acid that dripped down during the polishing process. The workshop was full of women all concentrating on their skill. It was a dark, hot, noisy place, grimy place with black dust that you could smell and taste in the air; any ideas of a glamorous career soon evaporated and Elizabeth felt her heart sink as she looked around.

The foreman explained that although they would be slow at first they would soon get used to the technique and before long be on a reasonable wage for their age. They would be paid according to how many pieces they polished per week and had two weeks to achieve the minimum number required. If they didn't reach this number they would be paid off. The new girls nodded their heads knowingly but all of them looked terrified.

They were all to start on teaspoons and be working under the tuition of an older girl. Elizabeth was assigned to a girl named Sara who smiled at her and nodded to her to sit down next to her, she knew exactly how the new girl felt and tried to make her feel at ease. Elizabeth smiled back, uncertain what to say, if anything, the girl broke the ice for her.

'Just sit there for a moment... I have to finish this.' She was working on a dinner knife, which was heavily embossed on the handle. Elizabeth watched her concentrate on the work at hand.

'There... that's another one done,' as she placed it on a rack lined with the dirty brown paper that seemed to be everywhere. 'Now let's get you sorted... you don't want to spoil that lovely hair so put this on,' and she passed her a red piece of fabric to wrap around her head. 'Bring a clean piece tomorrow with you.'

Elizabeth did as she was told and covered her hair tucking any wisps in that she had missed. 'Now your legs... and we will do your arms as well, seeing that you are new. We don't want any nasty accidents do we.'

Sara was one of the fastest buffers on the polishing floor, she was good at her job and her concentration never wavered. This was brought about by being the eldest of eight children in a fatherless house. Her earnings were more important to her than pride in her job, she had nimble fingers and used them to her advantage and Elizabeth could not have been placed with anyone better.

'How long have you been here?' asked Elizabeth.

'It seems like forever... means to an end really. I shan't be in here much longer, I want to go into the packing section. It is piece work in there as well but it is a lot cleaner... I hate this muck.'

'Will you be able to do that?'

'I reckon... the manager knows I am one of his best workers so he can put me in packing and know that he would still get the numbers through for both departments; his foreman sees to that... and apart from that... I think he likes me,' she laughed and winked at her new work colleague. 'Let's get on.' She picked up a blank spoon from a basket and a handful of the blackened sand needed to bring the shine up, as she set it against the brushes the dust started to fly.

Elizabeth watched her as she gently and methodically turned the item into the brushes, she moved down from the bowl to the end of the handle making sure the pressure didn't change. Miraculously the spoon started to turn from black to the required finish, the black dust moving itself from the spoon on to Sara's hands, down her nails and into her face.

From time to time she would bend down and take another piece of rag out of a covered bucket of water and wipe the damp rag over her face, neck and hands to clean off the black film. This was a luckless task, as soon as she started on her next piece the dust would start to build again. 'Regularly cleaning this off can stop your skin getting diseased, so bring some rag tomorrow and you can use my bucket. We can keep changing the water.'

'Thank you... it's not like I thought it would be,' she said a little crestfallen.

'No... I know it's not... well the sooner we get you started the quicker we will both be out of here. Now... watch my fingers, notice how I don't press the spoon in... hold it lightly... let the brushes do the work.'

She worked under Sara's supervision for the two weeks probation; the foreman kept an eye to her progress and reported to the manager. He would nod to Sara of his approval, she was right he did like her, she was not as rough as the others in the buffing shop with their colourful language, and she kept herself to herself. He also knew of her ambition to progress on to the packing floor and of her total commitment to her family that they depended on her.

He acknowledged the surroundings that they worked in were awful, the young fresh-faced girls who came straight in from leaving school soon turned into tough women who would take on anyone, they thrived on their reputation. They were poor to start with but this was a way to earn good money for the times if they could learn quickly. They risked dreadful scars to their faces, neck, hands and legs if their concentration lapsed and the acid that formed in the sand came into contact with their skin. If burnt they would put a rag round it and continue, ever fearful they would not reach their targets; they acknowledged their scars as being part of the job.

Finally, her first day at work ended, she had been relieved to leave at the end of the day and decided she would wait for Owen before she went into the house. When he had appeared on the lane she had ran to him and burst into tears. He had told Georgie of his concern regarding the surroundings she would be working in. They had both seen the buffer girls coming out of work, they would walk down the road in groups, with their blackened arms linked. He and Georgie were fair game for ribald comments if they were spotted on the street, the girls took no prisoners, their language and gestures were as colourful as their headscarves.

He put his arm round her as she cried into his shoulder, the dark dust left on her face forming black streaks down her cheeks. He let her stop crying before he said anything.

'Was it very bad... tell me.'

'I didn't think it would be like that,' she sobbed again. After a few minutes she blew her nose on a piece of cloth he had given her from his pocket, 'I will be alright... I just didn't want to go in to the house on my own and cry in front of him.'

Holding her close with one of his hands behind her head he said, 'I know... I wish I could do or say something that would make it easier for you. I wish you didn't have to work there.'

She pulled away slightly and wiped the tears away with her sleeve. 'The girl I am working with has helped me... she is nice... I don't know what I would have done if she had not been there,' and the tears streamed again.

He held her tight, then trying to lift her spirits, he said, 'Well, that's one good thing then, it is like Georgie being there for me on my first day. It will get better Elizabeth, it will, it's the shock of being in a horrible place after being at school. I know it is not want you want... it... '

He stopped mid-sentence when he saw his mother come out of the door with the jug in her hand, she looked up and quickened her pace towards them.

'He's in then?' asked Owen.

'Yes,' she looked at her distraught daughter. 'I have some hot water ready for you Elizabeth. Don't worry, I will help you, give me a few minutes it won't be too long before I can get him upstairs. I was hoping to get him out of the way before you came home. I will send Theresa out to tell you,' and she turned from them and started running down the lane towards the alehouse.

Owen stayed with her and they sat on a wall together, no further words were spoken, all she wanted to do was to sit in silence. Her brother knew she was in a dark place and he just held her hand in support as she had held his when they had been younger.

They watched their mother go back into the house and true to her word she sent their younger sister out to tell them when the coast was clear. Theresa was shocked when she saw Elizabeth, she was used to her older sister always being confident and in control, and to see her as distraught and dishevelled as she was upset her momentarily, she tried hard not to show it.

They returned to the house, the younger ones had been told by their mother not to say anything apart from to greet their brother and sister coming in from work. There was a bucket of hot water for Elizabeth to wash off the black dust and her mother fussed over her and tried to give her some comfort. She slept fitfully that night, a dark place, hot and smelly featuring in her nightmare together with distorted blackened faces laughing and taunting her with the black acid as she tried to reach impossible targets.

She and Owen were up before the rest of the household again the next morning, they left together. As they walked she said, 'Is this the way it is always going to be?'

'No,' answered Owen. 'It will get better... yesterday was a huge shock for you. Today you have a friend to work with and that is better than it was yesterday. Today there is no shock, you know what to expect. If you want to wait for me again tonight or walk to meet me that is alright,' and he explained which way he would be coming home.

'Yes, you are right, there is no shock today and I will walk to meet you,' she answered.

'Do you have everything?' he asked.

'Yes... scarf for my hair, cloth for my face... pack up.'

'Good, can't have anything spoiling those good looks and apart from that you might frighten Georgie if you come to meet us with a dirty face. Right, now go and show them what you are made of and what a toughie my sister is,' and he kissed her on her forehead and smiled. Then he watched her as she reluctantly turned away from him and continued to the factory.

She arrived in the buffing shop, Sara was already there and she smiled at her, 'Mornin... I wasn't sure if I was going to see you again.' She moved over to make room on the bench.

'Well... it was a close run thing I'll tell you. I'll not go into detail but I didn't want to let you down, one good turn always deserves another.' She smiled back, 'I don't know what I would have done without you yesterday... thank you,' and she held up her headscarf in one hand and rag to wipe the dust off in the other to show her friend. She covered her hair, gritted her teeth and said, 'Right... I'm ready.'

Sara and her protégé worked diligently through the following weeks. Elizabeth learned quickly and although she hated it she understood it was a means to an end. They became good friends and it was agreed that once Sara was in the packing section she would help her to follow her into that department and on to cleaner work.

Owen could see that she was growing stronger and becoming more focused as the weeks passed; he encouraged her as much as he could and readily accepted that she would never accept her lot in the buffing shop. As the months passed their alliance against their father grew stronger, they would arrive home together after a full day's work, if he was out all would be fine; on the days he was in, he would sit there glowering and muttering but they held their own and always had an answer to his sarcastic self-serving comments.

On pay days his cold dark eyes would hold steady on the door. He always had an indication as to what time they would arrive home as Theresa would put the kettle on the fire for her daughter to wash the dust off. He would wait for them to give their board over to their mother, then command her to help him up and to the door. This was her instruction to hand over the cash, he would take all the money she had been given and leave. After he had gone Elizabeth and Owen would then give their mother the difference they had kept back for her to buy food for the little ones. The routine worked well, it did not compromise their mother and saved them all getting involved in yet another violent argument.

'I ought to let a few of the girls from the buffing shop come home with me,' a wry smile appearing on her face, 'they would sort him out good style.'

Owen laughed back, 'Not half.'

Their mother looked nervous as she listened to their conversation. 'Only joking mother... don't worry... I would pay anything to get him out of the house and give us all some peace. Just relax and enjoy it, at least you know he will go straight upstairs when he gets back, that is if he can stand,' said Elizabeth.

'He wouldn't be like he is if it wasn't for... ' her mother started.

'Wasn't for what... exactly? He has never or never will be any different mother, get used to it, but he had better make the most of it because one day he will finish up a lonely old man. He will always be the same, a bitter, twisted, vindictive, nasty bastard... a bit of buffer talk there for you mother. I hope he is proud,' she took a cigarette out and lit it. 'It should be me and Owen that are bitter and twisted... that's the laugh of it... answer me honestly if you can... what sort of father or husband has he ever been?' She glared at her mother, '... and you defend him?'

Their mother couldn't hold her daughter's look and sheepishly glanced away and looked down.

'Come on Bets, don't upset yourself, he's not worth it,' said Owen gently taking hold of her arm. 'It's payday and the weekend and at least we get a break and it's on our terms.'

'Yes... you're right,' she answered and turning back to Theresa said 'I just wish you would stop defending him mother that's all. I am sick of having this conversation. I just wish you would acknowledge that he is never going to change... never!'

The younger ones listened once again to the on-going argument about their father in silence, they were relieved that as he was absent there would be no violent outburst this time.

Elizabeth had arranged to meet up with Sara as there was a funfair in one of the local parks. Owen was meeting Georgie as usual so he walked part of the way with her. 'Might come up and join you later... have fun,' he said.

'Well... some of the girls will probably be there so get ready if you do... you know what they are like. It doesn't take much to start them off, don't want Georgie getting frightened and running to me to look after him,' she said laughing.

Owen laughed with her, 'Yes... I'll tell him. But you just promise me one thing that you will never become a buffer girl in all its glory... salt of the earth that they are but my god they don't half make you cringe. You have to wonder sometimes if some of them are men, especially with the language.'

'Who me... and if so why not?' she answered sounding shocked for effect, before adding, 'No don't worry Owen... just a means to an end, it is just the first step. Mind you I have to agree it is one a hell of a step... have to say it's opened my eyes.'

'What looking like a man?' he laughed. 'Don't think you would get away with it somehow.'

'No silly,' came the reply, 'you can keep it quiet where I work if it embarrasses you, I don't mind, just so long as they pay me well. It will do in the short term.'

He watched her as she met Sara and off they went arm in arm, two attractive young women totally relaxed and a million miles away from their work environment looking to enjoy their weekend. 'Who would think?' thought Owen, 'my lovely sister... the buffer.'

They toured the fairground accepting the compliments and admiring glances as they passed, giving as good as they got with good grace and quick smiles. Sara had been on the lookout for their manager who had said he might come along, and before the end of the night she spotted him watching them on one of the rides. She waved and he responded with a smile and a nod of his head.

'Look Elizabeth... Samuel... he's here,' she nudged her friend sounding excited.

'You're blushing,' came the reply, 'do you really like him?'

'Yes, well I think I do... but this is the first time I have ever seen him outside work... doesn't he look handsome.'

'Yes, he does,' she replied, not for a moment would she have disappointed her friend by saying no. At the same time Owen and Georgie appeared at the opposite side of the ride. 'Oh and look, there is my brother and his friend as well,' and she waved over to them.

Sara turned her head, 'Goodness... now they are handsome, both of them... which is your brother?'

'The one on the right and yes he is, but Georgie is not bad either, he's lovely really.'

'What are they doing here?'

'They have come to fetch me... younger sister and all that, but I don't mind.'

'Should think not, you will be the envy of all the girls if they see you with the two of them. Heck... don't leave me just yet Elizabeth, I don't want to have to go over and have to say hello to Samuel on my own. He said he might come and if we go over to your brother first he might get the wrong idea,' a pleading tone creeping into her voice.

'No silly now would I? Don't worry, I know how you feel about him. When the ride stops we will go and say hello and explain my brother has come to fetch me, then we can either all go over to Owen or I can just wander off and leave you two together. Which would you prefer?' and she giggled as her friend decided which option to take.

'That's a good idea we'll both go over... thank you... am I still blushing?'

'Yes,' came the reply, 'so stop it.'

The ride came to a halt and they alighted; Elizabeth looked over to Owen and Georgie and mouthed for them to wait a moment. They both walked towards Samuel who smiled when it became clear that these two young ladies were approaching him.

'Hello,' said Sara still not able to stop blushing.

'Hello,' he replied. 'Hello Elizabeth,' and he doffed his cap to the pair of them.

Elizabeth looked at them both looking embarrassed and decided to grasp the nettle, 'Yes hello... my brother has come to fetch me home. Is it alright if I leave Sara here in your capable hands, or we can take her home if not?' she smiled sweetly.

'Oh... yes... that's fine don't worry. That is so long as you would like me to escort you home Sara?' he replied still fiddling with his cap.

Sara replied that it would be fine and bade her friend goodnight. 'I will see you on Monday morning.'

Elizabeth nodded, 'Yes... goodnight both of you,' and she turned and walked towards Owen and Georgie.

'Everything alright?' asked Owen.

Looking over her shoulder to see her friend turn and leave with her chosen man she replied, 'Yes... I reckon everything will be fine now. Are we staying here?'

'If you are happy to leave then let's go for some supper. What about it then Georgie are we up to buying supper for a buffer?' and laughed.

'You're on... so long as she hasn't got a dirty face and doesn't start swearing,' he said with a straight face and promptly received a slap on his arm in protest. Laughing loudly in response he bowed and offered his arm to her and they all walked out of the fairground together.

The following Monday morning Elizabeth arrived at work eager to see and chat with Sara; she arrived at their bench and smiled at her friend.

'Mornin... so do tell... I am excited to know. How did Friday night finish up?' she asked.

Sara looked around before she spoke then said quietly, 'It was lovely... he is so nice.'

Elizabeth hugged her friend and giggled, 'I am so pleased it worked out. So you are right he does like you. Do you like him now that you have seen him out of work?'

'Yes... I think I do,' and she giggled back, 'he seems to be a very gentle man... but with having no father at home how do I compare?'

'Hey... I have a father at home and wish I hadn't so don't let that sway you. After a moment she asked, 'Did you let him kiss you?' her eyes widening when she asked the question.

Sara looked embarrassed and demure, 'Yes,' she said looking down.

'Oh... what was it like. Are you seeing him again? Have you seen him this morning? Did he say hello?' after the rush of questions she then thought for a moment, 'He didn't ignore you did he?'

'No, of course he didn't,' Sara replied jumping to his defence.

'Good... that's alright then... I am so excited for you.'

Sara's relationship continued with Samuel although they were always discreet during working hours and kept it that way. Shortly afterwards she got her promotion to Samuel's department and Elizabeth was assigned to her bench and given new targets over in the buffing shop. She missed her friend but knew they would not let her down and within six months she was working again with Sara in the much cleaner environment of the packing section, life was getting better.

Beth & Owen: 1936

Beth and Owen were now married, they had their own rented house and had a young son. Beth was deliriously happy, she loved the house and never tired of the sight of her baby son's blue eyes greeting her first thing in the mornings. He was a happy baby, the image of his father and he knew he was loved. She had been determined to provide a better home for their son than she and Arnold had experienced with Ellen and lavished love on him on a daily basis.

Owen continued to work at Appleyards with Georgie who was now married to Annie. The four were still firm friends and helped each other out whenever the need arose, their respective houses were well decorated, clean and warm. Owen's greatest wish was for his son to grow up in the same loving atmosphere he had experienced in his grandmother's house and he felt relaxed that this was being achieved.

They had married with the minimum of fuss; Arnold had given his sister away, Adelaide and Annie had been bridesmaids and Georgie best man. The guest list had been selective, with only Owen's mother and his three older sisters and Georgie's parents. Mr and Mrs Newbould from the bakery also came to wish the newlyweds good luck but that was all, there had been no discussion of Ellen and Evelyn or Owen Snr attending. When the news was out both parties had been derisory and scornful, the loss of income being uppermost in both their minds. Ellen had enquired how Beth could afford to get married let alone pay rent and buy furniture. Owen Snr had also taken every opportunity to be critical and accused his son of having no respect for his family, that he was letting them all down and that he was an ungrateful wretch. Both had learned to bite their tongues and ignore any outbursts, taking heart that it was only a short time before they would be together under their own roof.

The day before the wedding, a major row had broken out when Owen had bought his wedding suit and left it briefly in the attic bedroom he shared with his younger brothers. He had gone to pick up the new shoes he was to wear and had intended to take them all down to Georgie's so he could dress there and keep the fleas out of them. His father had watched him bring the package in and take it upstairs and rightly assumed it was his wedding suit. As soon as he had left the house his father had instructed one of the younger boys to quickly go upstairs and bring the brown paper parcel down to him. He was waiting at the bottom of the stairs when the youngster reappeared and took no time in leaving and as fast as he could on his crutch, made his way to the pawn shop careful to make sure he wasn't going to bump into his eldest son on the way. Owen arrived back home, looked at the empty chair for a moment and without saying a word ran up the stairs to the attic. On his way down he bumped into his mother who had just returned home, he was furious.

'Where is he?' he asked his mother.

'I have just got in why...what's wrong?'

'The bastard ...he has taken my suit to pawn, is nothing sacred in this house...which one will he have gone to?'

His mother was taken aback, 'He will have gone to the nearest one I would have thought, but it will be all done and dusted now son. How long have you been out?'

'Fifteen minutes at most... he would have had to get upstairs and down again on his own with you not being here.'

'You can't get it back until you have the ticket Owen. You are going to have to wait for him to get back.'

'No, I won't, he will not gain from it if I can help it. I will swing for him... he'll be in the alehouse no doubt drinking it away, I'll find him and when I do... '

'Owen... don't,' his mother caught hold of his jacket as he opened the door.

Pulling away, 'Leave it mother... this has been too long coming. He cannot resist it can he... to make everyone's life a misery.'

Outside, he stood and thought about his predicament for a moment. He worked out that his father would have gone in the opposite direction so there would have been no chance of bumping into each other. He decided to head for the closest pawn shop in that direction and check to see if his suit was there; then he would trawl the alehouses. He would find him, he was determined.

His hunch served him well; as he approached the first pawn shop he saw his suit being hung in the window. He went into the shop and told the man to take it out and that he would be back to redeem it within half an hour. He knew once his father had the money in his pocket he would head for the nearest hostelry.

He walked into the alehouse and saw his father as usual holding court sitting in a chair with his back to the door. He had clearly bought the round, his drinking companions nodding in agreement with everything he said.

His father didn't see him as he walked quietly up to the table. The next thing Owen Snr knew his chair and the table was upturned and he was laid on the floor drenched in beer and looking up into his eldest son's angry blue eyes.

Owen bent down over him, gripped hold of his father's jacket and hauled him up and shook him and with menace said, 'Give me that ticket you bastard and the money you still have... now... otherwise I will not be responsible for my actions,' and looking around at his companions, '... and if anyone is thinking of getting involved to help they had better think twice.'

The other drinkers had quickly vacated their seats after watching in horror as their benefactor had been knocked clean off his chair; his crutch had gone flying and all the drinks had toppled off the overturned table and the glasses had smashed.

Dragging him up so he was standing on one leg, 'I am waiting... give me that ticket and all my money. Don't even think of saying anything, because if you do, as God is my witness it will be the last thing you ever say.'

Owen Snr saw the look of hate in his eldest son's eyes and fiddled as well as he could into his pockets hoping to try and diffuse the situation. He found the pawn ticket and threw it onto the floor.

His son was still holding him upright with one hand, his jacket was now round his throat. Keeping his voice low Owen said, 'and now the money old man... all of it,' and he tightened his grip. 'Make no mistake I will beat it out of you.'

With difficulty his father rifled through his pockets again and searched for the cash, 'That's it... that's all of it... if you don't believe me look what it says on the ticket,' he spluttered dropping it onto the floor.

He threw his father down on to the floor, picked up the cash and pawn ticket and without another word walked out to retrieve his wedding suit. The rest of the alehouse looked on in silence, nobody moved to help as his father attempted to get back on his feet.

Suit in hand he called in at the lane to pick up his shoes and see his mother, he warned her what had happened and gave her money to go and fetch his father his jug so that it was there already when he arrived home.

'That should take the heat out of the situation hopefully and here is some extra I want you to hide. It's for you and the kids so don't you go giving him any of it.' His mother's eyes brimmed with tears, 'Come on now don't get upset... I will see you tomorrow all being well.'

'Don't worry son... I will be there for you and if I don't have chance tomorrow to say it, be happy, we will miss you and thank you for this.' She kissed him on his cheek and put the money in her pinafore pocket.

He smiled at her and the rest of the children and turned to leave the slum that through tragic circumstances had become his home without any rancour whatsoever; he left feeling safe in the knowledge that a happier life awaited him.

He enjoyed his last night of being a bachelor with Arnold, Georgie and a few workmates; Beth spent her night at Annie's house with Adelaide.

Elizabeth had been instrumental in making the bride's and bridesmaid's dresses and a simple reception was held at their new house. It had been catered for by Mr and Mrs Newbould as a wedding gift and Georgie had provided the drinks; his parents had stayed back at the house to arrange everything for the reception.

When they had announced that they were to marry, Arnold had withdrawn Beth's savings from the bank and she had had a pleasant surprise when he had handed it over to her. 'So much?' she had gasped.

'Well... it is time you enjoyed it,' he had laughed. 'You have been working for quite a few years now remember and taken very little out. This is just a little security for your future, that is what we have been saving for remember?'

Brother and sister now stood waiting in the doorway of the church waiting for the music to begin before they started their walk down the aisle. He took her hand and said, 'My sister... all grown up and now a beautiful bride... be happy always. It is a good start that you and Owen have now for your life together.'

'I wouldn't have been here at all without you Arnold, thank you for everything as always. There is just one regret,' and she smiled.

'Yes... I know... I also wish it wasn't me standing here giving you away today.'

'Well, we can't change it can we. On saying that I couldn't have anyone better at my side... any tears I shed today Arnold will be ones of joy... so don't worry,' and she placed a kiss on his cheek. 'I hope you and Adelaide are just as happy when it is your day.'

'Yes... and now that you are settled it won't be long now. Her mother and sister are excited and busy with all the plans, looks like being a proper do... mind...will look a bit lean on my side though Beth with only you and Owen and Thomas as best man and his wife.'

'I shouldn't worry about that Arnold, like us it will be your nearest and dearest and the people who love you and that is enough. From what you have said they understand.'

'Yes they do.'

'And Adelaide and her family are your family now too, they all sound nice people from what you have told me.'

'Yes, they are, the best. But because they are all close I think they think our situation is all very sad, especially her mother.'

'Don't worry I am sure they will spoil you rotten and make up for it. You and Adelaide are not going home tonight are you?'

'Heavens no... god forbid... we are staying with Thomas and his wife. I have a week off so I will be taking her back to Burnley and looking for a job at the same time over there. Her father has been kind enough to put some feelers out for me. Anyway enough about us, today is your day.' The organ music drifted towards the door, 'So my beautiful sister, beautiful bride let's go... it's time for me to give you away with all my love.' He kissed her hands gently, then her forehead. He tenderly wrapped her arm through his for the last time and bursting with pride and keeping his tears under control he walked her down the aisle to a waiting Owen.

Adelaide and Arnold's wedding followed four months later; they arrived in Burnley to be met by Arnold at the station. They were greeted warmly by Adelaide and her family; arrangements had been made for them to stay with one of her relatives.

They had not seen Arnold for a few weeks. He had already moved to Burnley to start a new job on the railways; Adelaide's father had been instrumental in getting him an interview. Ellen had not been impressed when he had announced that he was also leaving, she was still annoyed that Beth had left and got married and now to be told that Arnold was leaving too. Falling on deaf ears her complaints and sarcasm were met with indifference until he finally turned on her, 'Well, after all the years of neglect when we were children and the fact that you have been milking Beth and I for years now, what do you expect? Typical of you I suppose always looking after your own selfish interests... furthest thing from your mind to wish either of us good luck isn't it? It's still all about you and Evelyn... well no longer... we have finally moved on after carrying you both for years. It's over, so get used to it... you are on your own now,' and he had left, suitcase in hand, without a backward glance.

Their wedding day was another celebration of love albeit on a much grander scale than Beth and Owens' day. Adelaide's family were Catholic, so High Mass was to be held. Beth was included in all the final day's arrangements at their home and helped to dress the bride. Adelaide's father had helped too and taken Arnold, Owen and Thomas to the pub out of the way of the women and all the fuss.

Everyone enjoyed the day; Beth sat through the ceremony enraptured with the surroundings and the music. She held on to Owen's hand when they pledged their vows and when he noticed the silent tears streaming down her face he held her hand tighter, no words were needed.

Before they left Burnley to return home, Beth had told them that she was expecting their first child; their news was greeted with delight and Arnold had congratulated Owen and hugged Beth. He was thrilled for his sister and Adelaide had quietly told Beth she hoped they too would be blessed with a child; Beth had held her hand and replied that she was sure they would be.

They bid their fond farewells and returned home to Sheffield. Beth felt tired but happy and content that both of them were now settled with a happier future to look forward to.

Their son had been born in the warm months of summer. Theresa had visited the next day anxious to see her grandson; she had held him close and had become lost in her private thoughts. She was momentarily transferred back in time to when her first born had arrived and the few precious days she had had to nuture him before he was lost to her. Beth acknowledged the silence and made no comment regarding the tears streaming down her mother-in-law's tired and lined face and consequently did not rush her to give him back for his feed.

Elizabeth and the girls appeared later in the day bringing small gifts for the baby and predictably fussed over their first nephew.

She kissed Beth then her brother, 'Okay... so what are we going to call him?' she asked looking into the crib and picking him up.

'Well... I would like him to be called Owen Arthur... but your brother says no definitely not,' said Beth in reply as if Owen wasn't there.

'Now then that is not strictly true, I would like him to be called Owen, of course I would, I just don't want you know who, to think it's after him. Poor excuse for a father that he is... I'm relaxed on the Arthur bit.'

Elizabeth looked at him, 'Owen for heaven's sake, name your son Owen and let him be proud of taking his father's name. It's got nothing to do with that old bastard, good god can you imagine him being a namesake for anyone. Go with it and be proud, let him be his father's son in name and you show him what a real father should be like. I will put the other one straight, don't you worry he won't say a word, there will be no gloating.'

Beth smiled at Elizabeth and nodded her approval to Owen, he laughed and picked up his son. 'So little man I am out voted by the women in this family... Owen Arthur it is then,' and he kissed him on his tiny forehead before handing him back to his mother.

Elizabeth

Life in the house had changed for Elizabeth after Owen had married and moved out to his own home. She was tired of continually trying to keep the peace at home when their father was there without her brother's support; it was a constant battle with him over money for his drinking. All she could see was her mother who had turned into a worn out old woman, continually harangued by her poor excuse for a husband when all she was trying to do was bring up her children and keep them fed and warm against all the odds. She didn't need convincing that if ever there was an argument against marrying a drinker or having children this was it in all its glory.

Owen Snr's humour did not improve when his eldest son had married and moved out. He still silently brooded over the episode of the wedding suit and the fracas in the alehouse but at least none of the family had witnessed it so as far as he was concerned it would be his word against his son's if anything was ever said. Since getting married and moving into his own house, Owen never visited anyway so he relaxed that it would never be mentioned.

He had been sitting in his chair when the news had arrived that a grandson had been born. To change the subject he had reached for his crutch and spitefully shouted at his wife to go and fetch him his jug. The reaching of the crutch was the sign that it might be used if his bidding wasn't carried out, the younger children watched and as usual became tense. Without question their mother left the house and quickly ran down the lane to appease him.

Elizabeth, not being able to hold her tongue, turned on him, 'Here we go again you cannot stand not being the centre of attention can you? It's a baby for God's sake... mind... never did have any effect on you did it a new life being born... even your own.' She stared him squarely in the face, 'Jug of beer... now that is something entirely different. Sell your soul for that father wouldn't you... or even better someone else's if you could get your thieving hands on it? Would make a change from suits don't you think?' she turned from his gaze, picked up her cigarettes and walked towards the door.

He didn't respond to her outburst but inwardly seethed about Owen leaving the fold. He didn't want to alienate his daughters for fear they too might leave and the money coming into the house would be reduced again. In his twisted mind his eldest son was once more to blame for creating this situation.

Elizabeth stood on the doorstep and tried to calm down, she watched as her mother hurried back up the lane with his jug of beer trying not to spill any. She moved to one side to let her in and said, 'Don't say anything to him when you go in... just put it down on the table and leave him to it.' Her mother nodded her head, opened the door and as instructed placed his beer on the table in front of him without saying a word.

She remained outside for some time, at least having his beer to drink would give them all some peace in the short term. She moved to sit on the window sill, lit another cigarette and cynically looked round at her surroundings. Surely one day she thought, one day it has to get better than this and her mind drifted to Owen's new family and then to Sara her friend at work and she smiled to herself. Sara had been planning her wedding, once again Elizabeth was involved in making the dress and she was genuinely pleased for her friend. Sara's family was poor, she had worked hard to support them and Elizabeth hoped that with Samuel she would find the happiness she deserved. She would now have her own house and a man who loved her after all the years of struggling and being the breadwinner of her family. Sara was one of the world's nice people who, even though she carried a heavy load, did not have a nasty word to say about anyone.

'Good Luck girl,' Elizabeth thought to herself and looking down the lane and at her surroundings. She inhaled her cigarette and mused, 'You never know... could be me next... can always live in hope I suppose.' She trod on the finished cigarette and went back into the house. Her father scowled at her as she came back into the house but he remained silent.

During the week leading up to Sara and Samuel's wedding there was the usual excitement at work and both of them took the ribald comments from the buffer girls in good humour. The couple were popular with the working girls, Thomas was a fair manager and they envied Sara acknowledging that she had done well for herself and bagged 'a good catch'.

The day before the wedding a visitor arrived in the packing section bearing a small gift; he worked for one of the company's customers and the gift was a token of thanks for the service they always received from Samuel. As the door opened Elizabeth looked up and was delighted to lock eyes with a good looking, extremely well dressed man. She smiled, he smiled back and said hello.

He asked for Samuel and stayed for about ten minutes chatting to him and passing on his company's best wishes to the happy couple. Elizabeth watched as he approached the door to leave and was amazed when he turned, looked her straight in the eye and said, 'Goodbye Elizabeth... hope to see you again soon,' smiled at her and walked out.

Feeling quite flushed she waited for Samuel to reappear, 'Who on earth was that?' she asked.

'That was William, he brought us a small gift from Tuckers as a wedding gift... wasn't that nice?'

'He is,' she laughed and winked at him.

'Well isn't that strange, he asked what your name was before he left.'

'Did he? Do you know him well then... is he coming on Saturday?'

'I have invited him for a drink afterwards, so you might be in luck,' he smiled and winked back at her. 'I have never seen you looking so flustered Elizabeth... goodness me are you actually blushing?' he asked as he walked out to find Sara.

Samuel had helped Sara's mother out with the cost of the children's clothes for the wedding so they all looked respectable, and the bride looked lovely in the dress that Elizabeth had made for her. A large contingent from the buffing shop had arrived at the church; they all looked completely different out of their work clothes and all cheered the young couple when they emerged from the church as man and wife.

Sara had thanked Elizabeth for her dress and for arranging her hair. 'I never thought I could look like this... thank you so much.'

Elizabeth had held her hand and said, 'You are very welcome... my way of saying thanks. You look lovely... he is a lucky man.'

'Yes, well, talking of men. William may call in a little later, Samuel told me that he had asked your name the other day. Do you like him?'

'Well, it was a shock when he walked through the door, we don't get many good looking men in do we, apart from your Samuel that is,' and she laughed. '...and I was stunned when he said goodbye to me by name... guess who he reminds me of?'

'Go on then... who?'

'Don't think I have gone nuts will you, but he reminds me of the Prince of Wales,' she said quietly.

'Who… the one with that American Mrs Simpson?' said a surprised Sara.

'Yes… you have seen him, he is having an affair with her. They are splashed all over the papers… he is very dashing… don't you think there is a slight resemblance?'

'Not sure… I will tell you if he arrives later… fancy that,' and she laughed at her friend.

'No, don't laugh at me, I said a slight resemblance that's all… not getting above my station.'

The reception was underway when William arrived. Elizabeth caught her breath when she saw him come through the door. She looked away not wanting to appear obvious, turned, lit a cigarette and started talking to Sarah's mother who was standing next to her.

William approached the married couple and congratulated them, Sara studied him and could see the likeness that Elizabeth had referred to. He was good looking, confident and suave, not like any of the men they knew from work. After the pleasantries he lit a cigarette and casually looked around the room until he saw her in conversation with Sara's mother; he studied her for a while, she stood out from any other female in the room. She had poise, was dressed fashionably and was incredibly lovely.

Elizabeth finished her conversation and was fully aware William was looking over to her. She turned and acknowledged him with a smile and a nod of her head; he picked up two glasses of beer and walked across the room.

'Hello Elizabeth,' he said handing her a glass.

'Hello William… well thank you.'

Sara watched from the edge of the room and smiled, her friend looked happy and 'Yes,' she thought to herself, 'there is a resemblance.'

The small reception came to an end and the few guests started to leave but not before once again wishing the couple well. William had remained at Elizabeth's side since he had arrived. They both enjoyed the light conversation and friendly banter and she silently hoped that they would be leaving together.

Taking his cigarette case out of his pocket he took out two cigarettes, 'That's nice,' she said looking at the monogrammed case.

'Yes… it was a present,' and he looked wistfully at the case for a moment before closing it and returning it to his pocket. 'Now… what are you doing afterwards, do you have any plans?' he asked as he lit the two cigarettes together and offered her one.

Taking the cigarette she said, 'Thank you... what am I doing? Nothing exciting, just meeting up with my sisters. We usually go dancing on Saturday nights.'

'Well, in that case why not come dancing with me instead?'

'I'd love to,' she replied without hesitation.

They said goodnight to the newlyweds and while William was chatting to Samuel, Sara took the opportunity to tell Elizabeth that she was happy for her. 'He's so nice... and yes there is a similarity. Look at the way he dresses, so smart and clean, look at his fingernails and not a hair out of place... a proper gent... he could be the Prince of Wales,' and she giggled to her friend, 'Mrs Simpson... eat your heart out.' They both laughed out loud together.

Elizabeth hugged her friend, 'Sarah it has been a lovely day. Now you are a respectable married lady and I am sure Samuel will look after you. Be happy always...you deserve it.'

'I will be, don't worry,' and she turned and took hold of her new husband's hand, 'and I will see you Monday as normal.'

As they walked William asked how long Elizabeth had known Sara and she explained what had happened on her first day at work. He had listened to the graphic description of the buffing rooms, the work that was undertaken there and about the injuries that some of the girls had sustained. 'I am pleased to be out of it... and it is all down to Sarah... I have much to thank her for.'

'Yes. I can see that. Well, those days have gone now so no need to dwell on them. I wouldn't even bother telling anyone that part of the story. To look at you they would have no idea, a natural beauty, you have a presence, so let's try and give you some sophistication.'

Elizabeth looked slightly bemused at him but really didn't understand what he was saying to her, then he said. 'Tell me about your family.'

'Oh... you can put them in the same box... no need to dwell on them either,' she smiled and casually put her arm through his. 'So... where are we going?' she asked changing the subject.

'Which dance do you normally go to?'

'Oh, nowhere special, only local... Edmund Road Barracks,' she laughed.

'Well, tonight my dear... Cinderella is going to the ball,' and offered her his arm.

They continued walking into the city centre and soon found themselves on the High Street passing Elizabeth's favourite shop Cole Brothers. 'That is my favourite shop,' she told him not offering any more information and she looked at the bench that she used to sit on and thought, 'Well, I'm not lying... it is.'

They reached the Town Hall and carried on walking until they were standing outside the City Hall. 'Here we are... this is where we are going.'

Elizabeth looked at him in astonishment, grinned, held her head high and said, 'Well, I'm game if you are,' and practically ran up the steps to the entrance.

He caught up with her and said, 'Just stay at my side and I will guide you through it all... where to go, who to acknowledge and where to leave your coat. As this is your first time here just enjoy the experience.'

'Don't you worry I will... lead on Prince Charming.'

Looking into the mirror in the ladies room she checked her make up and hair, took a deep breath and said to the image staring back at her, 'Well, Bets my girl... think we may have just arrived.' She turned on her heel and with head held high returned to William's side, flashed him a smile, and said, 'Right let's make an entrance.'

Smiling, he put his hand in the small of her back and whispered, 'You look lovely.' He escorted her through the arches that led into the magnificent ballroom. Inwardly she was nervous, mentally she took it all in; the chandeliers, the dresses and jewellery that surrounded her. Any casual observer would only have been aware of a beautiful lady on an attractive man's arm both comfortable in their surroundings and with each other. This image was reinforced when they took to the dance floor and never put a foot wrong.

As the evening progressed he introduced her to various couples and then to a group of men that were standing together but apart from the throng to one side. The group watched as William approached with Elizabeth on his arm. He introduced her to all of them personally, and each one kissed the back of her hand gently, 'Enchanting,' said one of the friends, 'and pray where did our William find you?'

'Never you mind,' came the curt reply, 'come Elizabeth.'

The enquirer watched them return to the dance floor, his gaze not faltering as they started to dance. His eyes never left them as he took an identical cigarette case to William's out of his pocket and lit a cigarette.

He walked her home at the end of the evening, Elizabeth having already worked out in her mind where she would leave him to finish the rest of her journey. There was no way she was going to let him see where they lived, she didn't want to run the risk of not seeing him again.

She stopped on the corner of the street where she had decided to leave him, took her arm out of his and turned, 'I will be fine from here William…time to say goodnight and say thank you for a wonderful evening that has ended a super day. Thank you again,' and she tilted her head for him to kiss her. The kiss she was expecting didn't happen instead he just took hold of both her hands and gave her a chaste kiss on her cheek before lifting her hands to his lips and gently kissing her fingertips.

'Yes, it has been a pleasant day. I will see you again soon and we will do it all over again. Goodnight my dear I shall watch you walk until you disappear into the darkness.'

His reluctance to show any more affection to her than he had, surprised her; she had not been short of admirers so was used to a long goodnight kiss at least, she was used to curtailing over amorous suitors. As she walked away from him she thought to herself, 'Don't rush it… let's just do it his way Elizabeth… the gentleman's way,' and she smiled, turned and blew him a kiss. 'Be a lady,' she said aloud as she turned the corner and giggled to herself.

Arriving home she looked at the usual scene that greeted her yet again, her father sleeping off his drink, slumped on the chaise. 'No change there then,' she thought to herself. She lit a cigarette and went back outside to think about her evening. Sitting on the window sill she looked up at the stars and smiled, 'Well,' she thought, 'what a day. What an evening… how about that… the perfect gent… the way he speaks, looks and how he treats me… like a lady.' After a moment's hesitation, 'Why me… what do I have to offer him… look at it here it's the pits… what would he think?' She finished the cigarette and threw it away with irritation, but their evening kept coming back into her mind. As she tried to sleep she relived their conversations, the way it made her feel when he held her to dance, perfect just perfect. 'Alright Bets, so just enjoy it while it lasts,' she kept telling herself, 'nothing wrong with that… I can always put it down to experience.'

William

He had been pampered to extreme, his every whim was indulged by his doting mother. She took him everywhere and called him 'her darling little man' while his father just looked on in his quiet and contented way having basically no input in his son's upbringing at all. William had been born to them after three miscarriages, they had given up hope of ever having a child so he was made to feel even more precious and was never out of his mother's sight. He sat next to her when her friends visited, accompanied her on shopping trips, she made no decisions without asking for his opinion first. By the age of six he was a charming, self-assured little boy with impeccable manners.

He was educated at private school, but his mother would not consider him becoming a boarder, she wanted him home every day after lessons and encouraged him to bring the 'poor boys' who were boarders home for tea forever reminding him that his mother would never send him away. Consequently, close friendships developed between William and his friends and within the school it was considered a privilege to be in his 'clique' and to be invited into his home. His mother was delighted with his choice of friends, they were all attentive to her and spoke freely of their admiration for her son. She in turn referred to them as William's Admiration Society.

As he grew older his friends became a chosen few; they kept close counsel and strangers were discouraged from forging friendships unless the invitation came from within. Sports were not a favourite pastime of the group they preferred the arts and in particular the writings of Proust, Oscar Wilde, Rimbaud & Byron. They discussed their collective works at length constantly, especially the authors' perspective on love. Known as 'The Pack' to their peers they continued their close friendships to the end of their schooldays; employment was guaranteed by positions being offered from within their own family connections.

As young men they were immaculately dressed and manicured, William styled himself on Edward, The Price of Wales, he had the same blond hair, suave clean shaven looks. His mother loved the similarity and from 'my darling little man' he was elevated to 'my prince.' She was always delighted when 'The Boys' as she referred to them included her in their conversations and asked for her opinions, even though it may only be about the weather or something just as trivial.

From his schooldays up to the day she died when William was twenty-four years old, she never questioned why his group of friends were totally male or why he had never brought a lady friend home to be introduced to her. She just assumed that she was and always would be the centre of his life.

1939

The mood of the nation had shifted from the shock and scandal of the abdication by Edward VII to the very real threat of another war looming with Germany; this was met with dismay and despondency. The last hope of the nation rested on the shoulders of Neville Chamberlain who returned to the country after talks with Hitler and Mussolini waving a piece of white paper declaring that all was well and the threat of war had been averted. The people watched and listened and hoped it was true. The raw wounds of the Great War were still evident every day; memories of loved ones lost in the conflict were brought to mind as reports of the continuing mobilisation by the Germans were still making headlines in the daily papers.

Beth felt her heart sinking, if it did happen again Owen would be conscripted and the memory of her father once again enveloped her. Little Owen was about the same age as she had been when her father had left never to return. 'Please God,' she thought, 'please don't let history repeat itself.'

Owen read her thoughts and tried to reassure her although privately he listened and read all the reports with great concern and only discussed them in depth and at length with Georgie when they were alone together at work.

The nation held its breath.

Elizabeth & William

It unnerved her slightly as it had happened so quickly, she had been shocked when he had proposed to her the week after taking her dancing and had laughed at the suggestion. He had then told her he was deadly serious, she would want for nothing and that there was really no need to wait. She stopped laughing when she realised that he was serious about it so, just as impulsively she accepted. Her agreement to marry him was sealed by yet another chaste kiss on her cheek. 'He's just being a gentleman,' she thought to herself and laughed when he held her hand and said, 'Let's go for a drink to celebrate… you have made me a very happy man.'

She told no-one, William made all the arrangements and gave her money to buy her wedding dress and a full new wardrobe. He was extremely generous, she had never seen that amount of money let alone ever have it in her possession. He told her to shop well and with style, she smiled to herself as she walked through the revolving doors and entered her favourite store to start her purchases. A whole new world opened up to her, she enjoyed every minute of being able to take her time and make her choices, being fussed over by the assistants was a bonus and a couple of times she had to stop and pinch her arm just to convince herself it was really happening. William had told her to have all her purchases delivered to his house apart from her wedding dress and trousseau, that she could have delivered to Sara and Thomas' house.

Conflicting emotions tormented her, one minute she was enveloped in excitement which gave her a thrill in the pit of her stomach, which was then replaced by the feeling of guilt for not confiding in her sisters or more so Owen. She had no reservations about not telling her mother and father, if the latter thought that there might be money to be made from exploiting the situation he would, she would inform them all after the event. The money William had given to her she kept on her person at all times even when she slept and tried hard to appear her normal self.

He had arranged the wedding to take place at the register office, and then confided in Thomas and arranged for Elizabeth and Sara to take the day off work. She was to prepare for her day at their house and Sara was to be her attendant and witness. On her wedding day she walked to work as usual with her sisters, clocked in and spoke briefly with Thomas who wished her good luck, she then left her workplace and headed for Sara's house.

Sara greeted her friend with mixed emotions. She was pleased for her friend but also there was concern, 'I cannot believe that this is happening so quickly... and why all the secrecy Elizabeth... are you sure you are doing the right thing? I only ask because I care about you.'

'I have never been as certain about anything in my life Sara... you took your vows and said, "for better or worse" well for me this certainly will be for the better. I would never have dreamt that anything like this could happen to me, it's like something out of the movies so be happy for me.' She paused, 'The secrecy... I have had to keep it secret because of that old bastard at home, he never misses a trick at least this way I can get married in peace and enjoy the day. Can you imagine him clanging his way through the door with his crutch, drunk as usual shouting the odds. Well, not today, it's my day,' and she hugged her friend. 'Now...wait until you see this.'

Sarah gasped when she saw the wedding dress. 'Oooh look at that... it's just beautiful... like something a movie star would wear,' and her concern for her friend was lost in her excitement.

Elizabeth was of small stature and had features similar to Vivian Leigh; she was petite and very attractive. The dress would cling to her body, it was the most delicate shade of pale grey matte satin, almost silver. From the shoulders it fell into a ruched cross across her back, the hemline fell into panels from below the knee; it fitted perfectly. Her shoes were the exact same colour again in satin and the outfit was completed by a small hair comb of orange blossom.

She had altered Sarah's wedding dress by adding grey seed pearls to the neckline and a satin pale grey sash that fastened at the back with a large bow, they complimented each other perfectly as they left the house in an ordered taxi for the drive into the city.

He was waiting at the register office when she arrived and looked his usual sartorial self. She knew he was bringing a friend to act as witness and recognised him as being one of the friends she had been introduced to at the City Hall. He turned to her and looking straight into her pale grey eyes said, 'You look beautiful Elizabeth... William is a very lucky man... he has my blessing,' and, taking her gloved hand, kissed it before handing it to William who escorted her into the Registrar's office.

The ceremony was over quickly and conducted by the Registrar in a monotone voice. After the witnesses had signed the marriage certificate the doors opened indicating that they were now a married couple and it was now time leave. Elizabeth felt a little deflated inside and she sought out Sara's eyes and looked at her despondently. At the same time William turned to his friend shook his hand and warmly embraced him.

'What's wrong?' asked Sara quietly taking hold of her hand.

'Nothing... really... just being silly I suppose,' turning away from her friend before Sara could notice that her eyes had filled with tears. Composing herself she added, 'I was just thinking about your wedding... this feels cold in comparison.'

'No... no it was lovely,' replied Sara a little too quickly. 'You look wonderful... it is probably down to not having your family here... your brother and sisters... don't worry, you'll be fine.' But she couldn't help feeling concerned for her friend on what should be the happiest day of her life Elizabeth was near to tears, it was unknown.

William had arranged lunch for the four of them at a restaurant near the register office. Sara kept close to Elizabeth and tried not to panic, she had never been in such an upmarket establishment before, in her mind this was somewhere purely for the Toffs not for the likes of her. They were congratulated on arrival by the Maître d' who obviously knew both William and his friend and they were shown to a discreet table already set and decorated for a celebratory lunch. Sara was relieved when she realised that the meal to be served had already been ordered; she waited quietly for each course to begin and waited to see what William did before she picked up any of the cutlery from the wide selection of knives, forks and spoons laid out before her. Unbeknown to her Elizabeth was doing the same, although as usual she carried it off with cool aplomb. The conversation was light and mainly between the two men. Every time Elizabeth caught Sara's eye she would smile wryly then cast a glance around the restaurant at the rest of the diners and think, 'If they only knew they were sitting in the company of two ex-buffers.' She winked at Sarah and lifted her eyebrow in satisfaction, picked up her glass and drank champagne for the first time in her life.

The taxi reappeared after lunch and they dropped a tipsy Sara off at home then carried on towards Williams's house. A silence fell in the taxi between the two of them and a strained atmosphere followed them into the house. It was a modest house but compared to the lane Elizabeth thought it was a palace, it was very tidy and impeccably clean. Unusual for Elizabeth her confidence seemed to disappear, she didn't quite know what to do so she sat on the settee in her wedding dress feeling slightly embarrassed. She sensed William's unease, he was looking through the window and had his back to her, he lit yet another cigarette then turned.

'Yes... well that didn't take very long did it. You have a lot to familiarise yourself with so I will leave you to re-organise everything as you wish and unpack your parcels. I shall see you later,' and out he went leaving her still sitting on the settee somewhat shocked.

She sat for some time in silence. Conflicting thoughts and feelings tormented her, should she go and tell the family that she was now married? Had she been stupid? No, she didn't think so... on the positive side she had moved from a flea pit to a very respectable house. Admittedly it needed an up-to-date woman's touch she thought looking around, but that could be remedied. There was no damp, it was clean and she had all the space in the world just to herself. Then the questions started to torment her. This is our wedding day where has he gone? Why isn't he here? Why has he left me? She felt the hot tears start to fall, they rolled silently down her cheeks onto her wedding dress and she started to sob, 'What have I done?'

She sat till dusk in the parlour of his house still asking the questions he wasn't there to answer. 'Why has he married me? Will he come back? What shall I do?' her cigarettes breaking the bouts of weeping and becoming her only support. She would dry the tears, take a deep breath, then start questioning herself again; she alternated one minute feeling terribly hurt then finally into anger.

Emotionally exhausted she dozed on the settee through the night. William returned early the next morning and disturbed her fitful sleep. He had glanced through the window briefly before opening the door then stood for a moment to look at her and was again touched by her loveliness even though it was evident that she had been crying and obviously had had a troubled night.

She sat up instinctively when she heard the door open and had to think where she was for a moment. Then, looking directly at him with tired eyes said, 'I think you owe me an explanation.'

'Yes I do,' he replied returning her gaze. He then came to her and took hold of her hand. 'I am sorry to say ours will not be a conventional marriage Elizabeth,' and looking directly into her tired grey eyes he went on to tell her that he did love her and could not make love to her, his sexual feelings did not and could not include any woman, ever.

Anger flashed in her eyes, 'Well, that is so good of you to let me know after the event William. I now understand why there was such a rush... thank you for that... it sounds as if you have it all worked out. Do tell me... how can you be sure that I can accept a life knowing that when you are not with me you will be with another man... and that I don't find that and you disgusting?'

'Because my darling, call me a little cynical if you will, but I think it will suit you to have everything you have always desired. You will never be short of money, you will have a desirable house, I will shower you with clothes and jewellery and there will be nothing for you to worry about... and the sex issue... I am sure you will have no problems finding suitors. It could be quite exciting don't you think, your security not threatened by you having affairs. You will be able to court whom ever you wish, I will not interfere or complain.'

She listened to his proposition in silence, her mind working through each suggestion he had made. No worries in this life, cossetted and dressed to perfection, able to have affairs with no redress... she could lose nothing, not that she had anything to lose as it stood. She could become a sophisticated woman given time just like the ones she had watched all those years ago. She didn't want children anyway, so that was a relief that William didn't want a son and heir... so why not? She shocked herself by realising that she was actually considering what he was proposing.

He continued and said he hoped she would understand that yes, on his part, it was a marriage of convenience in which as agreed, he would give her all she desired in return for her loyalty. It would appear to the world at large that they were a respectable married couple, she could take lovers he had no problems with that, all he would ask was that she be totally discreet.

When he had finished speaking she asked the question that had been tormenting her all night, 'Why me... why marry me?'

'Because I love your beauty and to the uneducated eye and all intents and purposes we make a very attractive couple... I need that.'

'No, William, let's be honest here, you need me to avoid prison… if you are caught with your lover… respectability and loss of reputation would be the price you would pay and you would never be able redeem that … why didn't you tell me before we married?'

'Because you might have been shocked even to consider such a thing. In the short time we have known each other I have the impression you are very much your own lady, you do things on your own terms. I think you will enjoy the comfortable life and being accepted as an attractive, extremely well dressed witty member of the elite here, you can and will grow into the role my dear, I am sure.' He picked her hand up again, 'and… I am quite prepared to raise a child as my own should you become pregnant from a liaison… so don't worry basically all the elements are there… you will have nothing to worry about.'

'Don't be too sure of yourself William, you are asking a lot.' She shook his hand away and turned from him, 'What if I say no?'

'I wouldn't want to contemplate that, obviously my reputation would be ruined, a divorce would be costly and undesirable to both parties. Just think of the headlines… where would you go? What would you do? If you accept, I could be your perfect companion.'

'Can I have time to consider all this? It is not the sort of problem I am used to coping with on a daily basis.'

'Of course you can, please take your time.' and he took both her hands in his and kissed them. 'My Elizabeth… please don't leave me… I beg you,' and sank to his knees.

She looked at the top of his head and resisted the temptation to stroke his hair acknowledging that he would not appreciate or welcome her touch. 'Give me some time; you may be asking the impossible for me to live without love.'

Lifting his eyes he replied. 'I do love you. truly I do… but I cannot make love to you… I can't… I'm sorry.'

'Do you have a lover at the moment?'

'Yes,' he replied quietly.

'Does he know we are now married?'

'Yes.'

Their wedding came into her mind and his witness saying that they had his blessing, she sighed, took her hand out of his, turned away and reached for yet another cigarette. 'Do you realise how hurtful this is…that he knew and was party to the deceit and I didn't?'

'Yes.'

'Leave me alone... I need some space.'

He stood and turned away from her and headed for the door; before he left he looked back at her, 'Will you be here when I return... please?'

Their eyes locked, Elizabeth's were full of sorrow, 'I don't know.'

* * * * * *

'Don't worry,' said Sybil, 'she's a big girl now, I'm sure that wherever she is it's preferable to here,' nodding over to her father in his usual position sleeping off his lunchtime beer. 'She'll surface soon enough I'm sure.'

'Well. so long as she is alright.' replied her mother ignoring the innuendos. 'But it's not like her not to come home at all.' She placed her two daughters' meagre dinner on the table. The younger ones as usual were all sitting in a line on the mattress and they watched their elder sisters eating.

'Don't look at us like that Dennis... I am sure you have already had yours.'

Her youngest brother dropped his eyes and didn't reply. He was six years old.

'It never stops does it?' said Sybil leaning back in her chair. 'I can remember sitting there and watching him eat his fill,' nodding at her father, 'and wondering why we were all constantly hungry.'

'Please... don't start... you'll wake him,' said her mother sounding anxious; she looked over to her younger children and instinctively touched her stomach.

The sisters noticed the gesture, stopped eating, looked at each other then in unison at their mother.

'You're not... surely... not again, not another one?' said Sybil looking at her mother. 'You can't be can you at your age? You have come to the end of those years haven't you?'

Their mother did not respond, she just looked at them with tear-filled eyes and turned away.

'Clearly not,' said Theresa breaking the silence, 'still life in the old dog too... more's the pity.'

'Well, what he lacks in being a father he certainly makes up for in having his oats obviously. My God mother why? Haven't you struggled enough... you can't really enjoy this existence.' She raised her voice, 'Fight him off if you have to... look at you a worn out old woman still with a family to feed and yet another one on the way... unbelievable!'

She stood and impulsively kicked at his good leg with all her might. 'You selfish old bastard.' She picked up her cigarettes and walked out of the door.

He jumped and instinctively reached for his crutch, the malevolent eyes watched her go.

'She tripped,' said their mother quickly placing herself between her husband and their children, 'it was an accident.'

'It better have been,' he snarled still holding the crutch and shouting after her. 'Did you hear me... you're not too big to sort out you know.'

'Happy days... here we go again,' said Theresa looking over at him. She shoved her chair back and went out to join her sister. 'Can you believe that?' she asked a fuming Sybil, 'It's enough to put you off married life forever.'

At that precise moment Elizabeth walked round the corner at the bottom of the lane, she approached them with half a smile, 'Hello you two.'

Theresa looked relieved to see her elder sister and said, 'Hey look who's here... you look nice... is that new?' touching the very fashionable coat they had not seen before.

'Here,' said Sybil passing her a cigarette before she had the chance to answer, 'you're going to need it... '

'Why... what's wrong?' she lit the cigarette and listened to her sisters in stony silence.

They came back into the house together. Their mother looked at the three of them and felt embarrassed. In her nervousness she turned back to the table to pick up the few morsels that were left on her older daughter's plates. The younger children watched with interest what she was going to do with them.

'Is this right what I have just been told?' Her father looked at her cautiously then with fear as she grabbed his crutch before he could. 'Never enough for you is it... the booze, the selfishness... you old bastard... congratulations another one on the way... that's right... another one... what is wrong with you... when is it going to stop?' she glared at him and he tried to move back into his chair out of her reach.

'So do tell us. Who is going to feed this one then?' visibly tightening her grip on the crutch, 'because I tell you now... I don't live here anymore so you can fund this one yourself!' With one swing of his crutch she knocked his jug of beer clear off the table and it smashed on to the stone floor. He looked mortified, his beer had gone and his eldest daughter was still holding his crutch like a cricket bat, not for the first time did he fear what she was about to do next.

He glared at his wife, 'It's nothing to do with me,' he shouted back hoping to deflect her anger, it had the opposite effect.

'No... it never is... is it... somebody else's is it... like always... we're all bastards then are we... yes?' and she nudged him with the crutch, her blazing eyes not leaving his. 'My God just listen and look at yourself, you are an absolute disgrace and do you really think that she,' pointing at her mother, 'has really got the time or the inclination to be having it away with everybody else. Boody good luck to her if she has, look at her,' she shouted at him, 'a worn out old woman... looking years older than she actually is and that is all down to you.'

Drawing breath she continued, 'You are nothing but a liar, a drunk and a bully who turns into a coward when we take you on. How does it feel father? No hang on a minute... a contradiction in terms, the word father as far as you are concerned, isn't it? Look at them,' she spat at him pointing at the younger ones, 'aren't you proud? And, another one on the way, well congratulations and seeing that announcements are the order of the day I have one of my own to make. I am now a married woman,' and she shoved her left hand under his nose. 'I am moving out as of now, so you,' jabbing him once more in the ribs, 'are now your own old man on the premise of one in... one out.'

The room was shocked into silence at this announcement; her mother, sisters and the younger ones had not moved since Elizabeth had walked back into the house. They were used to the shouting but realised that on this occasion it was different, they had never seen their eldest sister so angry. Time had taught them that there were bouts of anger, then a period of resignation and silence would follow until the next flashpoint.

Furious at the insults being thrown at him and Elizabeth getting the better of the argument, his anger made him put his hands on the arms of the chair to try and stand, but falling back he realised that she had the advantage and he could do nothing. 'Get out!' he roared. 'You have always been a troublemaker... you are just like that brother of yours... get out and never come back.'

'Oh, so he is my brother now is he. Well, according to you none of us... ' sweeping her arm around the room and encompassing all her siblings, 'are related to each other. We are all bastards with different fathers.' She threw his crutch at him, 'you are no better than a pimp living off immoral earnings you bastard... well no more. I will let you starve first, they would all be better off without you, so why don't you die and give us all some peace. In fact I will give you all the money in the world if you promise to drink yourself to death and let me watch. Yes, I would gladly do that and without any conscience. I have a long memory old man, I see you for what you are... a low life. Mother... I will be in touch,' and she snatched up her handbag and headed for the door. Her sisters followed her relieved to be out of the house but more out of curiosity regarding the announcement she had just made.

'Hey... hold up Bets. Christ that was some blow out wasn't it. You feeling better now?' asked Theresa and as she turned they were both shocked to see tears streaming down her face.

They both hugged her, 'Hey it's okay... stop crying... not like you after a run in with the old man.' Theresa took hold of her hand, 'So...c'mon my lovely sister let's go for a drink away from here and you can tell us all about this marriage. I think I am more shocked about that than our mother having yet another.'

They turned to leave when all of a sudden her sister stopped in her tracks 'No, you're not as well are you, hell fire!'

'Don't be ridiculous,' Elizabeth spat back. 'You know as well as I do I will never have any children. I made that pledge years ago when I had to help to deliver you and how old was I then?' she answered. 'Nothing has happened to change my mind after what we have all been through. Definitely not, so don't even go there...it will never happen.'

'Sorry. Bets.' a chastised Theresa replied. 'I should have known better... it's all been such a shock that's all... where are we going?'

Her sister sighed, 'I don't care...the first one we come to and I am buying.'

They sat in The Lancers, the nearest pub to the lane. 'Do we know him?' asked Sybil.

Elizabeth had regained her composure and chose her words carefully, 'No, you don't know him. I have only known him for a short while... it all happened very quickly...he swept me off my feet, whisked me off to the Registry Office and the deed was done. There you go,' and she held out her left hand to show the two beautiful rings on her wedding finger; both her sisters gasped.

'Will you just look at that,' said Sybil as they took hold of her hand. Then, looking at her directly, 'Would have liked to have been there Bets, why all the secrecy?' she sounded disappointed.

'Because I didn't want that old bastard knowing and making trouble like he did when Owen got married.'

'Was Owen there... does he know?'

'No he wasn't and he doesn't know either, only Sara as her Thomas knows him. I met him at their wedding actually.' Her sisters looked at each other with raised eyebrows concerned with her demeanour.

'Well you dark horse,' said Theresa trying to lighten the conversation. 'So do tell... what's he like this Mr Wonderful. When are we going to meet him?'

'When the time is right,' said Elizabeth looking away from them. 'I can hardly bring him up the lane can I, so just be patient.' She took a cigarette out of the packet and lit it. Her sisters both noticed a sound of resignation in her reply which indicated the end of the conversation.

They parted and she returned to her new home, William had already returned and was reading the newspaper. 'Hello,' he greeted her quietly.

As she started to take her gloves and coat off she turned to him and said without any emotion in her voice, 'William... I accept.' He noted the tone of resignation and the sadness in her eyes.

He looked relieved, stood and took hold of her hands, 'Thank you... you won't regret it my dear... trust me,' he said trying to lift her mood.

'Well it is not as simple as that is it. I really have no option William... do I?'

Still keeping hold of her hands, 'It will work darling... don't worry... look... if you are not happy say in six months' time, I will buy you your own house. I will support you always. What more can I say or promise you to put your mind at rest?'

She looked at him, her eyes devoid of any feeling, 'Not a lot... let's face it we now have a contract you and I to live a lie. You will be able to have your unlawful liaisons and I will be able to have my dalliances. I have agreed to pay the price for that, you have prostituted me... bought me off... I feel very shallow for accepting your money.'

'Elizabeth, you will have a lifestyle that will be the envy of others. I have already told you that, socially we will be accepted in all the right circles.'

Her mind flashed back to the argument with her father, 'Hmm yes... the right circles... whoever they are. There is the first obstacle, are you going to give me instruction on how you wish me to appear when we are in company... am I to be attentive, besotted, submissive... the quiet little lady... do tell William?' A note of sarcasm crept into her tone, it was not wasted on him, she turned away.

'That will not be necessary Elizabeth, one look at you on my arm and the world will accept that you are no shrinking violet I am sure,' he answered with a wry smile.

'Is that supposed to be a compliment or an insult?'

'Just be yourself that is all I am saying,' he sighed then continued. 'Elizabeth you are a beautiful woman, I am proud to have you as my wife. There is no need for you to appear submissive, for heaven's sake to an untrained eye all anyone will see is a married couple that complement each other perfectly... elegant... sophisticated.'

'There you go again, it will all be false and I can't promise to pull the sophisticated bit off, that will take time.' Reaching for a cigarette she looked at him again directly, 'Can I still work?'

He held his lighter to her cigarette, 'Do you wish to work? I am sure I can arrange something for you if you must. The allowance you will have will be very generous, why on earth would you wish to continue working where you are? I assume that is what you are actually asking me?'

'To keep my sanity that's why. Don't ask me to negate what I am all together William please, and don't even think of arranging a position for me elsewhere. I am happy where I am thank you.' She sounded determined and she turned away from him again.

He acknowledged her resolve, 'Alright... if you must... but I would prefer you not to mention it when we are out socially.'

'Well, like I would, let's face it I am not likely to meet any of your cronies there anyway, am I?' she retorted.

'No need to be crude about it Elizabeth,' he replied beginning to sound slightly frustrated.

'Me... crude... c'mon William whatever were you thinking. You married an ex buffer... what did you expect... really?' she raised her eyebrow in question.

'I would prefer you not to work... it is as simple as that,' he answered tartly.

'Sorry... no can do... I have to have something in my life that is real. Don't you understand that? Don't worry I shall not let you down.' She looked directly at him as she stubbed the cigarette out and he nodded in resignation. 'Fine... well now we have settled all that and unaccustomed as I am... I think I may just go shopping to lift my spirits,' and reached for her coat.

William smiled with relief, opened his wallet and handed her a wad of notes, 'Here you are my dear... enjoy.'

'Don't you worry I intend to,' she replied with a grin as she put the cash safely into her purse. He helped her on with her coat and before leaving she turned to check her appearance in the mirror then planted a kiss on his cheek 'See you later sweetie.'

The weeks that followed felt strange in respect of returning to a new home at night and not having the continuous rows with her father, but she also felt that she was slowly finding her feet. This new found independence together with the fact that she had enough money to do exactly as she wished initially unnerved her; she acknowledged that it was not to be a conventional marriage but she would not have wasted his money. They fell into a daily routine and she always left for work before he did not wishing to embarrass him as she obviously dressed down. When he returned she would be changed and presentable in her role as his wife. He had asked her to arrange for the house to be redecorated and gave her carte blanche to change or buy anything that she wished. He told her it was her house now and he would like it to reflect their taste and would leave it in her capable hands. When she had decided what she wanted to purchase, she was to let him know which stores were involved and he would open the appropriate accounts for her.

She appreciated returning to her own home and space after work and she had also started to think about the redecorating. She was excited at the prospect of the house taking on an Art Deco look and was influenced by the window displays of the stores she was now patronising, instead of the old dark Victorian influence that had been his mother's taste, it would be fresh and modern. They ate out regularly and she was slowly learning the etiquette of dining and growing more confident by the week. She loved dressing to go out and she felt that William was being considerate by not disappearing into his other life just yet and leaving her alone in the house all night; then again she appreciated that it was early days. What delighted her was the obvious reaction from other diners when they walked into a restaurant or arrived at a social gathering. The women would cast their eyes down her from her hair to her feet; the men would nod courteously and raise their glasses. William had been correct she didn't have to get involved in heavy conversation it was all just hollow social chit chat, she realised she could play the part to perfection.

At work she was unsure whether or not to confide in Sara regarding the arrangement of their marriage, then thought better of it. Whenever her friend asked how things were Elizabeth would just laugh and say things were fine. She saw her sisters on a daily basis but always kept their conversations short regarding her new life, once a week she would send provisions for her mother and the younger ones. 'I feel as if I have turned into our grandmother sending food parcels,' she said to Theresa, 'you remember those days?'

Theresa nodded, 'Could I ever forget... what a nice lady... thank God she was. She had the right idea giving him no money to drink away... she must have been ashamed of him.'

'Not by herself,' replied Elizabeth losing herself momentarily to the memories drifting back of their childhood. 'I cannot believe there is another one on the way... I reckon he lost the wrong bit in the war don't you?' and they both laughed out loud.

'Changing the subject Bets... you told Owen yet?'

'No, I plan to call and see them tonight,' was the reply.

Owen and Beth both expressed concern initially when she arrived at their house unexpectedly and announced that she was now a married woman. Concern turned to surprise when she told them where she was now living, he knew it was a good area. She was getting used to fending off the questions regarding her quick decision to marry someone they hadn't even met, did Owen know him, what did he do for a living?

'Stop worrying,' she said to him. 'I am a grown woman now and make my own decisions... its fine... I'm fine.' She lit two cigarettes and handed him one, 'I am very well looked after.'

He settled himself that she looked very well dressed and coiffured. 'Well, well...my sister, now married and a lady of means and property. I am glad for you Bets, it suits you.' He held her and kissed her on the cheek. 'We will look forward to meeting him... has the old man been round yet?' and laughed when the expected reply was returned.

Beth laughed with them. 'I'm pleased for you... be happy Elizabeth.' Owen watched as she embraced his sister but felt he noted just something in Elizabeth's demeanour that wasn't quite right. He brushed his thoughts aide aside and kept his own counsel; Beth would probably say he was being over protective.

She thanked them, then changed the conversation. 'Right... where is my nephew... I'm coming for you.' Little Owen giggled as she picked him up and tickled him. Still holding him she turned back to her brother, 'I assume you know the other news?'

'Don't let's spoil a good day Bet's, I can think of better things to talk about.'

She nuzzled the back of the little boy's neck and he giggled again. 'Yes you're right... okay baby... let's have some more good news then,' she handed him back to Beth before surprising her brother further by telling him that she would have a decorating job for him and Georgie at her new home.

'What a room?'

'No... the whole house,' and laughed at the look of surprise on both their faces. 'What's wrong?'

'Well from what I know of the area they are decent sized houses.'

'So what's the problem?'

'No problem at all... tell me all about it.'

He was delighted at the prospect of earning extra cash but told her that the work would have to be undertaken in the evenings after work and over a few weekends. He asked if her new husband would agree to that and Elizabeth had nodded and told him that there would be no problem. She had decided to leave the revamp of the house until the initial six months had passed and at times she felt nervous about William meeting any of her family. In the weeks that followed she realised that he would have thought it through and would carry off any introductions impeccably. He was fine with Sara and Thomas so why not Owen, Beth and her sisters.

She needn't have worried, he knew the day would come and when she told him she had asked for Owen's advice on decorating the house he readily agreed to meet them all and said, 'Yes, it is time we met, if only to put their mind at rest. Invite them anytime.'

She relaxed and knew it would be alright. When the day arrived he greeted them warmly and they all readily accepted him as their brother-in-law. She had one request of them which was that they not call her Betty or Bets in his presence and, although a little bemused, they all respected her wishes.

The initial six months deadline passed and she could sense that William appeared on edge. She had learned a lot over the short period they had been together and as he had predicted she did enjoy her lifestyle and in particular her persona that was accepted in the social whirl of Sheffield. Her two lives didn't conflict, no-one she met when on his arm in the evening would ever guess she worked in a factory during the day and she found that in itself satisfying and allowed herself wry smiles at the nonsense of it all. William always gave her a few days' notice when he would be 'otherwise engaged' as they referred to it and she quite enjoyed retaining her independence. If his plans fell over the weekend she would delight her sisters when she announced that he was away on business and she would join them at the Barracks for a fun night of flirting and singing with the band. She had two wardrobes full of clothes, one for socialising in William's circle the other was for work and going out with her sisters, life felt good.

She finally put his mind at rest and told him everything was fine and she was happy. She had decided on the new colour scheme for the house and asked if he would like to approve her choices. He had smiled, taken hold of her, and said he was delighted. He had every confidence in her taste and he would await the outcome with anticipation and pleasure.

She started on her plans to refurbish the house. She knew that she had his blessing to turn it into their home and to remove all vestiges of the Victorian era and his mother. She knew what she wanted to achieve and with Owen's advice on colours and textures the ideas flowed and came to fruition.

The hall and staircase were planned to make an impact. They used a bold colour scheme of silver and black with bold flashes of red and yellow. For the living room and bedrooms the prime colours were a mix of eau-de-nil, oyster, the palest of green and different toned beiges with the classic chevrons in black on the otherwise plain walls. The heavy light fittings were replaced with uplighters which complimented the overall effect. The furniture she chose was streamline in shape, and the drapes were soft folds of plain fabric which replaced the heavy velvet curtains and pelmets his mother had favoured. Owen had told her to start on the top floor and work down, that way there would be no damage to a newly painted staircase and to be patient as it would take a few weeks with them working during the day. She acknowledged that she had to contain her impatience and that it wasn't going to happen overnight. She was happy in the knowledge that Owen and Georgie would work as fast as they could, that it would be done right and that it would put money in their pockets. Whatever she removed from the house, if it was good quality, she offered it to them and kept things back that she knew her mother could use.

They started in the bedrooms first, the two smaller bedrooms, one of which William used on occasions. She had chosen a more masculine design in beige and black for him, her bedroom was a mix of eau-de-nil and a muted shade of damask rose, the geometric rugs complimented the plain polished floor, the old heavy wardrobes were replaced with a pale veneered finish, her bed throw was beige satin.

Georgie had been shocked at her plans and the capacity to convert her ideas into the actual. 'Well Bets... oh sorry Elizabeth... I have to say how well you have done. Where do you get your ideas from? Who would have thought... from the lane to this... it's marvellous.'

She had laughed as he had corrected himself with her name, William was not there so it didn't matter. 'The ideas... always aim high Georgie Boy... aim high,' and placed a kiss on his cheek.

The peck on his cheek took him by surprise and he blushed slightly, 'Well you can say that again, what do you say Owen?'

He smiled at her, 'I just think it's a good thing we are on the job here Georgie, otherwise she could have made a right mess of it'. Georgie laughed out loud and Owen ducked as she threw a cushion at him. 'Seriously... proud of you sis, you deserve it after all that has happened. Does William know any of it?'

'No,' came the reply. 'No need for him to know all the sordid details... or meet his father-in-law either... let's not go there.'

'Just don't let him in here ... ever,' said her brother looking directly at her. 'I am serious.'

'Goes without saying, don't worry,' and placing her arms through theirs said, 'Right boys...time for a drink.'

When the house was finally finished, she was delighted with the overall effect and so was William. 'Thank you my darling for turning this old house into our home... I love it.'

Beth & Owen: September 1939

After months of rumours and politicians rhetoric war had finally been declared and was confirmed by the wavering voice of Chamberlain on the radio. It was announced two days after the Germans had marched into and bombed Poland. The nation listened, then wept, as they remembered the horrors that had been unleashed twenty-five years earlier, the country was at war with the Germans again.

Although the spectre of war had gradually increased over the preceding months, human nature being what it is everyone had hoped that Hitler would cease his aggression in Europe thereby averting another conflict. The authorities had mobilised just in case, conscription papers were ready for mailing, gas masks had been issued, plans for evacuating children had been made a priority and Anderson shelters were being built in back gardens.

A strange feeling now enveloped the country after the formal announcement, everything seemed to be on hold and anything other than the essential industries went on short time, a complete blackout was enforced throughout the country. Although nationally the mobilisation continued there was no military action for months which led some to question what was happening and to declare it a 'Phoney War'. Owen and Georgie had time on their hands, there was no need to work Saturdays now as the work had slowed down, and Owen had started to enjoy full weekends at home. The money that he and Georgie had earned from decorating Elizabeth's house had been put to one side for a rainy day and it looked as if that rainy day wasn't far off.

As the weeks passed, each time Beth heard the letter box clatter and the letters drop to the floor she held her breath and prayed. Owen had noticed that she had become pale and appeared on edge over the last few weeks and had put it down to the war situation; everyone was tense so he didn't question her. Groups collected on street corners and in the pubs to discuss the implications of it all, it was the sole topic of conversation everywhere you went.

His conscription papers arrived in the conspicuous brown government envelope; it lay on the floor and threatened her. She picked it up then bolted into the kitchen to be sick, her young son watched her retch between the sobs then pass out. The toddler had screamed as his mother had slumped to the floor still gripping the brown envelope. His father was in the yard when he heard his son scream, he ran back in the house and called out Beth's name as he moved towards her lying on the floor. As he knelt beside her he saw the envelope in her hand and his heart sank.

'Beth... Beth... it's alright love... come on... please it's alright,' he cradled her head, held her hand and kept repeating her name. 'Beth... it's alright... I'm here... come on love... Beth.'

She came round, saw his startled eyes, and heard her son whimpering softly at her side. She remained where she was for a moment to collect her thoughts then tried to reassure them both, her son first by reaching for his hand.

'I'm alright Owen... don't worry,' she looked and sounded tired.

'I know you have been worrying about this for months,' he said softly taking the envelope from her hand and looking at it. 'I am going to ask you not to worry. I know that will be difficult, but it will be alright... you have to believe that. History will not repeat itself... come on... up you come.' He gently lifted her from the floor, her son clinging to her legs, she softly caressed the little one's head to give him reassurance.

He held her tightly but it did not stem the tears, she wept into his chest, 'I'm sorry... so sorry,' she sobbed.

'Hey... what is this. I was here so there is no need for you to be sorry,' he replied nuzzling her ear.

'Yes there is... of all the times... I am so frightened.'

'Everyone is frightened silly,' and trying to make light of the situation he said, 'anyway I might not be going anywhere yet. I have to pass the medical first haven't I?'

'No Owen... hear me out,' she shook her head. 'I was hoping it was a mistake but it's not, I'm pregnant.' She paused, 'What an awful time to be bringing a baby into the world. How is that for history not repeating itself... and what will become of us if..?' the tears rolled and she sobbed at the same time triggering their son into tears again.

'Hey shush... it's fine,' and he kissed the little one on his head. 'Right now let's go back, just for a minute.' He paused, taking in what she had just said and trying for her sake not to look too shocked. 'Listen... I will not have Adolf Hitler ruining the best news of the day, the month in fact... thank you,' and he kissed her. 'You cannot believe how happy that makes me.' He picked up their son and held them both tightly, 'Hey little man... did you hear that?' The little one chuckled as his father tickled him and quickly forgot his tears. He sat Beth down and put their son on her knee, 'Now let me get you a cup of tea then we will talk all about it and put your mind at rest.'

He knew he would have to let her talk all her fears through before she would relax, so they sat until dusk fell and discussed all the implications real and imagined. At the end of the discussion she felt drained but relieved that she had told him their news and that they had both openly shared their fears for what the immediate future held. They had opened the envelope together and read the instructions of when and where he was to report for the necessary medical examination; they both acknowledged that it was a very slim chance that he would not pass. It was a subdued weekend, with not many words being spoken, they were replaced by just a touch of hands or a gentle caress trying to give reassurance.

It had all happened so quickly. Owen attended his medical appointment and within days had received his instructions on which base he was to report to without delay. He and Georgie had gone for their medical on the same day, but to his horror Georgie had failed so was told he was exempt. Owen wasn't sure whether to sympathise or congratulate him until he realised that his friend felt humiliated and guilty about it; he felt people would think he was a coward or at worst a malingerer.

'Nothing could be further from the truth Georgie, don't be daft,' and hoping to comfort his friend said, 'apart from that I need someone here to keep an eye on Beth. We are expecting another baby and she is terrified of what might happen. Hitler is clearly a mad man, look at Poland... it couldn't have happened at a worse time for us. Oh Christ... she shouldn't have to be on her own at a time like this Georgie,' his voice wavered slightly.

Georgie, ever supportive, and putting aside his own upset, placed his arm around his friend's shoulder when he noticed Owen had tears in his eyes. 'Try not to worry about what is happening over here, you will have enough on your plate mate. Annie and me will always be there for you, Beth and your children... never doubt it Owen... ever.' They embraced each other like brothers and wept together, no further words were spoken.

Mr Appleyard had called him in to the office to wish him good luck and to pay him his outstanding wages. He had also enclosed a bonus in his wage packet for all the years of good service and wished him luck. 'Just a little something for the family Owen... take care lad and watch your back... always,' he said sombrely. 'We will all pray for you... God speed.' He had shaken his hand and turned away quickly so as not to upset him further; Owen acknowledged him and nodded his head and silently blinked back the tears. Appleyard watched him through the window leave the yard, all the employees had come out to shake his hand and wish him good luck and just for a moment he thought of the day that he had watched his wretch of a father storm out of the same gates on his son's apprentice day.

'Keep safe Owen,' he whispered.

The day arrived for him to leave. Few words needed to be spoken, they had already and tearfully said it all to each other. Trying to steel herself Beth kissed him then watched in silence as he walked away from her down the road; she held their son's hand and told him to wave to his father when she knew he would turn round to take a final look at them. Only when he had turned the corner did silent tears roll down her cheeks, there had been no marching, no cheering this time just a silent goodbye. A conversation drifted in to her mind from long ago, 'Always choose hope over despair,' and the policeman's face briefly came into her mind and she smiled. Her son looked up at her blue eyes looking for reassurance and smiled back at her, 'Come on you... let's go and find something nice to eat,' she said to him and he giggled in anticipation as they went back into the empty house.

His mother and siblings had embraced him before he left and she told him she loved him, was proud of him and to take care; Elizabeth had been bereft.

'I'm so worried about Beth... look after them for me Bets... please,' he had said as he had let go of her and turned away.

'I will... I promise... don't worry,' came the reply through her sobs as she watched him walk away.

His father had said nothing to him, he just watched the sad departure through the window, his dark thoughts were his own; he shared them with no one.

The months that followed were tense for them all. They listened to the daily radio reports of Germany's relentless advancement through Europe; they appeared not only invincible but ruthless with it. England was firmly in Hitler's sites, they all knew that it was just a matter of time.

Arnold and Elizabeth's husband were employed in reserved industries as was Georgie now. Arnold worked on the railways and William was involved in the production of steel in a management position. Georgie had given his notice in at Appleyards and used his father's influence to get him a job at Hatfields which was the only steelworks in the country to be producing 18-inch armour piercing shells. He worked permanent twelve hour shifts; in this way he felt that he was contributing to the war effort and more importantly supporting and protecting Owen.

Arnold kept in constant touch with his sister. If his roster took him through Sheffield he would work through a double shift so that his replacement would then pick him up on his way back, or he and Adelaide would use his concession and come to stay with her. They both asked if she wished to come and live with them in the short term, but she declined as Owen was initially based for his training at a tracking station on the east coast and it had been relatively easy for him to return back home on his forty-eight hour passes. Beth's pregnancy was proceeding well and she now had a date for the baby's arrival, it was due mid-July.

The Christmas of 1939 came and went, Germany's aggression continued apace in Europe. By May 1940 they had invaded both Denmark and Norway in order to protect their supply of ore from Sweden and to also give them a base from which they could break the British naval blockade that had been set up against them. Hitler then turned his attention to Holland and Belgium. Blitzkrieg followed when he gave orders to attack both countries and bombed Rotterdam near to extinction; both countries were then occupied.

Three days after the Blitzkrieg British politicians pressured Chamberlain to resign and Winston Churchill became Prime Minister, head of the wartime coalition government and ready to lead the country with strength and resolve. In his first broadcast he tried to calm nerves and declared that Britain 'Would never surrender ourselves to servitude and shame.' Coal production was stepped up together with fighter aircraft production. British troops had already been deployed to the Continent prior to the Low Countries being invaded, but no serious direct attacks on them had taken place by the Germans to date.

Overnight things changed and the nation awoke to the reality of Dunkirk; a government appeal had been broadcast for all private naval vessels moored on the South Coast to report to their local Royal Navy Reserve or other government offices. It appeared that British and French troops had been driven back by the Germans. They had amassed at Dunkirk on the beaches and were stranded with their backs to the Channel and at the mercy of German land and air forces. The evacuation of Dunkirk started; the nation waited in fear.

Beth listened intently to all the radio reports and each time she listened she had her son at her knee and her hand on her unborn baby. Owen and all the troops listened as well and were buoyed and cheered by Churchills' rallying and patriotic speeches after the limp-wristed appeasement stance of Chamberlain. The success at Dunkirk, that had rescued in total over three hundred thousand men, gave them a renewed confidence although Churchill did caution at the same time, 'Wars are not won by evacuations.'

Hitler was incensed at what he viewed was a humiliation and ordered Goering to make plans for the Luftwaffe to overpower the English with all the forces at his command in the shortest possible time. The attacks were to be directed primarily against the Royal Air Force and their ground installations together with the aircraft industries. Within a month a devastated France had capitulated and the British stood alone.

The run up to the Battle of Britain began on the tenth of July. Beth and Owen's new baby was due on the eighteenth, so Georgie and Annie moved in with Beth for support and to help with little Owen when she went into labour. The little one enjoyed having them around, although Georgie's shifts were onerous so he saw very little of him, but when he did he made fun the order of the day which delighted the little boy.

The midwife was summoned two days after the due date and before the end of the day a daughter was born to Beth and Owen. She was delivered already crying which seemed to reflect the times she had been born into. Beth held her baby and tried not to cry, but her emotions were shot and as her tears flowed Annie held her friend tightly with love and cried with her. She missed Owen dreadfully and looked at the little one in her arms and made a silent promise, 'You will give me the strength to keep us all well and away from harm until your father returns to us from this nightmare safe and well.' She kissed the tiny head and called her son into the bedroom to take his first look at his sister.

Owen had applied for and been granted a forty-eight hour pass on compassionate grounds. Georgie knew what train he would arrive on at the main station. Taking little Owen with him he held him high on his shoulders until the train arrived. Much excitement from the little boy at the sight of the trains which was surpassed when he saw his father in his uniform walking towards them. Georgie let the little boy go and he shouted with excitement as he ran along the platform into a pair of loving open arms.

Hanging on to his son and holding his hand out to his friend, 'Thanks mate... how are my girls?'

'Beautiful,' was the reply. 'So let's get you home to say hello to your daughter.'

Annie and Georgie returned to their own house while Owen was home. His time there was short but cherished and Owen spent as many of the few hours available to him with his son and newly born daughter. They didn't want to discuss the recent events in Europe and the battle for the skies that was raging in the south, but it was inevitable that Owen would be transferred overseas at some point; it was development neither of them relished but his concern was more for Beth and the children than himself.

'Whatever happens you must always look after yourself and the children first. You will make the right decisions I know you will... it doesn't matter that we won't be able to discuss it... ' she stifled a sob and held on to him. He held her tightly and stopped speaking for a moment until he had composed himself.

'Beth trust me... you will always be my motivation to survive... know that... I in return just need you to promise me that you will make the decision to move from here in order to keep safe. Don't worry that you might not be able to let me know... I will find you,' she sobbed again. 'It is important that I know that Beth... please.'

Sighing, then wiping her eyes, she quietly answered him, 'I will... I promise,' but her resolve left her once more and the tears came back again between the sobs.

'What can I say to comfort you?'

She shook her head. 'That you will come back to us... ' he looked into her tear-stained face and sad eyes and nodded.

'You know I will.'

'I'm sorry,' she started to again cry. 'I shouldn't be putting pressure on you... forgive me.'

'Hey... I am the one who should be saying sorry,' he said gently. 'You have been alone nearly all the way through this pregnancy... and with all that's happening…' he kissed her ear. 'Whatever that mad man throws at us he will get it back tenfold now that Churchill is in charge don't worry. It might take some time, but try not to dwell on what could happen, I will come back to you.'

He packed his kit and before he left put his son to bed and stayed with him until he fell asleep. He caressed the small, innocent face, listened to him breathing gently and kissed him goodbye. Before he had fallen asleep he had held him close and told him that 'Daddy has to go away… so be a good boy and look after your Mummy and your sister.' Beth had listened and the tears flowed again with the memories of her father's identical instructions to her brother so many years before.

He held, then kissed his daughter on her tiny cheek, and placed her back in her cot. He turned to Beth not able to hide the tears in his eyes. Taking her in his arms, 'They are beautiful… you are beautiful and I love you… you will be my strength… look after them… look after yourself… I don't want you to come to the door I just need to go. You are my life and my strength… all of you… love you… never, ever… ever doubt it.' He kissed her, let her go, picked up his kit bag and left with a heavy heart, closing the door quietly behind him. He held onto the wall for support, steeled himself and tried to muffle his sounds of anguish as he listened to the sound of Beth's loud sobs.

Georgie was waiting at the station and saw his friend approaching. His heart went out to his best friend, he looked desolate and was lost in his own thoughts. Owen didn't see him until a familiar voice called out.

'I'm here mate, don't worry,' and once again they held on to each other in despair. 'Annie has already gone to the house, she thought Beth might need her.'

It took a bit of time before they both regained their composure, then Georgie said, 'C'mon… you got time for a quick one?'

'Why not,' Owen replied. 'If I miss the train, then I miss the train.'

Elizabeth

Elizabeth had stopped work at the cutlery factory just after Owen had been conscripted and had decided, although William had tried to dissuade her, to take a job in one of the munitions factories.

'Elizabeth... you don't have to do this.'

'Yes I do and I am sorry if you don't understand or if any of your friends find out it wouldn't be considered... *acceptable*,' she stressed the last word and sounded indignant.

'Nothing to do with that.'

'Isn't it?' she stood, walked over to the coffee table and took a cigarette out of the box. 'Who are you trying to convince?' she lit and inhaled the cigarette. 'I'm sorry William... but please don't try and come the domineering husband.' Rather than argue with her he turned away and left the room, 'As you wish.'

Once again she found herself back in a dirty and dangerous environment where the chemicals turned the women's hair yellow and gave them skin diseases, she hated it. The money was good as it was precise but dangerous work; it had been good intentions that had made her apply rather than the money, she didn't need it. She was like Georgie and felt she was helping in some small way to protect her brother. Then one day walking home she saw a recruitment poster for Naafi (Naval, Army, Air Force Institutes) for both men and women to volunteer and organise canteens and entertainment for the forces to boost troop morale. Without thinking twice she called in at the address shown in the advert; the recruitment office was based in the Town Hall. The lady there explained that they needed civilians to man the mobile canteens that toured the bases or went out to meet the troops on manoeuvres; but what really gripped her imagination was the entertainment side of it where music, shows and dances were arranged for the same troops. She felt elated at the prospect of it, left her contact details with them and continued her way home with a spring in her step and eager to tell William her news.

William was delighted that she had had a change of heart and could see she was clearly excited at the prospect of contributing to the war effort in a way that he knew she would enjoy. He had never been relaxed about her continuing to work but accepted he had no option but to agree to her condition when they married. He had, however, become concerned when she had insisted on going into the munitions factory. He had reluctantly accepted that the lady he had chosen to become his wife was not only beautiful, but feisty with it and determined to do things her way. He knew there would be no further negotiation, he had given her his blessing to become a free spirit within their marriage and knew in time that she would do just that.

Feeling confident she handed her notice in at the munitions factory and to her delight it was only a few days before a letter dropped through the letter box requesting her to attend for interview to discuss the various options open to her within the organisation. When she had first called into the recruitment office she had been in her work clothes, for the interview she had really gone to town; she arrived with a smile on her face, her hair was styled in the latest look and she was wearing a stunning outfit. The same lady smiled at the transformation and nodded to her, 'You have understood exactly what we are trying to achieve here, just the job... well done and welcome aboard.'

There was an induction week which didn't tax her and she was issued with the uniform which she tailored to flatter. The mobile canteens were despatched to the various training camps and major train stations equipped with tea and coffee and whatever buns and cakes had been donated from the bakeries in the area. The object of the exercise was to have pretty faces serving the service men so that they would have a bit of banter and lots of smiles especially at the train stations where the troops were embarking for Europe. They travelled to the camps in Yorkshire, Lincolnshire and Nottinghamshire that were accessible in the day, it was an endless cycle of chat, laughter and flattery and word soon got round amongst the troops that the Naafi was well worth a visit. Elizabeth would chat and serve the coffees and cakes and in a quiet moment her brother would come into her mind and she would smile a bit wider and hope that there was someone similar in the camp where he was based to brighten his day.

The months fell into a familiar pattern. The routine was the same until the units' orders changed from the camp to the embarkation point. The girls would wave the troops off with beaming smiles and laughter and tell them that they would be there when they returned and to take care. Their joviality and waves would cease when the train left the station, silent tears would fall and prayers would be whispered as the track took its human cargo out of sight into the distance and eventually into certain conflict at some point in the near future. Elizabeth wept for them and imagined Owen in the same situation.

Beth & Owen

September 1940 and the Battle of Britain raged primarily over London and the South East of England; they suffered daylight and intensive night bombing. Hitler then changed his attack and gave orders to identify and bomb all the cities with heavy engineering industries that were working to full production to aid the war effort.

Owen was still based on the East Coast and one of the major functions of the base, as well as intensive training, was the radar and searchlight section. They would track the bombers coming across the North Sea from Germany and quickly be able to establish where they were headed; this hopefully would give the targeted cities time to sound the air raid sirens for their people to take shelter. The massive beams of light would arc across the night skies from one base to another revealing the German bombers to the defence gunners.

By November, the Luftwaffe had targeted Birmingham to try and destroy the aircraft and tank factories; Coventry was next for the munitions factories. Both cities were heavily bombed and the shock and devastation of the intensive night raids took its toll. Although people mourned their losses it also strengthened their resolve, production was stepped up and output increased.

As he watched the lights picking up the bombers carrying their deadly loads, Beth and the children were never out of his thoughts as he knew Sheffield would certainly be targeted at some point. The daily reports of casualties and the destruction of major cities brought home the full impact of what was happening and in private moments the thought of his baby daughter's first Christmas on this earth in these circumstances depressed him greatly. On the base everyone accepted that no one could allow themselves to be overwhelmed with emotion or become distracted when there was a serious job to do. They would pinpoint and track the deadly moving images approaching from the North Sea for the coastal batteries to target, then pass them onto the next tracking station and gun battery and hope they would be stopped before they could create further death and destruction.

After the Coventry bombings, Beth had looked at length at the devastation being reported in the newspaper then listened to the news reports on the radio regarding the attacks on Birmingham. Both cities had reported high casualties and extensive damage to houses as well as to the industrial sites that the bombers had targeted. Prior to the Blitz starting she had received a letter advising that she was eligible for evacuation as she had a serving husband and two children under five years old. She was convinced they were fine where they were, as it was easier for Owen to get home to them on a weekend pass and Christmas was only a few weeks away, surely nothing could happen before then.

Even though the Royal Air Force had been triumphant against the Luftwaffe a few months before, there was still a great fear that Hitler would invade. Newsreel pictures showing what had happened in Poland together with Germany's rout of France, Belgium and the Scandinavian countries instilled fear and dread; tensions were running high. Still convinced that they were better staying where they were for the time being, she decided that if things did get worse then she would consider evacuating with the children and keep the promise she had made to Owen.

Buoyed with the success of their raids on Birmingham and Coventry, the German bombers were given a new target; on the twelfth of December 1940 their target was Sheffield. It was a cold clear night, the moon favoured them as it was nearly full and on the wintry coastal base Owen watched them approach over the North Sea and fly through the gunners barrage and on into the heart of the country. As the light beams picked up the targets then stopped he held his breath in panic when he was told by the trackers that it was Sheffield that was being attacked. They had come to recognise where the bombers were headed with the direction of the light beams reaching high up into the night skies. On a couple of occasions he had held his breath but then sighed with guilty relief as he was told they had passed over his home town and gone on to bomb Manchester and Liverpool; but this freezing night of December was to prove fatal for Sheffield city dwellers, it was their turn to suffer Hitler's wrath and be subjected to long nights of intensive bombing.

As the warning sirens wailed again she picked up the baby and the readied bag, made sure they had their gas masks and warm clothes and told her son to hurry. Placing the baby in the pram they ran with others, all of them in panic, through the dark night towards the local school and into the waiting air raid shelter. It was noisy with fraught families already there calling out for relatives who were arriving late. They made room for Beth as she came through the throng looking for a place to settle down with the children to wait until the impending raid had passed. She hoped it wouldn't be long before they could all go back home as the sirens had wailed on quite a few occasions and it had come to nothing; the all clear had sounded shortly after.

Silence fell in the shelter as they heard the drone of the approaching bombers.

'They sound closer this time,' Beth thought to herself.

Incendiary bombs fell first, followed by the whistling sound of the falling bombs then huge explosions, the bombs fell indiscriminately. The lights in the shelter flashed on and off continuously with the force of the tremendous ground shocks; babies and children screamed and cried while their terrified mothers held them tight to try and comfort them as best they could. But given the frightening environment they were all in, the adults were as frightened as the children. The relentless pounding of the city continued for hours and it was four a.m. the following morning before the all clear sounded.

The Wardens finally opened the shelter's doors but there was a reticence by anyone to move back out into the open. People were frightened of what they were going to find, all were shell shocked and many were still crying after the horrendous experience they had all been through.

Beth let the throng move out before she felt she had the strength to stand and collect their belongings to take back home. She felt exhausted, she had held her son and daughter all night trying to ease their fears, whispering to them and kissing them softly. Little Owen had held her hand tightly all night, his large, frightened, blue eyes constantly searching her face for reassurance through the constant noise and darkness. She trembled as she moved towards the doors hanging on to the pram for support.

In the dark outside, the fires raged everywhere high into the sky, the air was full of smoke and the acrid smell of destruction. People were shouting and running everywhere, some were sitting crying in amongst the rubble silhouetted in the fires still burning, their children trying to help them to their feet. She was disorientated and felt she was trying to find her way out of a nightmare; everything seemed to be in slow motion. A policeman saw her through the smoke and ran over to them.

'Are you alright love?' and he took hold of her arm to steady her. 'It's alright ... where is it you want to go... are you looking for somebody?'

She looked him vaguely, 'I think we're alright thank you... no... I am not looking for anyone,' her voice sounded distant to her. 'I am just trying to find my way home... ' she turned her head to try and find her bearings. 'It's all so frightening... it's awful... oh dear... which way is Hanover Lane please?'

'Are you on your own love?' he ruffled the boy's hair and picked him up from the top of the pram and handed him his whistle to hold. 'Here young man... you hold my whistle so I won't lose it.' The youngster beamed, he then checked that the tiny baby warmly wrapped up inside was alright.

Beth answered him as he looked into the pram, 'Yes... my husband is in the army... I just want to get home now that the raid is over.'

'C'mon then I will take you... can't have you wandering around here on your own can we?' Privately he was hoping her home hadn't been obliterated in the bombing and erred on the side of caution with respect to her hopes that it was over.

'It all looks so different, I don't know where I am... its frightening... what will all these poor people do?' she said to him as they walked through the devastation.

They kept to the road slowly walking through the inches of glass from hundreds of windows blown out during the attack. Houses on either side had simply disappeared or were reduced to just rubble and still on fire or smouldering. She looked at the pieces of bedroom furniture that were hanging in mid-air as the floors beneath had been blown away exposing the decor and wallpapers on the internal walls. The flash of colours looked bizarre amongst the surrounding destruction; peoples' homes had been destroyed in minutes. People who had returned to piles of rubble were in shock and could not believe it had all just gone; many were trying to sift through the hot remains for any belongings or valuables that could be rescued. The awful sound of grief filled the air as they walked on through the devastation in silence. She looked at it all and thought, 'despair... it always sounds the same' and the sound of it momentarily took her back to when she was her son's age in the previous conflict.

They finally arrived at Beth's house, remarkably the building was untouched, the heavy taping on the windows that Georgie had put on for her had held so the windows were still intact. They looked around, the houses on the opposite side had not been so lucky the entire block of back to back houses stretching from the Lane to Hanover Street had disappeared into a huge mound of rubble still smouldering in the aftermath; the occupants were wandering around in disarray not sure what to do.

'You have been lucky love... not many round here can say the same looking at it.'

At that point Annie came running up the cobbles in tears and hugged Beth. 'Oh thank God, thank God you are all alright,' she took young Owen off the policeman and held him tightly still crying. 'I'm so sorry I wasn't here when it started,' she sobbed. 'I have been so worried about you.'

Beth held on to her friend and cried with her out of relief. The policeman gave them a minute to console each other then asked for his whistle back from the little one telling him he had done a good job of looking after it and ruffled his hair again.

'Thank you,' Beth said to him and planted a kiss on his cheek. 'Thank you so much... I doubt if I could have found my way back without you... I am very grateful. I have a historical soft spot for policemen ever since one told me many years ago "always choose hope over despair" and given the circumstances I think that it is appropriate again don't you?'

He smiled at her and touched his helmet in response, 'Always happy to help my dear. You keep yourself and these little ones safe. I am sure your husband is very proud of you all... give him my regards and tell him I shall keep a look out for you.'

'I will... thank you... would you like a cup of tea before you go... that is if the water and gas isn't off?'

'I would love one, but no I had better not given what's happening. There is a lot to take care of,' and he turned to go then paused for a moment. 'Good advice that from my old colleague... might use it myself... that's if you don't mind.'

'No not at all. What he said to me all those years ago has always been a source of strength, so please feel free to pass it on.' She held on to his hands for a moment, 'Thank you... it's a worrying time for all of us... I hope to see you again... take care.'

The policeman smiled at her again. 'You too and the little ones... keep yourselves safe for that husband of yours.' He touched his helmet and nodded, then turned and she watched him for a moment walking back towards the devastation.

The city hardly had time to draw breath when the full moon on the fifteenth of December brought the bombers back again. The sirens wailed invoking terror and fear this time instead of the previous apathy and the intensive bombing ensued once again. Owen watched the beams and the glow in the night sky for a second time from afar and prayed.

Beth and Annie were together this time when the siren sounded so, with the children, rushed to the shelter once again; it didn't lessen the fear. Annie held the baby and Beth her son, and once again waited for the tremendous explosions and grounds shocks to start. The Germans this time dropped thousands of incendiary bombs so when the all clear sounded and they emerged again it was like being in the middle of a furnace; everywhere was burning and the emergency services were stretched to breaking point.

'I don't think I can go through much more of this Annie,' she said looking round. 'I promised Owen I would make the decisions to keep us safe if I couldn't reach him... he must be frantic. I thought I was doing right by staying here but now I am not so sure.'

'Take them and evacuate,' said Annie back to her. 'At least we will know you are all safe... it's not like you are sending them away you will be going with them.'

Arnold arrived the following morning and the relief showed on his face when he found them and the house once again miraculously untouched. Beth burst into tears when she saw him so he just held her tight as she wept.

'Come on Beth let it out... it's alright to cry... I'm here.'

'Oh Arnold... it has been so awful...what if,' she sobbed.

He noticed her young son retreating quietly to a corner of the room; he looked withdrawn and constantly glanced over to his weeping mother and tried hard not to cry.

'No "what ifs" at the moment Beth... little ears and all that.'

After listening to how horrendous it had been and surveying the scale of the damage around the house he tried once more to persuade her to join them in Burnley or consider the offer of evacuation seriously. He gave her time to think about it then took his nephew to one side to try to calm the boy's fears.

'You know young man... a long time ago in the last war when I was your age... our father had gone off to war like your father, and I became responsible for your mother... because we had nobody else.' He put his arm around the boy's shoulder and just for a moment mentally pictured his own father then his brother-in-law. 'I just want you to know that we understand that it is frightening what is happening and when dark thoughts do come into your mind just remember that I, your Aunt Elizabeth and Uncle George are all here for you and your mother and sister. It is alright to be frightened, we are all frightened too and that is why it is important that we all support each other.' He lifted his nephew's tear-stained face and looked into his eyes, 'You will never be alone Owen... whatever happens... do you understand that?'

He watched the boy wipe a tear away, 'Yes,' came a whisper, he then turned and threw his arms around Arnold and wept into his uncle's chest. He held him until his tears stopped and gave him his handkerchief to clear his nose and wipe his face.

'Never forget Owen... we are always here... all of us.'

She made her decision to evacuate and was quickly offered a property in Tideswell in the Peak District. She was reassured that it should be a safer location than Sheffield as it had no heavy industries. She had thanked Adelaide and Arnold for their offer to move to Burnley and explained that it would be easier for Owen to reach them when on a pass, it was rural and would be much better for the children. She packed the same day and on arrival posted the address details to Owen straight away, and copies to Arnold, Elizabeth and Annie and Georgie.

Owen applied for a forty-eight hours pass on compassionate grounds after the Sheffield bombings and got a lift in a lorry travelling from the base to Doncaster. From there he took a train into Sheffield and walked to the house passing through all the horror and destruction of the city centre. He had to keep stopping and thinking of where he was and tried to find a familiar building to give him some bearings but it was dark and it all looked so different because of the blackout. There were huge mounds of rubble still smouldering days after the attacks and people still sifting through the devastation.

Relief flooded through his veins when he saw the house was still standing, this was short-lived when he realised they might not have been in the house when the destruction had started. Looking around he could see entire blocks of terraced houses had been obliterated. 'My God... just look at it,' he thought.

The house was in darkness and locked he banged and banged on the door praying for Beth to open it. He sat on the step for a moment and tried to be rational. He thought of where she might be and decided to go on to his mother's she might know something then Georgie's, she might even be there or at Betty's. Then looking around at the sheer scale of the damage he realised that they might not be there either, any of them, anything could have happened. He tried to quell the panic and feeling of nausea.

His mother was delighted and relieved to see him. 'You all alright... the children?' he asked and she nodded. 'I am looking for Beth... do you know where she is?'

'No, son I'm sorry... we haven't seen her... it's been awful there have been so many deaths... such much destruction.'

His father was sitting in his usual chair, they didn't acknowledge each other.

'I have to find her... the house is locked up no sign of them... I'll go to Georgies.'

'That's right look after your own, don't bother about us, selfish as always. We're in mourning, not that you would be bothered, never see your wife anyway so why should we know where she is.' The usual jug of beer was to hand and he refilled his glass.

Owen turned from his mother slowly, 'Well look at you... still the same nasty bastard... I don't have the time or inclination to get into a conversation with you... go back to your beer... I am not here to have a row.'

'What did I always tell you about him... selfish,' he shouted at his wife. 'He doesn't care that I have lost two sisters and a brother in the bombings... all gone...no respect.'

Owen looked at his mother questioningly.

'Come outside son... let's talk in peace.' His mother took hold of his arm and turned him back to the door.

'What was all that about... who's gone?'

'Your two aunts and his older brother... they were in your grandmother's house when the bombing started and it took a direct hit. His brother was... we think in Marples... direct hit again, full of people that couldn't get to the shelters when the sirens went. They thought they were safe in the pub's cellars but the bombs took the lot out cellars and all.'

He stood for a moment taking it all in, 'The Aunts... well I could say I am sorry but there was no love lost there... as nasty as him... made my life a misery... as for the other... don't know him.'

'Don't waste time on the dead Owen, go and find Beth and your children. Our Bet's might know and you have to pass her house to get to Georgie's... I hope they are all alright.'

'Yes... keep well mother and out of harms way. If he is too drunk to get to the shelter get yourself and the kids there, promise me you won't stop here, it's a miracle that anything is standing.'

'Yes, I will... you keep safe too... and come home to us son.'

He kissed her on her cheek, turned and walked back into the darkness.

Elizabeth's house was also fine, 'well that's three out of four' he thought and climbed the steps and knocked on the door. It was difficult to guess whether anyone was at home in any of the houses with the thick blackout curtains. After the raids the blackout rules were stepped up and people could face stiff fines for breaking the law and letting any light show.

He knocked once, there was no response so he knocked louder and out of the corner of his eye noticed a small chink of light at the bedroom window. He called through the letter box and within a couple of minutes heard movement inside the house and the sound of feet coming down the stairs.

William turned the lights out and opened the door, he entered and when it was closed again the light was turned back on.

'Oh... hello Owen... er how are you?' asked William. Owen thought for some reason he sounded on edge, he was dressed in a silk dressing gown and looked slightly dishevelled.

'I am sorry to bother you William at this hour but I am on a forty-eight hour pass and can't find Beth... she is not at the house. I thought our Bet's... sorry Elizabeth might know... is she here?' as he finished there was a sound of a door closing upstairs and Owen momentarily glanced up to the top of the stairs.

'Er... no she's not... she is with Naafi tonight and staying over.' He walked over to the table and took a cigarette out of the box, 'Would you like one?' Owen declined and noticed that William's hand shook as he lit the cigarette.

Feeling slightly uncomfortable he turned back to the door. 'Yes well... I will not intrude further if she is not here... give her my love when she returns and tell her to take care.'

'Yes, yes of course I will... she will be sorry to have missed you...she does worry,' he replied. 'Let me attend to the lights before you open the door... we don't want to be in trouble do we,' and laughed nervously.

Owen smiled, shook his hand, and left the house. Walking to Georgie's he thought about the conversation with William, 'bloody odd that' he thought to himself.

He could have wept with relief when he saw Georgie's house intact as well. He banged on the door, this was his last hope, and shouted through the letterbox, 'Georgie... its Owen...open up.'

The door flew open and an arm pulled him in, 'Get in here,' shouted a delighted Georgie and threw his arms round his best friend. 'What are you doing here?'

'I'm looking for Beth, she is not at the house and I thought she might be here with you... you're my last hope,' said Owen desperately looking round for some evidence of his wife and children. 'I got a pass because of the blitz to come and see that they are alright... I am running out of time,' Georgie could hear the concern in his voice.

'Come on through and sit down... Annie... look who's here,' he called upstairs.

Annie came running down the stairs and hugged Owen. 'It's good to see you Owen... don't worry everything is alright. They are fine.' They sat and chatted and she explained what had happened and where Beth had gone.

'Thank God,' he said with relief, 'at least I can go back with an easy mind... she has done the right thing. I just wished I could have seen them.' He rubbed his eyes in tiredness, 'I have no chance of getting there now anyway it will soon be time to start back and I wouldn't know where to look,' he sighed, then changing the subject, 'Are you still on shifts Georgie?'

'Yes I have to be on at six. Jerry's done some damage but not enough for us to have to stop production. The feeling is that they misread their maps and that is why there is so much damage in the town centre and surrounding districts. Let's have a glass of beer then you can get your head down for a few hours and I will wake you when I have to leave.'

'Great... we'll walk together and I can head for the station. At least the trains are still running albeit not to time. I am best going to Donny and then thumbing a lift.'

They enjoyed their beer and just being able to chat in relaxed mode escaping the nightmare of the situation for just a couple of hours. Owen told him about his grandmother's house taking a direct hit. 'That's my last connection with her gone,' he said reflectively, 'and my aunts... ironical that they should have been in it at the time...didn't do them any favours did it?'

Georgie asked him about training and the possibility of going over to Europe. 'Who knows when we will be ready... the main fear is invasion... thank God for the Channel. It is out of our hands Georgie boy, but I reckon Churchill knows what he's doing... he'll not let us go down without a damn good fight.'

'You're right,' came the reply, 'look, like I said before, we will always keep an eye on Beth and the children you know that. Whatever comes your way just keep that head down... you hear me?'

They looked at each other and slapped each other on the back. Owen broke the moment and looked at him, 'I will... it makes it easier that I don't have to look after your back,' and he laughed.

'Cheeky bugger... get your head down and I will wake you later.'

They set out into the dark, cold morning, the smell of destruction still hanging heavy in the air. 'I still don't believe what I am seeing,' said Georgie. 'Look at it all... shocking... reckon we have been lucky.'

'Yes, well just keep it that way, you hear me?'

'I'll try.'

'While I think about it have you seen much of our Bets? I called last night before I got to you, to see if she knew anything, but she was away on one of her Naafi stints. He was there and I am pretty sure someone else was too, he was on edge for some reason.'

Georgie looked surprised at him. 'I haven't seen her for ages. Annie has seen her a couple of times at yours. Why...what do you mean on edge?'

'What I say... on edge, nervous... said he was alone but I heard a door close upstairs. He was wearing a silk dressing gown would you believe... got the feeling something not quite right... I could be wrong.'

'Could have been the cat upstairs,' said Georgie eyebrow raised.

'Have they got one?'

'Don't ask me.'

'Forget it,' laughed Owen.

They parted at the train station, again no words, just a hand shake and a hug. 'You look to your back do you hear me... miss you,' said Georgie his eyes welling up.

'Same to you old friend... look after them for me,' and he walked into the station.

Georgie watched him go and hoped his friend didn't turn round. 'Don't want to make a fool of myself,' he thought, 'he has enough on his plate without me getting upset.'

Beth's letter reached him the week after giving him all the details of where they were. Annie had visited her on her day off to give her the news that she had missed him. There were tears and she felt guilty that he had had a wasted journey but was comforted by the fact that he knew they were safe.

Elizabeth: 1941

She had been delighted and excited when they had arrived at Owen's base for the first time and she had run into his arms laughing. The other soldiers had watched and there were a few ribald comments passed to which Elizabeth gave as good as she got. Owen just smiled and winked at them as they walked away for some privacy.

'Same old Bets... you look great in uniform,' he told her and spun her round.

'So do you... come here and give me a kiss,' she laughed.

They enjoyed their brief time together and she gave him all the letters she had brought from everyone, together with all the news. Beth had also sent up to date photographs of her and the children; he had held the images, closed his eyes, and sighed.

'Thank you for these…look how they have grown.'

She sat quietly at his side as he had looked again at the photos then, deciding to change the subject, 'Oh… and I have brought you a copy of my schedule so you will know where I am. Now let's go and get some of that tea I have brought.'

'C'mon then let's go,' he replied placing the pictures in to his breast pocket.

After the refreshments she asked, 'Do you have any idea if you will be moved out?'

'No,' he replied, 'we will be the last to know I should think, things change by the day. Some battalions are moved out at night with no notice so don't automatically think I am going to be here when you are next here... great if I am though,' he said raising his eyes.

'I understand... we have waved a lot off through the year... no doubt more will follow.'

'Well, if yours was the last face to wave me off I think I would be pretty happy. I would imagine you get lots of offers,' and laughed again at her.

'Never you mind you are not my minder anymore... big girl now... and married to boot.'

'How's William?' he asked cautiously.

Her answer was short, 'He's fine.'

He offered her his arm, 'Well married lady let's go for a beer... they will think I am the luckiest guy on the base.' Then he laughed 'I always knew that when you sang at the Barracks on a Saturday night you were practising for greater things.'

Their collective performance was received with the usual cheering and whistling. When it was time for them to leave he came to wave her off and gave her a letter and a bundle to take back to Beth. 'No doubt she can use this... it will save her coupons and they have to eat... tell her to keep well and keep themselves safe and I will try and get home soon.'

'Right will do... hope it's something nice for her.' It was wrapped well in brown paper and tied with string, 'It's not your dirty washing is it?' she laughed.

'No... ' he laughed, 'she'll appreciate it. I only caught it this morning so it's fresh.'

'What is?' she asked cautiously.

'A rabbit... she makes a nice rabbit stew... now... off you go.'

Her eyes welled up with tears and she hung on to his neck. 'Don't say anything,' he whispered, 'just get in the truck... it's easier that way.'

She did as he asked, but couldn't resist hanging out of the window and waving back to him. He stood and returned the wave and watched the truck disappear out through the gates. The strange conversation he had had with William when he had unexpectedly called at their house that night flashed into his mind. He still had an open mind on what was going on but certainly wasn't going to mention it to his sister; he had enquired about his brother-in-law and she had not furthered the conversation so that was enough.

The year passed quickly for Elizabeth; her schedules increased as the hostilities moved once again to North Africa. The British had routed the Italians the previous year but earlier in 1941 a collective force of German and Italian troops attacked Yugoslavia, Greece and Crete then Field Marshal Rommel led a collective force once again back into the deserts of Egypt and Libya.

Later that year and out of the blue the Japanese attacked Pearl Harbor; the Americans were totally unprepared and shocked at the death and destruction at the base. The Japanese aligned themselves with Germany and Italy and America had no choice but to declare war, join their Allies in Europe and open fronts in the Far East.

The GI's started to arrive by the truckload and were stationed throughout the country on standby, the impact it had on the locals when they arrived was mixed. The girls loved them and excitement came back into their lives when dances were arranged on the bases. All of a sudden there was no shortage of nylons, chocolate, cigarettes, whatever they wanted. The older generation watched with dismay as the local girls started relationships.

The girls' view was that after the years of austerity and no available men, the GI's more than compensated and they were defiant, 'Why not... there is a war on and life's too short... might not be here tomorrow!'

Morale needed to be kept high and Naafi did its best to send all the troops off with a smile and a memory of home. They modified their programme to include the current American hits when on a mixed base, and Elizabeth stepped up to the mark finding her forte once more. She loved it, all of a sudden glamour came back and rather than just performing in their Naafi uniforms she could turn her hand to creating outfits to perform in. The Americans brought their swing bands and covered all the Glenn Miller and Andrew Sisters numbers and for a brief moment in time, a few hours at most, life became exciting again and they polished their act.

Her eyes were bright and laughing as she glanced at the other two girls standing with her behind the curtain, they took their cue. The curtains parted, the first impression was that there were three Betty Grables on stage complete with swimsuit and hair coiffured in the same style as the Grable image in the iconic photograph that graced every GI's locker. The girls were standing together all looking over their right shoulder, hands on their hips. The Bugle Boy intro blared out, the Andrew Sisters could have been there in person such was the roar of approval that greeted them.

They were now used to the impact they were having on the troops and all laughed in unison and played up to the crowd. He was spellbound, the other guys around him called out compliments to the trio but his attention was all on Elizabeth and finally eye contact was made. She made it through to the end of the song aware of his gaze and on the last note turned her head slightly so she looked at him full on, slowly winked then laughed and blew the collective kiss at the end of the song in his direction. As the curtain came down he knew there would be contact between them at some point during the evening and she smiled.

He waited until they emerged through the dance hall to spontaneous applause and made their way to a table near the bar; the GI's whooped and shouted compliments as they passed. Taking her seat at the reserved table Elizabeth relaxed, took her time lighting her cigarette, sighed and turned to look back at the crowd milling around her colleagues.

'May I join you?' a voice asked.

She looked into the pair of warm brown eyes, 'Why not.'

'Well what can I say?' the American brogue was soft. 'I could have been back in the States watching the Andrew Sisters.' He laughed and leaned on the back of a chair, 'I would love to get you a drink... if I may?'

'Thank you,' she replied smiling at him, 'Yes... I would like that.'

'Hey Al... ' he called to the bar tender, 'a White Lady for the lady please...' Turning back to her he said, 'My name is Mitchell... Mitch for short,' and he held out his hand.

'Hello, I'm Elizabeth,' and she shook his hand, 'A White Lady... sounds interesting... can I ask what it is?'

He was still holding hand, 'Well, let's just wait and see if you like it first shall we. So... if I am not being too forward... are you going to tell me all about yourself?' He moved his chair closer to her as their drinks arrived, 'You will have my total undivided attention.' He looked into her eyes and smiled, 'Cheers.'

Oblivious to the rest of the crowd and both at ease with each other they just talked about themselves. He told her about his family back in the States, that he wasn't married as he hadn't found the right girl yet, felt that he had to join up and come and help 'you guys' and that at this particular moment in time was glad that he had. She had skipped the childhood memories, told him about Owen, explained that she was 'married but in name only' but didn't elaborate on the full details just left it to his imagination.

Concern came into his eyes. He took her hand again and asked, 'Is that enough?'

'No... not really,' came the reply. 'Don't get me wrong... materially I want for nothing... but it's not about that,' she replied leaning forward for him to light her cigarette.

'Will it ever change?'

'No,' she answered him without hesitation. 'Thanks for the drink I loved it.' Then she looked at watch and stood up, 'I have to go and get ready for the next number.'

'Hey I'm sorry,' he said standing up. 'I hope I haven't upset you?'

'No... don't be silly of course you haven't. I have loved the chat, but I have to go... they will be waiting for me.'

'Can I wait until you have finished?' and took hold of her hand.

She looked into the warm eyes again, 'Why not,' she smiled and touched his cheek gently.

The weeks passed and as the hostilities increased so too did their Naafi schedule, taking the troupe to all the camps in the area on a regular basis. The troops always welcomed their appearances; they were now well known on the circuit.

If it was a British camp their programme included the current hits by Vera Lynn, nothing too sentimental for obvious reasons, and they always finished up on a high note when all the troops would join in. For the Americans with their swing band it was a mix of Andrew Sisters, Glenn Miller and Tommy Dorsey numbers.

Whenever possible, whether it be a British or American camp, Mitch would endeavour to be there; he would stand more or less in the same place if the show had started so she would know where to look. He worked in logistics so kept regular hours compared to the troops on manoeuvres. It worked well for them and if he had to arrange cover he would do so. Elizabeth became his priority when he was not at work, she was constantly in his thoughts.

The intensity of their first kiss had shocked them both; he had kissed her with a passion and urgency, as if his very life had depended on it. His arms had enveloped her tenderly and she had responded to his need, the passion between them overwhelmed her. She broke away for a moment and drew breath, then felt his cheek next to hers, then his kiss urgently searching first her neck then finding her lips once again. He held her so gently but securely, she felt her legs weaken and let him take the weight and he swept her away with passion.

Their affair continued. He was the gentlest man she had ever met. He was protective, considerate, loving and very funny; given the dire circumstances that had brought them together he never failed to make her laugh.

Unlike William, who lavished expensive gifts on her, Mitch brought her small things which she cherished. It could be a flower, a poem or a book that was one of his favourites. She asked for nothing from him so loved it even more because she knew he had given it out of love. From time to time he arrived with provisions. She passed them on to her mother and Beth for the children, they were always grateful and he was pleased that he could make their lives a little easier and made sure there was extra chocolate for the little ones. She knew she was falling in love with him.

William accepted her frequently being away from home overnight because of her schedule, he knew she enjoyed it and felt happy that she was contributing to the war effort in a necessary way. He understood how serious things were becoming with the increased government orders that were being placed with the steel companies around the city.

As the months passed he sensed the change in her demeanour, she positively glowed with happiness. He knew she enjoyed being part of the vocal group but noted that she didn't seem to have any down days anymore and was even optimistic regarding Owen. 'I'm sure he'll be fine,' she would now say instead of worrying constantly where he might be. After thinking about it for some time he realised that she could have met someone.

He knew he couldn't criticise or make a scene as he had given her his blessing when they had married. He would have to accept the situation with good grace, after all she had accepted his continuing liaison as a condition when they married, and he had to be realistic she was a stunningly attractive woman.

She was sitting in the kitchen and had just lit a cigarette as she started to read her schedule for the coming week. William was leaning on the door jamb quietly watching her and caught the glimmer of a smile that touched her lips as she read.

'Elizabeth... can we talk?'

'Yes of course...what about?' she looked up at him and drew on her cigarette.

'Do I assume you have taken a lover?'

She looked directly at him and an eyebrow arched, 'Why do you ask? I thought we had – *an agreement.*' She stressed the last two words as she stubbed out the cigarette and looked straight back at him, her eyebrow remained arched in question.

'Yes... forgive me... I apologise... I am wrong to enquire. I know that,' he smiled at her and moved forward to the table. 'But you are positively glowing my darling... I really have no need to ask, I suppose what I really want to know is... is it serious and are you going to leave me?'

'I have no plans to leave you William... besides that... it is early days yet. I would err on the side of caution anyway and definitely not make any more rash decisions after being rushed into our marriage. Apart from that we are in a war situation so nothing is how it should be... is it? Then again I am used to that as well... aren't I?'

'Quite,' he replied.

'Sorry William, I didn't mean to sound sarcastic. Look... you have no need to be worried about the outcome... if it ever did happen. I am not saying it ever will, but in the event I would continue to play the game and take the entire blame. I am sure you will have a solicitor friend that would sort it out for you. Trust me, I would have no intention of creating a scandal... why would I... you have kept all your promises to me William... and for that I thank you.'

'Do you love him?'

'I love you William, but I am in love with him,' and standing, she walked over and embraced him, 'there is a distinct difference.'

'Yes... I understand.'

Maintaining the hold she told him, 'He keeps me sane I suppose in this dreadful time and to cope with our relationship, however you define it, can you understand that?'

'Yes, my darling, I do understand... don't worry... and thank you for being so honest with me.' He kissed her cheek, 'I shall always love you Elizabeth know that... whatever happens... and I also understand that if it is not enough for you...you must go.' He sighed and then continued, 'I do realise it is like keeping a beautiful butterfly caged and not letting her show her beauty to the natural world, it's very cruel, I acknowledge that.' She looked directly at him and was surprised to see tears in his eyes. 'Know this, I cannot contemplate my life without you now, but I also accept it is grossly unfair for you to live like the butterfly.' He took hold of her hands and kissed them gently while his tears flowed.

'It's alright William,' and she caressed his cheek. 'It is right that we can talk about these things and be honest with each other now. You will always be a part of my life too... always... I promise... so don't worry.' She held him tightly to reassure him, 'Feel better now?'

He sighed heavily, 'Yes and no... thank you my dearest. I will have to settle for that I know. Now, if I can compose myself, and if you are not booked for this evening, I would like us to go out for dinner.'

'So would I... tonight I am all yours,' and he offered her his arm.

Mitch was standing in the usual place and she blew him a kiss, she felt her heart skip a beat and watched him go to the bar and order the cocktail that had become 'her drink'. She found him after the set and he slipped his arm around her waist and brought her close to him, 'How's my girl?'

'She's fine thank you good sir... and you?' chinking his glass then taking a sip of her waiting drink, 'Mmmmm.'

'Never better,' he bent slightly and kissed her ear and ran his hand through her hair. 'My, but we're looking beautiful tonight... aren't I the lucky one?' their eyes met again and she felt her heart lift.

Over the months their affair intensified; they were in love. When her schedule required her to stay overnight he automatically booked a hotel. She had explained her marriage situation and he had listened sympathetically and with a sense of disbelief over dinner.

'Who else knows?' he had asked.

'No one... only you,' came the reply looking into his eyes. 'Remember it is against the Law.'

'That must be a very lonely place you're in.'

She paused and a tear rolled down her cheek. 'It was... before now, before you... William describes me as a beautiful butterfly in a gilded cage... I suppose I sold my soul.'

'But you didn't know as I understand it... did you have no inclination?'

'No of course not... Mitch... I had never met anyone like him. Of course I was flattered and it was all so rushed... don't get me wrong I have grown to love him but obviously it is only platonic. He's a good man really, he doesn't deserve to go to prison and I wouldn't want to hurt him unnecessarily.'

'Would you consider leaving him after all this mess is over?' he asked wiping the tear away from her cheek. 'Come back to the States with me? I mean it Elizabeth.'

'We'll see,' she answered cautiously.

'We'll do more than see... you have grounds for an annulment you know.'

'No I wouldn't do that... I would just give him grounds to divorce me.'

'Oh... is that where I come in?' he said and laughed. 'I would always be happy to help you. Know that no matter how many times it takes,' he held her tightly. 'I mean what I have just said... I don't want this to end when this war is over... I love you Baby... I want you in the States with me... you will love it.' He held her tightly and kissed her as if to convince her.

She drew breath and looked at him, 'And I love you and I promise I will think about what you have said, but for now let's just take it a day at a time. None of us know what is going to happen Mitch, it frightens me if I think about it too much.'

'Don't ever be frightened... I will always be here for you... always whatever happens... trust me... my love will always be with you. I knew from the first moment I saw you. Now come here and let me show you.'

Her heart lifted again and she relaxed into his arms.

Beth & Elizabeth: 1941

By 1943 the Allies had finally gained the upper hand. During the year the Russians had routed Hitler's fated troops on the Eastern Front, Field Marshall Rommel suffered defeat in North Africa and Sicily was regained. The plans for D-Day had been drawn up and mobilisation increased.

Beth listened every day to the radio reports and took heart that things were starting to improve, but she also recognised that the Germans would not surrender without a fight and when the push came all available forces would be in the thick of it, Owen included. She tried not to dwell on it and just concentrated on the children's wellbeing and writing letters to Owen always reassuring him that they were safe.

Elizabeth continued to enjoy her work although sadness overwhelmed her when reports of the deaths of Mitch's colleagues came through. She was grateful that he worked in logistics so wouldn't be sent overseas, but he knew he was going to have to tell her that when 'the big push' came he would be shipped out with all the other troops. The Allies were slowly making progress and there was an air of anticipation that one massive final assault in Europe could possibly tip the balance. The planning meetings he was involved in confirmed it, the supplies and armaments now being shipped over from America were massive. The time had come for him to explain to her what was going to happen and he chose his moment just after they had made love.

'It has to be all hands on baby when that day arrives, this war has got to be ended. I will have to go... there will be work to be done over there in support... that's my job but I am also a trained soldier don't forget that.'

'No I understand... we have been very lucky you and I. I suppose you could say we have had a good war, if that doesn't sound cynical. I can't imagine life any different now, if feels as if it always going to be like this, as if this is normality rather than what preceded it all.'

She snuggled up to him. He held her gently and kissed her ear, 'It will continue to be normal you'll see. You know what I have told you, when this is finally over you will be coming back to the States with me.'

She laughed, 'Oh... is this the GI promise?'

'Hey, that's unfair, you know I am serious about it. I don't want to live my life without you... I can't... now you promise me.'

'Yes I know. I have thought of nothing else believe me,' she kissed him. '... and I would also say... I think your plans might just be looking pretty damned good soldier,' and she laughed.

'Love you baby...come here.'

D-Day

The letters to next of kin had been written and placed in the administration files headed: 'In the event of'. All leave had been cancelled and all troops were on permanent standby. Manoeuvres were taken to a higher level to maintain fitness, equipment had been checked and checked again. It was now a waiting game, silent thoughts of fear, loved ones, and the unknown prevailed.

The sixth of June 1944, D-Day had finally arrived after the months of intense planning. Just after midnight British Army gliders silently moved in the darkness and landed with paratroopers on board whose task it was to secure the vital bridges in Caen; the Allied invasion had begun and Owen was part of this unit. A few hours later the Americans, Mitch included, started to come ashore on Utah and Omaha beaches, the element of surprise had been achieved but the Germans having built permanent fortresses were already entrenched and waiting for them.

The BBC Home Service announced later that morning, 'This morning the Allies began the assault on the North West face of Hitler's European Fortress.'

The correspondence then stated: 'The paratroopers are landing all around me as I speak... '

Beth sat and listened in tense silence, Owen was foremost in her mind and she tried not to weep in front of the children. She silently prayed, held them close and told them to think good thoughts of Daddy. Elizabeth also listened and felt physically sick; she knew the situation that she had discussed with Mitch must be on-going as all her schedules had been cancelled at the last minute. She had not seen him prior to the final mobilisation as all the bases were locked down and leave cancelled. She knew he would now be involved in the fighting and their last conversation drifted back in to mind.

'You're my girl... my little toughie... I knew it the moment I saw you up there on that stage. It will not be long now before we can start to plan our lives together sugar... so try not to worry.'

She had not questioned him, just held on to him tightly and told him, 'I love you.' She closed her eyes momentarily, he came into her mind's eye and a tear rolled down her cheek, 'Come back to me Mitch... please keep safe and come back to me.'

Hitler dismissed the D-Day landings initially as a diversionary tactic and insisted his generals make ready for a full assault on Calais. The Germans had wasted valuable time. The joint forces of British, Commonwealth and American troops were a major force to be reckoned with and now finally they were on mainland Europe.

The German sniper carefully took aim, steadied his shot and fired. His target dropped to his knees and rolled over, the bullet had hit him clean between the eyes, he died instantly.

Elizabeth: June 1944

My Own Elizabeth
'Baby I am so sorry you will be reading this, I need to try and ease your pain
so always remember:
    Our time together with love and a smile and know how much I loved you.
I loved you just for being you, your eyes, your laugh, all of you, you became
my world, my life.
    Fate has dictated I would only know that true love for a short time - how
good was it? It was the best.
    So when a soft breeze kisses the back of your neck know it is me, I will look
over you always, we will meet again you and I.
    I sleep with you in death, you will always be mine, I will be with you into
eternity – a GI's promise. Mxxxxxxxxxxxxxxx'

She stayed in her bedroom for a week and William respected her privacy and lived through her cries of anguish and despair with great sadness. When she did finally emerge pale-faced and red-eyed he just held her.

'I am sorry Elizabeth, so so sorry.' She cried into his shoulder and he held her until she could cry no more, fearing she would collapse.

'Can I do anything for you? Can I get you anything my darling? I am so worried about you.'

'No, what I need doesn't exist anymore,' and the tears rolled once more down her pale, distraught face. He put her to bed and stayed with her until sleep took her into a place of peace for a short while, where she could dream it wasn't true.

She stayed closeted in the house just wanting obscurity; she didn't want the pain of losing him to leave her. William had told the family and their friends that she was exhausted from all the Naafi schedules and devastated at news of deaths of colleagues on D-Day. He requested she be given time to rest and recuperate, the explanation guaranteed her continued solitude.

The next few weeks passed and her moods shifted like sand: one minute she would be angry and the despair would rise again, the next morose and despising the war that had taken him from her. Then in a quiet moment she would rationalise that without the war he would never have been part of her life 'life's cruel ironies' she thought.

Most days she didn't bother to get dressed, she just sat around in her dressing gown smoking endlessly. She sometimes caught her reflection in the mirror and just stared back at the dull lifeless image being projected back at her.

William was supportive, but only when she wanted him to be, he knew he couldn't do anything for her all he could do was remain quietly in the background and hope she would gently heal with time. Some days he would just squeeze her hand to let her know he was there. He knew one day that she would tell him about this love in her life, about her loss but it would only be discussed when Elizabeth was ready. Was he relieved that this figure in the shadows was no longer a threat, he really didn't know and in a quiet moment felt the guilt of even dwelling on that thought.

The days rolled into weeks and into the month of July. As she woke and looked round the bedroom her first thought as usual was now 'another day to get through' then as she turned on to her side to get out of bed she was aware of her breasts, they felt heavy and painful.

'Oh,' she winced, 'that's painful.' She sat up and thought for a moment and realised that she must have missed a period but because of what had happened she had not given it a thought. A slight euphoria set in but then she felt nervous, she stood and took her breasts in her hands just to make sure it wasn't her imagination.

'Oh Mitch,' she held on to the dressing table and looked into the mirror, 'please let it be.'

The tears started again but this time eventually the despair was replaced with a feeling of elation and renewed love. Later the same day William arrived home from work and was shocked to find her up and dressed, he felt a little cautious.

'Elizabeth my dear... how are you feeling?' he asked. 'It is lovely to see you up and dressed and looking more like yourself ... but this is so sudden, are you alright?'

She walked over to him and touched his cheek, 'Yes... and thank you for all your support I know it hasn't been easy for you.'

'No, I am just delighted to see you like this. Are you sure you are feeling alright?'

She walked over to a chair and sat down before answering him. 'Yes I am fine... I have had another shock today but of the pleasant kind, which leads me to believe that perhaps there is a God after all.' A smile appeared, the first for many weeks.

'I am not sure I quite understand... what sort of shock?'

'Against all my earlier principles William... I think I may be pregnant,' she looked at him directly. 'How would you feel about that?'

Surprised at what she had just told him it took him a few seconds to collect his thoughts.

He poured himself a glass of scotch before turning back to her, 'If that makes you happy again then I am delighted. You know what I told you when we were married... you didn't ask for this situation that exists between us and true love has been snatched away from you so cruelly. I had lost you Elizabeth... I knew that.' He lit a cigarette and continued, 'I would dearly like to turn back time and change the situation for you but that is impossible. You know I love you dearly and I would do anything for you; if you feel you want to leave here then leave with the knowledge that I will support you and your child always wherever you may choose to go. Aternatively, should you wish to stay here, I would be delighted my darling.' He placed the glass down and walked over and took hold of her hand, 'Please know I take no pleasure in what has happened Elizabeth, he must have been a very special man.'

'Yes he was.' The look of pain came back into her eyes and she wept once more into his shoulder.

He gently took her over to the settee and remained at her side for some time just holding her hand until she had composed herself again. 'William, thank you for understanding.'

'No need for thanks my dear. I would consider it an honour to bring up his child with you. Thank you for all your support all these years, I know at times it has not been easy and I could not have asked for more from you.'

'Yes, well as I said, this has come as a bit of a shock and I still cannot really believe it, but if I am pregnant it is more than I could have wished for. He is still with me. I shall never love anyone again as I loved him... this baby means the world to me... and I never thought I would ever think that way.'

'This is yours and the baby's home for as long as you wish it to be Elizabeth... and don't be afraid of the future... it will be all taken care of.'

'William... what would we be without each other?' her hand drifted to her stomach.

'I don't want to think about that, I was very lucky to find you. I will always love you for your discretion and understanding.'

'It works both ways William, your butterfly has come home.'

1945

It was a bright day, the sun was shining and the sky was littered with small white clouds moving slowly across the blue expanse being helped on their way by a warm breeze, a gentle day. His gaze moved slowly to the houses left standing after the conflict and to one in particular. Two of its inhabitants were sitting outside lost in their own childish thoughts and were totally oblivious to the eyes that took in the small scene of tranquil calm surrounded by the devastation around them.

The boy was now nine years old, he sat on a pile of rubble at the edge of the bomb site opposite his home and distractedly poked his stick at the spiders that were hiding in the dark shade between the debris and fallen masonry, and laughed aloud as he made them run. He had tormented his sister by telling her he was looking for a big one to chase her with so she had moved and was now playing with her doll and sitting on the newly washed and whitened step for safety so that she could escape into the house if her brother suddenly started to run towards her.

Owen watched him throw the stick down dismissively becoming bored with the spider game and move to sit on a house wall that had survived intact. His son had grown into a tall, good looking boy. He looked comfortable in his trousers that were just above his knee, his shirt was casually tucked in his trousers and the overall look was completed by one sock being around his ankle and the other one was holding up under his scuffed knees.

His sister, sitting on the step had long, dark golden plaits, they reached her middle back and after being carefully plaited had been finished off with what looked like new blue ribbons matching her blue and white cotton dress. 'Just like her mother,' he thought, 'always lovely in blue.' He stood for quite a long time just enjoying watching them play in safety now after the long violent years that had brought so much death and yet another generation blighted by the horrors of war. 'Thank God,' he thought looking up to the bright blue sky 'Thank you' and his eyes misted over as some of the horror images of the last few years flashed before his eyes.

He took a moment to compose himself and started to walk around the bombed area keeping his eyes on his children who were clearly still occupied in their own thoughts, oblivious to anyone. Young Owen kicked his heels on the red brick wall and looked around clearly bored. None of his friends were around so he resigned himself to the notion that it was going to be a long day. He glanced at his sister and thought of just running towards her pretending he had the threatened spider, but then thought again, she would scream and run inside to their mother and he would be in trouble for tormenting. He had glanced at the man walking round the bomb site who was carrying a suitcase and thought nothing of it; he was dressed in a pin stripe suit and was wearing a trilby hat. He didn't know him so his attention turned back to his sister and he tried hard to think if there was a way he could entice her off the step.

Owen maintained his step and turned on to the cobbled street. His son clearly didn't recognise him and his daughter was too wrapped up in talking to her doll.

A wry smile touched his lips as he continued towards the boy who finally raised his eyes and the realisation set in. He gasped before flinging himself off the wall and running into the arms of his father and bursting into tears.

'It's alright son,' said a voice full of emotion as he held him tightly. 'It's alright... don't cry... let's go and tell your mother and sister I am here...it's all over... I'm home.'

EPILOGUE

Owen lost his Beth after 56 years of marriage; she left this earth on a Bank Holiday Tuesday when the weather had been unusually kind. It had been a beautiful sunny day with a warm breeze blowing and she had been in the garden setting bedding plants. He stood beside her while she checked that all around was tidy when she collapsed without warning. He could not hold her weight and she died in his arms. He had lost his soul mate.

In the years that followed, he gently descended into the twilight world of Alzheimers losing the capacity to recognise his children, or family faces from photographs including Beth. That was apart from one, that of Eleanor, his grandmother, so strong was she still in his psyche. He died aged 91 years.

Beth had died long before her son Owen had decided one long, cold, winter evening that he would research the military archives of World War One to find out what had actually happened to Arthur's ship during the Gallipoli campaign. It took him eighteen months to complete and what he found surprised them all.

Arthur had actually survived the torpedo attack on his ship HMS *Majestic* and had been rescued by a hospital ship and transported to a military hospital in Alexandria, Egypt. Although his injuries were appalling he survived for a further six weeks in the hospital ward despite lack of air conditioning in the intense heat and prior to the discovery of penicillin. He finally succumbed to his injuries and died on the 1 July 1915. Enclosed in the information pack was a photograph of the headstone to his grave in the War Graves Cemetery in Chatby, Alexandria.

His grandchildren Owen and Lynne (Carol their sister had passed away) made the pilgrimage to his graveside to pay their respects. It was a tearful homage made to a grandfather they had never known, albeit 92 years late.

R.IP. Arthur Johnson – your story and that of our parent's early lives was my inspiration for this book, thank you all for giving us a loving, safe and happy life through your sacrifices.